SON OF THE GAMBLIN' MAN

THE YOUTH OF AN ARTIST

A Novel by
MARI SANDOZ

UNIVERSITY OF NEBRASKA PRESS
Lincoln and London

First Bison Book printing: 1976

Most recent printing indicated by first digit below:
5   6   7   8   9   10

Library of Congress Cataloging in Publication Data
Sandoz, Mari, 1896–1966.
   Son of the gamblin' man.

   1. Cozad, John Jackson—Fiction. 2. Henri, Robert, 1865–1929—Fiction. I. Title.
[PZ3.S2174So12]   [PS3537.A667]   813'.5'2   76–17066
ISBN 0–8032–0895–2
ISBN 0–8032–5833–x pbk.

☺

Bison Book edition reproduced by arrangement with the Mari Sandoz Corporation from the first edition published in 1960 by Clarkson N. Potter, Inc.

⊞ ⊞ ⊞ ⊞

To the early settlers who lived through those trying and turbulent times of the old Cozad and Plum Creek region, and to all those, well over one hundred, who contributed information and encouragement through repositories and by interview, letter, and telegram, I offer my grateful acknowledgement.

MS

The Family

■ ■ ■ ■

JOHN JACKSON COZAD, the Gamblin' Man and community builder by his true name, but only one of several that he used during his career.

THERESA GATEWOOD COZAD, the wife of the gamblin' man.

JOHNNY, JOHN A., the elder son.

ROBERT HENRY, second son, often called the son of the gamblin' man in his boyhood.

GRANDFATHER ROBERT, old Robert Gatewood, father of Theresa.

GRANDMOTHER JULIA, Mother Gatewood, mother of Theresa.

TRABER, A. T. Gatewood, brother of Theresa.

JOHN ROBERT, cousin of the Cozad boys, son of Van Gatewood.

THE DAVID CLAYPOOLS, niece and nephew of John Jackson Cozad.

All names of people in this book are those the characters were reported as using in life.

Preface

At the age of twelve John Cozad decided to be a gamblin'
man. He became one of the handsomest, most elegant, and
violent, of his kind, so adept at faro that he was barred from
many places and consequently traveled under various names
and gave out varying stories of his life and loves. He had
worked river boats, the plush palaces from San Francisco to
Canfield's in New York, the rudest smoking cars and the rough
gold camps of the West. Union Pacific railroad land agents, old
faro tramps homesteading in northwest Nebraska, and the cowboys of the lawless man who dominated the whole Cozad region
of the Platte River spoke of him less as a man fabulous at faro—
at bucking the tiger—than as a determined community builder.
But not even they knew that he was also a very lucky father,
and lived to see one of his sons grow into greatness as an artist,
and a teacher and leader of artists, a son he condemned to live
and die under a fictitious name and biography.

More than twenty years ago Dr. Robert Gatewood, nephew
of John Cozad, the closest remaining relative of the gambler
and his artist son, approached me to write the story of the two
men. By 1942 I had completed enough research to go to the
Cozad region to interview the old-timers. Several there must
have known the town's connection with the world-famous
artist but they studiously avoided any mention of this.

If the story had been one of exploitation of the helpless, or appropriation of the nation's lands and resources, I could not have hesitated, but in this I had to respect the community reluctance. I put the book aside until the story began to leak out. Van Wyck Brooks revealed the gist of it in his *John Sloan* in 1955 and the next year Harry B. Allen gave a brief account of it to the Cozad *Local*. So I felt free to tell the story that John Cozad, in letters to my father in 1903, characterized as "a most unusual one, and yearns for a Romantic Pen." Unfortunately he left his trail too shadowed and confused for the complete clarification demanded by non-fiction. I have kept to the facts available and only filled in the few holes necessary to reconstruct something of the crucible in which the dross of the son's youth was burned away and the gold of it freed to find itself.

MS

SON OF THE GAMBLIN' MAN

I

THE SUN BEAT DOWN on the frock coat and tall silk hat of the man striding westward across the prairie. It glinted on the gold head of the cane he carried as jauntily as though he were moving through a thousand watching people. But there was no one to see him, or to know that the man's special square-cut diamonds were gone from his cravat and his fingers, tucked carefully away. There was no habitation anywhere in sight, nothing much except the dusty old wagon trail under the man's feet and the laddered steel of the railroad track that stretched along beside him, following its line of telegraph poles toward the shimmer and heat of the far western horizon.

Back at the boxcar that served as a railroad station a scattering of men had watched the newcomer set out this morning, the two who had been sawing up logs for the fireboxes of the engines straightening their backs with their fingers as they looked after him. Their eyes followed this man as eyes always did, often soft handsome ones, with fluttering lashes. It had been so ever since he grew out of his awkward cowhide boots into that proud and arrogant cane-bearing stride that carried him through so many tight spots since.

It was one of the dog days of August, the earth dry and

baked, but this man had been in hot sun before. One summer noontime back when he was twelve and restless under the hand of his second stepmother, he had suddenly thrown down the tedding fork, wiped the clinging dust of the Ohio hayfield from his sweating face with his sleeve and left to find an easier way to make a living. He got away before his father's astonished anger could remind him of his duty as a son and as a member of a good, God-fearing family.

Since that day the man had never looked back. His high-bridged nose, the elegant goatee he grew, and his long slender fingers had led him through years on river boats, out upon the ocean to South America, around to California and back through the gold camps of the western mountains. He had worked the plushier cars of the railroads of all the nation, too, including the one whose tracks passed him here on the prairie. During the years his fingers had become so agile, so swift, or, as he preferred to think, his eye so shrewd across the card table, that one house of chance after another had barred him, particularly from faro.

"You don't buck the tiger around here no more," some told him, some of the cruder western element. But the more polite, "Not for you, sir," he had heard from New York to San Francisco and down the middle waters of the nation was just as final.

Today, however, his thoughts were far from the cards his fingers liked to caress in solitary hours. Today the man's handsome boots were grayed with the fine dust of the old Platte River trail and he barely noticed the occasional grasshopper heavy with late summer whirring up, to fall back into the yellowed grass. He did see the prairie chicken squatted in the shade of a telegraph pole under the humming song of the wire, panting in the heat, bill open, wings held away to catch any breeze. The man too was hot in his broadcloth. He drew a square of white linen from his pocket, brushed it

4

down his gaunted cheeks and over his mustache and goatee. Thoughtfully he wiped his high pinkening forehead and then ran the folds around the inside of his hat while the sun shone upon his dark hair and burned in the intensity of his black eyes.

The man liked to think of himself as lucky: Lucky John J. Cozad. Others of his calling had nicknames, like the chicken-headed little Canada Bill, with the half-witted way of twisting his ropy hair between his fingers to toll the slickers. Or Rattlesnake Jack, the favorite partner of another Ohio boy grown up on the river boats—the cardsharp, George Devol.

But somehow nobody nicknamed John Cozad, perhaps because he seemed lucky at larger stakes, larger sometimes than the $50,000 he was said to have picked up at faro this summer between trains at Omaha. Never given to talk about cards after the deck was folded away, he did not commit himself beyond saying, "It is true that the stopover at Omaha proved pleasant. I predict that city will become a great river metropolis."

Important, too, was John Cozad's luck with women, including his beautiful Virginia-born wife, who gave him two sons to survive the ills and epidemics that swept off the other three babies, along with most of the neighboring children. The sons were growing into fine boys, the father thought, particularly the younger, Robert, favoring the Cozads, and Johnny, the elder too, poised and soft-spoken like his gentle mother. Somewhere here on the open sunlit prairie he would build a vigorous new community for them, free from so many things that he, the father, had to see.

Perhaps this was the great day of luck for John Cozad, yet he had been lucky right from the start, from the days when a rope at a bridge or perhaps a waterfront gin pole might stop an overly successful gambler. He had seen a mob grab the man who had befriended him, back when he was a

5

frightened boy of twelve on his first trip down the Ohio, and started him in faro. He had to hear the dark murmur of the gathering crowd, listen to the anger rise into a roar.

"Hang the jack leg! String him up!"

He had tried to stand against them with his bare hands and was knocked off into the water as the mob dragged the man away to a pole and jerked him up, to dance the air. Even now, after more than twenty-five years, the apologetic, forward-tilted head of a hanging man anywhere, perhaps barely glimpsed from a swaying stagecoach or a roaring express train, always brought back that first time to John J. Cozad, made him want to run, run as he did at the sight of his friend, so long ago. Or to jerk out the revolver always under his coattail now, send bullets into the faces of the lynchers, perhaps even from the little pearl-handled extra pistol that fitted so neatly inside his waistcoat and had kept him alive a time or two.

But the luck that John Cozad courted most was not the gambler's at the card table or escape from lead and the lyncher's noose. His grandfather, the Reverend Job Cozad, had pushed into the remote western wilds of the Virginia colony to start a settlement. His son Henry moved on to lay out his town in Ohio, where young John later deserted the hayfield. But John Cozad had located a community in Ohio too, one of several attempts scattered as far as South America. Unfortunately his Cozaddale had been very close to the booming city of Cincinnati, much too close. The town was still on the maps but the builder had moved on.

"John Cozad shook the dust of it from his expensive boots quick enough when some fellows that got whacked over the head by his gold cane started paying him back with hard dirty fists," one of the neighboring Pearsons recalled later.

Nobody said this to the community builder's face, but the failure of the town was plain even to him. Too little space and too much competition, he believed, and so now, at forty-two, John J. Cozad had better and bigger plans, plans that would tax his dexterity of mind and fingers between trains, at Omaha, say. And other and larger places too. He would start one more community, one of many thousands of people, in a vast region fresh and new as an unbroken deck of cards. And clean, clean as the meadowlark watching him from a thistle, the black V sharp on the yellow breast that was bright as new-minted gold, but yellower.

Yes, he would build a strong, a spreading and prosperous settlement centered by a city of wide, tree-lined streets, an open and happy city, with a fine home for his family, a home finer than anything his wife could have dreamed even in the romantic fancy of her Southern girlhood, back before the war. He would display her like a diamond set by Tiffany's and it would be somewhere along the railroad running past his feet here, on the forty thousand acres he had arranged to buy.

When John Cozad was well out of sight of the men back at the little boxcar station, the west-coast express came roaring past, stringing wood smoke over the lone walker and letting out one apologetic, or taunting, blast of the whistle for him. After the rails stopped their humming, the man slowed a little and clipped the tall browning head from an occasional sunflower with his cane as he looked to the northern horizon, edged by hazy bluffs cut into folds that must be brush and scrub timber tucked into breaks and canyons. A mile or so to the south of him a low line of brushy trees marked the Platte River, and farther on a hazier line of bluffs, even and flat-topped as a great mesa, stretched all along the horizon. Between these two bluff lines lay the fertile valley of the Platte, fifteen to twenty miles wide and stretching westward from back at the Missouri River out across Nebraska to the Forks and beyond, deep into Colorado and Wyoming—long slender fingers grasping at the Continental Divide.

Except an occasional freight outfit few wheels cut the old trail this far west since the railroad went through, but the homeseekers would come soon. The Union Pacific Railroad had twelve million acres for sale strung through the Platte valley, a part of the government subsidy for building the tracks. Their land lay in mile-square sections* alternating with government sections in a strip twenty miles wide along each side of the right-of-way, a great checkered, forty-mile belt of U.P. prairie lands stretching westward across the public domain.

Somewhere in this vast empire, open, much of it free for the taking, John J. Cozad planned to make a good life for all who would join him. Here his sons would grow up without the lung weakness, the consumption, that still shadowed their father as it had so many generations of Cozads, sent so many to early graves. Here the sons would become the fine men his colonizing ancestors were, with some of the sound sturdiness of their mother's people—grow up strong and handsome, free from sickness and the evils of the waterfronts, a credit and an honor to their parents.

The man had been heading steadily westward, plodding, his jauntiness gone now that there was apparently no living thing to observe it, lost in his plans. Then a sudden whirring at his feet made him jump. He knew the sound—a rattlesnake. It was a big one, mottled and thick as his wrist, coiled, the great broad arrow of its head poised to strike. But the man did not raise his cane and after a long moment's lidless defiance, the snake slid off the road and away.

The gambler touched his hat. "You are a gentleman, sir," he said, and watched the grass shake a little, slowly, deliberately, with watchful pauses.

Before the man started on again he heard a faint yell far off somewhere and saw a deer start up from the brush below the tracks. The buck stopped, looked off southward, and was gone. The yihoos grew plainer and a rumble of hoofs rose on the light wind. The smudging of dust along the south horizon spread and after a while a dark string of cattle appeared,

* The eighteen odd-numbered sections of each township.

widened into a large herd that came spilling toward the river on a hard run, the cowboys riding to hold them down.

John Cozad slipped along a dry creek bed toward the Platte and stopped in a clump of brush. Spreading his handkerchief out neatly on a little cut bank, he seated himself to peer out. He saw the wide-horned lead steers hit the river edge, hesitate, and then leap the low bank before the push of bawling young Longhorns that crowded them into the shallow stream, but thrusting their dusty noses into the water even as they were shoved along. A couple of head were trampled down, but the cowboys worked to spread the running herd to avoid more piling up, whooping and whipping the dusty backs with their down ropes. They managed to line them out both ways along the bank for a quarter of a mile, the lazy water jammed with thirsty stock. Finally they let their faunching horses in too, the jingle of bridle bits plain as they nuzzled the water. Then, with outstretched heads, they drank.

After a while the men whooped the leaders on as fast as possible through a stretch of old quicksand and out upon the rich seed-topped grasses of the bottoms, the young cows belly deep and grabbing mouthfuls as those behind still came crowding. Gradually they spread out and fed for an hour, leaving the bottoms trampled, eaten down like summer range. Then they were strung out northward behind the chuckwagon that had crossed the loose-bottomed stream behind the settling hoofs of the herd.

After a moment of anger at this destruction of the fine deep meadow grass, free grass, perhaps even his grass, John J. Cozad watched the cattle go with satisfaction. The Union Pacific land pamphlets weren't exaggerating. Settlers better come in fast, for men who knew bovine husbandry were certainly taking over the free range and would try to hold it with gun and lyncher's rope, probably, as they did in Texas, if one could believe the stories. Most of the herd had been breeding stock, with around seventy-five young bulls of moderate horn plodding along behind, the rest of the two thousand or so mostly young cows and heifers.

With the last bellow of bull and dust of hoof gone the man with the silk hat rose stiffly, brushed his coattails, and hurried on. He must select his site and push the settlement, making everything as easy as possible for the colonists. He would put up an Emigrant House immediately to provide beds and meals for the homeseekers, and a livery stable with horses for rent—saddle or rig.

Weary from the unaccustomed walk of seven, eight miles in the growing wind and the blistering sun, John J. Cozad shaded his eyes to look ahead along the glistening tracks, impatient now. Finally, not far beyond a scummy little creek, he discovered the place described back at Coyote station that morning. There was, of course, not even a shack or dugout but the big sign stood wide and high, between two tall poles: The 100 TH MERIDIAN. Here the West began.

He stopped and, taking off his dusty hat, wiped his brow once more.

"I came along here a dozen times," he said, speaking to the sign as he would to the cards when he was working them alone, talking to them as to friends. "Here you are, so bold and plain and yet I never saw you. Too busy, I guess," he added apologetically.

From beside the sign as from the side of a trusted friend he considered the wide Platte valley. Most of the mile to the brush line of the river was a fine sweep of hay-length grass running in the wind like some green and shadowed sea along the bottoms but tawnier, and russet in seed toward the higher ground where he stood.

Gradually a quivering rose in the man, swelling until it seemed as powerful as the gusts of wind that shook the shaggy old willows at the river and ran over the great spreading cottonwoods standing alone out on the bottoms. But it was mostly inside, like the eagerness of a bird dog at a brush patch or the excitement that ran through the gambler when a good prospect for the faro box came up the plank at Memphis, or when cattle drovers appeared, their pockets arrogant with the heft of fat new beef money that had not yet taken time to root.

He felt that this day, at this sign, marked a sort of hundredth meridian in the life of John Cozad too, and eventually in that of hundreds, thousands of others. He could see a fine young city sprouting up here, with sweep of depot and loading pens far along the tracks, and rows of grain elevators craning their necks over the fields that now were only yellowed prairie. There would be factories, flour mills, and a packing plant, with greenhouses and a spreading nursery off at the far outskirts for the trees his city must have. In the center on the little rise, and facing toward the cheerful timber of the Platte, would be a fine white mansion, a mansion with pillars, perhaps, and a sweep of park before it. To each side in a sort of arc would be pleasant buildings of brick and stone, including stores, schools, churches, even the county courthouse eventually, although the station back east fifteen miles called Plum Creek was the temporary county seat now.

Of course that would soon be changed, as the prairie here would change to the wide streets of a growing city, streets filled with prancing horses, dashing carriages, gay, lively people moving along the walks under the green fountains of summer elm, the red and gold of oak and maple in the fall. And just a little above it all would be that great white house of John J. Cozad, community builder, and nowhere in all the city would even one gambling spot be tolerated.

In the sentimental moment he permitted himself to think of one more thing. For years newspapers and the halls of Congress had echoed with periodic roaring, like buffalo bulls in rutting time, from those wanting to move the national capital west to the Mississippi valley. John Cozad had heard men like

Sumner and Seward speak earnestly for this. Even the New York *Tribune* complained that locating the capital on the Potomac was a blunder "which even the great name of Washington can not hide." and predicted that a move was inevitable as the power of the West grew.

Now suddenly this year of 1872 brought a capital boom for Fort Kearny, not over forty miles down the Platte from him here. It was the railroad point nearest the center of the country; the military reservation, miles larger than the District of Columbia, lay at the vast public domain, with enough government land close by to finance an excellent New Washington, with a capitol building of unmatched beauty and eminence.

A flush beyond any disease rose to the cheeks of John Cozad. His 40,000 acres could make more than a hundred broken faro banks for him, more in cash, and bring signal honor to him and his family. With a great country estate and an elegant capital mansion his Theresa could be the capital's great hostess, his sons in highest position.

But John Cozad knew that he must shake all this off. The whole business was plainly too chancy for any gambler's eye. He must face the deck as it lay in the box now.

Today there were only the large sign here and the bit of siding for trains to pass on the single-track line. The late afternoon sun brought a little life. A small bunch of antelope, perhaps scared by the cattle herd, circled past the man and, leaping the tracks, were gone to the river. A flock of cackling wild fowl, prairie chicken or grouse, headed northward for the bluffs. Plainly it was also time for man to seek out food and water and a spot to stretch himself for the night. The timetable showed a train due about dark, but unless it took to the siding to let another pass it would not stop, not for the wave of a hat, even a silk hat by a famous hatter. Not today, but perhaps the time would come.

By now John J. Cozad was at least eight, nine miles from

Coyote, the station there without accomodations and too far away for tonight. But his pocket map showed another stop up ahead about five miles, with, he hoped, something besides a boxcar set out at the siding and dirty soogans on the floor for any stopovers who spurned the old buffalo robes usually crawling with graybacks. Yet even that much, with a little fried deermeat and squaw bread, would be better than nothing, and welcomed.

Doggedly the man struck out toward the sun already lengthening his shadow on the old trail behind him. Footsore, leg-weary, and hungry, he stopped at a little creek where chokecherry bushes hung thick and glistening black with sprays of the sweet, puckerish fruit. Farther on he saw a thicket rosy with golden, red-cheeked wild plums, their warm sweetness honey to the tongue. He ate without disturbing the wasps working busily on the down fruit, and then lined his hat with grape leaves and filled it with plums for the road. Once more he set out westward, really plodding now, weary, free from observation, and with nothing more to anticipate.

After a while he noticed a soft hum in the rails beside him. It grew, became the racket of light wheels on steel—a handcar coming up behind him, two men pumping hard, hurrying. At sight of the black-clothed figure beside the track they slowed down.

"Hou, Doc! Where's the pill sack?"

"Maybe he's one a them walking sky pilots—"

Usually John J. Cozad ignored such familiarity, but here on the empty prairie and so near sundown it seemed less offensive.

"I am looking for a location, gentlemen," he offered.

"Oh, a landseeker! Going to Willow Island? Hop on," the older man said, moving over a foot or so.

Pulling his coattails up, with his cane tucked under his arm, the hat, emptied, back on his head, John J. Cozad, Esquire, of Cozaddale, Cincinnati, and the wide world, hopped on. Almost before he was settled, the handcar started off with a jolly little *rrurrh, rhurr, rhurr,* as the men pumped it swiftly along.

Back at home in Cincinnati, John J. Cozad was greeted with proper formality but with warmth by his wife, her color heightened by his gift in a gold initialed mother-of-pearl box, a ring he had designed for her, the diamond like a great drop of sun-struck morning dew set in the imperishable gleam of platinum.

"Jewel of the Platte, I call it, for my Theresa in our new home," he murmured into her ear, and the wife of John Cozad was no less happy for the knowledge that the burning in his eyes was as much from the new dream he bore as from his love. A dream he must have, and if this lasted to an actual move to the wilderness, perhaps her parents could accompany her.

She took pleasure now in the excitement of the sons in their father's return from far places. True, Johnny was at the trying age, with a growing stiffness toward his father, and almost openly pleased by his many departures. But the boy was always happy to see him come home and was admiring the intricacies of the braided belt of dyed horsehair straight out of the wild west. The younger boy, the seven-year-old Robert, resembled his father more each time—the same thin temples, the dark glossy hair, the short chin, and the same intensity of eye. He had some of the Cozad excitability. Now he hugged his present, moccasins crusted in white and blue Sioux beading, and ran to fetch a drawing he made, showing his father sticking his head out of the train to watch a great herd of buffaloes streaming past the smoking engine, buffaloes that looked like humpbacked milk cows.

"The lines of your tracks and trains aren't very straight, dear," the mother said gently, apologetically. "Have you lost your ruler?"

Slowly the boy went back to his room. Slowly, too, he tore

his drawing straight across and then broke his drawing pencils, one after another, and hid the pieces back behind his stack of underdrawers.

Nothing was said all evening about moving out to this wild west the boys heard so much about, the west of the pictures they collected from *Frank Leslie's* and *Harper's Weekly*. But it was not proper to interrogate one's parents and so the brothers whispered about it long after all the house except their mother's bedroom was dark and quiet.

Within a week a new office was opened in downtown Cincinnati, small but making big talk around the piers and in the larger gambling houses, where John Cozad was well known. Other frequenters of the palaces had deserted their gaslit crystal and dark red plush, but setting up a real estate office was something new for a slick-finger like John Cozad. Even Canada Bill and Devol seemed to be joking about it a little.

"More room for the rest of us to chaw and spit," Canada said, but without giving John J. the customary rubbish nudge in the ribs.

The new real estate broker had an assistant, Capt. William Ross, to promote business. Some of this the sons were allowed to see, particularly the folio of photographs from the Union Pacific and the colonization bulletins describing the western railroad lands offered for sale. They watched the two men work up the rough draft of a big dodger almost as long as a circus poster, with thick black letters across the top: HO FOR THE GREAT PLATTE VALLEY!

"No pictures," young Robert said, in disappointment.

Soon there was only Capt. Ross around the little office. "Mr. Cozad is away on business," everyone was told firmly, even after rumors got around that the real estate operator had not turned his back upon his original talent entirely but was keeping more to the farther regions—Denver and the gold camps of the west, building up what was a substantial account at the bank, at several banks.

15

During the winter the Cozad boys hopefully gathered a good-sized collection of material, mostly pictures of the Great Platte Valley, as their father called it, including Indians, buffaloes, covered wagons, trail herds, and gunmen, lots of gunmen. Robert hoarded every mention of the west as he did stories he had been told, from the very first by his mother. Now instead of retelling the stories to himself during the hours between his bedtime and Johnny's, or when he must sit silent, as when his grandmother took him to church, he made up adventures with Indians, cowboys, buffaloes, and ravenous wolves and mountain lions.

Before long Robert suspected that his brother knew something that he didn't, something about "in the spring." He accused Johnny of this, but quietly, because their mother would have no loud or heated words between them.

"I will have no anger between my sons—" she had said, only once, that Robert could remember. But her face had been strained, her head proud as a great heavy blossom held sternly erect. He was only four then but he had not forgotten. Perhaps he had realized that there was already one swift and uncontrolled anger in the family.

"That's a murderous man," Robert once heard a loafer say to some others leaning against a building, "a violent and murderous man."

Although he had not understood this very well, he did sneak a look up to his father's face, and while he could see little except the goateed chin, somehow the teeth clenched, because the black bunch of hair stuck far out as the father held the boy down to the steady unhurried step.

Now, while Robert badgered Johnny a little about his secret, he brought it up gently, and repeatedly. "What is it that's going to happen to us in the spring?"

Finally Johnny answered him. "That's for me to know and you to find out," he said, and escaped to his hour at dancing school.

Robert had wanted to beg but he didn't, knowing his father's anger if he overheard even a coaxing tone. "Have you no pride?" he had shouted once, and the boy still remembered how red his mouth looked when it sprang open between the mustache and the tufted chin to let the words out. So now Robert went to the window to look after Johnny hurrying along the street. He kept hidden behind the velvet curtains, wishing he dared to cry, knowing he was too old, too grown up, and so he comforted himself in the heavy folds and tried to content himself with the waiting he had learned long ago, waiting, always waiting.

Then one day John J. Cozad came home in high spirits. That week he took Robert down to the waterfront where a boat was unloading mustangs, wild horses from the west. There were bays, sorrels, chestnuts, grays, zebra duns with striped legs, and paints, including a couple of striking snow-patched blacks. It was these two that drew the boy's adoring eyes. Cautiously, a little afraid, he moved closer to the pen where the young mustangs were held as they came galloping along the runway from the boat. He reached an aimless hand in between the planks as he watched the horses circle nervously around and around, seeking an escape from the enclosure, from the noise and strangeness, their heads up, nostrils flaring to the man smells, the enemy smells. Now and then they stopped, snorting, and then ran again, their long manes flying. After a while a white-polled calico with great white-lashed eyes slowed near the boy, turned his head toward him, ears sharp, his head tossing, testing the air. He even took a step toward Robert, then another, and finally paused a moment to sniff at the reaching hand. Then he plunged away but stopped and looked back over his shoulder.

"I think he likes me," the boy said, speaking foolishly loud in his joy and wonder.

"Would you want to go out near where these horses lived?"

For a moment the seven-year-old couldn't speak. "Out on

the Platte River, where you were?" he finally trusted himself to ask, making it sensible, quiet.

But he spoke too late. Already his father's mind was far away.

II

As the sun rose over the May prairie Theresa Cozad lifted the blind of the compartment and peered out at the land flying past the train. But as had happened before in the fifteen years of her married life, she could see little to remind her of the glowing description her husband had given her. Where were those dense, tall grasses of the Platte valley? All she could see were fire-blackened reaches, greening along the low places and on the protected slopes of the rises, but with the top of every knob bald and wind-bared.

Then she recalled the report of a great prairie fire earlier in the spring. She did not waken the boys as she had half promised she would the moment she opened her eyes in the morning. There had been a little trouble getting them to bed, not in actual protest but in dallying, particularly Johnny, who knew so well how to avoid her commands, with his meekly bowed head and a secret and loving little glance. Robert, at least, would be very disappointed that the grass was not shoulder high or more.

She drew the blind and slept again, until a shouting awoke her. Robert was jumping up and down beside her bed, excited, but trying to wait until his mother spoke.

"Shame, Son, all the noise and people trying to sleep!"

The boy quieted himself, standing still. "But you slept right through the hundredth meridian," he said reasonably. "I saw the sign whiz by—bz-tt—the place where we will live. And you were sleeping."

"*Perhaps* we will live there. Your father says Willow Island may be better. There wasn't anything at the meridian? Not even a hut?"

No, nothing except the big sign and two animals that stood looking. They were a little like deer in the zoo at home but with short horns and white behind when they ran away.

"Antelope," young Johnny interrupted, poking his neatly combed head into sight. "Antelope. The conductor said so."

Before young Robert's chagrin could embarrass him too much, the father came in, his eyes reddened from the night's work in the smoking car. He motioned the sons out and then laid a roll of bills and a palmful of gleaming double eagles into his wife's lap. "Our traveling expenses," he said, and stooped to kiss her.

"But we get a rebate on our fare for buying all that land from the railroad, don't we?"

Yes. However there were many other expenses, and for all summer. Besides their home would cost a great deal of money. And not even John J. Cozad's luck held all the time.

The train stopped on the siding at Willow Island to let the eastbound express snort through. Then the Cozads stepped down, their trunks and handsatchels set off behind them. The boys looked around. There wasn't much here either, the little boxcar station and maybe three, four more houses and a shed, all scattered out, none of the buildings amounting to more than the river-bottom shacks back along the Ohio. One of them was sod and faced the tracks, with a big weathered board above the door: SALOON, and a hitch rack with two horses tied, men in the door looking out.

"The trainmen and travelers can get something to eat there," John Cozad explained. "Even a little game now and then, stud, blackjack and so on. We won't concern ourselves with them."

There was something more, a stout tower with one of the big double-wheeled windmills that shifted as the big tail moved, turning the thickly petaled face always into the wind. The rod that thumped up and down was pumping water, John Cozad told his sons, and lifting it into the high tank near the siding, where the engine that had brought their train was filling the boiler. Sometimes the wind failed and then four men worked a hand pump to supply water for the engines. The big rick of wood was for the fireboxes. It was a long one, almost as long as the pile of bleached buffalo bones picked off the prairie and waiting for empty cars to haul them away.

Some distance up the track a couple of gandy dancers leaned on their tampers until the train was past the little washout they were filling. Costin, the section foreman, left them and came over to greet the Cozads while his sunburned children ran up to gather in a ragged row in front of the little section house. All but a couple of those practically grown were barefoot, and all of them stared at these dudes dumped on them by the railroad. John Cozad with his frock coat and silk hat they had seen before, and others not too different, but no such boys as these, with their neat caps, their wide white collars and flowing black ties, their knickerbocker suits. Or anybody as elegant as Mrs. Cozad, in maroon traveler, her white skin veiled close, a curly green feather blowing from her hat.

Mrs. Costin hurried out to wave a welcoming apron from the section-house step, and to motion her staring young ones back out of the way. At the boxcar depot the small red-bearded agent, who had been popping back and forth during the excitement of two trains stopping at the same time, now poked his fiery head out to call a greeting, and then jerked it back.

Up at the section house one end had been cleared of workers and Costin children for the Cozads. They moved in, with a tipi set up in the back for the two boys.

"This is fine," the father remarked, "but without a picket fence to Canada, maybe you ought to sew a compass into Johnny's nightshirt so's he can find his way back when he's been night-traveling."

All but Johnny laughed a little, quietly. "Maybe Robert will feel him moving and wake him up," the mother said casually, to the old family joke.

Before evening they went to look at the Platte River, rising with the new snow water roaring down from the Rockies. They went in the sturdy two-seater spring wagon the father had ordered delivered far ahead of time. There were half a dozen horses too, including a spotted pony for Robert, and saddles for them all. But these were for another day.

Costin left his boys to weed in the beans and the potato patch and drove John Cozad and his sons to the old dugout where a few soldiers had been stationed until not long ago.

"Against the Indians, sir?" Robert dared ask, hopefully and a little proud of his knowledge.

"Yes, Indians, train robbers and horse thieves."

"Oh!" the boy exclaimed, shivering with delight. He could see it all in his mind, just like the pictures from *Harper's Weekly*.

They drove to the flooded river on the old woodcutters' road, to see the willow-grown sloughs and islands, half under water now. There had been a shooting here between a few Pawnees and some Sioux. The Pawnees still liked to trap their old region for an occasional beaver or otter, and the mink and muskrats. But often the Sioux hunting parties came through, and early one morning the Pawnees running their trap line for the night's furs detected a camp of them on one of the little island spots. In the fighting one Sioux was badly wounded before they got to their horses and escaped. The Pawnees, afoot, hurried over to the depot to telegraph the tribe for help, afraid an avenging party would strike them before they could walk home.

For several days after that Pawnees kept getting off the tops of the cars bringing enough guns, lead, and powder, all together, for a little war, but no enemies showed up. A gun the Sioux had dropped when they fled looked like those that Duke Alexis of Russia had presented to them when he was out to hunt buffalo last year.

Robert listened with openmouthed astonishment, forgetting his manners, demanding to see the exact spot at once, and frightening himself by his boldness. But the father laughed with unusual good nature. "That can wait, Son. You have till fall. I want to see land for my colony."

The boy hid his disappointment, and relief, by looking all around. He was west, where Indians probably skulked in every willow, but there was a loaded rifle across the front of the spring wagon, if any came. Mr. Costin did show the boys how the gun carried. He took aim at a sand spot against a knoll a quarter of a mile off. Right after the great bang and the puff of stinking powder smoke, sand spurted up way out there.

"Always shoot against a hill or a bluff," the man said as he put the gun back. "Else you might kill somebody too far off to see."

"Would the bullet go right through, if it hit a bone?" Johnny asked.

"Oh yes, if within a mile or so. Blow a hole out the size of your fist."

From this the men began to talk of robbers, and of ranchers with cowboys who shot people, too—matters not to be interrupted, matters that left Robert feeling these were just stories, with everything about them as far off as when he was back in Cincinnati. But a few days later one story suddenly became very real, one that happened not far away, at the bridge over the flooded Elkhorn River, where they had crossed coming west. A roadmaster out inspecting the tracks had just been over it when a train came through with a car of open tanks full of live fish, $30,000 worth of them: pike, trout, bass, and so on, for propagation in California. The roadmaster had grabbed onto the engine to ride it over the flooded river. The bridge pilings crumbled and dropped the engine and the fish into the river, drowning the man.

"Just a few days earlier and it could have been us," Johnny said.

"Oh, one has to take a chance now and then—" the mother said, and stopped herself, flushing slightly at the meaning the Costins might place upon such a remark from the wife of a gambler.

But Robert was thinking about other things. Dead! A man drowned where they had crossed just before. He had a question, one that didn't seem prying, and yet he hesitated to ask it. "The fish—they'll live, won't they? They fell in the water."

Instead of asking this he went out to the tipi and drew a pencil picture of the engine toppling through the broken bridge, smoke billowing, and the man falling with outstretched arms, fish spilling, some already in the water and darting in every direction. He didn't show the picture to anybody. The lines weren't straight and it might be wicked to have the fish so merry.

Both the boys did feel a little cheated that there were no Indians, no buffaloes. Robert almost missed those that did come through. The Indians looked like ordinary horsebackers riding along the river. The buffaloes were no stampeding herd, only five calves in a pen riding a flatcar between gondolas going east by slow freight.

From the start the Cozad boys were set off from the Costins, not only by what they had to learn but by their city ways and manners, their neatly cut hair instead of shaggy manes, sunburnt and unkempt, hanging to the shoulder. Although they wore shoes and stockings, they washed their feet every night, which seemed an excessive scrubbing, even for beds with sheets. Mainly the barrier seemed to be the shoes.

The Cozad sons had too much exploring to do to notice the attitude of the Costins or to listen to their father's long talks with landseekers, railroad men, or with Josiah Huffman, who had come west in March and got control of the land of Willow Island station. A couple of times there were heated words between him and John Cozad, enough to reduce Theresa to a silence and a preoccupation that not even her husband seemed able to penetrate. Most of the time he was away from the region entirely, off at Denver or farther west, perhaps back with his diamond stickpin and ring shining, to stay a night or two and then head on to Omaha, St. Joe, and who could say where else.

"Do you have to keep going away?" young Robert once asked him, clinging to his father's heavy watch chain as he asked the question. But he let go when the Cozad brows drew down in a dark windrow across the man's face. "Times are hard this year," the father said sternly.

Yet he didn't take the opportunities that came to him. When three cowboys rode in from the west asking for the cardsharp, the gambler, it seemed John Cozad didn't really want to play cards. Robert had been out along the trail watching a bull snake trying to swallow a gopher. The men stopped, eased the guns at their sides, and looked down at the boy. One of them rode a fine, proud-stepping horse and a new saddle, at least new to the man, the way he had been all over it. He threw a quarter into the dust at Robert's feet.

The boy picked it up and handed it back. He guessed they meant his father when they said gambler, so he took them to where John Cozad was writing letters in the shade of his umbrella table.

"We hear you're honing for a game," the leader of the men said.

"Game?"

"Stud, draw, anything. Name your poison."

John Cozad acknowledged their offer with a little bow from his chair. "Gentlemen, I never carry such business into my home."

"We're staked to make it worth your time."

"No staking reaches that high," John Cozad told them, and settled himself back to his work. "Here I deal in land."

The leader of the men laughed a little, sharp as a cactus thorn, nodded to the others, and together they set their spurs. Robert looked after them loping past the saloon without stopping, sensing that there had been danger in their coming, some great and unknown danger. It made him remember overhearing his mother one night, late, in a crying voice, saying, "But John, you might be killed any day, any hour——"

The Cozad boys learned to ride like wild Indians, as Theresa wrote her mother. Johnny on his bay, Robert on his calico pony. They picked it up from the Costins, who were getting friendlier, and from the few Pawnees who came through. Mainly they learned from practice. The Indians had really been a disappointment to Robert, with nothing more picturesque about them than the dusty black felt hats pulled down over the scrawny braids. Only the braids, the moccasins, and the brown faces convinced him they might be Indians.

Apparently the boy did more thinking about Indians than the mother realized. One afternoon she heard a continued din and shouting. Glancing out the open window, she saw the Costin boys gathered in the buffalo wallow east of the house. They were running around in a tight little circle and pounding at something or someone with their fists as they came around, making all the whooping. She started to turn back to her reading but something stopped her—the sight of two shoe soles visible between the flying bare legs. She gathered up her skirts and ran out to see. It was true. Her Robert was down on his knees and elbows, the Costins striking his bottom as hard as they could every time around.

"Stop that!" she cried. Then louder, "Stop it, you hooligans!"

One of the older boys heard her and dropped out of the circling, yanking at the shoulders of the others to stop them as they passed. That left Robert, still scrooched down, his coat drawn up over his head, waiting for the punishment to start again.

At her command he rose, his dirty, flushing face even redder before her outraged eyes as he tried to brush the dead grass from his clothing. "They weren't doing anything . . ." he tried to explain.

"Half a dozen strapping boys picking on a smaller one alone?" she demanded angrily.

"Oh, please don't scold. They were just helping me get brave like the Pawnees——"

A few days later she noticed two deep roundish sores on the inside of the boy's wrists, one on each. She held them up to his view, once more demanding an explanation. Robert tried to hang his head, to mumble something not too foolish.

"Speak up like a man," she ordered. "Was this more of your plan to become brave as an Indian?"

The boy nodded miserably. "Yes, I guess so. Like the young Sioux warrior does. You put sunflower seeds to smoldering in a fire and then set them on your wrist with a stick and let them burn out."

"How barbaric!" the mother exclaimed. She made Johnny turn his cuffs back, showing nothing more serious than a few scratches from riding through a plum thicket on a dead run yesterday.

"There," she said. "You don't see your brother carrying the scars of the wild savage rites!"

Young Robert's mind was a confusion. Then slowly, reasonably, he tried to form his reply. "You always say we are

27

not to be aping each other, or anybody, but to keep the Three B's."

"Perhaps you can still tell me what the Three B's are?"

Robert swallowed, pulled at his tightening knickerbockers. "Yes, ma'am. Be kind, be thoughtful and be myself."

"Is imitating a wild Pawnee or Sioux being yourself?"

"No, ma'am," Robert admitted, and went out to the door-step to think about it.

With the Fourth of July coming the Costins scrambled to-gether old tents, a roll of buffalo robes and blankets, and willow hampers and tubs of food, to be loaded on the local for the big celebration at Plum Creek and the dedication of the new bridge over the Platte.

"Jerry says there'll be a bunch af Pawnees dancing, and all na—" Robert stopped, flushing—"dancing all in native dress, and painted."

The mother let it pass, her head bent over her embroidery hoop.

So the Cozad boys had to wait for a sign that they might go to Plum too, but it didn't seem probable that their mother would be interested, and when John Cozad was around he busied himself taking homeseekers out in the spring wagon. Sometimes with the boys standing up behind the seats. A few times he took Johnny out horseback to look over some farther sites, too far for Robert and his pony, the two left standing at the little pasture gate looking ruefully after the fast riders.

Then the morning before the Fourth, John Cozad looked across the late breakfast table set out in the shade, now that the Costins were all away, and made his plans clear. As the boys had suspected their mother didn't want to go to Plum Creek—not a whole day in dust and the crowd, with no shade and the sun around 100 at least. She preferred the ham-mock down near the river. The father had stopped off at

Plum Creek on business yesterday and protested the boodle the town was voting for herself. The county, not two years old, was sunk for $50,000 bridge bonds and now he heard about $30,000 more for a brick courthouse. With no deeded, no taxable land in the county except the railroad's it would be up to them and those who bought from them to pay the bills, mainly the U.P. and John Cozad.

"You didn't actually tell them this? Not to their faces?" Theresa asked, shaking her head helplessly, but smiling a little. "You have to get along with those county officials."

"No, I don't. I told them I plan to move the county seat to my town."

But John Cozad spoke less openly to her about some other things around Plum Creek, even last night when the boys slept. He had run into a couple of old acquaintances from Ohio among the good people who made up the original Plum colony. Jewett, one of the men, drove him down to the new bridge, shaking his head over the whole business. Not the bridge—that they needed—but not a mile long. There could have been graded approaches, with culverts, cutting the length down. He objected to the roadhouse and the new fly-by-night saloons in for the celebration, several just tents, with women and whisky and gambling everywhere. Not orderly, pleasant games of chance for a man of parts, but rough, drunken rowdyism. Jacklegs running the tables and sawed-off shotguns under the bars.

It was as the man said, like a tawdry little gold camp, on hot dusty ground, but with hitching racks tied full of fly-stomping horses. The bar at the sod roadhouse was lined with trail hands from a couple of herds just in, with some already at the gambling tables, their money hot in their pants.

The two newcomers settled at the one empty table in the dusky room. They weren't there much over five minutes when one of the owners stalked in, nodded to Jewett, and sat down at the table. Pushing his hat back, he spit on the dirt floor, scraped earth over it with his boot sole, and said there was no room for another gambler here.

"I have no desire to settle near such a place as this," John Cozad replied, pretending that was the only meaning of the man's words. "I am building an ideal community."

He got a loud laughing, particularly from a trail boss and his cowboys moving up nearer. "We got us a—a community!" one of them yelled out. "Plum Creek, the cowboy's friend!" and roared at his own humor.

But many were silent, determinedly pushing in close around the table—dark-faced men, some with the trail dust still on their faces, sweat-streaked like hillside gullies washed down into their whiskers, their eyes red, mostly still from the wind.

Calmly John Cozad looked up around them, tucked his cane under his arm, and rose, to stride out through the crowd, Jewett close behind, and nobody really standing against them.

Up at the depot, waiting for the train already whistling a mile or so out, several plow-gaunted settlers approached John Cozad—a little diffident at the sight of his hat and cane, but dogged. They were having some trouble, one said, and wondered what could be done. The Texas herds were eating them out, the fever taking their little starts in cattle, the better the stock the surer to die. Even the work oxen and the children's milk cows dropped wherever the Longhorns passed. And when they protested to the trail bosses, they got guns stuck under their noses. Lucky it wasn't worse.

"It will be," another added, raising his voice against the puff and grind of the slowing train. "Man down near the bridge been warned to get out of the country. Herd Law* don't do us no good. They got the county officials on their side."

John Cozad nodded as the step was put down for passengers, and, reaching a hand around for their calloused clasps, promised to do what he could as soon as he got his

* Nebraska Herd Law, passed 1871, made owner of trespassing livestock liable for damages, stock to be taken up and owner notified.

colony in. "By running the elections the courthouse gang can keep right on in office unless we throw them out."

The settlers looked up after him, and then scattered as half a dozen cowboys came spurring up, one shooting his pistol into the air, the others whooping. They stopped in a half circle, hands idly on their holsters as they watched John Cozad settle himself inside the open window, leaning back, not giving them a glance.

Theresa Cozad heard more of this from Agent Sanderson while she was out for an early morning walk than from her husband. He had picked up the story at the little saloon here at the tracks. Seemed too that there would be a lot of gambling at the dedication. Had an old army canopy set up for the crap games, and probably more going on so long as the horse blankets lasted. Pedro was guaranteed for everybody interested.

This fitted in with what John J. had told Theresa, mentioning faro particularly, a second dealer brought in from somewhere. Looked like an opium eater, his damask vest spotted, his hat a ratted, castoff old beaver. So they agreed that this, even more than the open drinking and prostitution, was not for the eyes of their sons.

"We'll all catch the evening train to North Platte, spend the Fourth there," she told the boys as they carried the dishes in after breakfast. "Your father says there are always Indians around," she comforted.

"Fighting Sioux Indians?" Robert asked hopefully.

"Fighting Sioux," the father called from his papers.

After noon great thunderheads rose in the west, and while not a drop fell at Willow Island, by sundown two trains stood silent and dead on the siding there. "Cloudbust up west a ways," Sanderson had shouted as he ran out, red beard fiery in the sun, to flag down the westbound express. "Gully washer took out a fill and left the tracks swinging . . ."

Once more the boys were disappointed, particularly young Robert. It was his first realization of man's dependence on the weather in the open country, his helplessness before its whims and violences.

The Cozad boys liked to hang around the depot watching Ed Sanderson send dispatches or gather up the strips of paper with the little dots and dashes cut by the needle. He was accustomed to boys. He taught the Costin brood a little reading and ciphering winter days around the depot stove in return for his board. From the first his eyes, fiercely blue in his sun-raw face, had glared in fondness upon the Cozad sons, particularly Johnny,who had little foolishness about him and soon learned to read the clicking keys as readily as the agent. Later the man warmed to Robert too because the boy drew funny stick figures along the paper strips hung to the telegraph hook. He only hoped he would never have to turn them in at the main office.

At first the boys had tried to make up to Mr. McMullen, the storekeeper, too. They noticed the Irishman working around his ramshackle building out on the U.P. right-of-way. He seemed a really determined bachelor, avoiding even the few women of Willow Island and the prairie schooners coming through, but he was all business the moment they stepped into his store with a purse in the hand.

The boys often watched him walk down the railroad tracks in the late evening sun, his dog beside him, his pipe puffing smoke over his shoulder like a wood burner going up a stiff grade, as Agent Sanderson said. Neil McMullen, a vegetarian, refused to kill anything, with deer, antelope, and small game all around. The flies buzzing in at his door were not poisoned or tolled to a strip of sorghum on a board and swatted. Instead he shooed them out with a leafy willow switch or a newspaper, if a paper came his way.

The storekeeper finally caught the field mouse nesting in

his stack of flour sacks. He carefully put her and her young into a cigar box and, taking Robert along, carried them far up the tracks to a patch of soft thick grass and left them with the blessings of St. Patrick to keep off any hungry bull snakes. He lit his pipe with a burning glass, concentrating the sunlight on the tobacco and sucking in his gaunt bearded cheeks until smoke curled up between pulls. Robert got him to order a burning glass for him but only on the promise never to try it out on the prairie or to lose it where the sun could strike it to flame. "All that black country you crossed coming out was just carelessness," he told the boy. "Carelessness sets prairie fires. Maybe some old empty bottle thrown away catching the sun like my glass."

Johnny, a little more critical of Mr. McMullen, called him an odd one but Robert liked to hang around there. Once when he ran an errand for the man he got a little striped bag of hard candy.

"Take no return for small favors you should be happy to do," John Cozad commanded his son. But Robert's mother, who grew up in her father's hotel, thought every service deserved a fee.

Robert liked to lean against the rough board counter at the store and listen to the passing cowboys talk, perhaps with awkward jaws as they juiced up a chew from a new plug of tobacco. In a couple of weeks they started to ask the boy about his father's plans to settle in the region, and about the homeseekers he was showing around, saying things like: "Mighty unhealthy business that your father's stickin' his nose into," making it sound like a sort of dare or threat.

The first time Robert had sneaked a look to Mr. McMullen, who seemed careful not to notice. When the men were gone he loaded his pipe and when it was drawing well, he spoke, short, and with too much anger to encourage questions. "Their cattle's spreading Texas fever among the milk cows too. Killed both of mine last summer," he said.

33

Robert could tell this was meant to be an explanation, but he was not sure what it explained.

Sometimes, before the summer's heat of noon, Theresa Cozad pinned on a wide rush hat and strolled out over the prairie for a glimpse into the lovely little nests tucked away in the grass, perhaps with small speckled eggs, or as blue as a pale prairie sky. She gathered armfuls of wild flowers for their room and for the scarcely marked little grave at the old Mormon Trail that passed near the station. She liked wild roses for this, to send their sweetness all around. Before long she was sunburned as a girl and as rosy-cheeked, complaining less and less of the trying wind. Even after she found the big rattlesnake near the boys' tipi the morning before the great thunderstorm and hail, she still went out over the prairie but with tough high shoes and a stout willow stick. Once Robert saw her beating the ground and hurried over. By then she was poking the stick at the broken snake, at the writhing tail plumed with eight rattles, and tucking her hair back where it had worked loose during the excitement and the pounding. The boy picked up her flowers, her shears, and a couple of her bone hairpins. Then with his big jackknife he slashed at the neck of the snake until the ugly wedge-shaped head, still blindly trying to strike out, was cut off, his mother pleading, "Oh, Robert, don't. Please don't. You'll be bitten."

"Jerry Costin showed us how to do it," the boy said easily as he cut off the rattles. "It's easier just to put your boot heel on the crippled snake's head and take the rattles, but I knew you'd be scared."

Theresa looked at her seven-year-old son, brown and agile, confident. "My, this country is good for you and Johnny," she said.

That evening Robert drew a page of pictures with his blue crayon. It was a string of plumed knights riding spotted horses like his new pony, but with rattles in their helmets instead of feather plumes.

During the drowsy heat of midday Theresa Cozad liked to loaf in her hammock down in the trees toward the river. "Have it hung where the wind hits a little," her father's note with it had suggested. "Cooler in the wind and fewer mosquitoes and chills, as you know from the Ohio. I hear the ague's reached all the way up the Platte."

Often she brought her mending—clothing that the sons went through like a Longhorn steer hitting a mosquito netting. Sometimes she read to the boys when they stopped by from a morning's ride or swim, or a little fishing along the river, with perhaps a great catfish from the set lines that the Costin boys let them run. Sometimes two, three of the smaller Costin children drew up closer to hear her stories, wiggling their dark, mud-caked toes in embarrassment if she called to them.

The summer promised to be the quietest, most restful one of all Theresa's life with John J. Cozad. Then one night, after he had been away for two weeks, he came tapping quietly, guardedly on the window. There had been no train for hours and Theresa was up immediately, alarmed at the thought of a stranger at her door here in the wilderness. Then she caught her husband's whispered voice outside and let him in, frightened by his instructions. "Sh-h-h, no light! They may have followed me here."

Silently, in darkness, she got him bread and meat and helped pull off his clothing that felt just rags and tatters to her agitated hands. She drew his silken dressing gown from behind the wardrobe curtain, held it for him, knowing that the softness of it, the richness of the deep maroon color that was so becoming to his black eyes comforted him even in the darkness of night.

Out of long experience she asked no questions. From his terse words, "Drunken cowboys on the train from North Platte——" she filled in the probable trouble, perhaps over cards. More likely it began over some real or fancied insult to her husband, followed by a swing of his cane or a show of his gun. There would have been an angry rush upon him, perhaps a struggle in the disarming or else he was thrown off the moving train. Very probably he was being followed.

"Oh, John, John," she wanted to cry, but she didn't. Instead she held his head in her arms as she wiped his face gently with a soft cloth soaked in warm water. Then she laid him back upon the pillow and with her arm over him, sat so until he slept. At last she stretched out softly beside him, staring into the paling dark of morning, listening.

III

JOHN COZAD had stumbled against the tipi of his sons in the darkness last night when he tried to slip unnoticed into his end of the section house. While he never permitted personal questions from anyone, he realized the boys should have some explanation both for themselves and for others, particularly with his face skinned, his hands scratched and torn, and the ragged and muddy clothing that Theresa had nowhere to hide from the sons. So in the morning he met the concerned and uneasy faces with an obviously exaggerated story, a tall tale.

"Seventeen Blackfoots ran me up a box canyon last night."

The sons hooted. "That's Jim Bridger's story! You told it to us yourself last winter!"

So he had, the father admitted, making it sound doubly rueful, as he unfolded his napkin, touched it delicately to his bruised lip, and then poured the syrup on each stack of pancakes and handed the plates to the boys. He said no more. Perhaps nobody else had heard him come home, or thought him full of red eye although he never drank anything stronger than a dinner wine or a glass of port.

Fortunately the little saloon at the tracks had been dark.

Somehow not even the teasing of the Costin boys mentioned the return in the night to Robert. The high-nosed air usually saved Johnny from questions, although not from resentment behind his back.

A week later there was a surprise. Theresa's brother, solid, square-built Traber Gatewood, stepped off the westbound train. "I couldn't let you have all the fun," was his only explanation, and although John Cozad must have realized that his wife had written of some uneasiness about him to bring Traber running, he met his beloved brother-in-law heartily and motioned the sons up to greet their uncle.

"Only a couple of weeks—I can't stay longer," Traber said. He pulled the lobe of Robert's sunburnt ear into a little twist and acknowledged Johnny's lengthening frame by tipping his head up as though following the growth of a cottonwood into the sky.

Traber went all over the country in the spring wagon with John Cozad, the boys perhaps along on their horses, ready to whoop out after the first jackrabbit or, with good luck, a coyote or some antelope. Sometimes they held down the back seat with the picnic basket underneath. They hunted arrowheads and birds' nests while the men sought out section corners and studied land maps, making notations here and there as they sank a spade into the ground or measured the standing grass up the handle. John Cozad still considered taking over Willow Island, even with the undesirable whisky establishment, for which he would substitute an emigrant hotel. But it seemed Huffman was determined to be unreasonable about selling his land rights, a truly bullheaded man.

"Why bother yourself with him? Your heart was set on the hundredth meridian from the start."

"Well, it was, but there's no harm hedging the bet."

Traber Gatewood, a dentist, was a easy-laughing man, and he laughed now.

Theresa Cozad felt more secure with someone besides the two young sons around, some level-dispositioned man if not a quiet one, even when her John J. was home. She wanted somebody plainly on her side, now that antagonisms against her husband were appearing, not only here from Huffman, but from others too, as was inevitable, she knew. Through talk at the Irishman's grocery store and from Ed Sanderson at the depot, she decided that the attack was probably from the cattlemen, as John J. seemed to think but did not say. He had had a big roll of survey maps made at the new land office at North Platte while he gathered information for his settlement, asking about mean temperatures, annual rainfall, frost seasons, and snow depths. Rumors of his plans for a big new settlement had been spreading like a stink on the wind, particularly since his stop at Plum Creek. Theresa knew that the agent was probably right. That was why, when John Cozad took the train home, half a dozen cowboys followed him on, jumped him from behind, tore up his maps, and threw him off at the trestle, five, six miles west of Willow. He hadn't had a playing card in his hands, the conductor told the agent, but out here there were things more dangerous than any amount of gambler's luck.

"Maybe you ought to try to talk Mr. Cozad out of it," the station agent told her. "You got two fine boys to think about."

Theresa Cozad considered the red-bearded little man. "You do not think that loyalty to your employers is part of your duty? My husband is the railroad's largest land buyer."

But she was not as casual about the future as she wanted Ed Sanderson to think, and when John Cozad left again before the end of the week, her brother had decided to stay on. He started to cut timber south of the station and rick it crisscross to dry for the brick-kiln fires that would be needed no matter where the new colony was finally located. He made a workmanlike job of anything he undertook and the boys hung around to watch him cut down great cottonwood trees, six, seven feet across. Sometimes Johnny pulled the far end of the big saw, for the fun came when the trees crashed down in a cloud of dust and leaves, with small birds darting out in fright. Then Traber prepared to split them into kiln lengths. He bored a hole into each great trunk with a two-inch auger, filled it with grainy blasting powder, fused it, and drove a stout plug into the hole. Together, with some of the Costin boys to help, they pried and sweated to roll the trunk over so the hole was underneath. Then Traber lit the fuse, yelled, "Powder!" and everybody ducked behind a tree or a rick of wood and watched the fuse sputter until it brought the explosion, bucking the trunk into the air, cracking and ripping it, perhaps sending the plug flying. Afterward the splitting and cutting into kiln size was easy but hot summer work.

"That's the way to pull a tooth, boy. Blast it out," Traber teased Robert and the younger Costins, gap-mouthed this summer.

One quiet August day while Theresa was dozing in her hammock down on the bottoms a cowboy came spurring through the river, yelling, "Indians!" as he passed her. At the station he slid from his horse and ran to telegraph his ranch boss in Chicago and then to Washington, and demanding troops to protect the scattered cattle outfits down toward the Republican River. There was a great Indian war beween the Sioux and the Pawnees, the winner sure to take over all the region west of old Fort Kearny.

"That includes us!" Johnny Cozad said, and ran to look after the horses before raiding Indians could set them afoot.

"The train will carry us out if there's danger," Theresa assured her sons when they came out to get her.

"But the Indians wrecked a train down near Plum Creek once, killing and scalping——"

While Mrs. Costin gathered her wash off the lines her husband, the section boss, not excited at all, sent a son riding to old Daniel Freeman, who had come into the Platte valley when there was nothing but Indians, the Sioux and Pawnees fighting all the time. Old Daniel was away, which alarmed many, particularly after Agent Sanderson got the news patched together. The Pawnees, around seven hundred, with their family dog packs and over a thousand horses, were chasing buffalo off southwest toward the Kansas line. They had been warned about the Sioux hunting nearby but thought it was a white-man trick to save the buffaloes for himself. When the Pawnees let themselves be decoyed up close with their families, the Sioux charged in, cutting off the fleeing people, sweeping the horse herds away. The Pawnee warriors fought hard to hold the enemy while the helpless ones got away, some of their women making a circle, singing the old brave heart songs for their brave men, the songs of death. But the warriors were forced to break and scatter. Now every-body had to run, hurrying down a long canyon, the few with horses cutting loose from the packs and the drags. Dropping everything but the young children and the old and wounded, they fled in a panic through the canyon and were about to be slaughtered, wiped out, when cavalry from Fort McPher-son up on the Platte came charging in.

"Around sixty, seventy dead, hundreds wounded, some get-ting clear up to the river. Dr. Bancroft of Plum Creek's got his hands full," the agent told the Willow Islanders gathered around his telegraph machine to hear.

"The fight was finished five days ago, wasn't it?" Johnny Cozad asked, just in from a ride and making it sound casual as he glanced to Robert beside him. After a while the boys slipped out to their horses at the hitch racks. They stopped by their place for a canteen and then at McMullen's to buy cheese, crackers, a can of peaches, and a jar of marmalade. Then they rode down the old woodcutters' road, racing a little as on an outing. They splashed across the shallow cur-rent between the sandbars rising in the Platte, and went south to a little dry creek, hoping they had made their going casual enough so no one would notice.

In the bottom of the old dry bed they tied their horses to a stub of dwarfed willow and, walking on the grass to hide their tracks, slipped into a washout opening back from a cut bank. There, practically invisible in the shadows, and un-moving, lay a Pawnee Indian, almost naked, gaunt-faced, with one leg stuck straight out, enormously swollen.

While Robert helped hold the man's head up and put the saddle canteen to his mouth, Johnny examined the torn flesh of his thigh, torn first by a bullet and then by crawling all the miles from the fight, mostly in the darkness, through the gravel and rocks of sheltering breaks and canyons and over the rosebrush and cactus of the prairie. With little hope of ever reaching the Platte he had to keep crawling as long as he lived. He had escaped from the fight because he could be still as the rest when the Sioux ran among the dead with their war clubs, but he was without a horse and unable to get to his feet, with the right thigh deep-wounded across the muscles and a bullet through the left ankle.

"I don't see how he lived the five days at all—almost no water, nothing to eat, with the bleeding, the infection and the fever——"

"The Sioux, they come find, they kill," he kept muttering, and Johnny knew that was perfectly possible and that this one Pawnee would endanger the entire handful of people at Willow Island. But they couldn't let him die here. Their horses had led them to him by their snorting this morning while they were chasing antelope. Now that they knew of him they had to try to save his life.

They held him up to drink a little more water and then put crackers soaked in the juice of peaches into his mouth. Finally, as the man's strength began to grow, they fed him thin slivers of cheese, and toward evening some of his fear seeped away. Through sign talk and the little English he spoke he made the boys understand how they could get him on Robert's quiet little pony, not sitting up but across the saddle, hanging to both sides. The little calico settled to her task like the good Indian pony she was. Then slowly they made it to the river and across to the tipi in the early dark. They got Traber to help lift the man down, unconscious but living. They stretched him out on the pallet inside fevering, delirious. There he lay five days, a danger from the avenging Sioux.

By then Johnny, with Traber to advise and help, had soaked the earth-scarred wounds, cleaned them of their thorns and the gravel worn into them. They worked the bullet and the shattered bones from the ankle. Then with linen thread from the uncle's dental bag, they sewed up the spread and torn wound of the thigh, after Traber had cut a few spots to raw, fresh bleeding, hoping these would start the adhering, the growing together. It was during these days that the boys saw something of the Pawnee's stoicism in the face of pain, something of what Robert had tried to learn when his mother stopped him earlier in the summer. With barely a grunt through any of it, not even when they drew the inflamed wound together, or probed deep at the shattered foot, the Indian had watched them, his eyes black, clear except a couple of times when the murkiness of fading consciousness clouded them. Two days after their work the swelling was going down, the open wounds granulating, the man wolf-hungry, with little fever even in the night.

By then Theresa Cozad and the rest at the station were very anxious over the rumors that the Sioux were scouting the prairie for wounded Pawnees as a hunter thrashes the brush for crippled quail.

"We must get him away to a hospital or at least to his agency," the mother told Johnny.

The boy was reluctant to let the Indian go. He wished he might watch the recovery, the foot stiff, to be sure, the muscles and nerves of his cut thigh slow to restore themselves.

But surely the injured leg would certainly become very useful again, as even Uncle Traber thought probable. Yet the Indian had to go, and so they carried him to the night passenger train and bedded him down for the trip to the hospital.

John Cozad watched his sons walking up from the depot with their Uncle Traber. "They are maturing fast out here," he told their mother. With misty eyes she nodded. "Soon we will lose them too."

"But not the same way, and not the way so many of my family died, of the disease that cursed me so long," John Cozad said with determination.

Although no one had been permitted an actual sight of it, dissension between John Cozad and the man who controlled the Willow Island site had been growing all summer. Theresa was glad when the time came to take the boys back to school. Her brother went along, aware that money for tooth cobbling would be mighty scarce in Cincinnati now, with times so hard, more and more wage cuts and layoffs, and runs on banks all over the country long before the panic of Black Friday in Wall Street, the week they left Nebraska. But as John Cozad said, it looked like a good time to organize an excursion to a new community in the west, with so many men anxious, even desperate, for a new start.

Now there was a final roaring blowup with Huffman, this time publicly, near the depot, John Cozad lifting his cane to strike and the site owner ordering him off.

"Next time I catch you with your dirty foot on my land I'll blow you full of holes!" he shouted.

It was very funny, such words from the indecisive Josiah Huffman, and on U.P. right-of-way at that. Even Agent Sanderson had to laugh at the sight and decided to put in for a transfer the moment the community builder picked his location.

John Cozad took the first train to North Platte and filed on a homestead adjoining the hundredth-meridian sign. Then he started to Cincinnati too, with a stopover at Omaha. Nobody got him into a game this time, no matter how much long green was flashed around, and there was plenty, as he had seen back in the early weeks of the panic of 1857, too, when everybody honed to recoup quickly.

He knew the hard times would start a great boom for the free lands of the west long before the snow cleared off. He must get his colony together as fast as possible, before outsiders came in and filed on the government land between his railroad sections. At Omaha he completed the contract for the 40,000 acres of land around his homestead, some for himself, the rest to sell to his settlers at from two to six dollars an acre, on the Union Pacific long-time installment plan if desired. Unstated but understood was that the U.P. would accord John Cozad the favored treatment that a colonizer of such caliber deserved—treatment never offered the most impressive railroad gambler. He had prepared carefully for this conference, with a more discrete watch chain across his vest, the diamonds of his ring and stickpin smaller and more select, his new cravat tied like the most important railroad magnate's. His appearance, and the 40,000 acre purchase, got him a hint that someday soon there might be an opening in the Union Pacific senatorship from Nebraska.

John Jackson Cozad smiled, letting no more than courteous interest show on his face. He would make his new community a success, build it into the metropolis of the great Platte valley, on what amounted to the center point of the entire nation. He did not say this, nor that he felt he had the deck shuffled for a take-all, and was sure he had the winning card in the box. Of course, the county was already formed and named Dawson some months ago, with Plum Creek the county seat. But these things could be managed by a man on his way to the United States Senate.

Handling his gold-headed cane with restraint, John Jackson

45

Cozad stepped up into the train, tipping his silk hat to the railroad officials who had come to see him off.

And after he was settled, he drew out the new edition of the *Guide to the Union Pacific Railroad Lands* describing the 12,000,000 acres for sale. Slowly, savoring every word, he reread the quotation from Whittier on the cover:

> I hear the tread of pioneers,
> Of nations yet to be;
> The first low wash of waves where soon
> Shall roll a human sea.

He looked at it a long time, stroking his goatee a little. A mighty fine come-on, this was, a mighty fine shill—but in this game every sucker would get his money's worth and nobody needed to copper his bet.

IV

IT WAS STILL FALL by the calendar but the trip from Cincinnati was a long winterish one, and as the settlements began to thin west of the Missouri, the hint of snow that had paled the prairie thickened to solid white. Gradually the low bluffs of the Platte drew away to each side but the river held its gray border of brush and trees close about itself and went its own curving way, aloof even from the railroad track that was only the narrow little ladder connecting one station to the next. As the puffing engine trailed the plume of smoke westward from the funnel-shaped stack, the stations became even smaller, lonesomer, until there was often nothing more than a weathered sign standing with its feet in the deepening snow.

An emigrant car fitted out with bunks was the headquarters and the living space of the thirty homeseekers that constituted John J. Cozad's first excursion. There were several families, including Theresa's father, Robert Gatewood, for whom young Robert was named, her brother Traber, and Dave Claypool, a nephew of John Cozad. None of them had seen much of the community builder since they got on at Cincinnati. He was occupied elsewhere on the train trying to break even on the expenses of the trip. Several of his excursionists had been cleaned out by the panic and bank failures. These had come on time, on tick, owing him the fare, the men needing to save the little hard money they had for the $14 government filing fee on a homestead* because they lacked even the small down payment on railroad lands. The five-year homestead residence requirement didn't worry these. They wanted a place to reside, to live.

As the train neared his townsite John Cozad returned to the emigrant car, his hat held to sit upon his wrist, the silk of it polished to gleaming, his linen fresh and white as when they started. He pointed out of the windows where only telegraph poles seemed to break the pure whiteness of the bright noonday sun.

"Watch for the sign of the hundredth meridian as we pass it. All around you here is the winter-fertilized ground of our new commonwealth."

The weary men and women acknowledged his words with a glance out at the weathered sign, and a nod or perhaps glum silence. But the glow on the dark face of John Cozad was not to be chilled easily, and Traber, as his brother-in-law, knew it was more than any lucky night at cards; it was this new venture, the newest, the most ambitious of the Cozad colonies. This time Traber hoped John would manage himself better, not blow up like a charge of that new stuff, dynamite, or build up animosities and opposition all around him by his big-bugging ways. The wish was not only for the sake of Theresa and the boys. Money John J. Cozad could pick up any time but he demanded more than that for himself and his family, much, much more, and now, getting on toward forty-five as John J. was, it should come soon.

At Willow Island the emigrant car was switched to the

* The Homestead Act, effective January 1863, allowed each bona fide settler 160 acres from the public domain for the $14 filing fee, and was patentable after 5 years residence and $800 in improvements, including house, tilled acreage, fences, wells, etc. Within the railroad land areas, the homestead was restricted to 80 acres, except for Union veterans of at least 90 days' service, who were eligible for the full 160 acres here also.

48

siding. The excursionists stepped down into the raw December snow wind of Nebraska and looked around the little station with the few scattered houses, huts to all but John Cozad and Traber Gatewood, just low, snow-roofed huts squatting on more snow.

The homeseekers walked around aimlessly a while, stretching their legs, watching the train take on water and wood and then puff away westward, and while not one sob escaped the women, their faces were serious too, as the men's.

By now a wagon was clattering across the tracks and stopping at the door of the car. Costin, the driver, was bundled up in a buffalo coat and a fur cap deep down over his ears. He wrapped the lines around the standard and jumped down over the wheel.

"Well, you made it, Mr. Cozad," he said, pulling off his mitten to shake hands with the leader and the others who hadn't gone inside the emigrant car. Then he lifted out the endgate of the wagon and drew down a big black army kettle smelling fine of hot beans, and a washtub covered with a flour-sack cloth that showed spreading grease spots. These and a bucket of coffee were carried into the car and the covers removed. Beans, steaming, dark and rich, Costin showed with pride. "Grew them pintos right here on the place, folks." In the tub was a great rib roast of fat buffalo. "Home grown too, but a little farther out," Costin added. "Roasted like the Indians do, staked over a bed of coals."

It was an excellent, a hearty, feast and afterward they asked questions of Costin and finally went to bed tired but happy.

John J. Cozad's colony had arrived, and this time there was plenty of room.

The early December snow cleared before that periodic stretch of warm sun that the Union Pacific land pamphlet promised sometime every winter. The icicles along the eaves dripped and fell, the earth pushed up dark and swollen along the edges of the drifts. By the time the new colony started out to look over their townsite and the railroad and government land, there was only an occasional strip of snowbank left clinging along the north of the rises and in the gullies. The ponies of the Cozad boys, shaggy with the early winter, were saddled and the stirrups let out. The teams were hitched to a couple of wagons loaded with supplies, implements, and enough lumber for a knock-together shelter. So John Cozad started out with his relatives; his assistant, Capt. Ross; Dr. Donough, the dentist friend from near Cozaddale; Sam Atkinson from near the colonizer's birthplace; and half a dozen others. The rest of the colonists remained with the emigrant car at Willow Island making plans, some discouraged to find the country raw and cold, others sending to Omaha or the home folks or friends in Ohio for necessities that the winter would demand here—warmer clothing, heavy bedding, maybe the loan of a little more money.

At the meridian sign the men stood around the wagons in the chill sunlight, some suggesting that they move the town farther up, with everything open and free for their selection, their choice. Here on this low ground they would find seepage in their cellars come spring, their wells probably tainted.

"But we have to stay near the railroad, and the siding here, where the depot's to be located," Dave Claypool argued with his usual reasonableness.

"And here's the hundredth-meridian sign," old Robert Gatewood added. "That's a mighty good card to draw to."

His words reminded the others of the handbills on the train boosting the center of the country as the proper place for the new national capital, and of the suggestion carried by the big sign here. So it was an easy victory for John Cozad's site, although nothing could have changed it anyway. He had signed the contract with the railroad to locate the town here; he owned much of the land where the city would spread, enough to make him and his family wealthy—help give his sons every-thing a man climbing as high as he was going could give them. And Theresa. No matter how far a man's fancy might wander in river town or mining camp, it was only his legal wife who could bring him the credit John J. Cozad must have. While he had known freer women, more seductive, and some who made him feel more overpoweringly passionate for a time or two, it was very easy to imagine the fine bearing of the hand-some Theresa in the velvets of a senator's wife.

By night a shelter shack had been hammered together, enough to shut out the cold wind, the roof boards weighted down by a few half-frozen chunks of sod. It was warm enough, with a smoke hole for the campfire set in the center, the flame kept low as Traber Gatewood had seen among the Pawnees camped at the Platte last summer. From that day the site was never to be deserted for an hour.

The pleasant days that followed the early December snow-storm were busy ones. John Cozad contracted for five hundred additional cords of wood to burn brick for his home, the clay discovered ready for the digging just north of the new camp. The shelter shack was put together more substantially. They even set the breaking plow into the earth and turned a little sod before the frost struck down. Laid up in walls that they roofed with willows held down by more sod, they had snug housing against the winter. The door and the window casings were of rough-sawn cottonwood off a pile hauled in from a little water-power sawmill down the Platte. The boards would curl badly but for the present they would do, at least until the carload of lumber John Cozad ordered arrived. It came, bright and pitch-piney even in the cold, and was unloaded at the siding.

By this time the colonists had lived through their first Indian scare. Sam Atkinson had hurried on ahead to file on govern-ment land not over two miles north of the meridian sign. He put the little money he had into a two-story house, of lumber hauled in from Willow Island, the carpentry done on exchange of work with other colonists.

The men had walked out every morning from Willow carrying their lunches, kept warm beside the trash stove while they worked. One day when they were up on the second floor, measuring and figuring, somebody heard a noise below —half a dozen Indians helping themselves to the lunches. Unarmed, the settlers could only keep silent and wait, even after the Indians had ridden away. In the first dusk they slipped back to Willow Island, hungry, cold, and scared.

Their story alarmed some of the colonists, particularly the women. But when Costin heard about it he laughed. "Might even have been the man the Cozad boys doctored last summer, if he can ride. Sure to be Pawnees. Hungry devils, ain't they? Friendly but hungry."

Even so, Sam Atkinson was mighty glad to see the settlers move in at the meridian. When the work was well started the railroad hauled the emigrant car to the siding there and then set out a boxcar for the station, the depot, with COZAD across the front and ends. The first substantial building, the Emigrant House, was going up fast as winter settled back upon the region. By then a couple of the men had returned to Cincinnati in disgust that the country wasn't a tropic idyl or at least as warm as they now remembered the Ohio valley. Several others had gone back to prepare their families for spring emigration. John Cozad was away too, organizing more and larger excursions, planning to send out one a month from January on.

While he was gone the Gatewoods circulated a petition around the camp for a post office named Cozad and prepared space for it in Emigrant House. They set aside a little corner room for a store, too, to be run by Julia Gatewood, Theresa's mother, when she arrived.

Two temporary wells were put down by spade to first water, very shallow, as some had predicted, the ones who had opposed John Cozad's site from the start. The red-bearded station agent, Ed Sanderson, got his transfer to the new town. The Cozad boys, off in school at Cincinnati, were pleased. Johnny tried to recall the Morse code that Mr. Ed had taught him and Robert hoped to loaf away pleasant hours around the station, and while he watched the sun make fire of the red beard, gathered stories to tell to himself later.

"Are we going pretty soon?" he asked. "I miss Grandpa and my pony. Can we go Easter?"

"Not until after school," his mother said firmly.

Late in January the boys went down to watch the second excursion start, Robert hanging back in the car to the last minute, hoping his grandmother would let him come along. There was room, with only about twenty-five likely settlers altogether, counting the grandmother and some other women who had been following their men for many years without question and would perhaps have to do it again. But John Cozad sent the boy out to stand on the platform.

When the March group, the fourth excursion, with some from Indianapolis and Philadelphia, arrived, the towns up and down the railroad began to take notice. North Platte, with the land-office business, and too far for competition anyway, welcomed the new settlement. Plum Creek, the only established town in the county, was a little sour, although some saw that the aggressive new community would help pay for the courthouse, particularly when the colonizer came striding in with his land buyers to register their deeds to taxable land—John Cozad still the only large landowner in the county except the railroad. When some stood away from him, he big-bugged it down the dirt road that was the one street and made it clear once more that he didn't consider a wild place like Plum Creek fit for the seat of his county. At the newspaper office he said,

"I issue a blanket invitation to all but the saloons to join our fair, our clean and orderly city. Come to Cozad and I will build you a fitting courthouse."

Nobody replied; nobody reminded him that the Plum colony was good Philadelphia stock that despised the drunks and the gun-packing outfits hanging around their town as much as he, and that many lumped the gambler, any gambler, with the worst.

It seemed there was a little dissension over at Cozad too, done before Theresa and the sons had to see it. More solid settlers were coming in now, some with several members of the family old enough to file on land, or with a large brood of growing young people, like Alfred Pearson. He moved out eight, nine miles north of town because, some said, the two bullheads, Pearson and John Cozad, had already clashed. Others thought that Al wanted room as the children reached twenty-one. In the meantime he could graze a spreading region as fast as he got his hands on cattle, already siding with the ranchers against the settlers although he had scarcely one cow brute to his name.

It was among the cattlemen that the Cozad colony caused the most concern, particularly among those who laid claim to the range around the town because their herds had passed through once or twice. Settlers like Sam Atkinson, with his two-story frame house, would be hard to shake loose. Better keep them from putting down taproots in the first place. Cowboys and some ranch managers hanging out at the cowtown of Plum Creek, or the road ranch at the new Plum bridge, sometimes rode around through Cozad although the place was dry as buffalo bones. They spurred in, arrogant and whooping, putting bullets into the hundredth-meridian sign or the frame of Emigrant House going up. Perhaps hard times and the collapse of cattle prices that had cut down the ranch jobs made the cowboys more anxious to prove they were worth their wages in other ways.

The seventy-five homeseekers in Cozad's April excursion found the Platte gray and sullen, the geese leaving for the north. By then the brick kiln was breathing heat and threads of smoke and carloads of lumber came in. Still, most of the buildings were sod, with perhaps cloth or paper greased with hot buffalo tallow for the window hole, the lamp a can of the same tallow with a strip of cotton underwear speared on a wire for a wick. Only half a dozen in town afforded the millionaire's light, the coal-oil lamp, usually bracketed to the wall, a tin reflector behind.

By the time Emigrant House neared completion it was packed with families sleeping in bunks, the children on pallets underneath or along the wall, waiting to move out to their land as soon as a dugout could be thrust into some bank or a building thrown up by a community house-raising. In the meantime the slips of geraniums, begonias, wax plants, and wandering Jew, nursed so carefully all the way west as a living symbol of everything left behind, were rooting in tin cans and axle-grease buckets picked up along the freight trails.

The last month of school the Cozad boys, particularly Robert, burned with western fever hot as any goldseeker's. They wrote to their grandparents every other day, the eight-year-old Robert's mostly fanciful little sketches along the wide margins of his stiff, badly spelled notes that were really little stories of adventures in the west. He had a new set of colors given to him at the Weber art school, after his mother took him to see the pictures that Frank Duveneck brought back from Munich. Robert liked the paintings, particularly one called *The Whistling Boy*, and he hoped he might paint something like it, someday. But Mr. Duveneck was a scary man, with the great mustache, the thick spectacles on his nose, and all that talking—a really great talker.

Robert put the painter into his new diary, written in a large and awkward hand, the spelling bad too, but he excused himself because he was only eight, really eight and three-quarters, practically nine for all other purposes. He liked the sketch he made of Mr. D., as he called the painter, better, the mustaches wonderously wild, like tangled Platte River slough grass.

They reached the west on a fine spring day, the sky far and blue, the eagle circling high up like a loose black eyelash floating. The smell of wild plum blossoms was heavy on the wind and the black and white bobolinks, as the Ohio farmers called the flying songsters, rose high into the air, dropping music as they climbed up, up and then drifted back to the ground where the nest was probably well hidden in the tufted grass. The Platte was roaring in the second flood of the spring, which, as the boys knew from last summer, was barely a beginning compared to the water that would come down from the snows of the mountains later.

The Cozads saw bands of dark plowing where last year there was only fire-blackened prairie. Here and there a man following his sod buster along a widening strip lifted his ox goad in greeting to the little local rumbling past, or his whip over the faster horses, the turned earth falling in a flat ribbon behind him.

At the hundredth-meridian sign the newcomers climbed stiffly down from the car, those who were returning surprised that so much had been done on the bare prairie of four, five months ago. But some of the new ones demanded a little evidence that the flowery promises of the Great Platte Valley poster and the population claims of five hundred people living within the environs of Cozad were not all just more western tall-tale stuff. A filling supper of roast buffalo, from the packs of meat rolled off the western trains every day or so, and the sight of a hunter coming in at dusk with a deer across his saddle, helped make at least that much of the dream a reality.

Mrs. Cozad and the boys settled in Emigrant House and visited around their relatives that evening, all passably housed, if not in castles, all offering John J.'s apologies that business took him on a hurried trip to the land office.

"Best places going mighty fast, ranchers covering the good watering spots with fraudulent filings," old Robert Gatewood said, his eyes bright in the sunburnt, wind-seamed face turned to his grandsons.

In three days John Cozad was back from North Platte with ten of his landseekers, all but two with the location they wanted, the others covered by cowboys for the ranchers, it seemed. He was expansive, going out to a string of covered wagons stopping, pleased with the hum of the new settlement here, After supper, when the colonizer could at last greet his family properly, he praised the boys on their showing at school, and promised them a fine summer, many, many fine summers here. Then they were sent to bed, the parents looking after them with their arms upon each other, almost like ardent young lovers.

That night there was a sudden orange gleam against the windows of Emigrant House and a cry of "Fire!" Everybody ran out but it wasn't in the little hotel. It was the depot, already a loaf of flame, the agent running out in his underpants carrying his station records and the telegraph machine he had ripped up by the roots, the wires dangling.

The men made a bucket brigade from the nearest well but the old boxcar burned fast. Afterward there was a light in the little Gatewood store until almost morning. It seemed that the fire had started on the west end of the depot—with the wind—and that there was a strong smell of coal oil on the sparse, trampled spring grass.

"Probably a cowboy or some Plum Creeker," David Claypool suggested, and while some men there nodded, those from Philadelphia protested a little. Why, there was solid stock from their home town in the Plum Creek colony, not the kind of people to go around laying fires. But an arsonist loose in the country was disturbing. Here and there an eye slid speculatively around those in the room, the shadows from the lantern on the counter moving ponderously, uneasily, against the wall.

At last the matter was left there for the present. Nobody outside of the family knew that there were bits of damp earth marked as from barefoot soles between the bunks in the Cozad part of the hotel, although everyone had gone to bed very early.

Traber Gatewood had used the saddle ponies some to take the winter friskiness out of them but they gave the boys a good run on their first spring ride. They let them out and raced for the river, Robert far behind on his short-legged little calico, short-legged but unwilling to give up until she stopped short at the riverbank and sent the boy over her head into a pile of flood-borne brush.

The boys were still wandering along the stream, watching for mink tracks, skipping flat stones across the gray waters or just standing, happy, when John Cozad with two rigs full of landseekers drew up at the river. Pointing with the buggy whip, he showed the fine hay bottoms and the beauties of the Platte, full of fish, a real resort spot for summer boating and bathing, winter skating. Soon there would be a bridge here, to bring trade from as far as the Republican River country and to hasten settlement over on the south side. Johnny listened, but his father did not add the other reason—that the cattlemen were getting a strong foothold over there, enough to threaten the settlement on this side, too. No use alarming the timid.

The boys were interested in the brick kilns, sending up meditative little whiffs of smoke to show that they were quietly at their work, their Uncle Traber said. He molded the bricks, ready when the kilns cooled enough for refilling. Afterward he started the hotel, carrying most of the brick and much of the mortar for the big barny building himself.

As he said, he wasn't as tall as some here, but squared out, only a medium distance from the ground so he didn't have far to lift the hod, and nature had provided a good resting place for it on those shoulders. Because his clothing was usually gray, whether for his dental trips and church, or his mason's overalls, he looked much the same except that the overalls got whitish from the mortar and dust, his hair thick with it too. His nephews liked to hang around, Johnny big enough to hand up tools and sometimes brick and buckets of mortar. Robert kept watching for the little animals he had molded from the wet clay and stuck in with the bricks for the firing. His nice prairie dog was somehow cracked in the kiln.

"Perhaps you will be better with your stories than your sculpture," his mother comforted.

It was about that time that J. D. Haskell, who liked to do a little writing, came to town. There was no depot, only stale ashes blowing where the boxcar had stood—and the five buildings far enough along to be worth the name. Robert, who met every daytime train when he was in town, was down to watch the car unloaded. He pushed up to see the twenty-year-old homeseeker who came with such a lot of goods. It seemed that Haskell had heard the colony was advertising for a butcher and here he was. He had a little two-hole stove in one end of the boxcar, to cook his coffee and fry flapjacks. The goods box full of his personal belongings served as a seat or table. In addition he had a horse, two milch cows, four sows, his butcher tools and a snarl-mouthed bulldog that sidled up to the Cozad boy. Robert stood his ground but held his hand up high out of reach. The dog pressed a cold velvety nose to the boy's black-stockinged leg and in a moment Robert was down in the dust, examining the dog's spiked collar, wooling the cropped ears, laughing at the low fierce growls of the dog and the spank of his stub tail.

"Robert! Be careful!" his Uncle Traber called from the street.

Young Haskell spit into the dust. "That dog only looks dangerous from off a ways. I fetched him along because a butcher just has to have a bulldog."

With his hand on the collar, Robert and the few loafers around watched this handy young settler work. He pulled a dozen heavy foot-wide planks from the car, leaned them in a double layer against the open doorway, and with the help of a couple of the curious, to push or to pull on the halters or lead ropes, slid his stock out, the cows first, groaning their ponderous complaint, the sows frankly willing to be dragged, slivers or no, the horse balking at first and then taking a final desperate leap off the ramp, to fall on his shoulder. For a moment Robert and young Haskell both thought he had broken a leg. But before long the horse sat up and then pulled his hindquarters up too. He limped a little, shook himself, and then reached for a mouthful of the scrubby grass at the siding.

It wasn't like watching the elephants being unloaded in Cincinnati but in some ways it was better, for this was their town, his father's first, of course, but belonging to the rest of them too.

Suddenly Robert remembered the manners that his mother, and his father too, when he had time, urged upon the sons. So he stepped forward as his father might if he were there. Pulling his cap off as his father did the silk topper, the boy held out a hand that lacked cleanliness but was friendly.

"Welcome to Cozad, sir," he managed to say. And then he ran, letting his feet carry him away in his embarrassment.

V

J OHN J. COZAD was back at Cincinnati glowing with confidence and well-being, striding in here and there where
he had been known perhaps since he was twelve or fourteen,
from around the time when his old friend the gambler had
been hanged here on the waterfront before the boy's naked
eyes. Now John Cozad was full of the ideas he believed no
one here had ever appreciated in him before. His sharp deep-
set eyes sought not only an occasional gleam of surprise but
some understanding, at least a little understanding, of the importance of his community, his dream, and of the force of this
dream.

It was true that he had a kind of power out in his town
that any swamper here would understand, a power beyond
any politician's. He controlled the sale of every lot in his
town, and was practically the king of the sixteen square miles
upon which it lay—a real, a personal metropolis, in addition to
the 38,000 acres of railroad lands he controlled outside. The
government land near the town was covered by his settlers,
including his own entry and those of all the Gatewoods
coming in as well as some Cozad relatives. Many took up pre-

emptions* in addition to the short homestead permitted in the railroad land belt. Some added an outlying timber claim** free for planting the trees.

As John Cozad strolled through his old spots in Cincinnati acquaintances, friend and enemy, pushed up to look at this new importance the man was giving himself. The land hungry were drawn too, particularly those with no money and no prospects in these panic times, young men and boys, some scarcely seventeen, eighteen.

"To buy railroad lands you can be any age, if you have the down payment," he told these. "For free government land you have to be twenty-one or the head of a family."

"Is there room for ladies too?" some dance-hall girls might ask, one way or another.

"Indeed for ladies," John Cozad always replied, with his usual bow for lady manners anywhere.

"I mean free land—for me——"

"Indeed, that is what I also mean," he might say, and move on a little more rapidly now.

Everywhere it was plain that the enthusiastic stories coming back from his colonists were not only making him a curiosity but bringing him new attention, a new respect. As the spring moved into summer with no easing of the hard times, he was swamped by requests for literature about his town, for help to get out to this "ideal community in the wilderness," "This New Canaan of the West," as one minister called it from his pulpit.

But with this enlarged reputation came resentment, too, at least John Cozad seemed to be the victim of more spite than he ever was as a gambler or the promoter of the struggling little

* Preemption Act. 1841–91, 160 acres of government land at $1.25 an acre, $2.50 within the railroad belt, payable in 5 years, to bona fide settlers not owning 340 acres.
** Timber Culture Act, 1873–91, 160 acres for planting (1874 on) 10 acres to trees.

community of Cozaddale outside of Cincinnati. Captain Ross, from there, expressed uneasiness.

"I hear some things I don't like," he tried to say several times, but the closest he got was to remind his friend that even as a land promoter he might still need his pistols.

Out in Nebraska there was a surprise of sorts waiting for the community builder's return, a neat pine board with the sign COZAD P.O. above the side door of Emigrant House. Robert saw this with a burning impatience to show his father.

"You sure got feathers in your britches these days, Robert Henry," his grandfather told him, speaking mildly, but the boy knew it was a warning about something. It always was when anybody used both his names. "Your father's due back next week, I hear," the old man said as he sorted the mail for Traber, A. T. Gatewood, postmaster, who was away to the western settlements pulling teeth.

But before next week a long telegram came for Robert's mother, and while she didn't read it to the sons, he knew she was concerned. He listened around the store and went down to Mr. Ed at the depot, but he could hear nothing about it, nothing more than his mother told some landseekers, "I think Mr. Cozad may be detained in Cincinnati a while." Afterward she sent Robert for Dave Claypool to show the gentlemen the land. The boy got to ride out with them, standing up in the spring wagon as they looked over the country and asked the main question: "Can a man make a living for a family here?"

Three days later Robert picked up the mail at the post office and the roll of newspapers. His mother was out with Johnny, gathering wild gooseberries and the early black currants for jelly. To pass the time, the boy spread the home papers out on the floor, looking through them for names he might recognize. On his stomach, heels waving aimlessly in the air behind him, he propped his chin in a palm and hoped for perhaps a little

63

item about General Custer going into the Black Hills looking for gold, or about hostile Indians in the west, which now seemed much farther out than it did in Cincinnati. Maybe there was something about the scandal he heard people whisper about there, and here too, his mother and grandmother discussing the Rev. Henry Ward Beecher, brother of the Cincinnati woman, Mrs. Stowe, who wrote *Uncle Tom's Cabin*. The grandmother once took Robert to see it, with a little girl called Eva to fly off to heaven. On the way home the Virginia-reared Julia Gatewood told the boy that the story wasn't really true. But he had known that. He could see the wires that dragged Little Eva up, as plain as day.

In the Cincinnati *Enquirer* Robert found some big poster advertisements about an animal show and wondered if it would be as mammoth as last year's—so much going on that he never saw near all. Idly turning the broad pages for something else interesting, a name jumped out at him, his own name: Cozad. "Todd versus Cozad" the headline said, whatever that meant.

Then his heart began to pound clear down to his belly, for it was their father that the paper meant when it said: "How Gamblers' Chickens Come Home to Roost." The boy's eyes blurred and he could hardly read the difficult opening words:

> The monotony of life of the region was varied by a spirited battle about midday yesterday. The circumstances of the quarrel were shrouded in mystery.

Robert went over this twice, pondering what it meant, and then read on, the story like something he might make up for himself when he was lonesome, with bad men and good. The newspaper said that the accounts were conflicting. One version was that a William Todd and a friend were sitting on the railing in front of Wehrle's about noon yesterday. John J. Cozad, an ex-gambler who had his office above, ordered Todd to move on in an insulting manner because he wanted no loud talk around his office. Cozad had transferred his talents to real estate but among his past victims was the young Todd, who was said to have been cleaned out of a $10,000 patrimony by the retired cardist years ago, and was out for revenge.

The crowd had included friends of both parties and so Todd and his companion left, but about an hour later they managed to encounter Cozad again, on the street, and challenged him. One eyewitness said the gambler drew a large pistol and aimed it. Todd grabbed the gun, broke Cozad's jaw and struck him several times over the head and nearly fractured the skull. Todd was arrested and taken to the police station, charged with assault and battery and released on $25 bail. Cozad's wounds were dressed at a drugstore and then he was taken to the residence of Dr. Donough, in badly damaged condition.

Cozad, it seemed, insisted that Todd and a companion were knocking their feet against his sign. He requested them to desist, in a mild way, which was the only offense he remembers to have given Todd, with whom he had had no word for years. Todd, a gentleman of wealthy connections, had always acted square in the past. All Cozad remembered of the attack was that while walking with Ross, his clerk, he was suddenly attacked from behind by Todd, who used a slung shot on him.

So the paper offered the two versions, stating no preference.

Slowly the boy came out of the illusion that this was a story. He sat back on his haunches and stared at the print as the suspense of the account faded and he had to realize that this was not something made up but an actual occurrence, and to their own father, the injury his.

Now the boy wanted to run to his grandmother's apron as he did when he was very small, but he knew they must never spread the father's business around, not to anyone. His short chin twitched as he tried to keep from crying, choking back the sobs that must not be heard by others in Emigrant House.

"Why didn't you shoot him, shoot him with your other

pistol?" he demanded, as though his father were there, lying bloodied on the ground. Then the phrases of the account began to strike him with their full meaning. "Broken jaw——" that meant broken and hanging down like the dog he saw after a runaway team went over him. "Nearly fractured skull" that was a cracked head——

The nine-year-old Robert knew people died of cracked heads, and now he could scarcely hold himself together, wanting to ride out to his mother and Johnny, run to Mr. Ed at the depot, anybody. But he did not dare and so he cried softly, huddled over the papers on the floor, letting himself slip face down to the print, sobbing hopelessly, as if he had always known something very bad like this would happen.

After a long time Robert awoke at a shaking from his mother's hand and sat up, rubbing his fist into his blurry eyes, staring at her and at Johnny with the bucket hanging from his hand. Then Robert saw the newspapers, the open *Enquirer*, still spread out around him on the floor, and, remembering, he started to cry again.

"Robert!" his mother ordered. "Stop this minute! What is the matter with you? You never cry!"

Finally they got the story out of him, and with her arm around the boy she read the account in the paper, read it aloud, murmuring in sorrow.

After she was through Theresa Cozad held herself to a silent moment, comforting the boy and looking over his head to the elder son. "The telegram three days ago told me a little about this, but carefully, so's not to start any rumors. Now it will be spread all over——"

"Oh, is he dead?" Robert asked fearfully, searching his mother's face.

"We don't say things like that. I told you he might be detained. That is all."

"But is he alive?" the boy wanted to ask, to persist for an answer, but he didn't dare, and his mother was still talking.

"Now go watch the store, both of you, and send your grandmother up here."

There was the Fourth of July to prepare for, but without much heart among the Cozads. Plum Creek was putting on a really big celebration, inviting all the people from down along the Republican who were using the new bridge to get to the railroad there, and everybody from Cozad, too, asking them to get up a baseball team against the county-seat nine. In addition there would be a grand picnic, speeches, horse and foot races, a fife-and-drum corps for the parading, and a grand display of fireworks at night. Many from Cozad went, some going up early as the Costins did last year, taking tents or covered wagons because they had county-seat business to dispatch before the holiday, perhaps land purchases or mortgages to record, maybe a marriage license to take out, or half a dozen other possible transactions. Several of the Gatewoods drove up and Theresa said the boys might go along if they wished. At first Johnny planned on it because the girls of the town would all be up there, but for once Robert hung back and so his brother decided to stay home too. They knew there would be gossip and snides about that gambler Cozad finally getting his just deserts. They remembered the troubles their father got into there last year.

When Traber came back he said they didn't miss much. Mostly there was just talk of hard times, drouth, the sod corn perhaps not sprouted at all, but feeding the tent-peg gophers, or if up, standing still, even shrinking, crawling back into the ground. It wasn't over an inch high except in the lowest spots, and already curled and rattling in the wind, where the range cattle and trail herds could be kept away. The prairie was dried out everywhere, and even the grasshoppers leaving it, moving thick into the garden patches where women had carried water to keep the beans or carrots green, and maybe a flower or two, bachelor-buttons or a clump of petunias.

By now not only young Robert but Johnny too watched the Cincinnati papers for news of their father, and if anything would be done to Todd. It seemed the town was getting mighty holy about gamblers when it was their breeding spot so long, Grandpa Robert complained. Some three-card-monte men, including Shang and Jarvis, men both Cozad boys had seen, were dumped off a train and thrown into jail. The little item made a chilly spot between Robert's shoulder blades and he sneaked a look at his brother, who was playing grownup and not letting anybody see what he thought.

Their father had written a little about one story in the paper, the great flight of passenger pigeons, dark as storm clouds over Ohio and now up in Michigan, dropping on the crops, cleaning them out slick. The farmers tried guns, traps, nets, and poison, and even built fires to start them flying again. Robert thought about the birds, hoping they would not come here too, pitying them. He begged a strip of wrapping paper from his grandmother for a long picture, showing the pigeons coming, settling, eating, the farmers hurrying out, their wives too with calico skirts flying, and the children and dogs while the hungry pigeons were eating and eating. He drew traps and nets full of birds, and piles of dead ones all around or being hauled away by the wagonloads. The last picture showed the fires and a few scattered birds starting up through the smoke.

The home newspapers had a little story about grasshoppers in eastern Colorado too, but that didn't interest the boys as much as the one about Canada Bill, the rube gambler their father knew so well. He was almost arrested too, only he was slick enough to sneak off the train at the edge of the town and take a streetcar. A Mr. Houh, accused of cheating a man out of $1400 was jugged, and suddenly Robert was frightened for his father again, with a broken jaw and maybe a cracked head. Maybe he was locked up too, looking out between bars.

Unable to stand it with Johnny there to see, Robert slipped

out the back way and down along the railroad track, running in the burning heat. After a while he got tired, sweat burning his eyes. He found a willow fish pole he had cut long ago, and with it he whipped off the drouth-browned sunflower heads along the right-of-way, whacking at them with both hands because they were so tough, their leaves dry and eaten full of holes, the grasshoppers pattering in a sort of rushing sound before his dusty bluchers.

When he came back a man just off the train from North Platte had gathered half a dozen wind-burned, gaunted settlers around him. Robert saw them standing together in a friendly knot and Johnny right up close too, not away as the boys usually stayed now, with so many dark faces blaming their father for bringing them here to starve to death.

Tad Matthews, the old buffalo hunter, was there too, and so Robert edged up, ready to stroll away as casually as he could, pretending he hadn't stopped at all. But they weren't discussing drouth or even hard times, some speaking easily for the first time since the rains stopped, it seemed, somehow alive again, one or another turning his mouth sideways to spit out the pale tobacco juice of hard times, but doing it fast, not to miss a word.

It seemed that a great old-time herd of buffaloes had appeared near North Platte, 50,000 head at least, some said, others putting it as low as 10,000 and shouted down for it. The herd had come charging in off the sun-baked prairie south of the river, the valley suddenly a great moving mass of the huge dark animals. Everybody who could find a horse to climb on and a gun, even an old muzzle-loader full of buckshot, headed across the drying Platte bed. A lot of ladies went too, sidesaddle, the skirts of their riding habits flying in the hot wind. But the buffaloes wouldn't stampede. They had come with their tongues hanging out for water and milled around in the river bed, blackening it for miles to the far eye. When they finally came out with their paunches full and round, they showed no inclination to move on. Run down, it seemed, trying to find water and from long chases by hunting Indians. Some had arrows still sticking in wounds that seeped a little blood, and a few of those that laid themselves down died there without a shot from anybody.

With rifle-armed troops from the fort and all the guns of the cowboys, old trappers and hunters, and the settlers, there must have been a real sight up there at the Forks—the puffs of blue powder smoke along the south bottoms, the roar of the guns lagging behind, and all the dust, the yells, and the running, and underneath the grunts and snorts of the great beasts trying to snatch a little grass even in the midst of the slaughter. Here and there a wounded buffalo chased a horse, one goring a couple before the bullets dropped him. The commander at Fort McPherson had sent out a squad to catch some calves. They got thirty by midafternoon, all they could handle, and had to take them in before the fun was half over. The cowboys who roped an old bull were mighty glad to cut him loose. Some of the settlers got calves too, picking them up where cows had been killed—the younger calves bawling over the carcasses.

When the valley was dark with dead buffalo, enough to feed the army half through the Civil War, skinners came in for the hides, summer-thin, but worth a little, and everything counted nowadays. The meat was free for anybody, all he could haul away in the hot weather, and still it seemed that none had been taken.

"You sure could dry it like the Indians do," one of the Cozad men said ruefully. "All this drouth and that hot wind ought to be good for something."

"My God, my kids could use some of that meat, if I was up there——"

It was a fine story, and the men at the Cozad depot found themselves looking southward, almost expecting a miracle to happen here where only a few scattered old bulls had crossed even at the height of the migrating season. They saw no streaming of dark herds down the bluffs south of the river. But there seemed to be something there—a curious silvery-gray cloud hanging along the horizon, probably the dust of a herd, most likely a Texas herd, to eat up what was left and spread the fever.

But the cloud lifted clear of the bluffs, moving, coming pretty fast on the southwest wind. Suddenly one of the men began to walk, head down in a soft-voiced cursing, repeating the same profanities over and over, quietly, hopelessly, as he plodded around in a circle, a kind of trapped and profane circle.

Finally one of the others spoke the evil word that was in the minds of them all now. "Grasshoppers," he said in a flat-mouthed way, disowning any connection with it. "Grasshoppers, by God, billions of them."

"Yeh, the Rocky Mountain grasshopper what's been eating up everything over along the Colorado line," old Matthews said. "I seen 'em before."

By now the cloud was lowering toward the river and next it was over the men, the air full of a light rushing sound and the shimmer of silver, the hoppers beginning to fall, spattering into the dust, more and more of them, sticking to everything, crawling over the men, over their hands, their faces, into the hair, the beards, in at the shirts and down the necks. The men tried to brush them off, some whipping the air with their hats, but the hoppers paid no attention, their jaws working, empty or full, moving, working.

The Cozad boys and their Uncle Traber ran up the dirt road to Emigrant House and helped the alarmed women carry the geraniums inside and slam the windows and the doors tight in the stifling air, to stare out at the chickens, first gorging themselves, now heavy and bewildered, some waddling reluctantly for shelter, others dropping in the road with grasshoppers all over them. A stray dog came running past, tail between his legs.

Robert couldn't stand it, with the hoppers still falling like hail all around. He threw a slicker over his head and bolted out toward the little pasture to comfort his calico pony and the other horses too, all running in wild circles along the pole fence.

By now there were low, ragged clouds of grasshoppers moving into the Platte valley as far east and west as anyone could see, but few took the time to look up. One woman was out swinging her broom of buckbrush against the tomato vines that she had kept growing by carrying water half the night. And still the plants bent and quivered with the hoppers, the gray earth all around moving with them, the curled and burnt grass covered with the struggling bodies, the jaws gnawing, all the air full of the gnawing sound, the creep of the legs, the snapping sounds of the jumps, and the gnawing, gnawing.

The telegraph rattled busily in the little station boxcar. Sanderson brushed his red beard over and over to clear it of the crawling and of the anxiety from the alarmed reports coming in. As far east as Kearney and west beyond North Platte, clouds of hoppers were dropping all along the route.

Evening came, and the night, and still the rushing sound, the flutter of wings coming down was there, the fires and smudges against them desperate little red points on the night prairie.

"Might as well burn the whole country now if you can find something to catch fire," Sanderson had said at supper, and pushed his unemptied plate back.

Robert ate, feeling ashamed of his appetite but somehow very hungry, although not even Johnny showed any taste for food. But Johnny always had to do what their mother did.

The bad news spread fast. By eleven o'clock Sanderson came running through the darkness with the yellowish sheet of a telegram. It was from Mr. Cozad, he said, and addressed to Mrs. Cozad, the Gatewoods, Dave Claypool, and all the rest of the colony:

> Tell everybody to hold fast stop railroad promised to haul relief goods free to drouth and grasshopper regions stop I have a great plan for employment for everybody in great local improvement. John J. Cozad

The faces around the room lightened, perhaps because even the vaguest relief plan was something positive this dark night, evidence of something being done when it seemed there could be nothing at all. But even more important was the assurance that John J. was recovering from the attack on him. He would be back soon and as full of vinegar as ever, making enemies right and left.

The comforting telegram was too late for two families who had been discontented even before the scorching drouth. Their wagons started east when the first sun set on the grasshopper plague, driving hard, hoping to get one of the women out before her mind snapped entirely.

Late that night the eastbound express stopped to take on an empty gondola from the siding, coupling it on behind the wood car, the brakeman throwing in a lot of shovels belonging to the section.

"There's been trouble with the wheels slipping, tracks too greasy from the grasshoppers," the conductor said. "We'll carry sand along to throw on the rails, give the wheels a grip."

Morning came, gray and hopeless, with the sky still darkened by the clouds of grasshoppers passing overhead and still falling, but it didn't matter much now. Everything was eaten bare, even the dead sunflowers Robert Cozad had whipped off with his willow switch yesterday. The potato vines that had stood dark and strong from the water carried all spring to keep something green along the tracks for the incoming landseekers were only holes in the ground, with grasshoppers still creeping futilely in and out. The ditches along the tracks

73

were level full, creeping, crawling, but many dead from sheer starvation. Sam Atkinson tried to set them afire but they wouldn't burn without coal oil poured over them, coal oil that would come mighty high by winter, no matter what the price.

It was an appalling three days, and when the wind changed and increased, the grasshoppers that had found something for their moving jaws began to lift like glistening winter mist from a frozen earth. The ground they left was barer than any field in January. By the next noon there were horses and teams all along the hitch racks, men and boys, even women too, come to ask if anybody knew of a shirttail patch of grass missed somewhere, enough to save a team or a cow or two until it rained and the grass could start.

Perhaps up north, along the Loup Rivers, and beyond, but not anywhere in the Platte valley.

And, as always among settlers, some were trading their last clutch of eggs or their last two bits from the pocket for late seeds, something that would still bring a yield. Turnips and rutabagas surely, maybe carrots or beets, with millet and fall rye for late pasture.

"You get rain enough to sprout the rye, you got rain for the grass——" Dan Freeman told the newcomers.

But something for the table, at least. It was a desperate hope—planting the ground that was bare and dry, and hard as the knobs of hell.

Mrs. Gatewood was caught short of seeds but she sent a hurry-up order to Omaha. Ought to be in by a couple of days or so. Long before the rains, probably.

In a few days the great stories that grow out of any calamity began to come in. Hoe and shovel handles had been eaten full of holes where grease and sweat from the palms had fattened the wood. Neat rows of holes were all that was left where horse-radish had been. Curtains, even whole rugs had vanished entire. Chickens, who ate themselves to death on grasshoppers, were stripped of feathers where they fell. Over

74

south of the river a man had been eaten bald-headed in his sleep. Skinned off clean as a prairie puff ball.

"I hear that the natives of Africa tamp the grasshoppers into flat cakes, dried and eaten. Taste oily, like some crisp oily nuts, ground up," Sam Atkinson said.

Nobody replaced the hopper-eaten handbills on telegraph poles and depots, not even those advocating the Platte valley as an ideal site for the New Washington.

By the time the real dimensions of the plague had been realized, John J. Cozad stepped off the train, pale, a brace around his jaw, with the new growth of beard beginning to curl around it. He was still weak but he brought news from Washington of seed grants next spring for settlers who lost their crops to grasshoppers. He walked firmly up the street, like a senator returning with special appropriations for his constituents. At the sight even those who had concentrated all their disappointment, all their suffering from drouth, hard times and finally the grasshoppers, in hatred for him, somehow took heart. Not all. Some were all ready to argue against anything he wanted to do for local improvement. One who argued about it before he knew what it might be was Alfred Pearson, from up north.

"In the name of the outlying settlers, I demand that we be given the same privileges and the same say-so as those close in," he insisted. Others tried to silence him. Nothing about local improvement work had really been said since the telegram. Did he want to spoil everything for them?

But mostly the talk was friendly enough, and it was late when the last one come to see John Cozad was gone. Finally it did not seem too bold for Theresa to show something of her feelings. Impulsive as a girl, she threw her arms around her husband's shoulder, but carefully—not touching the jaw brace.

"Oh, John, this time I was afraid for you, really afraid," she said softly, her handsome eyes wet and shining.

The sons, forgotten, slipped off to bed. Robert, very tired, was asleep in a few minutes. He awoke once and thought that Johnny was moving, perhaps getting up to walk in his sleep. The boy reached out and grasped a handful of his brother's nightshirt as he often did, so he would be awakened if there was a real movement.

But even before Robert was actually asleep again he felt his hand relax, and was too worn by the hard day to realize what he had done. When he awoke Johnny was gone, a bell was ringing, and his father was shaking him.

"Get your pants on. There's a fire. I think it's the depot again."

VI

John J. Cozad had come home, concerned about more than his lost goatee or the iron brace on his jaw that hampered his speech and put him on a practically liquid diet. The hard times were deepening. Jay Cooke and Company were bankrupt, mainly, some said, because he sank too much money in the Northern Pacific. To get new financing for that railroad, President Grant had been pushed into sending General Custer into the Black Hills to bring out the dramatic news of gold at the grassroots there, gold that every old-time mountain man had known about for years.

The Hills were legally Indian country and by treaty closed to white men, including, particularly, the army. But the Northern Pacific was going broke and by starting a gold rush to the Black Hills and pretending that they lay on the N.P. route up the Yellowstone, enough new money might be tolled in to save the railroad, and the shirts of the old investors.

Most of the talk that night of John Cozad's return had been about such far-off matters as this, and the panic in Wall Street and the bread lines everywhere. Mostly it was to avoid any reference to his appearance and to the attack at Cincinnati, which might so easily have ended in death and the collapse of his whole colony. To some that seemed to overshadow the outside problems, even the grasshoppers. It was typical of John Cozad that he passed lightly over the news of the plague. Of course the colonists were alarmed, Easterners that they were, and this gave an additional pry to the need for relief from the government. He did not say that he had seen grasshopper plagues before as he ate his late supper of a hearty buffalo soup, eggnog, and coffee. In the morning he would look over the crops, see the degree of damage.

Theresa had not been able to urge the calamity upon her husband's attention, not in the face of his pallor and the iron support of his jaw. Instead she found herself suddenly ardent as the young bride he had taken to Cincinnati with him sixteen years ago, but with a far deeper passion, and for a time even the braced jaw was forgotten.

Then suddenly dawn had come and the fire bell, stirring everybody out of bed, to run shouting and rousing the town. Robert had been awakened to stumble into his knickers and his shoes, only barely understanding what was said to him.

It was the depot again, the old boxcar stringing dark smoke over the dawning prairie, the flames roaring through the pine boards dry as kindling after two months of rainless summer. The bucket brigade was already working when John Cozad arrived, the Gatewoods, young Johnny, Dave Claypool, and half a dozen others, including the red-bearded Sanderson, handing the pails on from the railroad water tower. But there wasn't much saved except the station records that the agent had grabbed when the smoke awoke him.

Afterward Julia Gatewood stood at her door, waving her apron. "Come in for coffee!" she called through the hand cupped to her mouth.

But the people standing around the smoking strip of ashes that was the second station to burn here were slow to leave, the men talking, uneasy, arguing how this second fire started.

Apparently it came from some dry weeds and trash under one end of the old boxcar, but how?

Finally most of the watchers trooped up toward the barny hotel, all except Dave Claypool, who had sickness at home.

"It was pretty windy when the express went through," Sanderson said reasonably over his cob pipe to John Cozad when the others were gone. "Sparks, I guess, but there wasn't much to catch with the ground stripped so bare——"

At the last word, the community builder stopped his consideration of the fire to look around and for the first time he noticed the barren earth, gray and bleached, as naked as a desert. Abruptly he turned and hurried across the tracks toward the river bottoms, with only the wooden sticks of the weeds along the way standing, the grass gone, the trees even on the island bare as midwinter. Nowhere was there a living thing except a few dying grasshoppers among the dead piled up in corners and ditches by the wind—the last few who hadn't made it into the air.

Alone the man stood on the blasted earth of his colony, his black eyes smoky-hard. Once he looked back to the small cluster of houses and shacks that was the core of his dream, and then quickly away to the far horizon all around. There was only one movement on all of it, a covered wagon topping a little rise off south of the river and turning into the old Overland Trail. Such wagons were common. Some spring days fifty, sixty moved along the old trail across there, going west. This one was an exception, heading east, which would have been unnoticed if it were another year. Now it was deserting the fruitless land. And behind that wagon another appeared from farther west and then another. Early-rising bastards these were —men in a hurry.

Bowed, his hands clasped behind his back, John Cozad turned to look north, toward his town, his handwork, and now he saw wagons moving eastward on the trail there too.

He noticed that some of the shacks and soddies on the home-steads nearby already had the sad look of loneliness, of final desertion, about them, even from half a mile or so. All the dark anger that was never more than dozing in John Cozad rose up in him and throbbed in his healing jaw. So everybody had been waiting for him to come home, to watch him like buzzards waiting for a sick old horse to die. Not one of them had dared write him how bad it really was. Nobody had the courage, the fortitude, or perhaps the affection for him, not his brother-in-law Traber or his nephew Dave, the two who must have understood. Now it was already very late.

Swiftly he strode up the bare road toward the town, the dust spurting under his feet, the second burned spot of a depot all but unnoticed except that he crossed the tracks up-wind, to avoid the thread of lurking smoke and the shimmer of heat over the ashes.

At the Emigrant House he burst into the dining room, where the fire fighters and the others were sitting around the long bare pine table. Mrs. Gatewood, carrying in a great stack of pancakes, stopped at the sight of his face. Purposefully she set the plates on the end of the table and nodded him to his chair.

"You need coffee, Son," she said.

But John J. shook off the offer. "I've decided to bridge the Platte," he announced, speaking with difficulty in the jaw brace, standing dramatically against the light of the early sun outside the doorway. "I shall start the bridge tomorrow."

"A bridge, Mr. Cozad?" one of the men spoke up. "What the hell for? The grasshoppers got no trouble crossing."

But the town colonizer ignored the interruption. "It will encourage those over south to stay and bring their business here, instead of going to the Plum Creek bridge. Furthermore, I won't have any of my colony needy, starving."

Several of the men lifted their shaggy heads but not in hope, their knives and forks still poised. "It'll be a tremendous job,"

Sam Atkinson said mildly, his eyes thoughtful under the thick sandy brows. "Needs the whole county behind it."

"Plum Creek back it? Not a chance," Ed Young, the only real politician among them, said.

Traber Gatewood looked up. "Courthouse's not completed yet, over there. We might move the county seat, if we stick tight here."

"Well, any bridge over the Platte'll have to be a stout one, if it's to stand up come flood time."

But John Cozad didn't seem to be listening to any of them. "There will be work for all my settlers who lost their crops—or lost their customers."

Alex McIntyre, a distant relative of Theresa's, who had come out recently, spoke up. "I guess we'll unpack my tinsmithing equipment and try it a while," he said to his son Henry, who nodded reluctantly.

Several other men nodded too, slowly, not daring to be easily convinced, each desperately concerned with what John Cozad's announcement might mean to him, and perhaps to some hungry children at home. "Anyway, we're too poor to get away," one of them said.

By now the women had managed to get John Cozad seated in his place at the head of the table and his big mustache cup steaming with coffee before him. Most of the men were finished but they hung around, reluctant to go, even after they had pushed their chairs back and were done digging their teeth with broomstraws. When the colonizer had taken a long draw at his coffee, he eased his jaw brace a little and looked over to Theresa's brother.

"We'll want big spiles, Traber, a lot of them. From off up the Loup; I suppose that's the best place. And men to plow, cut and haul the sod."

"Sod?"

"Yes, I am planning the bridge in sections, the spans alternating with fill-ins where willows will be rooted to hold the earth. Water and fills, alternating, all across the river. But first the fills will have to be made of sod, the grass to take root."

"Sod? A goddamn sod bridge across the Platte River?" a newcomer demanded. "Such foolish talk, on top of them damned grasshoppers, sure cures me," he snorted. He paid for his breakfast and went out.

After a while Robert ran in to say that the man had piled all his stuff back into his wagon and was headed east, shouting and shaking his fist off across the river where the grasshoppers were coming again.

John Cozad went out to look, and refused to believe that this gray shimmering cloud could be anything but fog or pale, sunshot rain—not until the grasshoppers began to fall on him, clinging, exhausted, but their jaws working all the time. In a fury he whipped them off with his handkerchief and hurried into the house to lay his plans even bigger than he had anticipated.

The next week was a very busy one, even young Robert caught up in the excitement, the rush and hurry, carrying messages on his pony, running errands, or jumping on one leg in his impatience. Finally his father let him draw up plans, work them out with ruler and pencil until they were smudged with erasures.

John Cozad had forty acres of his river land east of the road laid out, to be stripped for the sod to make the long approach and the fill-in sections across the stream. Monday morning men with shovels on their backs, others with gaunted horses or ox teams, wagons and plows showed up, so many it seemed the country must really be settled, expect that they came from far away, as to an invitation on the wind. Before night the most difficult task of the day and of the weeks to come was turning away men who were strangers to the bridgebuilder, men whose need was great too, but he couldn't take on the whole state.

"I have to keep this to my own colony," he said, still speaking with difficulty, making it arrogant because he was very ashamed that he could not put bread into the mouths of all the hungry.

There were several heavy old freight wagons in the community, low wheeled, broad-tired, almost as stout as railroad cars. The long piling logs that Dave Claypool reported were available in Cedar Canyon, north of the Loup River, could be used as extended reach poles. The wagons went up and before they returned from the long and awkward drag, a flatboat with a small pile driver had been unloaded at the railroad and skated to the river on logs. Now even the skeptics who came to see began to believe, and John Cozad had to keep out of sight to avoid all the people he could not hope to hire.

Although there was little time for young Robert to look through the newspapers, and no son ever questioned John Cozad about anything as personal as the attack on him, the boy overheard a couple of the bridge men discussing something in the North Platte paper one had wrapped around his lunch. They stopped when they saw Robert listening but later he found the crumpled newspaper in the pile of trash and brush cleared off for the approach to the bridge. There it was, a letter his father had written to correct the story printed about the Todd attack. John Cozad objected to the statement that he used harsh words to Todd and his companion loafing on the real estate office steps. For some cause unknown to him, these men, with whom he had been on friendly terms, "made a small and cowardly attempt to assassinate me on my way to dinner." He complained that the Cincinnati papers wrote only from the assailants' side. No reporter had called on the man attacked. All except the *Enquirer* did finally publish corrections.

Robert thought about this and then hacked the letter out with his pocketknife. Before folding the clipping away he looked at it once more, and again on the way home. There was much left to be explained to him.

By now there were other things on the mind of the community builder, even though he still nursed his healing jaw and coaxed the curling beard to grow out into the customary goatee. One was the antagonism of the cattlemen even though no herds trailed through the blighted region now. With the grass so scarce it was not to be expected that the settler lucky enough to have any pasture or crop could hope to save much of either for himself. The ranchers let their hungry stock run loose to eat out every spear of green coming through. Their cowboys shot up the towns and settlements, sometimes dropping hot lead around anyone who dared to whoop range cattle off his land.

Then, over near Kearney, some cowboy put a bullet through the dress of a small girl driving Longhorns out of her father's corn patch. Now finally the settlers over there began to organize for mutual protection, arming and drilling against the more overbearing ranch hands who were often Texas badmen, mostly GTT's meaning "Gone to Texas," men who had fled there from the law or other vengeance.

Back before the grasshoppers it had seemed there might be shooting over range cattle around Cozad too, particularly with the trail herds eating a wide swath through land and crops and any settler's garden that happened to be within smelling distance, the lousy stock rubbing down soddies, falling through dugout roofs and into wells. A couple of settlers who did try to stand a trail herd off their homesteads found themselves outmanned and outgunned. What good was the state's Herd Law, which made the stockowner liable for all damages, if the settler was kept from taking up the trespassing cattle to hold for collection?

Now it didn't matter, with the whole region as bare as the bottom of a Pawnee papoose.

By mid-August the grass was starting again where a thunderhead or two had stood a while, with enough roaring and noise to send the timid cowering under the feather ticks. Usually the sky was one continuous rose and violet of lightning, cut by blinding bolts that forked down, the crash of their thunder hard upon them, shaking the earth, sifting dirt from the sod roof overhead to the dishes on the table or the kettle and the water bucket. There might be a scattering of drops big and heavy as silver quarters falling into the dust, and then a wind to blow the storm away, the towering white-topped clouds drying away to flying mares' tails—one more sign of a dry year.

The turnips and scattering patches of millet and other short-season forage sprouted where a little rain fell. But there was suffering even around Cozad and much more in settlements with no credit at the stores because the community had no mush-hearted gambling man to throw cash around. Only Cozad had one foolish enough to pay out good money for dumping sod into the Platte River from the tailboard of an old wagon.

The desertion from the western lands was so alarming that the U.P. repeated their offer to haul all relief goods to the denuded regions free of charge. Charity groups in older, more fruitful if still depressed areas gathered up clothing and barrels of flour, rice and potatoes to be shipped west. Congress was almost swamped by petitions demanding aid. John Cozad made all the work he could. The two-story brick schoolhouse was getting well started, the first floor for the pupils, the second for church services, lodge activities, and other entertainment. And not one cent of it from bonds or other obligations upon the taxpayers. He showed his further faith in the country by announcing he would build a substantial brick home in the fall, hoping this would help keep the desertion from spreading like a prairie fire fleeing before the blast of its own wind.

Robert ran to his grandmother when he heard about their new house.

"Granny, Granny, are we going to stay here this winter?" he demanded.

The woman smiled absently as she brushed her gray hair back and laid out new poison flypaper in the saucers in the window. Robert waited, but she said nothing and so he ran to his pony and rode down to watch the men dumping sod. People were still coming to see the work, to laugh a little, often anxiously, among themselves, and then maybe ask casually, "Where's Mr. Cozad at?"

One day the river began to rise, with rumors of a big cloudburst out west. At least a dozen wagons and horsebackers came to look at the water, plenty of water, the sudden gray rise of the crest rolling with piles of brush and submerged tumbleweeds, trash, trees and pieces of shacks and hogpens. Silently the men watched the flood, all that water—enough to raise crops over all the region, it seemed—all rushing off toward the Missouri and the Gulf, with no way to hold back one drop.

The next day the river was dropping fast, the banks muddy and soon cracking gray under the sun. Some travelers on the south side looked doubtful about attempting to cross, with the current still a swift run of dirty water.

"I'd think a while before putting a rig in on that loose bottom," old Robert Gatewood told his namesake through a mouthful of long nails sticking from the gray bush of his beard. He was hammering a shack together on his new homestead here at the bridge, where he could oversee the work and fulfill the residence requirements at the same time.

Over the pound of the hammer Robert heard a sudden splashing and ran to see. One of the teams from the south side was in the river, the little grasshopper buggy swaying as the current deepened, the man up and lashing his horses with the line ends, the buckskin Indian ponies quick as coyotes, taking the roily current in great simultaneous jumps.

"He'll make it if the doubletrees hold!" one of the old-timers said as he leaned on his shovel.

The ponies took the north bank in a final leap. The buggy jerked up, the doubletrees hit them and they shot ahead again, but the driver yelled, "Whoa!" and swung all his weight back against the lines, setting the team down in their breechings. They stood, shaking, panting, dripping.

The man wiped the water from his face and glanced over the workers. "Where's the boss? Looks like there's somebody with some get-up around here."

Before Robert could hear a reply his legs were carrying him away to the river, where there was more splashing and yelling. A wagon had just hit the current, the driver up and whipping his team. But he let the horses seesaw, one plunge ahead, then the other, the halted wagon teetering in the flood, the tail swinging downstream. As the wheels settled into the quicksand, the current swirling about it lifted the wagon box until it was swept out back of the wheels. At the last moment the man jumped forward and struggled to hang to the lines in the swift water, dog-paddling hard to reach the horses.

By now Johnny was following a couple of the men who jumped to their saddles and spurred along the bank. They sought a place to put the horses into the water but were cautious of the quicksand, one with a loop down ready to send it out, pull the floundering man in.

But the driver managed to grab a tail of his team, caught in the sand too now, and no longer jumping. He reached down, head under water, to unhook the tugs, and fighting the flood time after time, managed to free the team from the wagon. Then he got on a back and started whipping with the line ends, but the animals could only throw their heads, thrashing the water with their bodies, caught fast.

Now ropes came singing from the riders, and finally the driver got them down and under the bellies of his horses, like surcingles. With the ends dallied around the saddle horns the men on the bank spurred, the horses dug themselves in to pull low while the man in the rushing flood pounded his team again, yelling, cursing, and whipping them to jerk and jump until their legs began to work loose in the pull. Finally one was free, then the other, and struggling to the bank, Robert standing off to watch, a little afraid.

"Better make them broncs walk right away, see if the joints are pulled," an old farmer suggested. The team seemed all right, but played out, going down flat to the ground to rest as soon as they dried a little.

"You were lucky to have some bottom there," Lee Johnson, a herniaed old trail hand, told the man. "I seen horses sucked clear out of sight in five minutes. Down on the Canadian and the Arkansas—here on the Platte too. Sometimes it don't seem to take five minutes, after a big flood and the sand not settled. You just got to never let 'em stop or else ride the horses through a few times to settle the bottom a little before you hit the water with the wagon."

By now Johnny Cozad was back, shouting that the wagon box had washed out into shallow water.

"Flood'll be clear down in a couple of days, maybe you can dig out the wagon," Johnson said.

"We sure need that bridge," several of Cozad's sod handlers told each other as they went back to work.

The man in the buggy with the buckskin ponies had watched the rescue. "I didn't want nothing special except to look around and maybe shake the hand of the man behind this——" he explained, cutting a half circle with his buggy whip. "I'm from down toward the Republican and we would welcome getting a chance to trade at some new stores."

Dave Claypool threw his breaking plow out of the ground with a side twist of the handles and motioned to a couple of men riding up. "There're the storekeepers for you," he called to the man in the buggy. "Eli Russell's in the grocery business and McCarty handles hardware, even got that new barbed wire, and plenty sodbusters, even hoe handles and jackknives."

Before the end of the week the Cozad boys were helping the man from the south dig the running gears of his wagon out of the sandbar that had been new quicksand so recently. The sand turned wet and gruelly as they worked and kept filling in the hole until they borrowed some boards from the pile for the bridge to make a sort of curbing around the wagon and pushed it down as they dug the sand out underneath. They worked as hard as the new family of beavers that was damming up one of the side streams of the Platte. Their grandfather came to watch.

"Look at the boys!—working like nailers. Anything except what they ought to be doing," he complained, and went back to add up the men's time for their first payday.

John Cozad came up as the workers unhitched, his buggy team sleek, for all the grasshopper ravishing, two matched high-stepping bays with black and yellow fly nets quivering, the buggy whip mostly yellow too. He got out, threw the lines to Robert, and went to dump the contents of a big leather pouch into an empty wheelbarrow—silver and a scattering of gold pieces rattling against the metal of the barrow, the greenbacks falling like wilted leaves.

The bridge hands came up hesitantly and with sweated awkwardness before the clean linen of the builder, to accept money from the man some of them already owed. As the timekeeper, old Robert, checked the names off, John Cozad counted out the pay to the silent men, silent and some even a little surly, with all that money, ten times more than needed, there before them, the gold among it left to glisten in the evening sun.

But they took their pay and stepped aside, one after the other, until one man, leading his lathered team, caught sight of the pile in the wheelbarrow. "Why, the goddamn Copperhead show-off!" he shouted. Putting his hand on the back of one of the mares, he leaped up and, kicking her into a heavy gallop, left in a rattle of loose harness, his pay untouched.

A few looked after him curiously, and some enviously, it seemed, yet they stayed, holding out a calloused, perhaps a blistered hand in their turn, saying, "Thank you."

But they didn't say it to John Cozad any more. Risen tall and furious at the denunciation, he had stepped back and motioned Robert Gatewood to take his place. From beside his son and his handsome team, not twenty feet away, he stared coldly at the workers still coming up. Not one of the worn, gaunted faces turned his way, or one bloodshot, dust-rimmed eye met his. They took their pay from old Robert, mumbled their words, and hurried away.

At last all were gone except the relatives, come to stand around John Cozad, talking a little about the new team, the fly nets and the whip, and nothing more. The first to break away was Dave Claypool. He had to get home to his sick wife and the three small children, the youngest barely a month old and the mother not recovering.

That night not even Robert could approach his father as he sat silent at the late supper. Then the man went to work at his desk but only stared at the papers spread out before him. Finally he went to bed and that night the first death came to the little town, a death from a birth—Mrs. Claypool, the niece of John J. Cozad, dead.

VII

NOW THERE WAS A STORY to tell up and down the railroad and off beyond the Platte valley, a laughing story that somehow didn't make people laugh but only grow quiet at the thought of any money at all loose here.

It had been a hard ride into town the evening after the pay out at the bridge. Hard, perhaps, for everybody. The hitch racks around the depot, at the livery stable, and across from Emigrant House were practically empty. Nobody was aiming horseshoes at the new stakes out in front of Mrs. Gatewood's store, not one grease lantern bobbed—nobody returning from picketing the horses, it seemed, or the milk cows, or coming for thread, perhaps, or tobacco from the stores whose windows and doorways threw patches of light upon the dusty road that was the street.

When Robert came blinking into Emigrant House he saw his family still at the end of the bare table, waiting. No one scolded or looked up. When he returned from the wash bench and slid unhappily into his chair beside Johnny, his father passed him his plate and all began to eat, mostly poking at the food, the cold corned buffalo beef that Julia Gatewood did so well, with the new little beets and tender leaf lettuce. Even the green wild grape pie got little attention. Nobody really seemed hungry, late as it was, except John Cozad, his eyes even deeper in their sockets, as though turned inward, and yet he took a second helping of everything. Nobody came in, and all down the table the plates and cups were still there, turned upside down waiting. Not one of the regular customers had been in, all probably making a little cheese and crackers do. Once a cowboy did stomp up to the open door, but seeing no one but a family there, he mumbled something and went back into the darkness.

Afterward Robert lay silent and quieter than in sleep beside his brother. He thought about the day, the empty supper table, and the question that he had to face. Would they be leaving Cozad now as they left Cozaddale back when he was small, too small to understand what had happened there, or even knew?

In the morning John Cozad was gone again.

The next week or so Robert Cozad heard the word "Copperhead" used several times for some of the other Ohioans, when he had never thought of it at all except back in Cincinnati, where it was a dark thing, like the hovering shadow of a chicken hawk over a pullet, a word meaning some kind of treason, it seemed.

Many of the August excursionists went back in anger and in sorrow. "Nobody can really blame them," Theresa told her mother afterward. "All they see is the earth that was described so wondrously fertile only baked and bare."

"Yes, and those hateful little clouds against the hot sun aren't rain or fog but more hoppers," Julia Gatewood said in unaccustomed anger. The excursionists also knew that the greasy bodies not only made the railroad tracks slippery but turned the rough wooden steps of Emigrant House, even the step of the spring wagon, into something slick and treacherous to the foot. In addition they had seen the hoppers creep in everywhere, into the sugar bowls of those who had them, between the sheets, even into the pocket handkerchief and the purse.

But other homeseekers kept coming, running into strings of wagons and loaded railroad cars heading back east. They came any way they could, often with barely the money to be dumped off at the depot, money usually borrowed. They even came afoot and somehow they were fed for a day or two.

Gradually little rains started some late grass, and the railroad conductors once more recommended Cozad as a stopping place to the uncommitted. Young Robert took to meeting every train again, wondering about the people who got off as he watched their faces.

By September, the year after Black Friday, many city workers who wanted no familiarity with the plow were heading for the west too, for the far towns and stations, hoping for a new start. One of these was A. T. Griffith, who got off the early local with a little round-topped trunk, a carpenter's chest of tools, and $12. Robert Cozad saw his uncertainty as he glanced all around and finally shouldered the trunk and the tools. Plodding past the two boxcars now used for depot and freight station, he started up between the two little rows of houses, mostly sod, that were really the town. He was young and seemed to have a sharp eye out, particularly for Goodyear's lumberyard, the hardware store and McIntyre's tinshop. He stopped to look off toward the half-finished school building and the barny Emigrant House where, the conductor had told him, five, six substantial families generally were living until they could be sheltered by their own roofs. They would be crowded even though the hotel was two stories and around thirty by eighty feet, weatherboarded against the winters, but unpainted, graying.

After a while the young man set his burden down and asked the boy slowly strolling up from the station where he could find this Mrs. Gatewood, who kept boarders. Robert was happy to show the unexpected, unheralded homeseeker the place. "Really the only one, sir," he said.

That day John Cozad and Dave Claypool, real estate agents, went out with two wagons and the spring wagon to show the accumulated fourteen landseekers the country. Griffith went along, interested in the town's prospects. Next morning he asked what he owed Mrs. Gatewood and was told that supper, lodging, and breakfast at the hotel cost $5, which left him $7 and his ticket back to Cincinnati. Disheartened, he shouldered his trunk and tools once more and went back to the depot.

The eastbound train was late and in the meantime Matthews, the buffalo hunter, came up to offer him board at $3 a week. The old lady's cooking was nothing fancy—the meat mostly wild game, but hearty. With two weeks for his $7, young Griffith moved his belongings once more, this time to an unsold lot.

"Nobody's going to touch it there," the man assured him. "We got no little thieves. Big fellows that run off with horses, a herd of cattle maybe, or grab the entire range, but not anybody what calls for locks on the houses."

Griffith managed to pick up a few little jobs before his money ran out and finally he located on a place he liked, off east, near enough to town for his carpentry, although just now work was mighty scarce and had to be spread around, the family men getting first deal.

At schooltime the new building wasn't done and so classes opened at the Gatewood home for the Cozad boys, the Claypool young people, and a few others. With the poor equipment and the $35-a-month teacher it was plain that Theresa would have to supplement the education of her sons. They were accustomed to the best, with special classes in music, art, and dancing, all even more important now that her husband had such fine plans for them, for himself.

94

At last the hated sheet, the Dawson County *Pioneer*, the voice of the county-seat gang at Plum Creek, as John Cozad called it, carried an item on grasshopper relief. Traber Gatewood had tried to get more definite and complete information for the town's new paper, the *Hundredth Meridian*. He got plenty of rumor but no more than the same very general promise of seed help in denuded regions given to John Cozad long ago, although the adjoining counties were already on the relief list. Perhaps the ranchman influence on Plum Creek and the county officials was responsible. Every settler who had to desert his claim was a victory.

Now that the brace was off his jaw and his goatee grown out, John Cozad was off again. He took his grip, the gold-headed cane, and the big diamond stickpin so unsuitable for a senator and headed east for some faro where he hadn't been barred. The summer, with the building expenses of the town, his injuries and the work on the bridge, had gone through his ready cash like a Platte River flood through a dry wash.

"He will bring some information about seed and other relief, you'll see," Sam Atkinson, the calm, the judicious, predicted.

As the nights began to freeze a little, hunters brought antelope, deer, and elk to the Cozad butchershop when one was open or peddled it from door to door. Buffalo meat from the west was dumped off in great lots and very welcome because it was so cheap and considered excellent for those with stomach trouble. Many of the settlers had been sent west by their doctors to live closer to nature because there were reports of almost miraculous cures. Even bleeding stomachs, with the patients gaunt as boards cracked across the middle, bent over upon their misery, seemed to be recovering if the wild-game diet was fresh enough, particularly with some of the animal heat left in it.

While Robert was interested in every landseeker, Johnny liked to pick out the ailing ones as he looked them over at the depot, kept them under his eye if they stayed in the region.

Once one of these settlers complained to the colonizer, "That Johnny boy of yours keeps watching me like a buzzard on a stump, waiting for an old nag to die!"

But Johnny Cozad was watching for something else—for the first sign of a pound or two put on, the rise of a little ruddy color.

Along in the fall Theresa Cozad came to her mother and her aunt, the wife of McIntyre, the tinsmith, with sad news from the North Platte paper. It was a bare mention of the death of Mrs. Anna Mosby, "granddaughter of Governor Derceling of Virginia." She had recently married Colonel Mosby. Ten days later she threw herself under a train.

"Oh, how sad!" Julia Gatewood exclaimed, and hurried to make a cup of tea, Irish strong.

"Like newspaper stories, even this bit seems mixed up," Theresa said, a little sourly.

"Oh, I guess they printed what was sent out," her mother replied mildly.

"They wouldn't have printed it at all if they hadn't thought this was Mosby, the raider."

Perhaps not, yet how stupid and embarrassing, with the raider, Ranger John Singleton Mosby, married long ago, his house full of stairstep children. But it was very sad about Anna, the women agreed, carried back by the tragedy to the Virginia before the war, before their part of the state broke off as West Virginia. They talked of the Gatewood Hotel at Malden when the gay, vivacious Anna and her first husband came as guests to Theresa's wedding. They had all been so interested in the bridegroom, a dashing world traveler with visions of a better society, of building a perfect community somewhere. Many knew John J.'s father, Henry Cozad, born in Upshur County, Virginia, and the Cozad neighbors there, some of the Jacksons of Stonewall's family. "That was where

John J.'s middle name came from, his father once told me," Julia Gatewood recalled. He had hoped that the boy might have a little of the Jackson staunchness and courage. That, added to Henry's own vision of a better life, which led him to build a community in the wilds of Ohio, might stir young John to a larger dream, give him the power and the vision to build in greatness.

"We all believed it then, at the wedding," the aunt said.

Theresa did not look at her mother, but as always Julia Gatewood admitted no doubt about her son-in-law. "We believe it now," she said.

Yes, yes, of course, but it had all seemed so close, so real at that gracious wedding seventeen years ago, and with the infare, attended by a most important and elegant company. But somehow tragedy had come to so many, not only during the war and the Reconstruction in Virginia, but since, and now Anna's tragic end.

Julia Gatewood shook her gray hair back and looked into her teacup, at the little nest of wet leaves clinging together in the pattern of a shovel, a gravedigger's implement that some called the warning of great danger, even death.

"I hear John Singleton's turned Republican, and after all his raiding," she said, and washed the tea leaves around in a swirl of the cup.

Yes, and strange that he should, with so much of the South still under Northern troops, their boots still pretty hard to bear in places.

Big Alex McIntyre, coming in, stopped in the doorway. "Colonel Mosby is a politician as well as a raider. Now that raiding has been taken over by the politicians in power, switching parties opened a lot of rich territory to his well-known tactics."

As fall stopped garden, field, and bridge work, practically everybody who wasn't too busy, including any settlers in town, went to meet the trains. Everybody except Theresa, who never appeared there except to greet a friend or relative coming in. John Cozad stayed away too, unless some special homeseekers were expected. He usually sat behind the curtains of their second-floor-living-room window, where he could see everybody who came up the street from the station.

"Watching for homeseekers," Traber Gatewood explained once when a bolt of night lightning showed, in that one whitened moment, a tall man, not sitting but standing staring down into the street. Traber knew that for some reason, perhaps for several, his brother-in-law was always there around traintime, but not to be noticed, not to be seen.

One warmish fall evening the colonizer, in shirt sleeves and waistcoat, looked out upon the street for over an hour, waiting for the belated local to pass. Patches of light reached out from the windows, others came and went as doors opened and closed. The spreading glow of a lantern hung to a post lit the horseshoe pitching in front of Mrs. Gatewood's store. There was a shimmer of fall insects and dust through it as Traber, Sam Atkinson, and a couple of others tossed at the stakes, with several, including young Robert, standing watching. The only sounds were the thump-thump of the heavy railroad windmill and the occasional ring of iron on iron and an exultant exclamation, or a voiced regret in the game below the window, all formless sounds to the man watching.

Finally the train whistled in, and almost as soon as the brakes stopped grinding a man came stalking up through the lighted spots to Emigrant House. From the first glimpse John Cozad suspected who it was. Even with the soft hat instead of the plug of the old days, the man much grayer and older, he recognized King O'Dell, said to be a cousin of the other gambling O'Dells, and out now, after around twenty years in prison. Swiftly John Cozad ran his hand inside his vest to assure himself of the set of the small pistol, and then slipped into his frock coat, pulling the tail down over the gun in his back pocket. Then he stroked his hair back from his ears with the flat of his palms, smoothed his goatee, shot his cuffs, felt his cravat, and waited, facing the door to the little hall, standing so his right hand was on the outside, and free.

There was a murmur of talk downstairs, a screen door slammed, and steps went away on the hard-packed ground. The watcher jumped to the window but could see nothing beyond the light for the horseshoe pitchers. As he peered out, Julia Gatewood came running up the steps.

"Oh, John J.! A man was here for you. I sent him over to that meeting the Odd Fellows started."

The man nodded his approval, his gratitude, and met the woman's eyes in a moment of mutual understanding, of abiding affection. "I'll come down when he returns," he said.

"Theresa may be back any minute——" her mother said doubtfully.

Yes, he knew that, but he would come down. With his gold-headed cane tucked under his arm, John Cozad waited at the head of the narrow stairs. When O'Dell returned, Julia called and the colonizer came down slowly, confidently, the steps noisy under his solid tread, under his casual greeting, "Well, how do you do, sir!"

"I come for Kitty," the man announced loudly. "Last time I shot the wrong man. Now I got you, so trot Kitty out——"

"Kitty? Which Kitty? I seem to recall several."

"By God, Cozad, don't you mush-mouth me!" O'Dell shouted, jerking a pistol from his pocket. "I saw Kitty with you—last thing, twenty years ago—and me giving you, a scart kid, a start!"

John Cozad seemed not to notice the gun. "No," he said softly, his eyes very black in the sudden whiteness of his face. "No O'Dell started me. That was my old friend, strung up——"

"I come for Kitty——" the man shouted again, trying to make it a roar.

John Cozad smiled a little, his gaunt cheeks drawn back as none in his town had ever seen. But there were some who saw it now, men peering in at the door, even his two sons pushing their heads through between shoulders. The news of something on the wind had spread very fast, and as people came running up, Traber had hurried around through the back door, to be on John J.'s side, backing him up, facing those jamming the door and the windows too, all ready to duck but daring the chances of a bullet to see the two gamblers standing against each other in the bare little pine lobby. Both were armed, one with his gun ready, the other very fast—both still, silent, John Cozad's cane in his powerful left hand, the right ready, swift as a rattler. But something seemed to hold them both, O'Dell's ear tilted up a little, as for steps above him, the colonizer apparently preoccupied with some inner matter, perhaps some far sound, the angry King O'Dell before him almost forgotten.

Then Theresa came running in from the night, pushing through the doorway, her skirts held aside, blinking from one man to the other, her eyes black-deep from the darkness.

Quietly she stepped to the side of her husband. From that instant John Cozad was once more the confident man of the faro tables. "Pardon me," he said, with a bow. "I have been waiting for my wife."

Taking Theresa's arm, he started up the narrow steps behind him, turning his back upon the man with the pistol hanging in his hand.

A moment King O'Dell stood there staring after the woman, then he turned and with the gun still out, but foolishly, he pushed through the people in the doorway, past the unrecognized sons of the gambler. They watched him go, young Robert taking a step or two after him as he went down toward the depot and off into the darkness of the tracks.

But he might be back, he or his kind, be back any day or night.

VIII

YES, THEY'RE AFTER MR. COZAD NOW like buffalo gnats after a pink-eared dude," Sam Atkinson admitted to Griffith and a couple of other young fellows donating a little work at the schoolhouse. There had been an increasing disrespect for the community builder since the drouth and grasshoppers struck. Particularly since that matter of the money in the wheelbarrow, grown to a pile of gold coins a foot high in all the retelling.

"And the charge of 'Copperhead' shouted against him by a man from Ohio who maybe ought to know," one of the helpers said.

No, not Ohio, Pennsylvania, young Griffith thought.

Sam Atkinson sorted out a sheaf of nails for his mouth. "That man was a Hoosier," he said. "But it could have been almost anybody now, with 'Copperhead' a bad word handy for any dirty tongue, like 'niggerlover' and 'scalawag' in the South, or 'Tory' after the Revolution——"

The others nodded as they measured and sawed. Nobody mentioned King O'Dell, perhaps because he and his accusations made such racy talk now where there had been too much gloom. People were ready to enjoy the discomfiture of the more fortunate, particularly off around Plum Creek, with some talk of raiding the settlement of that notorious gambling man Cozad.

"After the evil places running open around here?" the Plum Creek doctor asked, but privately. He was known to be from Ohio and a friend of some at Cozad.

The talk was evidently only talk, for outside of a penny-ante game down at the livery stable now and then, or perhaps a little crap shooting on a horse blanket in the back stall, men honing to risk a bit of money had to look elsewhere. Then one evening late a covered wagon came in from the east to the back lot of the livery stable. Before the tugs were down a folded table was lifted out over the endgate, carried inside, and maneuvered up the narrow steps to the hayloft, the whole front end of which was emptied, ready.

From that night business seemed to boom at the stable, although the stalls were seldom filled and few rigs except the schooner stood in the back lot. Horsebackers tied to the hitch rack outside and went in. Some spanking teams waited there too, particularly nights, and some of the Cozaders took to slipping down.

The colonizer was still away with his little black gripsack and Traber off on a round of dental stands, so old Robert Gatewood made an errand down at the stable. Somebody must have seen him coming. The four, five men around there were at an empty stall, acting ready to start for home. He took his neats-foot oil and stopped in at the store to talk to his wife and then to Dave Claypool at the *Meridian* office. A few minutes later Dave drove off to the river with him, caught up one of the bridge horses, and rode away through the brush.

Nothing was said to Theresa. She had kept closer to her work the last couple of weeks and the boys avoided the jibes about King O'Dell too. This afternoon the mother had let them give their fattening horses a good run. They went south across the river, straight into a late-flying swarm of buffalo gnats. They stretched out a quarter of a mile, like a shimmering veil in the autumn sun, fine as dust and biting fiercely, with winter so close—getting into the eyes and ears, the horses faunching and wild, unable to outrun them. At a more prosperous settler's shack the boys begged a few drops of coal oil for the corners of their red bandannas. With these under their hats, the stinking corners out and flying, and with some of the oil wiped lightly over the ears and faces of the horses, they started home, singing a little, the gnats dropping away from the hated stink.

Outside of Emigrant House they met one of the Pearson boys with some of his friends from Plum Creek, just riding past, they said, and stopping in at Mother Gatewood's for supper. They made a laughing meal of it, with jokes and riddles, and telling about the gnats the Cozad boys ran into, the old buffalo bull the others had tried to locate in the breaks off northwest. Then they sat around and listened to one of the boys blow his harmonica while Johnny pulled at the accordion a landseeker had left as security for his board bill.

When the Plum Creekers said they had to start home, Johnny and Robert went along to the livery stable for their horses. Inside, they heard laughing up in the hayloft. The stablekeeper stuck his head down the trap door, motioning them to come up. Johnny hesitated but the older boys went, and stomped around up there, laughing so that Robert was curious. He climbed the narrow steps far enough to see a lantern hanging to a rafter and a big poster with a snarling tiger. A man was standing next to a rack with pictures of playing cards on the tabs. It was an odd contraption and the boy took a couple more steps to see, and then clear up into the smoky loft beside the other boys. They were watching four, five men sitting around a rickety old table opened long. The top had pictures of all the spades on it, ace to king, in two even rows, the seven out at the side. A couple had chips on them. Back of the table sat a red-faced man with a deck, face up, in an open-topped box, his fingers sliding the top card out at a slit in the side. He laid it on the soda, the exposed pile, next to his stacks of white, red, and blue chips, while the marker checked it off on the contraption against the wall.

Johnny followed Robert, tugging at his coattail, but the boy had to watch as the dealer slid out the next card. A trey came up and one of the men at the table pushed the tall stack of blue chips on the jack from him, turned, and stumbled past the boys and down the steps.

Those left at the table looked around at the newcomers and, settled back, easing their seats. The dealer reached under the table for the whisky bottle, offered it around, drank, and set it back. The livery-stable keeper turned his head toward the spittoon. With his mouth emptied, he told the gamblers who Johnny and Robert were.

"Just dropped in to see a little fun," he added.

"Welcome," the dealer said, and motioned Robert up closer, to see better. "As you know, Master Cozad, faro's a mighty easy game. All you got to do is pick the right card, win or lose, any way you bet it."

While he talked he emptied the box and, adding the pile, shuffled the lot slowly, clumsily, compared to the swift and even flow that the Cozad sons had seen when they caught their father unawares a few times—keeping in practice, he called it, for when he got his hand on a deck.

The dealer replaced the pack in the box. "Now you figure out what value the card under the soda, the top one, will be, and lay your bets."

Robert nodded, grinning, pleased that it was so clear to him, but not moving to a bet. The Plum Creek boys did buy a few chips, white. "Not stacks, just five, six each, and a red too," one of them said, laying the money down.

The dealer nodded good-humoredly toward the marker. "We'll deadhead the young sports a little," he agreed.

The boys placed chips on a scattering of cards while one

of the men at the end piled reds on the queen and placed a penny on top, coppering the bet.

"He's mad at the ladies, betting on the queen to lose," the dealer told the boys, winking a thick-lidded eye.

Now Robert did move up closer, resisting Johnny's more urgent tug. This was just like seeing a story acted out. He watched as the dealer slipped the soda card away and the losing card came up, not a queen but a six. The coppering player turned to the few reds he had left, fingering them as the next card, the winner, showed up a ten. It paid one of the Plum Creek boys. At the sight of the house chips pushed toward him he looked back to the Cozads, his eyes suddenly gleaming in the lantern light, as he nodded to let his bet and the winnings ride.

When everything was down, the ten was drawn out and dropped to the soda pile, exposing the second losing card, the copperer losing on the queen again. The ten repeated and the downy-cheeked young Plum Creeker whooped and let his redoubled stack ride once more as the counter racked up a second ten with a win.

Now the nine-year-old Robert Cozad felt himself pushing in against the table, resisting Johnny's whisper "Come *on*." He was fascinated by the game, by any game, but by this one particularly. The dealer offered him a stack of chips. "Complimentary," he said. And when the boy couldn't take them, he was offered the loan of a twenty-dollar bill. Embarrassed further by this generosity, and by his brother urging him to leave, Robert managed to say that they were not permitted to accept gifts of money or to borrow.

There was talk and sign-making over the boy's head until the livery-stable keeper reached out for the bill. "Let me have it," he said. "I owe Robert's father some back rent on the place——" He folded the bill down small and slipped it into the boy's breast pocket.

"The rent," he said.

Robert was uneasy about this but he had often picked up payments on land sales, sometimes adding up to more than a hundred dollars before his father returned, so he said "Thank you" to the man and remained at the table.

While the game was resumed, one of the men went to the big hay door of the loft, worked to slide it back a few inches, and spit out, although he had been using the spittoon beside the table. As though surprised, he jumped back out of sight from the street and hurried to the dealer, saying something to his ear that sounded like "Three, four coming——" the rest lost in a shouting and roar downstairs, a stomping up the narrow steps. Suddenly Robert felt cold all down his belly for it was the silk hat of John Cozad that appeared in the trap door, with a couple of heads behind it—Dave Claypool and Traber—the latter there only a second and then gone.

The colonizer came up with an ax in his hand lifted high. He took one look all around—the fierceness of it shriveling his sons, and apparently the men beyond them too. All they did was jump back as the man brought the ax down upon the table, crashing through its rickety center, then again and again, splintering the wood to kindling, scattering the cards from the box like leaves to the wind.

By now the surprised dealer had drawn his gun. John Cozad took notice. "So you pull a gun on me on my own premises, you broken-down would-be jackleg!"

There was a stillness in the loft, with Robert perhaps the only one not afraid because he didn't see the pistol, remembering only the bill in his pocket and that it was called rent money. He picked it out, still folded close, and tried to hand it to his father, who stood towering in contempt over the dealer and his gun but glancing to the man back at the hayloft door and making a motion to someone below. Immediately there was a noise of running boots, their stomping coming up the stairs until a burly man with a deputy star on his coat appeared, gun out, three others in a row just behind him.

The gambling men and the stablekeeper lined up almost before they were given the order, pushing the furious John Cozad back beside the Plum Creek boys. Then, almost as though he knew what to expect, the man with the star stalked to the youngest boy there, Robert Cozad, and jerked the folded bill from his hand. Opening it, the man grinned sourly.

"So, Mr. Cozad, you not only run a gambling hell for the young but put counterfeit money in the hands of your innocent kid, to——"

"Counterfeit?" the colonizer demanded, and after a glance at the bill he ignored the man as though he and his gun were not there. "Where did you get this?" he demanded of his son, his voice filling all the loft.

And to the dealer's shout, "From his pocket!" all Robert could do was motion to the stablekeeper. "I wouldn't take it from the card man, and so he loaned it to Mr. Joe, and he gave it to me on the rent——"

"He's a damn liar, like his old man!" the dealer shouted. "Put the cuffs on Cozad! String him up!"

Now suddenly the colonizer saw his danger and cooled, became the man of faro. He looked all around the loft, as the stablekeeper, long ago ordered out the first of next month, at the man with handcuffs dangling, ready, and to the one with the star, his pistol still upon John Cozad.

"Ah, gentlemen," the man of faro said genially, rubbing his palms together as becomes a good host. "So you have gathered for a little game?" He stooped to pick up several of the cards, arranging them, but looking under his heavy brows toward the trap door, where Traber, the red-bearded agent, old Robert, and several others were coming up in sock feet, silent under the noise, and armed, even Johnny there, peering out from behind the others.

Now John Cozad scooped the last of the cards together and as he straightened up, his hand shot out, grabbing, not the gun but the star, grabbed it, jerked it off.

"Frauds! All frauds and impostors!" he roared, and motioned toward Traber and the double-barrel buck gun in his hands, the agent behind him holding up a telegram.

"He's a fraud all right," Sanderson said. "I telegraphed Sheriff James at Plum. He has no deputies out."

It was far past Robert's bedtime when the livery stable was finally dark and the boys scolded for letting themselves be trapped like that, scolded now, to save their mother knowing more about this than could be helped. Leaving old Robert, Traber, and Johnny to sleep in the stable, to watch, John Cozad and Robert started home, the light of the lantern flickering over the ground before them. The boy hopped on one foot and then the other, forgetting himself in his excitement, making a singsong of the evening, but out loud. "Now I know, now I know, how to make $50,000——"

The father stopped short, the light thrown upward from the lantern on his face, gaunt, hollow, his eyes suddenly empty holes. The boy saw and trembled, for the anger there now was greater than any all this night.

"I didn't mean it——" he started to say, trying to keep his voice from whimpering, but his father grabbed him by the neck and marched him across to the family stable, and in at the door. There he set the lantern down and took the yellow buggy whip from the socket. Once, twice, three times he cut it hard across his son's stockinged legs, until the boy was gasping to keep from crying out and then crumpled sobbing into the straw.

Slowly John Cozad replaced the whip, his face bone white in the lantern.

IX

ALL THROUGH THE LATE SUMMER and fall Mother Gatewood was interrupted now and then by customers who came with sheepish step, men with hungry children and hoping for a little credit to be worked off at the bridge, if not this year, then next spring. They came, even though they might turn out not of Cozad's colony at all or anyone connected with it.

"I got a good right——" the man might argue, one way or another, meaning as good a right as anyone to feed his family. "God knows I got!"

But the work at the bridge would soon be closing down for the winter, and Mrs. Gatewood had to pay her bills promptly or get no more goods. Would it profit the community if she bankrupted herself trying to feed all the needy? Even if she sacrificed every cent she had, it wouldn't add one drouth-shriveled kernel to the vast graineries of food needed for the hungry now.

Many left, if they could get out of the country, seeing no humor in the parodies on "Rock of Ages" or on "Beulah Land":

> We do not live, we only stay,
> We are too poor to get away.

Robert Cozad liked parodies and sometimes mumbled the funny words in church with his grandmother instead of those in the hymnbooks. "Why can't you behave like a gentleman, like Johnny?" she complained, as others did, sometimes, particularly since the faro gamblers were down at the livery stable. But Johnny was too smart to be around at church time——

There was another song Robert heard this fall, one that he felt guilty about because it kept bounding through his head to the trot of his pony:

> The night is dark and you're alone
> Alone with your doubts and fears,
> For you are the bride of the gamblin' man,
> And your lot is sorrow and tears.

At first he had grown hot with anger, knowing why it was sung around Cozad now. But those things were not the lot of the gamblin' man's bride at all, he thought. He could recall only a couple of times when his mother's lot seemed really sorrow and tears, that is, outside of sicknesses in the family, and deaths, which come to everybody. Maybe those two, three other times were because of the gamblin' man; he couldn't be sure, like when old King O'Dell came with his gun demanding a woman called Kitty. They were sleeping outside then, Johnny and he, and so Robert didn't know if his mother cried that night. She wasn't down the next morning before he went on errands to the bridge. He did manage to overhear Traber and Grandfather Robert talk about O'Dell, from back around Cincinnati, a river gambler who had married a pretty redhead from down the Mississippi somewheres, with those soft-talking, big-eying, Deep South ways. Soon her husband was quarreling with everybody and finally he shot a man dead on a street somewhere, a man, it turned out, who had never seen her.

"Must have thought John J.'d married Kitty, until he saw Theresa," Traber had said. But a fool like that wasn't easy to satisfy. If he couldn't run Kitty down, he might be back. "You know John J. and women——" Then, perhaps feeling disloyal, he added, "Before he married Theresa."

Robert had wanted to shout out a defense of his father, even at exposing the shame of his eavesdropping, but he held himself together, to think. Kitty's lot as the bride of a gamblin' man had certainly been sorrow and tears, but they were all wrong about his father, so often called a prince of a fellow until this bad summer. Robert wondered a little about the son of a gamblin' man. What did the songs say about his lot? If there was no song, maybe he could make one up, one to laugh. He liked to laugh, make everything he did fun.

Among those who lived through the summer of 1874 and still believed in the Cozad community was young Jim Haskell, who had shipped in his car of stuff last spring, ready to be the town's butcher. Of course he had to give that up, with no feed for the killing stock, nobody with money to buy the meat. But during the winter he wrote fine letters to the newspaper at Oxford, Ohio, about the Cozad region, ". . . the richest, the most fruitful agricultural lands in the entire Union," open and mostly free, the winters so mild that large Texas herds were brought up to winter and fatten. Wheat harvested before the grasshoppers came was plentiful; later crops were scarce and high-priced. Buffalo, elk, deer, and antelope sold for two to four cents a pound, the skins practically given away—a great opportunity for tanners, harness makers, beef packers, and processors of related products.

Robert read these letters back in Ohio. They hadn't kept the trouble at the livery stable from Theresa and she took the boys to Cincinnati. "Just going a little early, to prepare for the holidays," she said. "Christmas is always so pretty there, and our old friends full of plans."

To her husband she made one plea: "Give all this up. The next time there may be bloodshed," knowing it was futile.

John Cozad was with them through Christmas and Robert begged to go back with him. The boy felt he must make it up to his father somehow, make up for the humiliation that came from the men in the hayloft, and the danger that he was just beginning to realize, danger so terrible, with the talk of lynching, that it made his insides go like muddy water to think about it.

But there were no words for this. The father left and once more his weather luck failed him. The mild winter suddenly turned ironhard for the January excursionists. The thin scattering of snow, whipped up by a bitter northwest wind, cut the face, and yet most of the homeseekers took up land. By now last summer was recognized as a dire exception even by the government, and settlers eaten out by the grasshoppers were relieved from residence on their homesteads to July, to enable them to find work, if possible. Should the hoppers come again, the leave would be extended another year. Unfortunately the U.P. couldn't postpone the payments on their lands. The railroad was about broke.

With planting time near and no sight of the promised seed from the Relief Commission, settlers protested to Washington and the papers. They got a promise—a general would be out to investigate. Always a general under Grant's administration.

"What's a Brass Bound know about our needs? He probably never saw hungry homesteader kids, or hoppers eating the roots out of the ground, or care if he did," the settlers protested, one way or another, all over the blighted regions.

Work was so scarce that some decided to try the outlawed gold diggings in the Black Hills, still Indian lands, the army throwing miners out, and the weather forty below. They hunted up old buffalo coats and headed for the Hills, preferring to face the scalp knives of the Sioux to waiting on Relief Commission handouts. Some settlers trapped a little, or hunted until the price of meat dropped to a cent a pound for hindquarters, the rest thrown in, peddled from the wagon. A couple of the colonists taught school over near the Missouri River, one leaving his pregnant wife alone on the claim because the pay was too small to take her along. She had her baby in a blizzard, her first child, and got through it somehow, but when her husband saw her he promised himself she should never be left alone again.

Jim Haskell of the enthusiastic letters and a couple of earlier settlers went mustanging in the sandhills north. If the snow laid on long enough to weaken the wild herds, they could rope good short yearlings and brood mares heavy with foal from their faster grain-fed horses. Later in the spring they might shoot the stallions that kept the small bands apart. With a big herd together, they could plant drivers over the usual range, the first one to run the horses hard for ten, fifteen miles, the second to take over, and then the third and so on. After two, three days and nights without rest, food, or water many could be lassoed. They might trap some in the canyons too. After handling and riding the horses a little, they could be sold, the stronger ones to the new ranchers coming in; the quieter, older mares to the settlers; most of the younger stock to eastern markets, wild-eyed and spooking, like those Robert once saw with his father at the Ohio wharves, the time the white eyelashed calico came to the boy's hand.

Robert got the mustang news in a letter from his cousin, John Robert Gatewood, at Cozad, and for a week Theresa was afraid the boy would slip away to the west the first time her back was turned.

With the worst of the winter past the government finally sent out some castoff army clothing and blankets—nothing for the women, but some pulled on the clumsy old cowhide shoes too, and the blue overcoats with the flying shoulder capes that they tied up around their heads, perhaps with an old diaper or a dish towel. Some flour and beans were issued too, althought the less desperate objected to the weevils and mouse droppings.

"They think we're Indians, to dump such stuff off on us," one sodbuster complained.

But most of the hungry sifted the foreign matter out if they could borrow a piece of screening somewhere, or picked it out by hand. After all there was plenty of time these long nights with no light better than badger or skunk oil in a sardine can, the wick a strip of underwear speared on a wire. Some had only buffalo tallow, hard as rock in the frozen winter. Those without a hunter went to bed at dark, and saved fuel too. There were many jokes about the weevils and the long night hours without a light, but John Cozad ignored those that reached his ears because no amount of roaring anger was a remedy here. Besides, few even greeted the gambler now, who, some whispered, had tried passing a little counterfeit through one of his boys.

By April the trails were dark with wagons crawling westward, the settlements pushing out, in spite of the reported starvation. "A man gets just as hungry in a soup line in New York—where they go 'round the streets with big wagons every morning, picking up the poor devils who's died of exposure in the night," one homeseeker told John Cozad.

The colonizer took the twenty-five homeseekers of his April excursion to North Platte to file. Jeremiah Cozad, a cousin, was along and a couple of other relatives. Jerry filed on a pre-emption some distance from Cozad and was given a hearing date in May, along with a couple of others who had filed on the same land. That proved how fast the country was settling up.

John Cozad made the rounds of the newspaper offices and

the saloons for news of the narrow-gauge railroad to strike across the country toward the golden Black Hills, and about the raging flood coming out of the west. He went to look at the bridge, the last one this side of the Wyoming mountains. The cold gray waters, barely clear of winter ice, were rising again, around an inch an hour. He worried about the causeway to his bridge down at Cozad and telegraphed Dave Claypool to have brush and stumps dumped off the end, to protect it.

Because no one could believe in permanent drouth with reports of the Platte running a mile wide in flood, John Cozad wired the Relief Commission once more for the spring seed promised his settlers. Finally he ordered 300 bushels of good wheat seed out of his own pocket.

May found the town of Cozad growing again, for all the bad publicity, and with desirable land getting scarce, particularly now that the rains were back. There was never a pleasant word about anything of Cozad in the Plum Creek paper, but the North Platte *Republican* commented on the work of Colonel John Cozad. The colony he started two years ago had grown to nearly 500 population, with the adjoining country settled by the very best class of citizens. Cozad City was a living monument to the builder, and the crops, largely from seed he donated, looked good. Building boomed. Bricks were being fired for the colonel's $5000 residence. There was to be a big Independence Day celebration with everybody, all of North Platte, invited, the town baseball team challenged by Cozad's first nine.

"Come one, come all!"

John Cozad snipped the item out with the tiny folding card scissors that fitted into the back of one of his cufflinks. He sent the item to Cincinnati; it would please Robert to see his father called colonel in the expansive frontier manner.

Theresa and the boys returned as soon as school was out, although many had predicted that she had "a real belly full" of her husband's town and ways. She brought some of her furniture, only a few sticks, the barest necessities, she said. These included her cheval mirror, her golden dressing table, and the square rosewood piano too, this because many around Cozad liked to sing. At the station Johnny and Robert leaped from the train and ran to the grandparents to show how much they had grown. Young Robert had gained the most, at least in maturity, almost ten now and carrying the air of a young gentleman of much greater years, the grandfather said gravely, his eyes twitching at the corners. Johnny seemed a man in all but the hated short trousers and his way of teasing his mother, and trailing after her.

"Johnny's got a girl," Robert whispered to his grandmother. "She's tony," using a Platte valley word, and snickering.

"Robert means she's letting her skirts down a little early, but she's very womanly for fourteen," Theresa explained.

There was talk around the depot when John Cozad didn't show up to greet his family—was off at the land office again, it seemed. "Good places are getting scarce; you have to file fast," Dave Claypool explained, but that was to be expected of him.

Up at North Platte the colonizer heard some disturbing news. It seemed that the Union Pacific property there, including the coal sheds, the engines and the rest, was seized by the sheriff for the unpaid 1874 taxes, $19,131.62. They hadn't been paid elsewhere either—hard up. If the railroad went into receivership John Cozad might lose the favored-agent position to which his vast contracts entitled him. And perhaps never get the senatorship that had been so seriously endangered by the drouth and grasshoppers, and by the recurring attacks upon him. Some at least were planned to run him out, like that faro outfit that would trick a man's nine-year-old son, plant counterfeit money on him. There was a time, before he had to think of his family, his community, that John J. Cozad would have thrashed the scoundrels, left that jackleg dead among his miserable cards, even if he got some bullets himself. But that was exactly what those who put up such jobs wanted.

There was a long telegram from her huband waiting for Theresa in their quarters at Emigrant House, welcoming her return, regretting his inability to lift her from the car step. And the boys—he was hungry for a sight of them. Perhaps the two might like to come up for the circus and animal show stopping at North Platte a couple of nights. There were Indians around, lots of Sioux.

Theresa sent the boys off with some settlers going to meet the colonizer at the land office, warning the sons to remember their poise and manners. They arrived in time to stand beside their father as some Sioux chiefs came through from Washington, where they were to be compelled to sell the Black Hills. It hadn't worked, but the Indians looked angry and dark-faced, even the shy and pretty young woman Johnny mentioned several times later. Afterward they rode down to Fort McPherson and then hurried back for the circus, which wasn't half the size of the ones in Cincinnati. But Robert liked the Sioux camp down on the river bottoms, the painted tipis gay, some with feathered warbonnets out on stands, the drumming and dancing around big fires in the night. Several old trappers were selling buffalo meat around North Platte, like hard-up settlers, and talking about the good old beaver days. Robert made his first sketch since last fall—in marking pencil on stiff rawhide—of an old trapper, the wild hair over his shoulders mixed with the dirty gray beard, a great grizzly-bear scar down over one eye. At least the man said it was made by a grizzly.

The Cozads were barely home when King O'Dell showed up again. He came in on the eastbound train and strolled up the dusty street in full afternoon light, ignoring the recognizing faces at the hitch racks and at the store as he had at the depot. He went straight into Emigrant House and back to the colonizer's little office as though expected. John Cozad had seen him from the window above and came down, unsurprised. This time King O'Dell showed no fight. He was after money. Kitty was dead. Laflin, who used to run that palace in Cheyenne, told him she hung herself.

"Oh!" John Cozad exclaimed. "Not hung!"

O'Dell saw the sudden agitation in the man who had sat so calmly before him, and replied cooly, his whisky-flushed face held quiet as in the old days when he broke faro banks too.

Yes, his Kitty hung herself, and with one of big John Cozad's neckties.

"My tie?" the colonizer shouted, red to the cheekbones. "That's a damned lie and you know it! As a gambler you're a disgrace to the profession. You're meaner than the trashiest old jackleg, and sure stooping mighty low now, coming here with blackmail!"

Oh no, not blackmail. He just had something to sell, something, under the circumstances—gesturing with his long card-sharp fingers to take in all the town about them—pretty valuable. "I got the letters you wrote to Kitty."

"That's a double-damned lie. I never wrote her a scratch!"

The man unbuttoned his coat and took out a package tied with a faded claret-red ribbon. "I want $25,000 for the lot," he said, tapping the bundle on the desk.

Now John Cozad did what few had ever seen—he threw his head back and laughed aloud, his little goatee bobbing up and down in time with his adam's apple. Then before King O'Dell could do more than jump forward, he was at the door, calling, "Robert! Robert! Get your mother and all the rest together in the lobby here," standing tall in the doorway, blocking it as he sent the boy running, smiling back to King O'Dell with the ribbon-tied package in his hands.

"You're still good on the bluff, Cozad, but you don't work it on an old hand like me. You don't dare let anybody know about the letters!"

Still the colonizer smiled, waiting for the tramping of feet

118

that came into the bare lobby and the light step overhead starting down. A dozen or so gathered, Theresa standing at the foot of the little stairs, the Gatewoods, all but old Robert there, and the Cozad sons in the doorway, with more people coming to peer from behind them, even Handley of the new livery stable, and one of the Pearsons.

Now John Cozad took the old gambler's arm and led him out, the man trembling under his hand. "King O'Dell comes to me with what he claims is part of my shady past and I've gathered you to hear him tell it."

"You can't bluff me, Cozad," the man protested again. "You know you can't let me blab it all out about you and Kitty."

"Of course. You must tell them."

Slowly the man's watery blue eyes slipped over those in the room and to John Cozad. He tried to shake off the hand on his arm but it was firm. Suddenly he dipped his head forward and opened his mouth. "She hung herself," he said. "She did it with one of Cozad's neckties!"

There was a sort of gasp, an exchange of glances, shocked, some embarrassed, some exultant. But the community builder was not disturbed by them.

"You have proof that the necktie was one of mine?"

"I got better. I got the pack of letters you sent her right here," O'Dell shouted out, still clutching the ribbon-bound little bundle.

There was a small sound from Theresa, but she recovered herself. "May I see them?" she asked, putting her hand out.

But the man jerked back from her approach. "I got to have money for the stuff. They lost my Kitty for me——"

"He wants $25,000——" John Cozad said, stroking his goatee gently, speaking reasonably as about a wasp buzzing on the window sill or about a pocket handkerchief.

For a moment there was silence in the room, then Dave Claypool exploded in a snorting. "Damned blackmailer!" he yelled, and jumped for O'Dell. They scuffled but the man who had spent twenty-five years in a hard prison had learned some good tricks there. He was like a swamp eel, slipping from Dave's hands, through the crowd and out the door, running, with the people pushing to see him go.

Inside, John Cozad stooped to pick up the bundle O'Dell had dropped. "Come in!" he called, and when everybody was back, and more crowding around outside, he handed the package to Theresa.

"Open it, my dear," he suggested, speaking softly.

For a moment the woman hesitated, her fine eyes very dark in the whiteness of her face. She pulled at the ribbon, tugged and then deliberately broke it between her hands. Slowly she unfolded the wrappings. Inside was a small stack of paper, sheets of newspaper, cut and folded the size of letters. She leafed through them, handed them toward her husband, who nodded to Julia Gatewood. The old woman took the papers, barely touching them with more than repugnant fingertips and passed them on, to go from hand to hand around the room, one face after another lifting to the Cozads, standing together, watching.

Slowly, one after the other turned and went quitely through the door and away, even the sons, Johnny calling back, "We're riding out to tell Grandpa before somebody else does——"

Robert followed his brother, thinking about his father and the one moment of doubt, of uneasiness, that he had seen on the handsome goateed face as his wife opened the bundle. "I must grow up fast," the son told himself. "I must grow up very fast."

X

ALTHOUGH THERE WAS RAIN EARLIER, it dwindled by June and many began to think about that dry-land stock, sheep. Haskell and a friend from Ohio had gone by wagon to the Ozarks and were trailing 600 sheep back, holding them nights in corrals of muslin stretched around footed posts. With a rifle and shotgun they got through coyotes, wolves, settlers, and cattlemen and were now camped over across the river. Half a dozen young fellows rode down that way to see. Johnny and his cousin John Robert Gatewood made a race of it, far out ahead of the younger boys, kicking their slower mounts along.

"Find out all you can," John Cozad had told his sons. "After the grasshoppers all we need is a lawless sheep outfit eating us up."

There had been nothing lawless about Jim Haskell all the year since he came to Cozad but no telling to whom he might sell the sheep. Robert forgot this and was happy to see his friend unchanged except that he had a thickish sun-streaked beard and two busy shepherd dogs instead of the big bull proper for a butcher. The boys watched them work the herd and then decided to stay for early supper of fried quail, helping to scare the flock out of a brush patch and then plucking the birds, sending the soft feathers flying on the wind.

They rode home through the late evening sun, their hurrying shadows stilt-legged monsters with long lean giants in the saddles. Jim Haskell had said his sheep were already consigned off north of the settlements and he could have sold a thousand more since the hot winds blew out of Kansas again. And down near the state line they saw the ground alive with hatching grasshoppers no bigger than cabbage lice but livelier.

"Hell, I seen them too—almost as small as buffalo gnats last week, and millions, like crawling gnats," a man up from the Republican said.

"Yes," Sam Atkinson added softly. "I hear that up on the Niobrara River the hoppers are so thick they're damming the whole 300-foot-deep canyon, dropping pebbles in, to flood the country and grow their own green stuff."

It was meant for a little laughing, and some did.

The high point of the Fourth of July was the baseball game out on the prairie, the diamond worn a little by last-minute practice that stiffened the old players like a string-halted old mare. The young men around Cozad were willing but few except Jake Schooley had ever played. The North Platters were mostly McPherson soldiers, every man ready to argue the rules and to back up his opinion with fist and perhaps with brass knucks or East Side New York shiv. Finally, to avoid bloodshed, the batter was permitted nine balls and four strikes or swings at them, the pitcher delivering the ball where the batter called for it, generally by pointing to a spot in the air with his bat. If the delivery didn't come near enough to suit him, it didn't count and there was more argument. One wild pitcher put in almost an hour getting a batter to strike at his balls.

But if it hadn't been for the threats and the small encounters between the backers of the baseball teams, and a couple of real ringtail roarers out on the diamond, even Robert Cozad would have lost interest and wandered away as the parasoled ladies did right after the first ball, and many of the men too.

The day passed with the picnic lunch, the orator from North Platte, a few races, and a lot of noise and popping of firecrackers in the heat and dust. By midafternoon thunderheads rose, high and vaulted like great piles of egg meringue, pink lightning flickering through them, a long rolling sausage of gray cloud underneath. Sudden gusts of wind tore the sparse celebration bunting into streamers and carried them flying off across the prairie to catch desolately on some thistle or rosebrush. Rain fell in a few dirty spattering drops that sent the last hardy picnickers running. There was a far-off roaring and rumble that might be a buffalo stampede and excited Robert very much, wishing he could ride out to meet it, see the running animals close, for a painting.

"Hail!" an old-timer said tersely, tilting his browned mouth up to hold the tobacco juice. He had no particular concern. He had quit trying to make a crop here, even to raise a garden.

No hail fell near Cozad although there was a sudden coldness as of snow on the wind. Then the sun came out to set, cool and clear, while the telegraph reported a tornado not far from North Platte: clouds, dust, and roofs flying by like some cowboy's bandanna jerked loose. Shacks moved around too, but nobody was hurt much.

John Cozad and others pointed out that two years ago most of the region west of Kearney was considered unfit for anything but cattle, at least by the ranchers. Now much grain was produced farther out, well beyond there. Newspapers outside of the cattle-dominated towns carried big stories about the fruitfulness of the Platte valley. Adam Rankin was reported to have a thousand acres under cultivation near Cozad, showing what a crack farmer could do. He had won a thousand-dollar prize from the agricultural society of Illinois before he came west and it showed plain here.

The cattlemen were pushing their herds out over the government lands clear into Wyoming and were preparing to hold the range they used free of charge against any homeseeker and even the government, if anybody in Washington decided to get legalistic. Bratt, the big rancher from North Platte, predicted that the U.P. would carry 1500 carloads of cattle east this season, in addition to all the herds going to feed the Sioux and to stock the new ranches starting up as fast as the buffalo was cleared out and the Indians driven to the reservations.

John Cozad had to see the herds come bawling into his region again as the rains returned, overrunning his land with the rest. Taking along Robert, like a smaller edition of his father on a spotted pony, the colonizer rode out to leave warnings here and there, including Alf Pearson's. He made it clear he was armed as efficiently as any ranch hireling, and as prepared to shoot to kill. He was not the man to waste lead on the cattle as the more timid settlers did.

"That tinhorn can be dry-gulched like anybody else," one of the Texas cowboys said, almost loud enough for Cozad to hear. "Or picked off from behind some shack right in his place, without sheriff or constable, even."

Goldseekers were going through both ways this summer, hopefully westward, many dark-faced and angry heading back, ordered out of the Black Hills until after the Sioux conference for their sale in September.

That wasn't far off now, and John Cozad and his nephew Dave drove out northward, a shovel along to set up little markers of sod along the trail if they located a good route through to the gold regions. Kearney, to the east, was outfitting contraband miners heading off northwest through the empty, unguarded sandhills every day. Why not Cozad, much closer?

124

Suddenly interested, Johnny and his cousin John Henry went down to watch the miners passing through, some with pick, shovel, and gold pan tied to their packs.

"That's what the boys want to be this summer—bonanza men," Theresa told her mother, speaking bitterly. "There seems no quieting the wandering heart of the male."

Julia Gatewood had a touch of her indigestion and was a little short-tongued with her daughter. "You have seen it all your life around the hotel. Picked the biggest wanderer of all for yourself," she said impatiently. "When spring comes the dog will run, no matter what his age or what he has at home. You know that."

But it wasn't that simple, and not just in the spring. Theresa wanted to cry out, now that her Johnny showed signs of wandering too. Instead of arguing with her mother she gathered up her skirts and escaped to the commotion out behind the store, where the Gatewoods' Prince dog and Robert had discovered a half-grown skunk under the old piano crate and were raising a tremendous noise and stink. A passing cowboy shot the skunk and Theresa sent the boy and the dog down to the river with a bar of her mother's wood-lye soap.

"Don't come back until you are presentable," she ordered, with such unaccustomed anger that the boy stumbled back from her, his eyes searching her face. Then he turned and ran, not stopping for his horse, but running, the dog in a lope behind.

In a week John Cozad was back with stories of the road ranches booming along the Kearney–Black Hills trail. One, priced a little above the usual pick-and-gold-pan boys, offered fine wines and whiskies, also billiards, and games of chance, including, on short notice, banco and pedro. To those who asked if Cozad might start a roadhouse too, hinting at the faro discovered in his livery stable, Dave Claypool answered, "Uncle John J. never mixes gambling with his community."

"Most of the route would be through Indian country," John Cozad said at home, "and the Sioux may make a stand." He really had another worry. Everywhere until they got into the deepest sandhills, sooner or later a horsebacker appeared on a ridge, watching, and once, when the colonizer got off to sink his spade into the thick sod of a valley, a man came riding down, with pistol in his holster and rifle in the boot.

"This is Stappler range," he warned, "Keep off!"

"You can't bulldoze me!" John Cozad had replied, but the man was already gone, his horse kicking up sand in the pass.

Old Robert filled his pipe and listened and said nothing about the tobacco sack with a couple of .45 cartridges hung to his door down at the bridge while the colonizer was gone. Johnny had found it when he went to make up the weekly time sheet for the bridge crew, but he didn't seem to know what the shells meant.

It was a rattlesnake year, hot, with the towering thunderstorms that always make prairie creatures restless. Besides, as the settlers became acclimated they were more observing, saw more, including more rattlers. Tall tales grew up fast, the tallest about Cozad. Perhaps because two, three were killed in the region every hot day this summer, a rumor got around that the town was invaded by venomous snakes, people taking to the roofs, the U.P. canceling the usual train stops there as too dangerous, even refusing to pick up those bitten because they would die in half an hour or so anyway.

Robert thought this a fine tale and was immediately set straight, but not by his father, who took no public notice of gossip or "other gross exaggerations." Some thought the snake story was spite work by the Plum Creekers, who were worried by Cozad's rapid growth. Soon the town might have the votes to take the county seat, as that gambling braggart had promised.

The snake scare didn't keep Julia Gatewood from her usual berrying. When the chokecherries were darkening and the wild plums began to turn she got up an expedition into the northern breaks, taking the Cozad boys and John Robert along, all in high boots, leather gloves, and with a sealed bottle of whisky for emergencies in the grub box. They stayed two nights and had a very fine and lazy time but afterward Johnny regretted going. Dr. Marshall, chief physician at the Buffalo Lung Infirmary, with nearly three hundred of his patients traveling the west for their health, had stopped off to see John Cozad. He brought a number of his patients into the little Cozad parlor and told them in his floweriest language of the accomplishments here.

"And Mr. Cozad, the builder, was a lung patient. Ran in his family, many members dying. He too went west for his health."

Yes, that was true, the colonizer started to say, but the doctor interrupted. "Note carefully how well Mr. Cozad looks now, erect, full-chested, no fever in the cheek or the eye, no transparency of skin. Sound as a nut, a black walnut —require a mallet to crack."

When the doctor and his patients were back on the train, the colonizer, standing bareheaded in the evening sun, looked out over his region. This year the grasshoppers had lifted earlier, with the summer a windy one, so windy that the great double wheel of the railroad pumping station seldom was still. The rod pounded night and day, the gears often without oil, so much of the railroad without care.

But the town did seem pretty solid now. Even the Odd Fellows had finally organized, men like Atkinson, Russell, Dave Claypool, and Traber among the charter members. Robert Gatewood too, an old-timer in the lodge. True, there were still trail herds coming through this late but several of the bridge hands had rifles in their scabbards and could hurry the Longhorns on.

Unfortunately there were conflicts in town, violent encounters that should be rare without a real saloon in miles, nothing more now than the hidden jug down at one of the livery stables. The worst was the shooting of Jerry Cozad. He had the family's arrogant temper and in a hot moment he threatened John McIntyre with a knife and got a shoulder bullet that cut an artery, the blood spurting. John Cozad was away and by the time he returned somebody had found the severed vessel and by thumb pressure had saved Jerry's life so far; somebody else had telegraphed the sheriff at Plum Creek. Others had been at work elsewhere too, for there were dark knots of men down at the livery stables, particularly the new one, where a couple of outsiders up on a wagon shouted about lynching McIntyre, stringing him up. Even the more sensible men of the town seemed to be there, nodding, motioning their approval when one of the loudmouths held up a rope, lifted the coils of it high.

Then slowly the groups of men began to move together, two, three taking the lead, stalking up the street for the house where McIntyre was said to be hiding, with more men and boys joining along the route. From his window up in Emigrant House the colonizer saw them come, out in the middle of the street, his nephew John Robert at the fringe and his sons running up to fall in behind.

For a moment John Cozad was back at his first sight of this savagery that seemed so close to the surface even here—back hearing the sullen noises and the march over the waterfront cobblestones as the mob dragged the friend of his boyhood away to hang from a rope, the legs and arms jumping, then the head fallen forward, stilled, a lonely figure swaying only a little.

Suddenly now, here in his own settlement, John J. Cozad found himself running down the steps and out into the street, directly into the path of the mob of men.

"Stop! I'll have no such violence here!" he shouted.

Before his words the lead men slowed, wavered, looking down at the colonizer's hand. He looked too, and saw his pistol there, although he had no recollection of drawing it at all.

In an hour the sheriff rode into town, guns strapped on, the star on his chest shining. He brought McIntyre out, put him under arrest. Next day the man was free on $1000 bail and Jerry Cozad already healing. All it had required after the pressure on the artery was a little digging with Traber Gatewood's thin steel wire to draw the bullet out.

But for John Cozad there was a defilement in the dark knot of men who had marched up the dust of his street, a coil of rope in the hands of the leader. And not until years later did Robert understand the father he saw that day.

XI

THE SUMMER MOVED INTO GOLDEN OCTOBER, the Platte with its banding of timber and brush lay like an endless silver ribbon edged in yellows, russets and reds flung carelessly through the tawny stretch of the great valley. Then the prairie fires started, pearling the horizon by day, burning the night sky to red and orange. One of these fires not far west brought out the entire region before the wind finally drove it into the fall river. But there could be worse, much worse in scattered settlements like Cozad's. Scarcely two years ago ten school children were burned to death over in Saline County because a terrified woman took all the pupils related to her out of school before the furious onsweep of a prairie fire. She took them out against the urgent protest of the teacher, and all were overtaken and burned to death, the woman with them. The teacher and the other pupils had run to the safety of a plowed field nearby. Ironically, tragically, the school-house that the dead children had deserted was not touched by the flames at all.

This story, told one of those burning nights, stirred the Cozad boys. Johnny asked how they died—from breathing smoke and fire into the lungs or actually burned, mulling over what could be told, the tender skin of the small ones coming off as the woman, already afire too, tried to rip their flaming clothes away.

"Of course, tender and delicate," the youth exclaimed, "like the skin of a young grouse or a quail, very thin, like tissue paper, and cooked in a second."

"John A.!" his mother cried out in horror. "Don't say such things!"

Robert thought of the burnt children left scattered over the blackened prairie and wanted to know who had started the fire.

"Mr. Matthews says anybody that sets a prairie fire ought to *dance*," the boy remarked, and got the flat of his father's hand across his mouth. Hurt and astonished, he clapped a palm to his lips, and then fled from the house.

A long time afterward he slipped into his chilly bed in the tipi and lay looking up into the darkness. It wasn't that he hadn't been slapped before, often, for sass, slapped and more, like that time with the buggy whip, but this seemed different. Once he thought Johnny was awake and, drawn to his brother in his confusion, he whispered, "What did I say—what was worse than yours—about the tender skin of the burnt children like young quail?— What——"

But he let his voice trail off, for Johnny didn't seem to hear.

A slow fall rain stopped the fires, the air grew colder and fringes of anchor ice glistened along the morning edges of the river. John Cozad took his family to Omaha for winter clothing and a look through the Union Pacific museum collections. At dinner with the railroad president the colonizer spoke of a trip to Washington, with no mention of his need to recoup his cash reserves. The September conference to buy the Black Hills had ended in a near-massacre of the commissioners by the Sioux, but with the buffalo about gone the Indians would have to give up. Toward that time John Cozad had a plan, still hazy as a frost-misted January morning along the Platte, but sure to clear fast enough under the sun of opportunity.

He was applying for an allotment of land near the Hills, something like the old Spanish grants for colonization, to build an ideal community as a sort of contrast to the wild mining towns to come. Such a grant was practically impossible under the present land policy but perhaps during that momentary interval between the end of the Indian title and the absorption of the region into the public domain something could be done.

The other plan he did not mention: for a land subsidy like the U.P.'s to finance a stub railroad from Cozad to the gold of the Black Hills. He hoped he could run a railroad better than the U.P.

The land grants seemed unlikely but the community idea lent respectability to his trip. John Cozad realized now that he must leave faro behind him very soon, before it ruined his chances for a senatorship and became a handicap to his sons. There was something else that he had not mentioned before Theresa or Robert: when the Indians gave up the Hills there would be a Dakota Territory, with the officials from the governor down appointed by Washington. True, in Wyoming and elsewhere under Grant these had been political hacks and out-of-job carpetbaggers, but John J. Cozad carried some mighty good letters in his hand valise.

Nothing came of the Washington trip except some Cozad luck at cards and a fine full-length camera portrait by Mathew Brady, made between the political calls. The picture, framed in old silver, he put on the top of a box well packed with excelsior containing gifts for the sons: a pocket microscope that Johnny would probably use most, and a New Improved Magic Lantern, with a cabinet of glass slides including such titles as The Seven Wonders of the World, Great Paintings, and In Darkest Africa. When he arrived home with nothing of his misty plans achieved he found Johnny and Robert running magic-lantern shows once a week in the lodge room, Robert passing one of his father's silk hats for contributions to send Bibles to the benighted Africans.

For all the failures and the incredibly bad luck of his community, or perhaps because it was like a gambling defeat, John Cozad was elated, excited. He spoke highly of the town's progress, with the bridge well started and the colonists of too little courage largely frozen out by the stiff ante that the grasshoppers and the hard times proved to be. The tougher, stronger stayed and strengthened more. Even in his own family the sons were sturdier if not actually robust. Theresa, too, was strengthening, less dependent upon her parents, it seemed, although her closeness to them had pleased him from the start, with Julia Gatewood soon a mother to the man who had known only stepmothers, old Robert a second and less demanding father than his own. Henry Cozad as a community builder the son learned to respect greatly but only after he had wandered far from the hayfield and the tedding fork.

Further, the last year had brought John J. Cozad an unexpected gift, one that was good for his sons to see, a gift that comes reluctantly to a man of his profession, even to a community builder. During the last year he had found a friend, one who asked nothing for himself, and what this friend gave no man ever bought for money or favor.

John Cozad had known of the elder Schooleys back in his home county of Vinton, Ohio, and Jake had been with the colony for some time. But Jake's younger brother Sam had gone with the parents to Missouri where he fevered and shook with malaria. Desperate at twenty-two, he and his brother-in-law, Bill Claypool, had headed west in a covered wagon with no aim except to find some relief from the burning, shaking ager. In Kansas, Sam heard it was healthier farther north, so they headed to the Platte and westward up the river, stopping wherever there was game. While Bill went directly on to

Cozad to visit Dave Claypool, Sam Schooley took a slower pace, hunting, camping on windy rises or on the western side of stream bends, said by many to be healthier because the poisonous night vapors seemed to travel on the eastward wind. It was true that Sam kept feeling better as the nights grew chillier and he got farther on. Near the town of Cozad he turned off to camp at the river and saw that part of the bottoms here had been stripped, the sod dumped into the stream in a sort of raised approach. With the pile driver at the far end it looked like some narrow, flat-bodied prehistoric reptile crawling out into the water, the uplifted head turned to look back.

So the sod bridge his brother Jake had described in his letters was actual. It pleased Sam Schooley that such an unlikely prospect, such a dream as a sod bridge over the roaring spring floods and the barefaced sandbars of summer could be true. From his enthusiasm, his delight, Sam realized that he was feeling pretty good, perhaps better than any time he could remember. He built a little fire and roasted a slab of rib and back from the fat young doe he had shot in the breaks. Then he rolled up in his blankets and slept, knowing what is given to very few so young—that he had come home.

It was months before John J. Cozad realized that the man who was to be his most loyal if not his blindest friend was this newcomer who had found his own fool way to the town.

January of the new year, the centennial year of the nation, brought snow, eighteen inches to two feet on the level around Cozad. While this would have caused much consternation the first year of the new colony, those who had seen the drouth years welcomed every drop of moisture no matter how it fell, even in great isolating drifts that blocked the roads and stood against the snowplows of the railroad for days. When the storm cleared the Odd Fellows installed their new officers and threw the lodge room open to the families and invited guests.

There was a welcoming speech, with a few wry jokes about hard times and ragged pants, then some songs, with the Cozad boys standing up in a duet that ended fine and strong enough to make up for Robert's quavering start. The ladies applauded charmingly. Someone began the old songs with "The Merry Golden Tree" and finally Robert Gatewood blew on his pitch pipe and started "Old Bangum and the Boar" with the men roaring it out and then falling into parts, singing as many of them had back in Virginia, Ohio, and on the way west, singing as they should have been singing here every week, old Robert Gatewood told them.

To relieve the nostalgia, a newcomer started the trembling agony of the "Bride of the Gamblin' Man" and turned purplish as from a blizzard wind, gulping painfully in the middle of a note when he suddenly remembered the source of John Cozad's income. But the colonizer was in fine humor and joined in, singing heartily, propping up the newcomer's voice until it grew strong as a U.P. whistle on a frosty dawn. Together they shook the dust from the bare rafters and brought on a stomping of cowhide boots. Afterward Mother Gatewood sang some of the ballads of her youth in a sweet, plaintive falsetto and was embarrassed by the applause. She hadn't sung any of these except while making green tomato preserves in many, many years.

Later in the evening a music club was organized "to capitalize on the latent talent smoked out here tonight," Ed Young said, with singing practice once a week at the Cozads', who had the only piano in the town. Everybody nodded. Some had seen the small squarish instrument of lovely age-toned rosewood with a garland of golden inlay back when it was unloaded, and opened right at the depot so a traveling man could play it while the engine was fueled and watered.

A couple of fiddlers finally hauled out the instruments they reluctantly admitted they had brought, while somebody went to get the accordion still left at the hotel for the board bill.

The dancing started, four, five men standing along the walls for every woman and girl present, including little Maggie Claypool in red hair ribbons. Skirts flew out, boots stomped. Next time a drum would be added to the music, one carried at Shiloh by a boy so small he spilled no Confederate blood, which counted here, with half a dozen from Virginia who had relatives buried in the Gray, among the many who had worn the old blue overcoats long before the relief barrels came. Afterward coffee was carried up from the kitchen in a copper-lined wash boiler, the coffee bag floating. Johnny and Robert brought dishpans piled with fry cakes just out of the fat—lard, not buffalo tallow.

It was almost dawn when the guests muffled themselves for the zero weather, the frost pushing in cloudily at the opened door. The snow squeaked under the heavy overshoes, the horses' feet, and the wheels. There were a few sleighs too, their runners singing, a sleigh and a buffalo robe, it seemed, for every girl old enough to wear her hair up. Before long the Cozad sleigh wouldn't be loaned out. Johnny would be wanting it for himself.

Along the Platte, February had once brought preparations for great hunts, for tribal wars. This year it gave Cozad the town's first compliment from the horse thieves who had raided all around for years. They came in upon the stock of an emigrant train camped for the night near the river, perhaps because the firelight glistened against a new Studebaker wagon. But the horses proved worn and gaunted from the long winter trip west, and the thieves merely scattered them with a loud and contemptuous whoop. They did pick up half a dozen good head at the older ranches around Plum Creek, including a fine pacer that had been cleaning out the sports around the trotting circuits from Grand Island west to North Platte.

"That's one fancy stepper that will be pulling a sodbuster for some hoe man in Kansas in a few weeks," Costin predicted.

136

Out beyond the grasshopper regions the clearing snow left the prairie deep in dead grass. Once more prairie fires started, driven by the winds freshening toward spring. The Cozad boys were out in one of the worst in years. Their father had taken them along to North Platte to see some buffaloes loaded into a railroad car for a wild-west show in the east somewhere. The buffaloes didn't arrive, perhaps because of the fire scare. For a whole day and night a prairie fire swept up from below Frenchman Creek toward the Forks of the Platte. If not stopped at the frozen river, the town would go up. Then if the wind turned to the west, every settlement down along the Platte might be cleaned out too, with no stream of size before the Loups big enough to stop the racing flames.

John Cozad, busy with contest hearings at the land office, hired a couple of good saddle horses for his sons and turned them loose. "Be back for the late train," he said absent-mindedly.

The boys got a lunch for the saddlebags, crossed the bridge, and headed for a look toward the fire from the high backbone against the far southern sky. The smoke was boiling up grayish off beyond them, pearling as it climbed higher and, finally turning white, it trailed off in windy clouds. The boys settled down to their sandwiches, the smoke rolling up nearer and nearer, although everybody within fifty miles must be out fighting the flames. North Platters had been hurrying down from the first pale streak on the horizon, more still going, people running like ants over the prairie, troops trotting by from McPherson.

And then suddenly the two boys were gone from the ridge.

Toward evening the wind strengthened to sixty miles an hour and a warning spread that the Forks of the Platte might not stop the roaring blaze, that North Platte and everything beyond might go. Now even the land office closed and the last of the able-bodied men hurried out, taking the last of the breaking plows, held back to lay out fireguards for the town.

Some of the wagons rumbling over the bridge were solid with standing men, following loads of water barrels, hoes, spades and gunny sacks to backfire at the guards thrown up by the sodbusters, the teams whipped along by riders, the men between the handles running with giant steps to hold the bucking plowshares in the dry, tough sod.

Suddenly John Cozad appeared at the livery barn where the only man left, a peg-leg, was hurrying to get the Morgan stallion out to a plowed field.

"My sons haven't returned?"

"I ain't worried only about them horses," the man shouted, running in his gimping lope to gather up ropes and blindfolds.

So all John Cozad could do was hurry from hotel to store, to street, and back. No one could listen to him or hire, loan, or sell him a horse. Down at the bridge he tried to stop those back from the fire, worn out, but they knew nothing of two boys who were strangers.

"Everybody's a stranger, with the singeing and the soot," one said, through burnt lips.

By night messengers were spurring in to say that none of the fireguards were holding, the high gale sweeping the fire over them, the bending flames clearing them like rabbits jumping a ditch.

"Boys?—Lots of boys around——" was all the reply John Cozad could get.

Then suddenly he saw the west leap high in a solid red wall as the fire topped the bluffs stretched across the south and stood against the sky a moment. Then it swept down the broad valley. Troopers, the last to be spared from McPherson, galloped out to replace men who had fought to exhaustion, to dropping, their faces fire-blackened, their lungs smoke-poisoned. Wagons full of these were unloaded at the depot, the churches, anywhere that there was floor space.

And nowhere could John Cozad find his two sons, one of them only a child.

Women rode out now with the last of the boys and the old and the sick, and still the fire came on. No one could face it, particularly not in the dried marshes of the bottoms, with all the old accumulations of dead and rotting vegetation. The best the fighters could hope to do now was slow the fire a little, keep it from hitting the frozen river with such speed and heat that one smoldering tumbleweed could be skated across the ice, or one bit of popping diamond willow be blown across into the old slough grass and rushes where none could fight this fire and live.

It was nearly nine before the last tongues of flames sullenly turned to follow the riverbank, north and south, half into the wind, and were pounded out. Here and there in the darkness a little blaze sprang up from the smoldering grass and leaves and was put out too.

So North Platte was saved, but even John Cozad's goatee got a little singeing in that last stand at the river, throwing himself into the defense with the rest, using his great coat to slap out the sparks and new little flames, the smoldering. Afterward he made one more anxious round of those from the fire, seeking and inquiring, and then to the saloons, full, with so many parched throats to wet, so many who needed a little cheer now.

"Takes a lot of wetting and cheer when you know everything exceptin' the ground's gone up in smoke," one of Bratt's top cowhands said. He was riding early next morning, helping throw the Bratt herds north of the river, up toward the sandhills for grass, now that all the range here south of the Platte was gone.

"Damn it, somebody must have seen my sons!" John Cozad kept interrupting, here and there, and finally he had to put his fears into words. "Could they have been caught somewhere and—been lost?"

A couple of the men looked at each other. "Not likely, but possible," one admitted.

Then suddenly the boys were there, out in the light-patched street, on the horses, both singed a little, but with clean-washed faces.

"Where have you been?" the father demanded, the agitation in his face an astonishment to them.

"Why, you said be back for the late train," Johnny explained.

"I meant the late evening train—I've been a crazy man——"

"We were fighting fire with Sergeant Poole, from McPherson. He's a dandy——" Robert added, his excitement held in as long as possible. "*He* said it was worse than when all the school children and the lady with them was burned!" Then he had to admit the truth. "But I guess nobody died in this——"

With the first real thaw, the country was in a roaring gold boom, with big parties heading into the Black Hills from every direction, towns springing up on the winter rock of Custer City and Deadwood Gulch, the miners gophering everywhere, the army apparently helpless to keep them out of the illegal territory. John Cozad, at the land office with his March settlers, hired a couple of horses and slipped away in the night to Fort Robinson, up toward the Hills. An old Cincinnati friend there got an army ambulance, a prairie wagon, and with a couple of officers along and some enlisted men to make it look like a reconnoiter, they went to Deadwood. But the Hills were too confused and lawless for John Cozad. On the way home he put an item into the North Platte paper saying Cozad needed a good blacksmith, realizing that good blacksmiths would try the gold fields first.

It turned out that Cozad might be needing some Indian fighters more. Up on the Loup, near little Fort Hartsuff, thrown together to protect the settlers pushing into the Indian country, a few soldiers were ambushed by the Sioux and one killed. Alarms spread, skulking warriors were reported as far down the Platte as Willow Island and Cozad. Settlers streamed into the towns, or threw up sod forts with loopholes and barrels of water stored inside for a seige. Robert Cozad was in a boiling excitement, remembering the wounded Pawnee the boys had discovered not three years ago. Maybe there would be more.

In a week the scare was gone like fog before the sun. Spring was upon them and settlers who knew nothing of the Indian threat darkened the trails, filled the tourist cars of the railroad. They had to be taken out farther now that most of the land near Cozad was covered by filings. Unless there was another big gold strike, it seemed the Platte Valley would be all settled by fall. Or unless the cattlemen started a real war against the settlers like that reported in parts of Texas—settlers found face down on their homesteads everywhere.

John Cozad was out almost every day, often until late at night. Then before dawn one morning there was a sudden smell of pine smoke, and immediately a smother of it, and the terrifying leap and crackle of flames. At the same time two stores and the hotel blazed up, reddening the clouds overhead. There were shouts, the ring of the fire bell, and the glint of buckets as men came running, crying, "Fire! Fire! Everybody out!"

Finally John Cozad and his wife appeared through the flames and smoke, clutching their dressing gowns about them, with their arms full of clothing. For a while there was a cry to save Robert, the sleepyhead, but he burst out too, a coat over his head, scattering sketches and drawings as he ran.

There was no need to worry about Johnny. He had been one of the first out to the fire again, right after Sam Atkinson, riding in late from over south. Now, with the bucket brigade strung out, the water hit the flames in glistening arcs, making momentary bits of darkness, but nothing helped and down-wind everything went, all Mrs. Cozad's clothing except the dress and coat she had grabbed up. The gold dressing table, the piano, everything of the house was lost except the handsome Brady photograph of her husband. That she clutched close under her arm. There were rumors of a great roll of money burned too, the recent faro winnings that were to pay for the summer's work at the bridge. Not the gambler's showy diamonds; those were in the pocket of his frock coat across his arm, but Theresa's diamonds were gone, the magnificent Jewel of the Platte that her husband had designed for her too, and the emerald of her engagement.

Slowly the men of Cozad searched the edges of the dying fires for clues to their origin, but they found nothing to implicate anyone. No cattleman hireling, no Cozad enemy, no malicious mischief-maker. Perhaps sparks from a burning chimney had been blown upon the roofs down-wind, the direction the flames spread.

There was talk of the Cozad losses in the morning while the family stirred through the cooling ashes so carefully, with some whispers about the town's future. This might just be the final slap of circumstance, the final undercutting, as the Platte might undercut the greatest cottonwood.

Then suddenly everything was changed, for the raking struck a body in the hotel ruins.

Theresa Cozad stood up well under this, her eyes suddenly haggard, searching all the crowd for someone missing. It was poor John O'Neil, who fell into bed insensible as a stinking log every night from the rotgut, the redeye at the new livery stable. Two years ago O'Neil had still been a passable booster for the town and selling real estate, even though no longer able to practice law.

There was other talk too, with hints that one of the stores had lost too much money these hard times, and was well insured. One of the newspapers said two boys were arrested for arson after O'Neil's body turned up, but that seemed more Plum Creek gossip. True, the sheriff had been up but that was for the man killed. Plainly drunk all the time, as some of the women said, those who were members of the new W.C.T.U.

and loud in the denunciation of the Demon Rum and the poor victim.

As the wind sifted the light wood ashes along the dirt street and off past the houses left in Cozad, it became clear that the fire had burned more than buildings, money, diamonds and even human life. It seemed to have burned hope.

XII

John Cozad seemed to look upon the fire as one more attack by the enemies of his town, although Traber tried to say that there were Plum Creekers as alarmed as anybody over the domination of their town by cattleman tools and money. They particularly hated the growing influence of large outfits from the unorganized territory north, outside of Dawson County, ranchers who made Plum their shipping point, their headquarters. Entirely too much rough element bulldozing the citizens, Dr. Hudson complained when he stopped by to set some bones broken in a buggy runaway.

With his usual vigor John Cozad had put men to work rebuilding two days after the fire, first of all hammering together a big hollow structure as barny as Mrs. Trollope's old Bazaar in Cincinnati for temporary use as a hotel, until the brick one could be put up. He kept the men working through another Indian scare, a roaring spring flood, and even a big expedition from Ohio stopping off on the way to the Black Hills to visit with old acquaintances and brag a little about golden millions. He pushed the work so the roof was on the new hotel and the doors hung in time for the June excursion and Robert's birthday.

At eleven Robert Cozad was a lean and thin-wristed boy, still with the short chin of his father and the same dark eyes that already seemed to carry their own light. Several times he had started a diary and usually kept up the decorations, the little pictures, longer than the words, perhaps because there were so many things that it was not nice to speak about. He did insert little stories of adventure, stories a little like those the mother had read to the boys years ago.

Diffidently he showed her some of these one evening when it was drizzling outside, a dull, lonesome evening. He offered her the open composition book, standing before her, holding it out gently but insistently.

The mother laid aside her embroidery hoop with its Battenberg centerpiece and took the book, waving Robert to his chair and to patience. Then she glanced at the ink blots, the blackened corrections, the bad spelling, rocking a little as she read, and reread, pursing her full lips in consideration of one sentence, one paragraph, turning the book to follow the gay little drawings along the margin.

She took a long time but Robert's dark eyes did not leave her face, holding himself back, wanting to cry out, demand a word, even if she had to say the stories were bad—anything. He resented his brother Johnny's standing beside their mother, slapping his shining boots with the new quirt he had made. He looked very tall there while the mother read, the lamp-light touching his smooth cheek, scraped clean of down, Robert knew, with the razor he bought years ago, through an advertisement. He had practiced holding the genuine bone handle turned back daintily with his little finger against it as they had seen their father do, but not stopping as the father did, at the clean line of the goatee.

Robert wished for his father now, but John Cozad was off in the new gold town of Deadwood Gulch again, making needed cash, with the hotel burned, the money lost, and rumors of grasshoppers hatching again. Perhaps he was out at

Denver and the mining camps of the Rockies, working up markets for the hay that stood deep and green along the river, or would if the hoppers didn't come. Robert knew that money was important but he did wish his father were back just now. He wanted his special friend here, as Johnny had his, their mother.

"With Mr. Cozad away so much, I do lean on Johnny——" she had said to some missionary ladies coming through a few days ago. Then perhaps because Robert was there, passing the little sandwiches, she added, "And his brother too, of course."

Suddenly now Robert heard his mother speaking, and speaking for some time. "Oh, Son!" she exclaimed. "Aren't you interested that I think your little stories are rather good for a young boy?"

He took the book with trembling hands, and wanted to dance a little waterfront jig, but he held himself quiet. "Thank you, I shall work on neatness and spelling."

Suddenly the kind of news that infuriated John Cozad beyond anything else—news of a lynching, came from Plum Creek, his own county seat. It seemed that Tom Hallowell, living on a homestead on Donelson Island near the end of the Plum Creek bridge, was to be thrown off his land by the county authorities. When a deputy sheriff and two assistants came to order him and his family off the place, he retreated to the house and promised to shoot the first man who touched anything. The deputy sheriff ordered the door opened. Hollowell refused. They battered it open with a fence post and as the hinges gave and it crashed inward, the settler put a charge of buckshot into the officer, brought him down dead. The other two tried to push in and Hollowell cut flesh from the lower jaw of one. But now his double-barrel was empty and they whipped him down with their pistols while he begged to live. He was ironed and brought to Plum Creek.

The district attorney hurried to the town to prevent violence because Plum already had a bad name for lawlessness. He was stopped in the darkness outside the town limits by some of the armed, masked men riding in from the ranches all around. He tried to slip in from the other directions and found guns stuck in his ribs.

In the meantime a mob of the masked men surrounded the courthouse, seized the jailer, bound him, knocked the lock off Hollowell's cell, gagged him, and with a rope around his neck took him out to the outside stairs leading up to the courtroom on the second floor. There they strung him up to the railing and left him in the darkness of midnight, still in handcuffs, his feet not eighteen inches from the ground.

When John Cozad heard the news he spoke out in cold fury, his eyes white-ringed as those of some outlaw horses. "A man's home is supposed to be his castle, his homestead his kingdom," he roared.

"Depends on who wants the place," Sam Atkinson said. "Remember the troubles over near Kearney a couple summers ago, the settlers arming after the little girl who was keeping the Longhorns off her father's crops got a cowboy bullet through her dress?"

"There's more than one story on that," one of the Pearson boys said. He was working for a Loup country rancher now, not far from his father's place up north, and feeling mighty big with a gun on him.

"There's always more than one story," John Cozad said bitterly. "But the end's the same——"

Once more the grasshoppers came, almost as bad as in seventy-four. This time Robert Cozad felt the desperation without having to see it on the faces about him. At nine he hadn't understood the full meaning of the great clouds of the hoppers, clouds even bigger than the passenger pigeons he saw once in Ohio. Since then he had observed something of the devastation, the human suffering. He remembered one time when with Johnny he went looking for antelope to chase, if they could find some grassy spot missed by the hoppers. They stopped in at a dougout off southeast of the river to ask for a dipper of water. The woman and her two small children there were like skeletons, with nothing left but roots to eat, and grasshoppers. The husband was away, had taken the team to try to find some work or food, it seemed.

"He can't come back if he's got nothing——" the woman said with the dullness, the low hoarseness of the starving.

Robert had a little money along, $4.20, it turned out, all they had expected to need. They rode off to the store at the Plum Creek bridge and bought flour, baking powder, a little can of sorghum, brown beans, and a chunk of salt pork, all they could talk the storekeeper into letting them have, promising to send the rest of the money immediately. Then, their horses packed, they returned to the woman and, unloading the stuff in front of the dugout, they left before she could start to cry.

It was late when they got home and Johnny did the explaining. Their mother had been sympathetic. "It was kind of you," she told them, "but you can't feed all the hungry. It would take billions——"

She had not satisfied Robert, but there was nothing he could say. Since then grasshoppers flying always brought up those little skeletons he saw in the dugout that day, the sunken eyes, the wrists like sticks, and a fury rose in him. But in many around him now there was more anger against the head of the community than against the gnawing jaws of the hoppers. Even Ed Sanderson, the red-bearded station agent, spoke out against John Cozad lately in spite of going into the real estate business himself, booming the region to those who might be talked into buying railroad lands off beyond the Cozad holdings.

It was the summer of the Sioux war but the times were so

troublesome in Dawson County and in the Cozad community that the troops going through the Yellowstone and Powder River country caused little stir. Not even the news of the wipe-out of the Custer force brought much discussion, particularly not among the settlers from the South, or from states like West Virginia and Missouri. True, some border men were rabid Custer partisans but not when they walked through their first crop in three seasons and then had to watch it fall to billions of hungry jaws.

The grocery stores that had been giving credit all spring and summer on crop prospects shut the books when the first gray shimmer of grasshoppers appeared in the sky.

"Just when my kids will be hungriest," one settler said bitterly, yet he could not blame Mrs. Gatewood or the rest.

Traber came in from a dental trip over north. The wild currants, yellow and black, were fine up back of the Loup, bending the bushes to the ground. "Seems we ought to get them before the hoppers move in up there," he said.

The next morning Theresa Cozad and a couple of her friends started north in Schooley's covered wagon, the boys riding their ponies, with some friends along and this time, a girl. Maggie Claypool's cousin Mollie, sidesaddle, had so suddenly become a young lady that she made Robert bashful, but not Johnny. He was teasing her about the sidesaddle, a concession to her Aunt Theresa. Usually Mollie wore a divided denim skirt and rode astride, much safer on these half-wild Indian ponies, but not ladylike now that her hair was going up and she was about to teach school.

Mrs. Gatewood waved her apron from the doorstep and then went back to turning flapjacks for her breakfast boarders. That night John Cozad came home unexpectedly. He had hurried down from Deadwood the moment he heard of the grasshoppers and knew there would be a real stampede out of the country this time unless he could somehow hold the people to the land that had already cost them money, time, work, and so much anxiety. He had dodgers printed at the *Hundredth Meridian* office announcing that work at the bridge would be stepped up immediately, extra work in his community's time of need.

But before night several of the notices just tacked up were torn from the nails, one stained with large splatters of tobacco juice.

"Probably the cowboys riding through, hoping we'll quit the country," Dave said.

"Yeh, plainly it was some plutocrat, somebody on a pay-roll. None of us been mouthing ambeer as rich as that in a long time," a gaunted settler agreed.

The handbill in the depot was one that vanished almost as soon as it was posted. John Cozad went down there in a fury and tacked up one himself, with shingle nails driven deep through washers to hold it firm.

The berry pickers came home toward evening, tired, but with tubs of fruit. That night the fragrance of boiling wild-currant jelly was on the night wind from half a dozen open doors, women straining sample glasses very carefully for entry in the fair, come fall.

The Cozads went to bed early, but some time after the train stopped several men came stomping up to the makeshift hotel, and then a couple more later, just about the time there was a running up the back road. In a little while Johnny slipped into bed with the waking Robert, who had put out an automatic hand to detain the sleepwalker. Then he sat up in the darkness, but realizing that his brother was awake, he settled back into sleep, never really out of his dreaming.

At breakfast there was a conference and then, with his coat brushed, his British boots softly gleaming, John Cozad strode down to the station to accost the agent.

"What do you mean, driving my son out of the depot last night, from a public place?"

"He wasn't in the depot, Mr. Cozad. I caught him along the wall outside."

"You mean you accuse him of spying on your tricky ways, grabbing the landseekers I brought here—trying——"

"Hell, no——" the red-bearded agent interrupted.

"You don't deny you were talking to the men that I arranged transportation for, talking them against me and the land I offer?"

"That's got nothing to do with last night. I was protecting the depot from going the way the other two went, the way your own place last spring—burnt to the ground!"

For a moment John Cozad's anger held him. Then he lunged at the agent, who struck out with his fist, missing, but squaring away with determination as he began to curse the community builder. "—you goddam crook!" he shouted. "You overbearing bastard of a cardsharp, coming in here——"

John Cozad's angry face bleached to its bone whiteness at this public affront. Then he jerked himself together, the pistol from inside his coat out and firing, but into the plank flooring at Sanderson's feet, driving the man back, to cower with an arm over his face.

Then a sudden gasping noise behind John Cozad made him do a very dangerous thing—glance back. He caught one glimpse of a young face, blank, horrified, and then it was gone—Robert, his feet running, running hard.

Behind his gun the colonizer backed to the depot desk, felt for the drawer, jerked it open, and with the agent's gun in his pocket he went out the door. He looked all along the street that seemed empty, making it casual, the gambler cool in a great loss.

There were saddle horses and several teams at the hitch racks, and a few people out looking toward the depot, mostly curious, with shooting so common, the nearer faces suddenly stiffening. But Robert was gone, nowhere in sight.

Johnny was coming along the street with the Gatewoods'

Prince dog beside him. He began to hurry when he saw his father, the boy's handsome face pale and anxious. "Is everything all right?" he asked, looking down at his father's hand.

Only now did John Cozad realize he was still holding the gun. He slipped it away and together they went up the street to reassure Theresa.

For the next hour the man who had acted swiftly in a hundred tight places could think of nothing to do. He could not send anyone to find Robert, not the boy's brother or anyone, not go himself, for that kind of humiliation was not to be put upon a Cozad, not even a knee-pants youth. All he could do, it seemed, was hope that the boy had not been driven to the desperation that had shown on his young face that moment in the depot doorway.

The story of the encounter, the Sanderson version, ran over town like a dry-land whirlwind, dipping here and there. The Gatewoods and particularly Sam Schooley and Dave Claypool listened to it with sobered faces but said nothing. And no one seemed to know that a Cozad son had been anywhere near.

Then at supper the grandfather looked at Robert's empty place and said the boy seemed to be getting moony, been down at the river most of the day, in a clump of willows, staring into the water.

"Out fishing alone? He knows I don't like things like that," his mother complained.

"No, he didn't have a pole—just mooning."

"Mooning? Now John J., you will have to speak to him," Theresa urged.

But John Cozad's ear was straining for footsteps that didn't come until near midnight. A long time afterward the father tried to catch the pattern of the boy's breathing, hoping that sleep would come to his troubled mind, but all night it seemed no one lay beside young Johnny, and in the morning the boy was gone early.

"He's checking in a couple of men coming from the south side around sunrise, to get back home before dark," old Robert explained at breakfast.

So it went, and somehow nothing was ever said between father and son about the morning in the depot and the bullets around the agent's feet.

Whether the story of the fight with Sanderson got to the railroad headquarters nobody around Cozad really seemed to know, but in a few days he was transferred. By then the financial difficulties of the U.P. were very public, with employees laid off, cut to half time or shifted. There was uneasiness about the bloodthirsty Sioux, who had stopped General Crook, well known and liked throughout the Platte valley and wiped out Custer. Finally they sent Crook on his hungry march to the Black Hills instead of punishing the scattered Indians of the Little Big Horn. The second conference to buy the Black Hills gathered and the agency chiefs again refused, but this time they were locked in the stockade and told there would be no goods or food for their women and children or for them until they touched the pen. It was done, mining in the Hills became legal, and in addition a vast prairie empire was opened to settlement, but not if the cattlemen, already pushing in upon the new grass, could prevent it.

John Cozad hurried off to Omaha and to Washington, about his model settlement but more hopeful for the Cozad–Black Hills railroad. He took along a map Robert helped make, and a lot of literature comparing the Cozad route with those from Cheyenne, Sidney, North Platte and Kearney, in mileage and in the regions crossed, both for ease of spanning and the dangers, particularly in the west, from the hostile Sioux still out under Crazy Horse. He outlined the excellent space for sidings and warehouses in his town, the unlimited supply of superior labor. With the financial alignment he offered, backed by the push, the confidence and enthusiasm of a John J. Cozad, the short line could not fail. If the government should prefer a company already in operation he was ready to promise the U.P. all his facilities, his fullest cooperation.

At Washington he got courtesy but no action on the railroad idea or on his application for an appointment to the government of Dakota Territory, so he returned, realizing that after election it would all have to be done again.

In the darkness of a hard winter at Cozad after three practically fruitless summers, misfortunes elsewhere were rolled on the tongue like ripe chokecherries, puckery but very sweet. Particularly sweet was the growing money trouble of the railroad, after overcharging the little fellows on the short haul all these years. They chuckled about Swan, the New York broker who skipped the country with maybe $300,000 from trust funds. They repeated the scandals of the Grant administration, and argued the undecided presidential election between Tilden and Hayes, with inauguration day just over the hill, and sympathies here very split. They laughed at the troubles of James Gordon Bennett, the newspaperman who came hunting buffaloes and wild-west romance a few years back. He had lorded it all up and down the Platte but now it seemed he had been horsewhipped by the brother of the woman he left waiting at the church.

"Apparently just didn't show up for the wedding," Gene Young, the town's talker, told the waiting crowd at the post office. Bennett had ducked out on the second date too, and the girl's brother went for him with a bull whip right in public, in New York. Now there would be a duel.

"Just like in stories," Robert whispered to his cousin back behind the crowd.

But John Cozad spoiled that. "Dueling is against the law," he said crisply, and several there recalled that, according to rumor, he had been in several duels himself, less public but more scarring than Bennett's would probably be. That was back before the modern and less romantic attack by young Todd when he broke Cozad's jaw.

Toward the spring of 1877 the sky pilots and revivalists came. "They always follow on the heels of hard times and eat up the few chickens left," Matthews, the old buffalo hunter, said.

While some of the women around Cozad seemed to have other plans for the hens they managed to fatten, and their spring friers, the wandering preachers kept a revival running forty-one days down at Nebraska City. The toughs around the livery stables told the story to each other, wondering if there was a sweet ham, a fat hen, or a virgin left in the town.

But there was more important talk for the desperate, talk from rainmakers, and from the windmill salesmen who pointed not to the heavens but out over the bare earth and made it spring up lush and green before the imagination.

"Hitch up the hot winds from Kansas, put them to work pumping water for the crops they been burning up," was their ditty.

"Yes, but keep away from the peddlers. All they want is a small note secured by mortgages on your team, wagon, plow, milk cow, sow pig, even the gold fillings in your wife's teeth and your own eternal soul," Grandpa Gatewood told Robert, although the boy couldn't tell how he knew. Windmills were really very good. In Cozad they were thick as flowers in a garden, with green plots around their spouting water pipes.

Others talked of damning creeks and even the Platte itself, with great flood-filled reservoirs, and canals going in every direction. Suddenly John Cozad recalled the old Stump Ditch, already well grown over when he came walking through here in 1872, unused for hundreds of years, probably from back in prehistoric times. He got a railroad line engineer, a professor friend, and the boys and rode along the route of the old ditch, from its start far up at a northern creek and down its fine gradual course southeastward, with just enough drop to keep the water moving along, laid out as competently as any engineer of 1877 could plan it, clear to the Cozad vicinity, where the corn and squash patches probably were.

"Indians?" Robert dared ask, incredulous.

"Yes, I think so," the engineer said.

It was very exciting and Robert made some notes in the little account book he carried to list his expenditures, notes for a nice story of how the ditch was, back before a horse or a white man had come.

That night, at the head of the long table in the barny hotel, John Cozad talked irrigation. That was the improvement he would undertake as soon as the bridge was completed for the south settlers. Water! All the water that came rolling down the Platte floods, washing out bridges and silting the bottoms as it passed. What couldn't a man do with that much! A new Canaan could be brought to flower here, such a one as his grandfather, the Reverend Job Cozad, had never envisioned when he moved westward, a Canaan free of stone or heated desert wind, free of war or disputes of rivaling peoples.

Robert bent forward to look past Johnny to his father in warm admiration. This sounded better than any story he had ever read, or imagined. He didn't notice the two men at the foot of the long table, busying themselves spreading butter on their hot bread, sopping up chicken gravy. When their plates were clean they rose together, threw the money for their supper down in silver dollars to roll along the pine table, one spinning off and over the floor. By then the stomp of their boots was gone.

"What rude men!" Julia Gatewood complained, as the Cozad boys gathered up the money for her.

Traber tilted his chair back and told a little of what he had heard about them. "They are two of the Olive cowboys, that big Texas outfit that's moved in, stock, furnishings, family and all, spread the herds out north of the county line. The boss, Print Olive, set up headquarters at Plum Creek and's already about to run the town. Tough outfit, I hear. Olive himself's tough enough to be run out of Texas."

Traber didn't mention that the Olive herds had been moved in on a region pretty well given up by the local ranchers because it was full of solid homesteaders, many with good crops growing, and that Print Olive was giving the settlers notice he wanted the land, no matter who owned it legally. Or that the man was credited with around eight or ten of the most inhuman murders ever committed in Texas, inhuman enough to scare out even the hardiest settler.

XIII

Now John Cozad and even the twelve-year-old Robert were warned not to set foot inside of Plum Creek, their county seat, or they would "get it in the guts!"

Although sprouting a long time, the trouble finally ripened over the growing land boom. Without any newspaper talk of irrigation, of windmills and canals, the land office at North Platte was receiving over a hundred letters a day from home-seekers. At Cozad Johnny and young Robert helped to get out the promotion sheets to the land hungry who wrote to their father. Robert liked this task. In this there was none of the fighting he was growing to hate so much.

Growth brought problems to Cozad. It was not legally a town, only a precinct, larger than Rhode Island, but a precinct. To get money for school, for the law enforcement needed now that cowboys and other outsiders were pushing in, and for civic improvement, John Cozad and many of his town worked for a bond issue. But those who were against him united with those who were against all taxes—most of the childless, the few with property, patented lands, usually railroad lands, and the cattlemen who wanted Cozad, his community, his locating activities, and his settlers squeezed out. Not that the ranchers paid taxes in the precinct on the cattle running there, or in the county. Usually they hadn't even bothered to file on the land under their ranch buildings. Nobody in the county turned in much taxable property except the Union Pacific and John Cozad, and the railroad wasn't paying.

Because the precincts were run by the county commissioners, John Cozad, with Claypool, Atkinson, and several other old-timers, meaning those in the region four years, went to the commissioners' meeting at Plum Creek. They took the two boys along mainly because Johnny wanted to visit with Dr. Hudson, and Robert because he was eager to go anywhere, any time.

Conspicuous in his summer broadcloth and plug hat among the roomful of ranchers and their hirelings, John Cozad was sour-faced from the start. Against Sam Atkinson's advice to "talk pleasant" he praised his moderate community and spoke openly of the lawless crowd hanging around Plum here. For this he got a loud and noisy laughing, particularly when he added some of the newcomers in the room to his complaint, men like Print Olive and his gang, "Driven out of Texas, I hear on good authority, and drawn to Plum Creek, gentlemen, because Mr. Olive found his own kind here."

So the hated man from Cozad infuriated the town once more, particularly the better element, already angry and of bad conscience about the lawlessness that had taken them over. As the meeting progressed there was some unexpected opposition to the bonds from Cozad's own community, including a couple of men from his bridge crew. "Eating offa him," as some said, as recently as last week. Nevertheless they spoke openly against him and everything he wanted, and when it came to heated words, John Cozad was gaveled down.

"There will be no shooting at any man's feet here!" he was warned. "Nobody will be run out like your agent Sanderson here."

The tall, erect colonizer in summer black and gleaming

linen looked around the packed room, most of the dark-faced men with guns at their sides, half a dozen known to have killed at least once. Deliberately John Cozad folded up his papers, put on his hat, and stalked out—and found young Robert being held at the door by the town marshal. The boy's arms were locked from behind but he was kicking hard, his hat down in the dust of the steps.

"They called you names!" he shouted as his father and the others came out.

"What's going on here?— Unhand my son!"

The marshal released Robert's arms and jumped back. "Now hit the road, Cozad! Don't put a foot across the city line again, you and your hell-cat kid," the man ordered, tapping his gun, "or you get it in the guts!"

John Cozad's face went the flat white that Robert had seen in the depot just before he drew his pistol and fired around the feet of the agent. Frightened for his father, surrounded here by enemies and guns, the boy tugged at his arm. "Come, oh, please come," he whispered, begging, and with the others from Cozad behind him, urging him on, they got the colonizer out of the crowd and away.

Now John Cozad was doubly determined to work for the county seat, or, with a population large enough, to split the county, get the new one named for him. That might help toward a senatorship but, more important now, it would get him and his family out of the power of that gang around the county seat, before there was real bloodshed.

First, however, his town must be made a legal unit. The colonizer went to the state capital and in a few weeks Cozad was legally a town, managed by appointed trustees until election. The newcomer Jim Ware was town marshal and would have been mighty helpful the night of the faro tramps in the livery stable, with their counterfeit money and fake deputy sheriff, and—John Cozad firmly believed—their plans for a lynching.

There was little work for the marshal, with practically the only lawbreakers the cowboys who came tearing through, banging away at the old hundredth-meridian sign and spurring up the street, yelling, grabbing up any loitering chicken by the neck from their running horses, shooting through false fronts of stores and into the dust, sending people flying. There were reports of shots put through this or that settler's night window, and rumors that somebody was to be picked off in each little settlement as a warning, like a dead owl hung out to scare the rest away, or a prairie dog left to rot at his hole.

To be sure, the cowboys weren't all lawless, not the working cowboys, many sneaking off to homestead for themselves, good men who wanted to settle down. But these only stirred up the worst of the cattlemen to greater determination, to more swift, more drastic action. Former cowboys among the settlers made scaring anybody off much harder.

Some of the ranchers were turning to the courts to help them clear out the homesteaders, as many newspapers along the fringes of the cow country warned. Right now there were half a dozen men waiting to be tried at Plum Creek for rustling cattle. Some were outlaws, some had children hungry because their crops had been destroyed by range cattle, some nobody could believe guilty of any crime except the exercise of their legal right to a homestead, sometimes crime here enough for a hanging.

But these cases were still from off north and down around Plum Creek, not from Cozad, and none of them were from that prime group of enemies of the cattlemen, the locators who found land for the settlers.

The Black Hills were the one booming spot. Sidney alone sent almost $25,000 in gold dust to New York the week of

July 4, and no telling how much went out through Cheyenne, Pierre, and in the pockets and gripsacks of stagecoach passengers. But freight was falling off everywhere, and the U.P. increased the rate a dollar a ton on the short haul, say from Cozad to Omaha or from Ohio out, while long hauls, California to Chicago or New York, were reduced. In addition, large shippers got rebates. Thousands of little fellows protested. John Cozad protested, but nothing helped.

Once more the Union Pacific cut wages, five to ten per cent this time, and the strikes spread west to Omaha. Troops were called out and because in the East some of them seemed to fraternize with the strikers, President Hayes, precariously seated by counting out most of Tilden's Southern electors, termed it a revolution and ordered cannons turned on the strikers.

For weeks men like Young, Atkinson, Traber Gatewood, Sam Schooley, and the rest talked about this reversal of the duty of the peacetime military. Formerly troops were the protectors of life; now there was powerful precedent for their use against life in the protection of property.

Young Robert listened to this talk at the bridge over the lunch buckets, at the horseshoe pitching, or the hitch racks and along the street in the cool evenings. Then West Virginia demanded troops against her strikers too.

"What's happening down there?" old Robert Gatewood demanded. "Asking for bluecoats, while most of the South's still trying to get the Federals off their backs! It's not long since that was Virginia——"

During one of the arguments, young Robert sat back on an old raisin box and drew a picture of a row of soldiers in blue shooting into men trying to stop a smoking engine that pushed through a crowd, the cowcatcher cutting a swath a little like a mowing machine, the men falling to both sides. Off at the edges of the crowd others were going down from bullets too.

Traber Gatewood held up the picture for the men to see,

and showed them some others from the boy's folio—a big fire sweeping down upon a town, North Platte, Custer's men surrounded by whooping Indians, and cowboys shooting up a town. There was a special one of Daniel Freeman crossing the Platte. Old Daniel, the first settler around the region, had been one of Robert's early friends when the Cozads came west. Recently he ran a freight line from Cheyenne to Deadwood and when his lead team of mules got into trouble crossing the flooded Platte up there he jumped in, and was struck on the head by a heel of a struggling mule, and swept away in the flood.

It was a sad picture and Robert soon pushed it back under the others because he liked to laugh.

"Yes, Robert is quite a young artist," Gene Young, the schoolteacher and chief arguer of the town, said. He got a mild protest from Theresa.

"You haven't read his stories, I suppose," she told him. "They are my pride."

Johnny and John Robert, the cousin, shook their heads. With his writing and painting Robert wasn't much fun any more, not even at pitching horseshoes. "Mostly he just moons around. Almost as moony as Maggie," Johnny complained, meaning Bill Claypool's pretty ten-year-old.

"Robert misses his visits with the agent," Traber suggested. "I think he liked Ed Sanderson. I noticed the change right afterward."

It was half teasing, perhaps half blaming too, but not entirely of the boy. Still, Robert flushed and, jumping up, let the drawings on his lap scatter over the ground. He left them and ran off between the houses, and for once John Cozad did not order him back to apologize for his conduct or to gather up the pictures and put them away from the wind.

January came with a kind of chill hopelessness, with the cold frown of the retrenching U.P. falling heavily upon

Cozad. The snow had deepened and crusted with the cold. The wood gave out, none of it much better than green cotton-wood and willow from the bottoms anyway. Coal had been ordered long ago but the U.P. pulled a whole fuel train right through town, refusing to drop off even one car at the siding. It was a desperate time, with epidemics among the children and sickness from cold and exposure everywhere. Those who could, sent their ailing families back East, perhaps selling the team for the fare, or mortgaging them, with no hope of the travelers' return anyway.

Traber Gatewood wrote this East to John Cozad and added that he got a committee together, armed with rifles and shot-guns, to hold up the next freight of coal cars. At first the trainmen thought it was a joke but the dark scowls and the guns were convincing. They set out a car. Bobsleds and wagons were waiting, even a couple of galvanized washtubs that the women dragged home with ropes, one over a mile. Their men were away hunting work and sending back only news of flophouses and hunger.

Traber wrote that they weighed the coal out and turned the pay over to the railroad, with a warning that the town must be kept supplied. More coal came but some said the U.P. never got the money for the first car.

John J. Cozad, the Union Pacific's chief colonizer, took it all as a personal affront. He must make other, firmer connections.

Toward spring there were rumors that the gold in the Black Hills was pinching out. Around March some busted miners stopped off to talk about sodbusting, so despised on their way west last year to become gold millionaires. As John Cozad hauled them out over the cold gray prairie they spoke of the smallpox epidemic at Deadwood and flour a dollar a pound when the trails were snowbound.

"There are a lot of holdups—road agents, up around there, I

hear," John Cozad said. "They make hauling harder, perhaps."

Oh, they had ways of dealing with road agents up there. Like that triple hanging at Rapid City some time back. Three strung up on the rise the same time, left swinging. One of the men in the landseeking party here helped pull the rope.

"We sure put them through a pretty flyin' dance," the rope puller said, easing his cartridge belt a little.

None of the men seemed to notice John Cozad's growing anger as they talked on—his fury. Suddenly he lifted the whip against the men in his spring wagon. "Get off my land!" he shouted. "Get out of my rig!"

Before the violence of the colonizer's words, the darkness of his face, the men hopped out, their mining boots heavy and awkward as they stumbled away, looking back at the man known as a gambler.

Dave Claypool motioned them over into his wagon when John Cozad had whipped off alone, the wheels of his light rig bouncing over the rough prairie as he took a short cut to town.

This year John J. Cozad's handbills extolling the fruitfulness of the Platte valley and particularly his community began to sound true. In the spring the drifts had not gone out in one great roaring of gray water down the gullies, merely to anger the Platte, send it in sullen spreading over the bottoms on its way to the wild Missouri. The winter snows had thawed very slowly, drawing the frost from the earth, mellowing it to turn dark and smooth and fat behind the breaking plow. Every unoccupied quarter section within a day's wagon travel from the railroad seemed footworn by homeseekers, some hurrying from place to place, like a pretty girl with many beaus turning round and round and settling down on nothing. Some dropped the harness from their teams gratefully at the first place vacant, perhaps leaving the wagon there as though to hold the land while they took the train to North Platte, or jumped on one of the horses and rode there, going bareback if there was no saddle, hurrying to file on the place.

Saturdays and Sundays the boys of the town were out on their horses, riding like a bunch of young colts turned out, racing, trying stunts, even falling and keeping the injuries hidden as long as possible. Sometimes they all stopped at the Cozad-located settlers, leaning over the horn a few minutes to ask how things were, particularly if there were young people around, perhaps shy young girls in blue calico, at first hiding their bare feet from the grand young men.

It was a fine spring to sell land. There was rain—true, with a gray rolling sausage cloud of hail underneath sometimes, and a far rumble like a buffalo stampede to scare the farmer, hurry him to the house or shed. Perhaps he ran to cover the window with blanket or wagon sheet to save perhaps the only cash outlay of the whole soddy, or to stand in the doorway to watch, cursing or praying, each according to his nature, that the thrashing white hail might pass him by.

Most places rye, oats, and wheat on the older backset fields stood in tall green seas that ran in waves before the wind. Corn throve too, on old ground and sod, and some sang the old Ohio snap-out song:

> Corn knee high by the Fourth of July,
> Farmer fly high.

Robert enjoyed being drawn into the circle of singers at playparties and picnic dancing on the grass, dancing that even the good Methodists and those with Methodist feet liked to join. Johnny usually refused, growing a little impatient with "country" doings now that he had long pants and had been down to the roadhouse at the Plum Creek bridge with one of the Costin boys and seen things not for his young brother's eyes or ears. Besides, no one could imagine Mrs. Cozad leading one of the dance songs at a play-party, and never Mr. Cozad.

Not that the couple weren't always handsome in the waltzes and quadrilles—the proper place for their elegance.

But long before the wheat began to turn that wonderful golden yellow of the first good crop in any region, there was the problem of harvesting and the exorbitant costs of the implements. Not even going in together, as those who were Grange members back in Ohio planned, would give them enough cash money for the new harvester, the self-binder that was such a boon in the bonanza areas. Cutting by scythe was hopelessly slow in fields of these dimensions. In the dry heat the mowing machines available to some with the hand tying later, would shell out too much of the fine grain. Left standing overripe, it would shatter and lodge, especially in the richer, heavier fields, even without wind or hail.

But necessity meant to use what they had, and everybody who could turned out to hurry the harvest. The Cozad boys helped their cousin, John Robert, a little with the shocking behind the tie-men, until they showed their mother the rattles cut from half a dozen snakes in one day. Then she made urgent town errands for them.

Somehow most of the wheat was finally harvested, even as far up as Clear Creek in the new Custer County along the north line. Clustered stacks of bundle wheat, fat and round, were browning in the summer sun, fine, symmetrical, rain-shedding stacks if Whit Ketchum, a young Iowa settler up there, could be obtained to top them out.

Now there was another problem—keeping the range cattle away from the grain, and also the sheep. With the grass so good, sheep were being herded through in flocks of around a thousand each, eating their way north from Missouri, perhaps, and up the Platte valley. Usually they cleaned out everything in their path, grass, crops, even gardens and grain or hay on their way to the new ranges out west, mostly in Wyoming. The market animals were shipped at their best weight, say at Sidney or Cheyenne, if some irate settler or cattleman hadn't run them over a cut bank or scattered them to the coyotes and wolves before that.

But no sheep put on much fat on the Cozad lands. Johnny and Robert were usually out on their horses, eyes open for trail herds and trespassing range cattle. Sheep were harder to locate but the boys usually saw them in time to whoop the timid creatures on in spite of the rifle-carrying herders.

Stopping trail herds of Longhorns was harder. Most of them had at least one slick-fingered gunman in the outfit, and none of them admitted knowing or caring that Cozad owned much of the local railroad land. They cared even less about the Herd Law, certain that nobody would dare take up any stock from a trail herd for damages in the face of the gun-armed crew, and the ranchman officials at Plum Creek. Not if the herd ate up the whole county.

The first time John Cozad tried to drive a Texas herd off his hay land this summer he was suddenly surrounded by dark-faced men with their hands on their guns. Evidently it had been planned, because every trailer popped up right there, instead of riding his position strung out a mile or more along the cattle. There was nothing the colonizer could do but retreat, knowing this was one tiger he couldn't buck. His body pumped full of lead, even on his own land, wouldn't get the murderers one uncomfortable minute from the law at Plum Creek.

In the meantime the Cozad sons had seen the Longhorns too, and managed, by riding up a dry creek from the Platte, to come out in the midst of the loose, spreading herd, whooping and waving their wet bathing suits. The wild stock jumped into a run, the trail boss spurring over upon the boys as he motioned his cowboys out after the cattle. He set his big horse down before the young Cozads and cursed them out until he was breathless, threatening to put holes through their goddamned ignorant carcasses any minute.

By now the colonizer was within shouting distance. "Don't

you dare touch my sons!" he roared out, the sun glistening on his pistol across the horn. "You and your gang of outlaws just bulldozed me off my own land and now I catch you cursing unarmed minors also on their father's property. It's cowardly, rascally cowboys like you who attack helpless children, like the small girl over near Kearney."

"I am the boss, not a cowboy. We make no war on women."

"There was a bullet hole put through the little girl's dress, but I notice you dropped the trail over past Kearney since the settlers got organized and armed. It's coming here too, with your bulldozing lawlessness. Now get off my land and stay off!"

Although the heavy Colt sagged at his side all this time, the trail boss made no move to draw. Without the backing of his crew, he turned, set spurs, and headed off toward the rising dust and rumble of his running herd. John Cozad nodded to the boys and slipped his pistol back into his pocket, but not even Robert thought that the matter was ended, not even before the father spoke:

"Tomorrow I'll see you both get saddle holsters with pistols and a rifle for Johnny. Matthews will show you how to defend yourself."

XIV

ALTHOUGH THE SUMMER was one of rain and crops, it was also a season of extremes. When a total eclipse of the sun in late July darkened the heavens, a couple of settlers from the north breaks happened to be in town trading eggs and garden truck. As the sun whitened into a chilly disk of blank ice and a duskiness spread over the town, the men fell to their knees in the middle of the street, praying and shouting, trembling, sweating in their awe and fear.

"It is the end of the world as foretold!" one of them was repeating over and over, tears of dusty water streaming down his face.

"Confess your sins, Brothers and Sisters! Embrace your Lord Jesus before it is too late!" the other entreated.

Sam Schooley and Gene Young, out watching the sun through smoked window glass, became concerned about the weeping men and those who gathered around to taunt them, shouting exaggerated warnings of fire and brimstone.

"It's the years of starvation and hard times," Sam said. "Enough to unbalance almost anybody."

The two men were even more pitiful when the sun was clear again and Mrs. Gatewood's chickens got off their roosts and ventured out into the street again, looking around foolishly. Slowly the men lifted their bottoms up to the layer of willows laid over the old running gears of their wagon and started their ponies homeward.

There was much violence of man against man too, this summer. Not that anybody seemed to be shooting many of the horse thieves who came fanning down from their headquarters up along the Niobrara. Doc Middleton, their leader, had regular places that put him up for the night along the Loups and at the Olive Ranch. From there his pony boys swept off stock to sell in Iowa or Wyoming, the horses stolen there taken to the other end of the runs. They sent Indian herds flying toward Kansas and brought angry Sioux warriors on their trail to the Platte and beyond, scaring the timid settlers. Some counties tacked up reward notices for capture of the horse thieves. Extra guards were stationed at the trotting circuits and yet some good stock was stolen, including fine sulky horses, one whole stable emptied right out at the track—three prime pacers gone.

All the gold talk drew more agents to the Black Hills trails, and every new report of holdups attracted more hopefuls. Even the Iron Clad, the gold coach with Winchester-armed guards riding shotgun, was held up, men killed.

August brought a mad-dog scare throughout the country, with wolves, coyotes, and skunks rabic. Theresa cautioned the boys to be very careful, stay on their horses when out this hot weather. But she knew they could not, particularly with the work at the bridge and the hay flats.

Then one afternoon a homeseeker whipped into Cozad shouting for a madstone to apply to his arm where a stray dog he tried to pet had bitten him. No one knew of a madstone nearer than down at Fremont and the new doctor just settled at Cozad was away on a forty-mile call. When Johnny came in from the river he surprised everybody by saying that he had a madstone, at least it had been taken from the stomach of a deer by Daniel Freeman. It looked like the Virginia stone

Johnny had seen back at Malden once, years ago. He fetched it from his room, a hair ball, with the grayish limy surface chipped off here and there, exposing the close-packed hair.

To Theresa's surprise, Johnny knew just what to do, or thought he did. He sent Robert for a syrup bucket full of milk while he opened the dog bite wider and much deeper with his razor, cutting across it both ways, squeezing the wound to a free, clear bleeding. Then he applied the hair ball, which didn't cling well, but he washed it in the milk and laid it on the wound again and again, the milk in the bucket turning greenish from the blood, as milk does.

"It's coming—sucking the poison right out!" one of the gathering spectators exclaimed, in surprise. "Look, the milk's turning——"

That was all anybody knew to do for the man and although Johnny and several of the grown people urged him to catch the train for Omaha and the hospital, he refused. No money. In a few days the wound began to heal fast and Johnny was called a natural-born doctor, although even the boy knew that hydrophobia could be developing in the body long after the wound was grown over and forgotten. But in a few days the dog showed up in town, a little shy and touchy but with no frothing at the mouth, no stagger, and no fear of the water Mother Gatewood set out for him. In fact he soon adopted her and came every morning and night to the dish she kept there now. He followed her with his soft brown eyes during the day until Julia had to give up and adopt him too.

By now there was a long rick of baled hay waiting for empty cars, good hay, cured to a fine and fragrant green. There were Indian rumors again, this time some Cheyennes jumping their reservation down in Indian Territory, raiding and burning their way up through Kansas. The baled hay at the tracks would make a handy fort if the raiders came in this direction, old Matthews, the buffalo hunter, told the loafers around the livery stable, although he doubted it would be needed. He knew these Indians; they just wanted to come home.

The old-timer proved right although there were fights, with the Indians pursued by troops and some killed, starting a swift and bloody raiding through northwest Kansas. From the Nebraska line the Indians moved as fast as they could, crossing far west of Cozad. For ten days prairie fires burned almost all around, reddening the sky of night. Set by Indians to hold off pursuit, some said; set against the Indians, others claimed, to destroy the grass for their horses, burn the red devils out of hiding.

But most of the fires were in central and eastern Nebraska, too far from the Cheyennes. Over near Wisner a widow and her daughter who had fought to save the schoolhouse were overtaken by the flames on the way home and burned to death. Their stable, stock, and most of their hay went too, leaving almost nothing for the three orphaned children. The city of Lincoln saved itself only after a day and a half of backfiring, and Hastings was completely surrounded by prairie fire and yet saved.

All this time there was nothing for those hoping for rain, for fall moisture, nothing but smoke to sting the eyes and turn the setting sun to blood red. Finally a blizzard swept in from the northwest. It helped the army trap the fleeing Cheyennes, at least part of them, up near the Black Hills trail and stopped the prairie fires. But it did not block the sweep of bank failures through the nation and it didn't stop Print Olive's gang from lynching and burning Mitchell and Ketchum, two home-steaders up on Clear Creek, in Custer County. They were good farmers, Ketchum the man who put up the fine wheat stacks for himself and others. Both had proved hard to scare out, even on the charge of cattle rustling, the Olives claiming they found some of their stock in the settlers' corral one morning—some of the Olive cattle that were always in the crops of the two men. Nobody seemed to recall that, to get damages under the Herd Law, the stock had to be taken up and stabled or corralled.

Many were disturbed that after only two years up from Texas the Olive outfit had taken Plum Creek over so completely that the two settlers could be pulled off the train there and, instead of being protected by the officials, were turned over to the Olive gang who hauled them across the line to Custer County, hanged and burned them, and left their shackled bodies for the wolves.

John Cozad was away when the news spread over the nation. In a week he stepped off the train from the East with his silk hat full of newspaper clippings denouncing the Man Burners. He was so furious he could hardly speak at first, his eyes smoky hard. He emptied the hat on the counter at Julia Gatewood's store and strode rapidly up and down in the little space between the open boxes and barrels.

"No man is safe with such lawlessness permitted, encouraged, at our county seat!" he roared. "Olive seems to claim he found some of his stock in the settlers' corral. Maybe they had been taken up under the Herd Law. Anyway, over at Plum Creek the cattlemen control the courts. They could get a verdict against anybody. It isn't punishment of rustlers they want but terror, to scare us all off our land. Half the women in the country will be crying to get their men out, afraid they will be next."

"You can't blame them much," Sam Schooley agreed. "I guess all we can do is get the county seat moved to Cozad somehow."

The men talked late into the night, even Robert permitted to stay up as long as he wished; no telling how soon every boy might have to grab a gun and need to know what the deal was. John Cozad recalled the time they went down to Plum Creek to get their bond issue past the county commissioners —in a room filled with ranchers and cowboys, their holsters heavy with their guns, the commissioners plainly in their pockets. And outside the threat of a bullet in the guts if he or his son stepped across the city line again.

Before the lamps were finally turned down for the night, Robert went with his father to check every gun in the store and the hotel, the two new ones of the sons as well. Then he got a pocketful of big ridgepole spikes and inserted them as pegs into the holes that Claypool drilled in the casings of every outside door against possible intruders. Tomorrow John Cozad would have the doors reinforced with planking, and have locks put on them, his first locks in Cozad. He even thought of bars for the windows, in this, his ideal community.

The Mitchell and Ketchum burning brought really nation-wide notoriety to the Platte valley, particularly to Plum Creek, the home of Print Olive, and notoriety to all of Dawson County. It cut down on land applications to the Cozad region too, cut deeper than the drouth, hot winds, and grass-hoppers together. Even men who had signed up for the Cozad excursions canceled out. Some already negotiating for rail-road lands refused to sign up and a couple of them renigged on the payments. They insisted that they had been sold the land under false pretenses—that Cozad had represented the Platte country as a good, law-abiding region for their fam-ilies. Well, he could bring up his sons in such lawlessness if he wished but others had scruples.

When John Cozad threatened suit they dared him to take the matter to court. An early acquaintance from near Leb-anon, Ohio, had signed a contract for three sections of rail-road land as a center for a little settlement of ten families with the adjoining land open to entry. He even had a name picked for the post office—Rosalind, for his wife. When John Cozad protested the cancellation, he got a fast reply:

> I refer to your own dubious early career and to the violent lawlessness of your county officials, who not only offered no protection for the shackled prisoners, the settlers Mitchell and Ketchum, but who evidently

connived openly to turn the prisoners into the hands of a lawless man-burning mob. In such a situation no man settling upon a small piece of land can feel safe in property or in life. I could not ask any of my colony to expose himself and his family, even his small children, to such lawless bullets and be himself always threatened by the lyncher's noose. Worse, by the man-burner's torch.

You represented your region as one of order and law, yet now we discover that there have been frequent acts of violence right in your county seat before this latest outrage. It seems that the destroyers of Mr. Mitchell and Mr. Ketchum are still at large and living openly near the court house of your county seat, with no attempt being made to apprehend them and bring them to justice.

This was a patent piece of misrepresentation of the situation and you may consider yourself fortunate if we refrain from instigating legal action for the recapture of our losses, reimbursement for our expenditures and commensurate damages for our mental anguish.

Mental anguish! He read no farther.

With the letter was a sheaf of clippings pinned together, items from a dozen Eastern newspapers about the man-burning, including some most sarcastic comments from the New York papers.

John Cozad stuffed the clippings into his pocket and with the letter crumpled into a white ball in his long, slender fingers, he stalked to the office of the *Hundredth Meridian* and threw it down on Dave Claypool's overflowing desk.

Slowly Dave smoothed it out to read, and then the clippings . "Well, as a lawyer, I'd say you could collect but not without a lot of very damaging publicity to the region. As for the clippings, there'll be more," he said as he turned them back, one after another, scratching under his chin thoughtfully afterward. "Now would be a mighty fine time to grab the county seat if we had more votes over in this end of the county——"

176

John Cozad nodded, his mind busy on this hope.

The next national publicity for Cozad's Platte valley came almost immediately, and once more was nothing to encourage colonization. The Cheyenne Indians captured in the fall had been massacred, men, women, and children, when they refused to return to Indian Territory where they had been dying of disease and starvation. Fuel, food, and water were cut off to compel them to give in. Instead they broke out of the barracks at twenty below zero and ran over the moonlit snow, the troops picking them off and then following the remnants for almost two weeks until the last of them were finally surrounded and destroyed. The general newspaper protest to this inhuman butchery aroused more cancellation and delay among the Cozad excursionists, even among those who considered the only good Indian the dead one. Besides, such butchery would surely bring bloody revenge upon the settlements, some were convinced, recalling the old, old stories of Indians burning villages and towns, of a bloody, flaming sweep over border settlements in reprisal.

But the Cheyennes were forgotten in the news that the Olive outfit was finally arrested in their own Plum Creek by a handful of men under the deputized brothers of Ketchum, and without firing one shot. Practically nobody expected Print Olive and the rest to serve a day for killing the settlers, and even some of the quieter Cozadites were ready to ride out with ropes to settle the outfit before they could be rescued by sympathetic ranchers and their cowboys, or spirited away to the strong bars of the penitentiary until the trial came up. And if they were tried who expected a conviction?

"Let's string them up now," old Matthews argued, patting the scarred buffalo gun on his arm.

But John Cozad was up on his feet immediately, shaking his cane, shouting. "I'll have no such talk here!" the anger of his words echoing through the barny hotel. He seemed twice his own tallness within the black frock coat, his pale face like bleached bone, the violence in his eyes beyond anything his friends here had ever seen.

Johnny, back at the wall, slipped away, and Robert wanted to run too, but he did not dare, and after a while Sam Schooley got the man quieted a little. "You know, Mr. Cozad, none of us can go doing any lynching, no matter how we might hone for revenge."

But old Matthews wasn't through. "You know damn well that outfit will never be convicted, with most of the cattle country rallying behind them. Witnesses will be scared out or left face down on the prairie, the jury stuffed!"

Yes, he knew that, John Cozad agreed, but the rope must not be used, never the lyncher's rope. Those like Dave and Traber and a dozen others knew that gamblers were often threatened by the rope and maybe got it. Even the innocent-appearing Canada Bill, one of the best known of the gamblers, was almost strung up at Cincinnati once, and who could say how close the rope had come to John Cozad himself in his thirty-five years among gamblers, what close shaves in the hanging days back in the height of river boating, or in South America, or during the wild vigilante days of San Francisco?

Violence seemed to have become epidemic, spreading like typhoid in a summer plague. Almost every paper carried a story or two of men shot or strung up. Two were found near the Laramie crossing of the Deadwood trail, hung by one rope, it seemed, one man on the ground with no mark except the rope burn around his neck, the other still swinging. Then two missing landseekers from Missouri were found up in the Loup country, near the Olive ranch, both men and team full of bullets, unrobbed, untouched except by the lead.

That's the way it had been done in Texas in the Olive region, before Print Olive left there, almost three years ago now, and bodies still turning up in dried-out reservoirs and such places on his old range. It was curious how the man operated. With so much of upper Nebraska unclaimed by any cattleman, hundreds of miles of long-grass sandhills without a settler, he had to push in on a range practically given up by the local cattlemen because so much of the land was homesteaded by men with homes, families, fields.

Some of the settlers talked uneasily about the dead Missouri landseekers. Their deaths were probably intended as a warning to any other newcomers who believed the story that Mitchell and Ketchum were killed for rustling cattle. Some as far from the Olives as Cozad left their claims, afraid other ranchers would follow the Olive example, particularly with the cowboys much bolder since the man-burning. Many did not want to be there at all when Print Olive and his outfit got off scot-free.

Yet so great was the land hunger that more and more settlers came as the winter finally mellowed a little. By then John Cozad had taken Theresa on a trip to Washington and New York before the last end of the social season. It had been a trying fall and winter for her and so he arranged invitations from one of the West Virginia senators—old family friends of the Gatewoods. This included half a dozen brilliant balls and soirees. There were several opportunities to make short addresses to various senatorial committees and government commissions and then they went on to New York, still with nothing definite on the short-line railroad to the gold fields.

Theresa sent back frequent notes of their activities, written with more gaiety as the troubles of Cozad, Nebraska, receded. She sounded more like a girl than like their mother and assured the sons that she was not worried about them. They were almost grown men and she had given up trying to keep track of their comings and goings very closely. It was the traditions she had tried to instill in them that would guide them now or fail. She did not say that if it were summer they would not be left alone, not even with the guns now always in their saddle holsters, not with the ranchers and their herds pushing in everywhere.

But this was still winter and she sent back dance programs, menus, and souvenirs, including a cut-glass salt cellar from the White House. When were they coming home? Ah, who could tell? she replied, and then by the end of the week the boys saw her get off the train, her husband at Cincinnati working up his excursions.

The three walked up the street together, a son on each side of her, their handsome mother with velvet roses on her hat. She actually did seem like a girl, a flirtatious mysterious young woman from far places.

Before John Cozad returned, Robert had found a picture of the burned bodies of Mitchell and Ketchum in the Kearney paper. He put it aside to show him when the news of the excursion had been told, with, Robert hoped, the enthusiasm of a money belt heavy with gold.

But the boy was not prepared for the towering rage of his father at the sight of the horrible photograph. He lifted the gold-headed cane and the boy threw his arm over his head trying to duck the blows that came fast and hard. Finally he escaped out the door and down the alley toward the tracks and the river. He hid near his grandfather's shack until he was half frozen, his feet and hands numbed from the winter evening. The shack was padlocked to protect the bridge tools, but finally the shivering boy managed to pry a window open, and built a fire inside.

It was by the low-spreading smoke of late evening that his father found him, and pounded on the door, commanding that the boy lift the heavy bar he had dropped into place.

Trembling so he could hardly lift the plank, Robert drew the door back against himself in an unconscious sort of shielding, the father tall and dark and vast in his buffalo coat, almost filling the doorway, shutting out most of the evening sky.

The boy was unable to speak, wanting to back away from the hand that reached for him, yet knowing he must not let his feet move, nor run. That would never be forgiven.

At last the father spoke, sadly, in quietness. "Oh, Robert, my son," he said, "don't you see you almost drove me to doing you real harm? Don't you understand that I'm bedeviled from every side?"

Slowly he closed the door and in the duskiness of the room he let himself down to the bench at the glowing hearth of the stove and, pushing his beaver cap back, buried his long fingers in his black hair and sat there, silent and still, the firelight flashing in the diamond of his ring.

At last the stove cooled and the son approached to push more wood into the firebox. When the pipe chimney crackled and roared with the wind-drawn flame, he slid down to the dirt floor beside the stove, the two silent as the early night crept into the room, the only light the moving flames behind the mica windows of the little stove.

A long time later they started back across the freezing earth bound very close, for better or for worse, bound close as seldom comes to a father and son.

XV

It had been a skating winter, with Johnny and his cousin John Robert in what amounted to a winter-long race. Sometimes half a dozen of the boys, including perhaps even one of the Pearsons, skated up the river as far as Willow Island station on Sunday, the two fastest boys stooping low, shooting ahead, stroking fast, their skates clinking, glistening in the cold air as they wound from side to side following on the solid ice that was like glass. Sometimes John Robert's plaid blanket coat was in the lead, the red of it just a tinge of color as Robert and the others struggled to keep in sight. Sometimes it was Johnny with his long striped orange and blue woolen comforter streaming out far behind, even though it was heavy and double-knit, the wind whipping the long fringed ends.

Always, even in the coldest weather, there were holes in the ice, with winding narrow strips of dark preoccupied water showing where the current was swift. One break-through or one slip and the skater could be dragged under ice that was two feet or more in thickness.

"Throw yourself, if the ice breaks. Throw yourself cross-stream," old Matthews told the boys. "It works until the ice gets soft. I've done it on the Yellowstone and even the Missouri, up north, with dangerous current, deep and swift. But when the ice starts to rot a whole acre may bust down with you and you're a goner too."

If Theresa worried about the skaters they didn't realize it too much. She knew there was as great a danger in riding like wild Indians over a prairie full of badger holes and gopher and mole tunnels. She suspected that the boys sometimes raced through prairie-dog towns as she saw the Costin boys do, their horses dodging this way and that as they whooped and whipped. John Cozad had looked after himself at twelve, and she couldn't shame him now by overanxiety about his sons, with Robert almost fourteen and soon out of knee pants too, a break easier to face now that Johnny had outgrown them. She put aside the loss of the other three children. These two had come through childhood and grown to vigor and strength in this raw and violent region—passing over the violence quickly because her husband carried the seed and the flower of it within him, as many women before her had put such thoughts from them and many more would after she was long gone.

One Sunday the boys from Cozad were met by a big fire on the bank at Willow Island, with over a dozen other young people, including the Costin girls and their friends. They all seemed to be getting unexpectedly pretty, in their shoe-top dresses and long braids under the velvet hoods with the bands of winter-whitened rabbit fur around the faces. There were three towheaded Richter girls, a big brother, and their long-pipe-smoking father from the German table. They had brought a dishpan half full of little pig sausages to be roasted on sticks over the coals, and there were potatoes, turnips, and ball squash baking in the hot ashes around the fire.

The day was a fine crisp one to show off on the ice, and this time it was Robert who hung back when the others started home. Johnny and John Robert tried to hurry him but he kept sitting on an old log near the cooling fire apparently staring straight ahead. Actually he was looking at the youngest of the Richter girls across from him, her pale braids thicker than the wrists of her hands folded in her lap, and her eyes the dark blue he once saw on a Steller jay flashing through the bare willows. But the girl was very shy and would not lift her eyes again until he started to leave. Then suddenly she was up and running to him, holding out her hands. With her fingers curved down she reached out for his, hooked over them, and started around in a witches' dance, leaning back, her feet close together against his toes, both bodies swinging out and away, whirling fast, very fast, around and around.

At a sharp "Anna!" from her father, the girl slowed and, dropping her hands, turned and ran for their wagon, the boy looking after her, dizzy, his head still flying.

Finally now the three boys started the six miles to Cozad, their shadows like elongated jumping jacks darting over the sky-reddened ice before them. The moon came up, almost round, but a bank of clouds moved swiftly out of the northwest over all the purpling sky. The boys skated as fast as they could, but soon it was impossible to see more than the pale direction of the river in the darkness. They knew how dangerous it was, with the current wandering here and there, but nobody suggested taking to the road, walking. They tried to make torches but even the driest willow just smoked when carried, without the light a good pitch-pine knot might have given them. Because they had to keep going in the deepening cold, afraid it would start to snow, turn to a roaring blizzard, they cut thin willow poles to push ahead of them with one hand, the other on Johnny's long comforter, off his neck now and stretched out between them, Robert holding to the middle, the older boys at the ends.

But they couldn't manage the poles with one hand and when they finally got under way again they moved slowly, in a diagonal line so they wouldn't all go through a hole at once. They had skated about a quarter of a mile with Johnny leading, when Robert's skates broke through, both together, everything under him going so fast he forgot to throw himself crosswise. Instinctively his hands clung to the comforter as he plunged gasping into the icy water. He went down deep, choking, struggling to kick himself upward under the weight of the heavy clothing. He rose and bumped his head, gasping to realize he had been swept off under the ice. His lungs were full of freezing water and bright lights whirled behind his frozen lids. He tried not to cough as the current dragged at him, still struggling to swim, raked and bumped against the solid ice above him, yet kept from sinking deeper by something in his hand. But he was growing heavy, slowing, holding his breath, his head spinning with lights as he fought the numbing water until his lungs seemed to explode. Coughing, choking, the shooting lights under his lids faded, as he spun away in the heavy darkness.

After a long time he felt a bouncing and shaking, a choking, his mouth full of water, bitter water. He struck out with a hand to free himself and heard somebody speak, far off, then closer as he was let down to something hard, like frozen ground.

Ground—so the water was gone. He was out. Numbly he tried to sit up and was suddenly sick to his stomach, sick all over and vomiting like a two-year-old.

Afterward he felt a little better and as a fire flared up beside him it lit the strained faces of his brother and his cousin. Gradually they made him understand that he was safe, that he had somehow clung to the long comforter until they managed to crack a patch of thin current ice over him with the heels of their skates, grabbed him and dragged him out just as the comforter was almost cut in two.

"We sure thought you were a goner," Johnny said, and suddenly found his voice breaking into a silly childish squeak.

They thawed Robert out and when he was drying drew

the fire along, leaving warmed earth to sleep on, taking turns keeping the blaze going, and to answer if anyone should call for them in the night.

They got back to their horses at the bridge early and rode hard for home, but were met by Traber Gatewood and his brother Van about halfway, their worried faces full of anger long before the boys could see.

"What do you mean, not coming home?" John Robert's father demanded of him.

"Robert went through the ice—almost drowned," Johnny explained for his cousin.

The men sat back in their saddles, silent a moment. Then they turned their horses and led the lope into town.

The March thaw drew the snow back from dead cattle in draws and canyons and out on the empty prairie. It was a hard revelation. Men who had plunged into debt at the tail end of the beef-bonanza days, hoping to make a few quick millions too, had fallen, instead, into the panic and grasshopper years. Now much of what little they had left lay bloating in the noonday sun.

This year it wasn't only the unacclimated Texas herds. Many settlers had brought a little start in Eastern cattle, perhaps just a couple of milk cows, and even some of these died. Then almost as soon as the winter snow cleared off, the prairie fires began again, and after the late storms hit the blackened regions few of the starving cattle were left.

The first warm spell of March had brought another scourge —horse thieves. With the dark of the moon Doc Middleton and his gang made a flying trip into Dawson County, running off twenty horses, eleven of them from the good stock around Willow Island, five from Cozad, and four from farther east. In the past some had wondered whether Doc wasn't being blamed for a lot of stealing by others who made their work look like his, an old trick often used on the Indians, the Sioux blamed for raids along the Platte that later proved to be the work of painted and feathered white men.

But if this new round of thievery wasn't Doc's, it was by somebody who knew horseflesh just as well, and also knew where it was. Apparently only three head had been stolen from around Cozad but toward noon Robert's grandfather came to school to ask when the boy had been at the bridge stable last.

"Why, yesterday evening, after school. You know, when we all rode down to measure the floodwaters. The horses came nickering to the fence and we took Pirate and the others from the stable to water," Robert said.

"That's what I thought. Well, now he is gone. Seems Doc Middleton turned up his nose at the rest."

Of course no horse thief who knew about Pirate would overlook him. He was a fine white-stockinged dark bay, the one horse John Cozad liked to ride, perhaps because the gelding was tall, and powerful enough to make a picture of ease and dignity carrying a long-legged man. He stood for shooting too, and could carry his rider away from any other horse in the region. It was mighty hard to lose him, and for once John Cozad choked back his pride and telegraphed his loss to the sheriff at Plum Creek. Not that he expected any help from there, he admitted, but he wanted to give the county-seat gang a chance to expose their corruption in the face of crime.

Nothing was done by the sheriff, and Robert Gatewood went out to sleep on his place to watch the remaining horses, laughing a little, ruefully, that he had let Pirate get away.

In a week the horse was back in the sod stable at the bridge, a little gaunted down from long winter travel, but still sound. A slender tow-haired man with a soft Texas way of talking had brought him back, dropped the lead rope into the hand of Robert Gatewood, running out to see.

"I didn't know who he belonged to," the man said. "Mr. Cozad done me a good turn once at North Platte, and I wouldn't want to put a gentleman like him to any trouble."

Johnny brought the news into town, a cloud of frosted March air following him in at the evening door.

"That was Middleton," John Cozad said, in satisfaction. "I'm mighty grateful. He's known as a gentleman but sorely tempted by good clean horseflesh."

Young Johnny wanted to know more, to ask a question.

"What did you do for him?" he finally dared to say.

Although John Cozad was too pleased with the horse to warn against prying questions, he still gave no reply to them, and so all that got around town was that Middleton had once more repaid a favor.

Eugene Young, one of Cozad's early excursionists, had settled south of the river on a homestead and a timber claim, and became a good friend of all the family. Gene had studied law and taught school in Kentucky, and when the grasshoppers got his sod corn here he took up teaching again. This spring vacation time, he went back to Kentucky and returned with a pretty bride. For a while they lived at the new brick hotel where the Cozads made their home. The young Southern girl was gay and full of song and laughter and soon had both Johnny and Robert trying to run errands for her.

There was a shivaree the first Saturday night. Just about the time the Youngs were undressed, the stillness below their window exploded with the boom of an old big-bore muzzle-loader, the banging of dishpans and washtubs, and the ring of a spike maul on the anvil left behind by a blacksmith starved out by the grasshoppers. Robert got a trumpet to blow with all his might. He had hoped for a steam whistle and found he needed steam. There were some powerful voices in the shivaree crowd, including Wild Bull Potter, who could imitate a fighting brindle Longhorn from down on the Concho in Texas and to be heard about that far off, those who nicknamed him insisted. Now Bull leaned back and let go.

By the time they all settled down a little, singing "Love Is Such a Funny, Funny Thing," and "Nettie of the Light Brown Hair," accommodating the song to the bride's name the couple inside were dressed. Then everybody was invited in for popcorn, coffee, and doughnuts that Julia Gatewood had ready, still fried in hog lard, not the settler's usual buffalo tallow. Afterward they danced, even Wild Bull, about as graceful as that brindle Longhorn on the Concho. It was daylight when the last went home.

After they were arrested, Print Olive and his men were taken to district court at Hastings in an adjoining county to stand trial. Many predicted that Print, said to be the wealthiest or nearly the wealthiest man in all of Nebraska, would never need to face a judge. The whole Platte country was aroused. The settlers were certain that if he went free they would be fair game for any cattleman who wanted their land, anyway he wanted to take it. Others, with no land to covet, were shamed by the man-burning and hoped for conviction to wipe out the stigma of such inhuman crimes going unpunished.

The Cozad sons wanted to go down to the Olive trial but Theresa said there would certainly be violence, hoping that settled the matter, particularly now that her sons carried guns on their saddles and were becoming bolder, more forward. Others feared violence too. Settlers from as far as two hundred miles away rode in with their guns in the boot or ready across the saddle, determined that no gang of cowboys and ranch gunmen would rescue the Olive outfit. A dozen or more from Cozad, including Jim Haskell from his new horse ranch up north, came to stand guard too, taking their places beside the neighbors of Mitchell and Ketchum, some of whom had walked in, one over a hundred miles from his little job.

But the gathering of cowboys and men whose professional guns were known to be for hire increased so fast, grew so threatening, that the citizens of the little border town became

189

uneasy for their lives, particularly after an open threat that the Olive outfit would be rescued and Hastings burned to the ground, the judge and other officials shot down like rats as they fled the burning courthouse.

The local sheriff, determined to keep peace, called for the militia. The governor came out to see, took one look, and ordered troops in, to camp there until the court session ended.

Suddenly now Dawson County and Plum Creek got more newspaper space in a day than they had received all the time of their past, even more than after the man-burning, which really took place over the line in Custer County.

John Cozad leafed through all the papers he could reach with his long fingers, each paper carrying two, three or more columns about the Olive trial every day, with a running story in the Chicago *Tribune*, daily reports in the New York *Herald* and almost everywhere else. In St. Louis a newspaper reprinted long stories from the Texas press, stories of the many horrible crimes attributed to Print Olive in his days down there.

All this about men of his own region, his own county seat, shamed and infuriated John Cozad so much, did so much damage to his hopes, that Theresa and her parents and even strangers became concerned for him. His face was gaunt and sunken as in the depths of the consumptive attack, his gestures so violent, that surely he would burst a blood vessel if he didn't try to control himself.

"Dear, even those wild mustangs that Jim Haskell traps can kill themselves in their fury," Theresa said gently. "Perhaps you should get away a while, go back to Cincinnati to work up your next excursion."

"—with the papers there full of scorn and sarcasm for all of Dawson County and the Platte River valley?" he demanded.

Then why not go to Denver, Traber Gatewood argued, build up his hay market for the summer, or take up faro a while again? If the grasshoppers returned the money would come in handy.

But John Cozad could not tear himself away, although he would not expose himself to the insults and probable bullets of the Olive hirelings at Hastings. The Gatewoods went, and Schooley, Claypool, and a dozen others, mostly early, with their guns. Finally, when the grandparents took the covered wagon the Cozad boys were invited along.

"Yes, go, go," the father finally said to Robert's pleading. "Maybe you should see that there are really such men."

"They haven't been found guilty yet, Mr. Cozad," the new minister pointed out quietly.

"Have you heard that any of them deny their guilt? They want it known everywhere, to scare out settlers, not only up there in their range but here, everywhere."

In a few days the Gatewoods brought the boys back to school and told of the men who turned state's evidence against Olive to save their own skins. Even so the verdict was only second-degree murder for Olive and his foreman.

"Seems when his threat of guns and fire brought the militia, old Print turned to bribery. We heard that the jury verdict cost the outfit seven, eight thousand dollars in bribes alone. They plan to buy a reversal or a mistrial from the state supreme court for Olive and his foreman," Traber said. "That will come higher."

John J. Cozad rested no easier that night. Olive would be out in a few months at the most. Second-degree murder for the hanging and burning of two men and letting varmints gnaw the bodies. "It's an open invitation."

"It will pass," Theresa tried to comfort her husband, saying it quietly, softly in her Virginia way.

But perhaps he knew she would be pleased if he were even more discouraged; less violently angered, yes, but discouraged enough to give up the whole venture here. She spoke of this to Johnny at breakfast the next morning, just a mention of it, stopping when Robert came in with his paint box, ready to start a picture of the courtroom at Hastings and another of the crowd outside, with the blue coats of the militia standing in a row against the cowboys. He sneaked a glance at his mother. He knew how she felt, but he couldn't bear to think of failure for his father. They would just have to work harder to help him.

As he ate and listened to the pleasant talk between their mother and Johnny, Robert wished idly that he could get up in time for some of the breakfast visits too, but somehow he couldn't manage it.

"He's like a hibernating badger," Johnny once complained. "Like that one we dug out up on the north section before the ground froze hard. He didn't liven up until we had him clear out and the sun in his eyes."

In May the man-burner case was still in the papers, the other members of the Olive lynch mob found not guilty. The North Platte *Republican* jeered the jurors. Unless Dawson County contrived to do better than Hastings, Nebraska would be eternally disgraced by her farcical dealings with criminals.

"We must get the county seat away from Plum Creek or no telling who will be next," John Cozad said once more to his ear-worn friends.

Apparently many people in Plum were concerned too. Print Olive had been at least half drunk most of the two, three years since he came swaggering out of Texas with a whole ranch on the move. It was the whisky, many thought, and so the next election they voted liquor out of their town. There was boot-legging and illegal sale, of course, but not too openly at first. Most of the drinking was at the roadhouse down at the bridge, well beyond the town limits, and along the Loup trail to the Black Hills. Those places a man could get anything.

Spring was upon them, with the geese going north, one day swans floating majestic upon the still pools of the cold gray Platte and gone the next. The cattle losses of the winter were a heavy stink upon the wind that blew over the flowering hillsides and through the canyons and gullies suddenly white with chokecherry and wild plum bloom. Other years these sweetened the air for miles and drew thousands of butterflies in snowy flight or in clinging, fluttering orange. This year there were the flowers but on the air only the carrion stink that drew the wolves, magpies, and the buzzards too, circling.

The snow that killed the cattle had soaked the earth with promise. That, and the continued hard times and unemployment, made many in the east forget the violent story of a rancher named Olive. Once more homeseekers came westward like ants running to a sorghum boiling.

The wet spring brought stories of tornadoes that lifted the buildings, twisted off great old cottonwoods, crumpled windmills like paper out west, and of a hailstorm that took nearly five thousand windowpanes at North Platte. One hail did strike near Cozad, pounding a twenty-mile strip under five, six inches of hail white as snow until the rain behind it washed the stones into deep drifts that lasted for days, a store of ice to freeze a bit of ice cream for the children, and keep the butter cool. When the hail thawed it left the fields of wheat, oats, and young corn gray and bare, the gardens too, and even the prairie.

But outside of that one hail the crops were so good that a self-binding harvester was brought in. Picnic parties came for miles to see it work, the buggy horses frightened by the pound and fury of the machine, threatening to run away. The rows of golden shocks of wheat set up behind the harvester were beautiful to see—that much grain safe from wind and hail, from all but fire or range cattle wandering, or, more likely, driven over that way in the night.

Gunplay became more common over the cattle regions after the news of the Olive crimes. Like an epidemic spreading on the wind, shooting and lynching burgeoned all over the cow country, with several hangings up along the Niobrara River—thieves and those called thieves strung up. It increased with the arrival of the first herds from the south in the spring, but after a couple of swift murders among the cowboys of the roundup, more and more law-abiding cattlemen refused to hire gun-carrying ranch hands at all, not for their roundup crews or for the regular summer work with their stock.

Horse thieves were thick, as usual. Doc Middleton seemed to be working from Sidney eastward past Cozad to Grand Island quite openly, although there was around $1000 out for his capture, some said $2000. Most of this was from Nebraska and Wyoming, but some from Texas too, from back when he traveled under another name.

This time Doc picked up another horse at Cozad. John Handley, who had worked on the sod bridge, now ran a livery stable. Some time back the sheriff had come through on the way to Plum Creek with a Kentucky-bred race horse named Rob Roy that he left at Handley's stable until the owner paid a bill of around $200 that the sheriff had for collection. Before the matter was cleared up a man came to hire a saddle horse for the fourteen-, fifteen-mile ride to the county seat. Rob Roy was the only good horse Handley had in, and needing exercise anyway. He let the man take the horse.

The next morning Middleton had Rob Roy. As soon as Handley got the news he and some others who lost horses picked up the trail. It led, as usual, to the broken Niobara.

In a few days another story reached Cozad. It seemed that Doc, tired of being on the run, had agreed to meet with a U.S. marshal to work out his surrender. A sharpshooter was set along the route to pick Middleton off from ambush. But there was a mix-up; Doc got suspicious and fired into the hiding place. The ambusher sent back one wild bullet and hit for healthier country, leaving the marshal and Middleton to shoot it out. They picked each other off their horses and, both wounded, crawled off in opposite directions like a couple of snakes in a big hurry. But Doc had to have medical care and so he surrendered and was sent to the penitentiary. Rob Roy, ridden something like a hundred miles a day a couple of times during the flight from the officers, was never fit to run again.

Robert Cozad heard the story, and half a dozen other versions with disappointment. He had started a fine series of incidents called "Robin Hood of the Plains," with pictures in color now that his grandmother had given him a fine new set of crayons for his birthday. But the story was spoiled; how could his Robin Hood end up in the pen?

True, Middleton's gang went right on under somebody called Kid Wade. Unfortunately for Robert's story the Kid lacked Doc's cleverness with horses and his native gallantry. Nobody told stories of the Kid returning horses to the needy or to anybody else as Middleton had returned Pirate to John Cozad. Nobody sat around the sandbox in Julia Gatewood's store to tell stories about the Kid as he chewed and spit. So Robert put the unfinished account into the bottom drawer of his desk and looked around for other material. In the afternoon he slipped away to talk to Pirate a little, tell the nickering bay the story of Doc. Finally he made a sketch of the capture, and one last little story to go with it, with Doc still the hero, mainly because he liked to finish everything off. Robert was very busy these days with the hay press down on the bottoms and counting the bales as they were hauled away to the empty railroad cars waiting at the siding.

"Have to get up all we can before the herds come through to eat out everything. I look for a lot of gunplay now," John Cozad told his son, speaking very bitterly, and glancing toward the boy's horse, grazing slowly with the reins up. The gun was in the holster at the horn, even here at the hay press.

XVI

THE JUNE DAY THAT ROBERT was fourteen he rode off south with Johnny, just to look around, see the new dugouts and soddies and the new strips of breaking, with crows and an occasional sea gull following the turning sod, pecking at grubs and worms. Perhaps a chicken hawk swooped in now and then to catch a mouse or mole uncovered by the plow, or even a snake, maybe cut in two. In the meantime plovers might rise ahead of the first furrow, or curlews come to light on some knoll with their peculiar cry of *kurloo, kurloo*, the lovely brown of the long graceful wings folded high over the backs as they settled down, the pink of the underwing turned out, pink with a little apricot mixed in. It was a sight Robert wanted to hold in his mind, to be recalled on his birthdays to come—that lovely pink of the praying wings.

The boys rode back by way of the little dry wash where they had discovered the injured Pawnee from the Massacre Canyon fight six years ago. Then they came back by the little prairie-rose flat, a sandy patch with sparse, lank grass and squat clumps of rosebushes not over ten, twelve inches tall, the blossoms large as palms and the pale pink of a baby's hand.

They crossed above the bridge, where an old sod shack had fallen apart many, many years ago. Around the crumbled walls the ground was heaving with mushrooms. The boys got off and spread a slicker out on the ground for the supper treat they would bring to their mother. They turned the first of the great caps up, fragrant, the large ones a handsome brown underneath. Robert sat back on his heels with a couple of the fat young mushrooms in his hands, the fluted underside pink. A sudden excitement ran through him. The curlew's wing, the roses in the grass, sunset on the ice of winter, and now, from beneath the black earth, these young mushrooms, all with the same lovely pink with a tinge of apricot repeated over and over.

The boy was silent on the ride home. They took it leisurely not to bruise the mushrooms that ballooned Johnny's slicker out behind the saddle. At the stable Robert busied himself dragging the saddle off and rubbing down his present, his new Darby pony.

"It has been my best birthday ever, I think," he said to his brother, without looking at him.

This summer there was one conflict, one exciting fight that didn't have their father in the middle of it. John Handley, the redheaded hotheaded Irishman who was always going up like a Roman candle Fourth of July time, ran the new livery stable where most of the malcontents and the local anarchists, as some called them, hung out. John had made several fusses about the way things were done at the bridge, angered too, because Cozad once dumped all the money into a wheelbarrow and distributed it from there, just the most arrogant of many vulgar displays Handley called it, arrogant in the face of men who didn't own so much as a shin plaster, let alone a red cent to buy a hardtack for their hungry children.

But in one thing Handley agreed with the community builder—in his anger at range cattle running loose. The livery-man's homestead, over south of the river, was on the trail from Texas to the new Indian reservations up north, just across the Dakota line. The hungry herds ate him out as they did the other homesteaders along the route. Cattle had to have grass, no matter who owned it, no matter at all. Young corn, wheat, oats, and even cabbage patch were all grass to the·wild Longhorns walking for so many weeks—jucier grass. Hungry, spread-horned, they would not be driven off, tossing their heavy heads, perhaps chasing the women and endangering the children, particularly the stock herds of cows with calves— very dangerous even if there were no insolent gun-armed cowboys around. The settler's best defense was to put a few loads of buckshot into the trespassing stock, preferably without witnesses, but often that really brought the gun-packing cowboys down upon him, and so the shooting of loose cattle was done at night if possible, or of strays. Sometimes a stray was taken up and hidden for later meat or if slick—unbranded —for an addition to the starting herd. Legally there was always the Herd Law, giving the homesteader the right to take up part or all of any bunch of cattle he caught on his land for damages.

At last Handley, with some neighboring settlers to help and a couple dozen others who joined later, cut out a parcel of steers from a herd allowed to scatter over miles of homesteaders' fields and started them on the run toward the river. Robert Cozad and his cousin, John Robert, saw them from the bridge and jumped to their horses to help. With a solid line of riders, Handley managed to haze the spooky Longhorns through the river and to some sheds and a corral at his livery stable.

At first the wild-eyed steers kept running round and round the corral, their horns banging. Pushed into the darkish interior of the sheds, they quieted, as stock did when packed into cattle cars. Then Handley took his witnesses to the justice of the peace, and a man was sent to the owner to serve the notification of stock taken up for damages.

In a couple of hours the rancher's cowboys came riding

hard, pulling their horses down at Handley's Livery, their hands on their guns, demanding the cattle.

The redheaded Irishman appeared in the shed door, his new Winchester across his arm, several other settlers behind him with their rifles too. "Pay the damages we got put on them and they're yours," Handley shouted.

The cowboys weren't fools enough to match their Colts against the rifles, and, cursing, they rode off. But now there were the cattle to feed and water, and that would soon eat up their value. John Cozad sent Johnny down with an offer of hay, glad the take-up was done, and by someone besides himself. So bales of hay were rolled off the long rick at the tracks and hauled to the sheds. Finally the ranch foreman came, talking mighty polite, with a wad of bills from which he peeled off enough for the damages.

Then the cowboys whooped the steers into a run, turning them up the main street of Cozad, the big roan leader dodging from side to side, scattering those out rubbernecking, and the chickens, a cow or two on picket ropes, and the barking dogs. But not all the dogs fled. A little bench-legged English bull from over north got away from his owner and was at the nose of a big blue steer, clinging as he was swung off the ground, to the whoops of the boys loafing around the buildings, including Robert, who had been sent home by Handley at the first sign of gun trouble.

The steer bucked and ran but still the dog hung on. One of the cowboys pulled his gun and shot, missing, the bullet spurting up fine dust. The foreman yelled, and spurred in before there was another chance to aim.

"Damn fool! You want to get mobbed? Hold your lead! You'll get your day."

There was a lot of good feeling in the Platte settlements over this victory—one homesteader daring to use the Herd Law, take up trespassing stock for damages in the face of the cowboy guns. John Cozad was so pleased he strolled down to the livery stable in his silk hat, swinging his cane in the sun to compliment Handley in public.

But the good feeling between the two men didn't last.

"It never does with John J., you know," Theresa said slowly to her mother when it seemed there would be trouble again. It came, a real clash between her husband and the fiery redhead from the livery stable. Out of this grew a story to be told and retold up and down the river and particularly at Plum Creek.

According to Handley's story, Cozad had hired him to haul some stacked hay in off the island near town. Johnny Stevenson claimed that some of the hay was his property. He had John Cozad arrested. In court the colonizer acted as his own attorney and called Handley as a witness to testify that he was hired to haul hay from the Cozad stacks only, and had touched nothing of Stevenson's. Instead of testifying one way or another on this, Handley launched into a complaint that he hadn't been paid for the work.

"Irrelevant, irrelevant," Sam Schooley protested from the audience. He had read law and had advised John Cozad, but this was a surprise.

Irrelevant, maybe, but probably true, some whispered. There were others, however, who recalled a time, only a few years ago, when Handley's family would have had nothing to eat if Cozad hadn't taken pity on him and hired him, although the Irishman was outside of Cozad's own settlement and not his responsibility.

When the justice of the peace had gaveled down the noise, John Cozad was calling Handley a liar. He had most certainly been paid.

By this time the Irishman was up on his feet, standing behind his chair to make a statement. If the court would not protect him from this violent man, he would do it himself.

"I'll repeat my statement once more, and it had better not be disputed. *I have not been paid for the work.*"

"You are a liar!" the defendant snapped a second time, considering this final.

But not Handley. He swung the heavy chair off the floor and upon John Cozad. Trying to shield his head, the man caught the full force of the chair on his arm and went down, the bones broken in two places.

There was a roaring in the courtroom. Young Robert pushed through the crowd as fast as he could and stopped at the sight of his father on the floor, his arm stretched out, twisted like a snapped stick in the black sleeve.

"You—you crippled my father!" he cried, diving for John Handley, to claw and kick. But Traber Gatewood grabbed him by the shoulder and pulled him back, still fighting.

"I demand a charge of attempted murder be entered against my attacker!" John Cozad shouted from the floor.

But it seemed that the court would not allow that, couldn't, and so the charge was changed to assault to do bodily harm. Handley was fined $20 on the spot and had about fifty cents in his pocket, or so he claimed. James Ware, marshal of Cozad town, and, it was said, anxious to clear the crowd away before more animosities broke out, came forward to pay the fine, and for the time the charge of Stevenson against Cozad was forgotten.

The fight in court split the Cozad colony more than ever, and yet even the faithful Sam Schooley saw something of the ridiculous side of the matter. One of the country's foremost masters at faro with an arm in a cast, and broken by a man who objected to being called a liar but was called worse every day around his livery barn.

Robert was quiet under the frown of his mother because he had been drawn into one of his father's fights, in spite of her plea that he keep away or learn to control himself. But John Cozad was pleased with the boy and let him write the new poster that was to build up the excursions again. The boy revised the wording of the old ones, and after his spelling was corrected, the lot was printed. Robert made some two-color sketches on a few, and emphasized the railroad fare, only $22 one way, Cincinnati to Cozad, round trip $35, first class and good for 40 days on any train, tickets to be purchased from the Cozad representative at the office above Wehrle's. That was where the other trouble that got him a broken bone started, young Todd and his fellows rowdying outside there, and then breaking the colonizer's jaw, for ruining Todd at cards long ago, the man claimed. There was little danger of John J. Cozad ruining anybody now for some months, he thought sourly. It was too bad because the boom at Leadville, Colorado, was holding up. At least he could get some hay contracts in the camp, tucked just under the Continental Divide with no place to grow the feed for the mine mules. Not that he lacked buyers for all the hay he could put up. The heavy losses in cattle last winter had taught some of the ranchers a lesson. Horses could paw the snow and live but not cows.

While Johnny worked with the father in the office, answering the swelling correspondence, Robert mailed out the promotion sheets and kept track of the hay baled and shipped. He felt very grown up, a man, with an embarrassment before every girl since the one with the dark blue eyes had whirled him in a witches' dance. An embarrassment and a growing interest in them, even if they were considerably older, like pretty Mollie Claypool, really a distant cousin of sorts. He thought about these things while he lathered the fuzz of his face from the new shaving mug with the fragrant soap in the bottom. But sometimes he looked back a little enviously to

the children of the town, particularly when the wagon peddler came through on his way to Cheyenne and back. The
man carried a general line of merchandise to interest women
of the section houses and small stations without a store, and
for settlers not too far off the trail. What Robert liked most
was the trinkets and treats for the children in the big packs.
He remembered his old excitement when the man drove in,
swinging his four-horse team and the heavy wagon in a fine
U turn in the middle of the street, making a great show of
it and shouting to the horses, a signal for all the young ones
to come running.

With his lead mares tied to the hitch rack or to an anchor
iron dropped in the dust, he went around to the back, lifted
the padlocked bolt, and swung the double doors open, exposing the big trunk-sized telescope bags and beyond them
the dusky shelves. First he dragged out the big bright-brown
case, with the top fitting down over it all the way. This he
lifted off and turned up on the ground to receive the goods as
he showed them. First there was a tray of safety pins, buttons,
thread, hooks and eyes, beauty pins, needles, and darning eggs.
Under this was usually another tray, with a few of the children's favorites—lead pencils, jew's-harps, mouth organs, and
so on, with tops, balls, and perhaps jumping jacks and teething
rings for the babies. Here usually went the savings of the
children, the shin plasters, the pennies, nickles or even dimes,
clutched in sweaty, undecided hands. But those who had been
through this clung to their money even more tightly, knowing
that at the end, an hour or two from now, there would be a
last little box, with pretty, shallow trays of special things that
broke your heart not to own, and your money already spent.
Of course, sometimes parents could be induced to buy here.
Robert knew by experience that this did not work with their
mother or even the grandparents. Although the boys always
had money in the pocket, often more than a settler with a
family could turn out of his old snap pouch when he came to

the store, the funds were not to be augmented at the last trays if they had spent themselves broke.

"Plan your expenditures to fit your purse," Theresa Gatewood tried to impress upon her sons, but it wasn't always easy, with the big-talk ideas so close around them.

Robert remembered the first time he saw the peddler, with children standing around him that summer at Willow Island station and during the early years here. He recalled the man measuring off calico and sateen and unbleached muslin, yard after yard from his outstretched finger tips to his nose, and this or that woman protesting, measuring it to her own arm. He remembered the women dickering for tin pans or at least patching material for the pans, or some notions they needed. If a woman felt flush or was angry with her husband, she might buy a petticoat of Irish green or some red stockings, and fight it out with him later.

And there was the last little chest, to be unlocked with a key on a string around the man's neck. Inside was tray after tray, from "genuine imported French lace handkerchiefs" to beads; jeweled combs, cuff links, perfumes—Jockey Club and Ashes of Roses—rings, bracelets, and the better mouth organs, slender, perhaps, and sweet toned, so that the one bought for fifteen cents only an hour earlier now seemed no better than a comb with a piece of tissue paper over it. There might also be a piccolo, to be put together and blown with a fine screeching sound.

And when the covetous eyes let the last breastpin or the last mouth organ be locked away and the big cases were lifted back into the wagon, the children followed their friend out to the west end of town, stirring up a great dust behind the wagon with cans and barrel hoops on long strings and old ropes looped over the rear axle, holding the ends in their hands so they could let them slip when they got tired running, their hoops and cans stopping in the dust, to be picked up for another time. Later the hoops might be rolled along the street by somebody's small sister, the ropes used for lassoing or jumping, the cans tied to the tail of any stray dog lucklessly wandering within reach of the noisier, bolder boys, who, Theresa hoped, never included her sons.

Now Robert looked after the peddler's wagon and laughed with the elders at the children running along behind. He had bought two of the harmonicas for a couple of small boys in a settler soddy off toward Willow Island, where there was never any money because the father had come down with typhoid almost a year ago and was still only yellow skin over the bones, not able to do more than sit in the shade.

There were few of the earlier settlers this good crop year who needed work on the bridge but some who came too late for seeding were happy for the few dollars, or those luckless enough to be in the hail strips. But with the south bottoms settling fast and the only bridge around still the one at Plum Creek, John Cozad knew the importance of capturing this south trade for his town and their votes for his county seat. The latter was a more hopeful prospect now, with the tar of the Olive crimes on Plum's record, on top of the county officials' refusal to arrest the man-burners, who walked openly on the street until outside warrants were brought in.

So the work on the sod bridge went steadily on, Robert Gatewood overseeing much of it from his homestead shack. From there he saw how often the fording was made at real danger to rigs, horses, and even lives, although in late summer there might not be enough water to wet a Pawnee moccasin.

When school was out Eugene Young moved to his homestead on the south side, his Nettie fast becoming a fine horsewoman able to ride her half-wild mustang anywhere, even with her sidesaddle. She crossed the Platte any time with only their hunting dogs along, even when it had to be swum, feeling safe because her dappled gray never got himself into quicksand. If the river was roily he reached down to sniff the water anxiously, his nostrils flaring, his ears pricked forward. If he smelled danger he refused bit and lashing reins rather than step into it, selecting his own route across. He was sure-footed in an antelope chase and took as much joy as the hounds in a good run.

One afternoon the Cozad boys saw Nettie Young come past the bridge workers, her gray riding habit falling gracefully over the dappled sides of her horse, the veil of her hat blowing a little. As usual the greyhounds trotted obediently behind, their curved, bony tails bounding lightly as they came. She lifted her little saddle quirt to Grandpa Gatewood and the boys, who ran for their horses to escort her across the river whether she needed it or not.

Out on the south bottoms they turned back to their work, waving to their friend over their shoulders. Afterward they regretted their unusual concern about their tasks. About a quarter of a mile farther on the dogs scared up several antelope and started a run as the animals whistled and flashed their white rumps. Nettie let the faunching gray out, forgetting her natural caution in tall grass, eager to keep up with the dogs cutting in on each other, gaining fast. Just as the lead dog was ready to snap at the heels of the slowest, the horse stumbled in a badger hole and went down, throwing Nettie over his head. The dogs stopped at once, surrounding her as though in protection, and wouldn't go on, no matter how much she commanded them. By the time she got back on the horse, the antelope were too far away.

But it had been a fine chase while it lasted and made a good story to tell around. A couple of new settlers saw it and spread the news at the bridge and the post office.

"Woman riding sidesaddle, going hell bent after them dogs right on the heels of the antelopes," one said, admiringly.

"Dangerous, I claim. I wouldn't let her, was she my wife——"

The next day Robert Cozad sneaked away a couple of times

hoping to locate the little herd and then perhaps borrow some dogs, or get a hunt started, and be invited along. But the animals were gone, probably scared out of the country. They were getting scarcer every year. Robert could remember when fifty or more came regularly to drink at the Willow Island game crossing.

By the time winter was sending out warning signals, powdering a little snow for the dawn, or icing the edges of the water holes, John Cozad's arm was free of the cast and useful again. There had been an angry boiling in him all this time, but he contained himself and kept out of trouble with Handley since the court assault. Some were saying that the Irishman from the livery stable had taught the overbearing bastard from the faro table a good lesson.

Then one gray chilly afternoon, John Cozad saw Handley coming along the street on top of a high jag of hay. He grabbed up his bull whip and ran out to even the score with the Irishman. The result was a set-to that was talked about for months, even years, with no real agreement on what happened.

Because Handley was a talker and there was the usual human enjoyment of discomfiture in high position, the liveryman's version spread fast, particularly around Plum Creek. He told it there himself to a gathering audience at the Johnson Hotel. According to him, young Robert grabbed one of his horses by the bit and stopped the wagon while John Cozad popped the bull whip up around the top of the hay load, yelling, "John Handley, some time ago you almost killed me and did break my arm in two places. Now I'm going to collect my damages!"

Handley said he hooked the lines around the standard of the rack, grabbed the pitchfork, and rolled off the load with the fork ready for business. At the sight of the gleaming tines, Cozed and his boy hit for an alley, the father yelling, "Run,

Robert, run! That damned fool will kill you!" with the Irishman close behind, hurrying Cozad along with a touch of the tines to his broadclothed rear.

It was that last that brought some doubt to the story. It was just too much, spreading it on too thick.

XVII

THE YEAR 1880 started bleak enough. There had been a lot of fall fires that left great stretches of prairie like black moiréed velvet. But even before the cow chips stopped smoking, the wind began to lift the soot and ashes in dark clouds and to tear at the bare knobs, blowing the grass to the roots, leaving it to stand on weak and wavering stilts. Then came December, with diphtheria sweeping through the settlements of the Platte valley. Often new cemeteries had to be started, so healthy and hardy had the people been. True, the settlers the last seven, eight years were mostly the young and the strong, or perhaps those with bad stomachs and weak chests, sent west to become strong, and usually did.

But by now there were many children too, either brought out as soon as a shelter was up or born here, and many of these, particularly the infants, were dying. At one time most of the school at Plum Creek was down, the women worn with the nursing and anxiety, the few doctors in the entire region helpless to make all the rounds, even if there were much they could do. But anybody with a saw and a hammer and nails could make a child's coffin from a few rough cottonwood boards.

Theresa Cozad took her sons to Cincinnati for the Christmas season, leaving early to get them away from the diphtheria that was hitting their town too. With the epidemic and the bad storms the holiday season was a quiet one at Cozad. The few landseekers who arrived just before New Year found plenty of room at the brick hotel or half a dozen other places happy to take them in for a little cash money, much less cash money than Riggs at the hotel.

By early January the region had been swept by weeks of terrifying blizzards and what the hotel lacked in paying guests the streets made up in the unwelcome jamming by snow-caked Longhorns drifting down from the ranches north, some from clear up on the Loups. Theresa and the rest had just returned. Robert still awoke easily to any unusual movement or sound from the time when he was to stop Johnny walking in his sleep. The night of the drifting he heard curious scrapings along the buildings, and a dull pounding of hoofs. He ran out to see beyond the frosted windows. Men were plunging into the driving storm with overcoats thrown on, swinging brooms and clubs and yelling against the snow-whitened cattle gathering in vague shapes along the walls out of the blizzard wind, crowding, threatening to push them in, knocking windows to pieces with their unwieldy horns, or overturning smaller buildings entirely. And still the cattle came, driven with the wind, ice-caked, blinded, plunging into piling snowbanks in front of the hotel, struggling everywhere in the deep drifts, perhaps pushed down by those behind, more and more coming, running in until all the street was rising and falling in white backs, the hoofs a muffled rumble in the roar of the wind.

It was dangerous to be out in the daytime too, particularly for women and children. The Longhorns, wild from starvation, lurched at everything that might be feed, or, maddened by the approach of death, crashed through the crusted snow upon anything that moved, seeing it as the enemy that, by animal instinct, they knew was near.

One of the earlier storms of the winter caught several men out unprepared, men who never got back home. One of these was Elisha Clark, an old-time hunter and trapper. He had been a colonel in the war, and with his wife dead, he had returned to the free ways of his youth, following prime furs anywhere, going wherever there was game. Early in December he had camped with his wagon and two big greyhounds in the deep protection of the Powell Canyon region, in the breaks up around the Loup. A couple of weeks later a man hunting cedar for fuel saw him carrying an armful of hay from the stacks of Goodyear, a Cozad hay contractor who cut some up there too. It was a full three snow-drifted canyon miles from the stacks to Clark's camp but nobody worried about that, not until the man's greyhounds were found dead at Goodyear's hay, frozen in the appalling cold of that winter. There was no sign of Clark but he was an old-timer——

The first of January more cedar haulers with bobsleds had found the trapper's wagon and team. One of the horses was dead, still tied solidly to a tree. The animal had gnawed the bark from the trunk as high as he could reach and all the twigs and bushes around. The other horse had eaten off the limb to which he was tied and escaped.

But there was still no sign of the man, not even a wind-blown track in the deep snow. Although far below zero, the settlers rode out to search many miles of drifted breaks and canyons and didn't find him. There was talk of a bullet in the back, as with the hunters up farther two, three winters ago, and the Missouri landseekers, all within reach of Print Olive and his gunmen. But now Olive was locked up at the pen in Lincoln. Of course his killers were still loose.

The county commissioners offered $50 reward for the body of Clark, but nobody came to collect, not until spring. Then a man out after stray horses saw a coyote run up a steep canyon wall ahead. Below was the body. Apparently Clark had gone for more hay and in the blizzard got into the wrong maze of breaks and ended at the head of a bare, steep, drift-choked box canyon, still half on his knees, the gun at his side, trying to crawl into a narrow cut for protection from the cold. A mile or so more and he would have been in sight of a ranch, if the storm had broken.

Many were a little relieved that the body was not found until spring. The women had been uneasy enough as it was whenever their men had to be out this winter. That a hunter, a plainsman like Clark, could die in a storm showed how justified their uneasiness had been.

Although Robert Cozad never seemed to tire of the story about the trapper Clark and his death, the boy's father found other events of the winter more disturbing. One was the killing of Curly Grimes, whom he and many others along the Platte had known and liked. Curly, accused of robbery up toward the Black Hills, was captured by a couple of detectives and killed on the way to Cheyenne "attempting to escape," as they called it. Even the Black Hills *Pioneer* agitated for an investigation and the jury found that Grimes was killed "without just cause or provocation" and recommended that the "officers" be tried for murder.

It reminded John Cozad of the fake deputy sheriff who appeared at the livery stable with the faro tramps, and of all the other killings the last two, three years, mobs and individuals taking the law into their own hands. He made up a large file of these. In addition to the Hallowell hanging at Plum Creek, the Mitchell and Ketchum burning, and the others laid to the Olive gang, there were at least a dozen more lynchings and unsolved shootings within the Platte region alone and lately several bodies found up around O'Neill. Now in addition to Grimes there was the man found dead on an island near Ogallala, in the Platte Fork, the hogs eating him. Murdered too, and not identified.

"No man's life is safe anywhere around here," John Cozad

roared out, pounding the newspaper story with his fist. Perhaps he should run for the legislature, or a county office, as soon as they got enough votes in the west end of the county. But then he could have the county seat.

Perhaps a senatorship was still possible, with its prestige. There was still talk of moving the national capital to Fort Kearny, but the lynchings were a mighty black mark.

While most of the February excursion went back or hurried south for warmer climate, the March group would certainly do better. At last, hours late, the train stopped at Cozad but the passengers had to take the conductor's word for it, so thick was the spring blizzard. E. D. Owens, the young well borer who came to the region a year ago, was scooping the growing drifts away to the train step to welcome his mother and brothers and sisters. His cap and eyebrows were frosted white and he looked mighty rough in his worn old coat but mighty healthy, a sound, sturdy young man. He helped with the grips and, taking the arm of his mother, guided her toward the Riggs hotel, the rest close behind, all bowed into the driving snow. Behind them was the Cozad excursion, led by John J. himself, his beaver-collared coat thrown open to the whitening storm.

"Healthiest climate in the world," he shouted against the wind. "I was a consumptive, you know—hunted all around for a cure, South America, California, everywhere." He thrust his chest out, his face handsome in its ruddy color, ruddy enough so not even the darkness of his hair and goatee, the intense blackness of his eyes, could pale it today.

The hotel was suddenly packed, with cots set up in rows down the main room stretching through the entire building. At supper everybody gathered in the dining hall north of the brick hotel. It was a narrow, barny frame building, with a bare pine table twenty-five feet long down the center. There were large chairs near the head, and benches around the rest for the settlers, with men in working clothes toward the far end today, some in old muskrat caps with the ear flaps pushed up—the one concession to the indoors and dining.

The Cozad family sat at the head of the table, napkins in silver rings at their places, the plates white bone china instead of the tinware farther down. As always John Cozad came in a little late, hurrying, his black frock coat well brushed, a heavy gold chain around his neck and across his chest to the watch pocket. At one side sat Theresa, handsome in dark blue worsted that set off the pinkish glow of her cheeks. Across from her were the two sons. Johnny, handling much of the desk work of his father's land dealings, always liked to size up any new prospects, particularly those who came through the storm today. He favored the Gatewoods in appearance more than the Cozads, but his features were more delicate, his bones thinner and longer than his grandfather's or his Uncle Traber's. Beside him sat young Robert, still much like his father, perhaps more than was casually visible. The short chin of the boy was hidden by the skillfully lengthening effect of the goatee in the father, but who could tell what of the father was hidden in the son?

The Cozads made an imposing picture in the light of the wall-bracket lamps flickering a little in the wind that crept in here too, a picture imposing enough for a white-pillared Southern mansion in the Virginia of Theresa Gatewood's girlhood. But that was unbelievably far from the unfinished pine-board dining hall at the edge of the winter wilderness and from the guests, for no matter how nearly broke the excursionists might be, how actually penniless, they ate at this table with the Cozads. Tonight there were some really ragged settlers too, and a couple of section hands and some cowboys caught in town when the blizzard struck.

After the first talk had quieted a little, young Owens called attention to his relatives. "I want to introduce you to Mr. Cozad, the builder and owner of our city——"

214

Later he whispered to his young brother out of the corner of his mouth. "He's a king of faro and poker——"

The boy looked toward the head of the table with new interest, and considered the son they called Robert, about his own age—one of the sons of the gamblin' man. He glanced in pride at his mother. Why this was better than seeing President Grant that time, a few years back.

The Owens boy was still excited about the Cozads when his father arrived, bringing the carload of stock, farm implements and household goods with which the family was starting life in this new land, a land whose earth the well-drilling son had found fertile and very deep.

Robert Cozad received a new stock of notebooks for his diary from his Uncle Traber, and a bottle of clear red ink to go with the blue he had for illuminating the letters of the page heads. He wanted to make some in his diary look a little like those of his mother's Bible. He wished he had a pinch of gold leaf, which he needed badly to put with the red and blue. But gold leaf was very expensive, a traveling photographer told him. Joseph Brander, portraitist, as he wished to be called, confided in Robert that he was really an artist. He traveled around making money to buy time for his own painting. He had reached Cozad late one evening and drew up between a couple of houses on the main street, his wagon a little darkroom with folding steps that dropped down to accommodate the ladies. Inside it was fitted up with a romantic backdrop and a fringed chair for taking and developing studio portrait photographs.

Robert hung around the photographer all he dared and in return for this he drummed up a little trade—getting his grandmother and as many of the rest of the Gatewoods, the Claypools, and the Schooleys and anyone else with the money to sit for their portraits. In addition Mr. Brander let Robert ask about painting.

"Here, where you can look at your father, and yourself, in the bright sunlight, you would naturally approach portrait painting by thinking about the eyes. That's what I see when I look at you outdoors, or even here," the man said, holding out the hand mirror that he carried along for the ladies, who liked a final touch to the hair before sitting.

Robert took the glass and saw himself with the bright lamp shining into his face. "Why, my eyes are glittery as a mouse's," he exclaimed, a little uneasy.

"A very big mouse, and without the fear that a small creature has in a world of great monsters—cats, dogs, people."

Young Robert laid the mirror down and glanced at all the sample photographs pinned up inside the wagon—pictures of actresses and suchlike, with curls at their necks, black stuff on their eyes, and their dresses cut very low, as he had seen on actresses in Cincinnati. He knew there were other women too who walked around dressed like that out among people in the places where his father went, and in towns like Deadwood and Virginia City, as he had found thumbing through *Harper's Weekly*.

But perhaps with a special way of seeing people now, and with his father's eyes, and his own too, to remind him, he might begin to make pictures of people from that point of view. Or was *aspect* the right word? From that *aspect?* Anyway, it was a new discovery, an exciting one, and he wished that he had known it last winter, when he saw the Richter girl with the dark blue eyes at the skating party at Willow Island. He often thought of riding up there, but what could he say to get to go. And everybody would just laugh.

In a week or so the artist-photographer hitched up and moved on. Robert had looked after the disappearing square back of the little darkroom on wheels as long as he could see it.

"A boozefighter," Sam Schooley said sourly as he came along the new piece of board sidewalk, cottonwood, but fine in wet weather.

Others were mad at Joseph Brander too. He sold stereo-scopic views and the Cozad boys and John Robert had each bought some to be passed around the family, views that complemented each other, the photographer had said. And it seemed that they would, from the titles. But "Elephants in Indian Jungle" and "Elephants in Central Africa" turned out to be the very same pictures. The American Indian views they bought were an even greater disappointment. Johnny's "Red Cloud, Sioux Indian and Wife," John Robert's "Crazy Horse and Squaw," and Robert's "A Pawnee Chieftain and Daughter" were all three exactly the same photograph to the last hair and bead, just pasted above different captions.

"A common cheat and blackleg!" people said.

Robert finally had to admit that they were right but it seemed to him that perhaps Mr. Brander was really an artist, anyway. No matter how hard he tried to be angry, Robert found himself looking at people, even horses, in this new way, starting with the eyes, but now seeing much more besides. Even Tabby blinking in the spring sun in Mrs. Gatewood's store window had a new fire, although she sat on the same pile of folded overalls, carefully away from the papers of pins and needles, and the scissors and crochet hooks. He caught a sort of inner burning in the eyes of his father, and a cool remoteness in the far-focused ones of the older, the hard-working cowboys stopping by, or perhaps a wavering and a weeping if they were real old-timers and had faced too many years of wind. He noticed a sudden gleam rise sometimes in the faded eyes of his grandmother. But when he looked at his mother what he saw was the line of her throat to the poised chin, and from her nape to the top of her soft upswept hair, and with this came a sudden wateriness in his breast.

As the geese came back and the grass started the Cozad sons with their cousin and perhaps the new Owens boy or someone else their age took long rides on Saturdays, sometimes clear off north to the cedar breaks and the Powell Canyon region where Clark froze to death last winter. Sometimes they went to an old Pawnee village site, looking for arrow and spearheads and the many beads in the anthills. Once they found a broken grinding stone, worn deep by generations of corn-grinding women and girls.

On these expeditions the boys usually carried their lunches in their saddlebags or a frying pan, a little jar of lard, and some salt to cook the young cottontails or prairie chickens they shot with the .22 rifle in Johnny's scabbard. But they didn't talk about their guns around their mother because they made her uneasy. "I cannot approve of your carrying weapons, not with your father's temper and only the frail judgment of youth——" she once told them. "Oh, I couldn't bear it if you got into trouble——"

No one reminded her of what she knew, the need of self-protection here now. The boys had nodded their sober understanding of her concern. Old Matthews had tried to teach them well. "Never draw a gun unless you mean to use it."

But otherwise they were high-spirited as young antelope as soon as they were out of sight of town, trying tricks like reaching down and snapping off dried sunflower heads on a gallop, or picking up a handkerchief. They put their horses over washouts, if they could make the sensible creatures try it, or rode hard through prairie-dog towns, the horses dodging the holes this way and that, the boys barely staying with the saddles. Perhaps Johnny whooped off into a sudden race with John Robert, leaving the brother and his plump Darby far behind. Nor was Darby as tough or wild as the other horses, particularly Jerry Gibson's buckskin Indian pony that some said was stolen from the Sioux and traded down to the Platte by old Doc Middleton's gang.

But these fine days were getting rarer. The Cozad sons had to grow up under the responsibility of more and more of the bridgework and the haying to oversee. Often the two stayed at the bridge overnight, to guard against the theft of tools or of mischief against the equipment, even the pile driver itself. There were rumors, too, that somebody planned to blast the bridge out by the roots with giant powder or the new explosive, dynamite.

As the animosity against John Cozad grew, the threats against his dream, the bridge, also increased. "A lot of those men were glad enough to let me bring them out here, find free land for them because they were dead broke, and then needed help to put bread into the mouths of their families when the grasshoppers cleaned out everything. Now they have crops, a little work elsewhere, and so they think they can afford to call me a bastard, a jackleg gambler, an overbearing s. of a b."

Anyway there was no use taking chances, both Schooley and Traber Gatewood argued. The bridge must make real progress this year and should be completed no later than the next summer. Robert saw the concern in their faces as they said this, and so he worked up the plans on paper. He sketched a map of the location and of the bridge, then made side elevations to show how the finished work was to look. He drew these carefully, to scale, and shaded the completed portions, half-shaded those in progress, and left the projected sections in bare outline. He wrote a detailed description to go with the map and the elevations and then took the whole folio out to the bridge to check it. Some of the earlier sod fills were solid in grass by now, with willows blowing along the sides, their roots to hold the earth. Some later work had the young planting and the surfaces down; several stretches, still to be widened and raised, stood naked and bare in rain-washed earth. The last sections were not yet started, the final spans to leap the stream.

It was curious how much clearer it all became, with the plans and the sketches here in his hands, how much more just drawing them had made him see. It was not only the bridge that became more solid, with more meaning. The boy lifted his dark head and looked off across the river and then back to the town and the far, far blue line of bluffs across the north. Suddenly it was all new—always there, of course, but he had never really seen it or comprehended it until today. All the valley here, the people and all, were no longer just a sort of accidental accumulation, like the leavings on a flood plain of the Platte. Even with so many of them strangers and rolling angry, suspicious eyes, suddenly they were all a part of a pattern, a part of a community as his father had always seen it, a body of people and ground and sky, with the earth as thirsting as the people felt when the rains did not come.

Spring had warmed the gentle prairie around Cozad if not the river, rising fast and cold from the snow water rolling down out of the far mountains. The first swim the Cozad boys dared take froze their naked marrow but it was very exciting. They tried standing on the bridge over the first gap between the sod sections and looked down into the gray current boiling up so high that it had to fold in upon itself to squeeze through the narrow space. One after another the winter-skinned swimmers dove in, were caught in the tow and shot through the gap, to come out sputtering in the spreading water far below, breathless, purple with cold and pounded sore. But it was a sort of test among themselves and each one had to pretend he was eager for another dive into the roaring, freezing water and then yet another, until the grandfather appeared to stand with his hands cupped to his mouth.

"Come in! There's work to do!"

There was a great deal of work, with John Cozad away again, signing hay contracts up at Denver, Leadville, and elsewhere if the deal was good enough. In the meantime he was open to a little faro, but only with men of quality and aplomb. He hoped he would never get involved with another young fool like that Todd of Cincinnati. The wild young fellow had lost his money because he wanted to lose it, and then years later broke a man's jaw for it in the street, the jaw of a man now with a reputation as a community builder. Young Todd should have been grateful he hadn't fallen under the rougher mercies of a Devol, King O'Dell, or Canada Bill. They would have cleaned him out. But in those days Todd certainly would not have looked at Canada. He was a snob and no man whose come-on was a rube outfit would have attracted him, no matter how easy the rube might promise to be. Others made that mistake with Canada Bill but not Todd in those days. He liked to lose his money to a man "who looked like a genuine senator or an English lord."

With so much work upon them when their father was gone and their mother suggesting that they put in five hours a day in reading, studying, and thought, Robert had little time for his drawing and writing, or even the diary, and that only at night. It was true that Johnny's handwriting needed improvement and Robert's spelling was abominable but beyond that neither believed, secretly, that he needed improvement. Yet one did not say this to Theresa Cozad or at least Robert knew he could not. Johnny, as the elder son and therefore more privileged with the mother, might, but this, too, Robert realized, one did not put into words.

Yet even with the work of the bridge and the studying, the sons found time for a little play and some critical appraisal of their surroundings. When John Cozad was away the meals Riggs served at the hotel fell off noticeably. Robert, always a little fussier about his food when his father was gone, grumbled about the meals, particularly after the swift June rise in the Platte stopped the work on the bridge and gave him time for impatience. After a few days of idleness he announced he was going to board with his grandmother.

"But our meals here are included in Mr. Riggs' rent on the hotel," Theresa told him. "At your grandmother's you must pay, and out of your own pocket."

Robert felt himself pulling into one of the sulks his father never tolerated. He wanted to say that his mother would never treat Johnny like this. But it was true that his brother would put up with the Riggs table so long as the mother did, no matter how bad it became, and so Robert paid his own board bill without protest.

Along with the normal spring flood a violent rain and windstorm hit the Platte country, driving the river even higher and blowing the pile driver over. Nothing was damaged, but the tower and the flatboat had to be pulled back upright by a long string of teams and a stout block and tackle borrowed from the railroad. Work soon started again on the north side and as the foreman, Sam Schooley, pointed out, the rains did promise crops and hay. There was a hail too, with stones big as hen's eggs falling here and there. Coming straight down, they bounced around very foolishly and unless a window was hit or a lamb or fleeing hen there was little damage. Robert ran out with the new nine-foot bull whip that Mr. Gibson had made for him and tried his aim on the hail before the rain started. A few people watched the boy with amusement from doors and windows. But not everyone. Ed Winchell, the new grocery and drygoodsman, had heard some of the stories about John Cozad and the bull whip that he took to people who offended him.

"Like father, like son," Ed said as John Handley ran in out of the storm, just beating the rain coming from the west in glistening white sheets.

When John Cozad came home he ordered Riggs and his whole kit and caboodle out into the street. The man went promising revenge. Next day he opened a little hotel across the street in the old house where Goodyear, the hay contractor, used to live.

Now at last the Cozads had a little more room. They took all one end of the hotel, their sleeping quarters on the second floor, the downstairs cut into a parlor, a business office for John Cozad and Johnny, and a small den for Robert, big enough for his printing press, his desk, and his paints and papers. Now they all took their meals with Mrs. Gatewood.

It had been a very bad spring for poison ivy, as wet years could be. Many around the bridge began to itch and the bathers too, particularly those who liked to stretch out on the bank to dry off and get a little sunning. Robert's poisoning had spread until he was feverish and sick. The doctor finally gave him sweet spirits of niter, to be diluted with equal parts of water. "It's being used for almost everything nowadays," the town's new doctor said, grinning a little. "But I guess in your trouble it's really indicated."

The niter helped and by his fifteenth birthday Robert was healing and beginning to peel. It was a time for celebration anyway—the end of knickerbockers and a beginning of grown-up resolutions. Most of these were thrust upon him by his family, his relatives, and Mr. Schooley, but the one Robert really hoped to keep was his own, out of the memory of the dead-beat photographer, Mr. Brander, who could make so many invisible things take form before Robert's eyes.

"Don't let yourself be stopped by foolish little ways and mistakes that set people's backs up against you," he had said. "Go along with their little notions and then you can make a real stand for something important. That's why I cultivated good manners——"

It was true about Mr. Brander's manners, and too bad that he had turned out a petty cheat, selling mislabeled stereo views for the miserable pennies of boys. Suddenly Robert realized that the man who had told him to look for the eyes, always the eyes, was unable to keep his own resolution not to be stopped by foolish little mistakes, and that he would probably never reach his goal—never be an artist.

So he, Robert Henry Cozad, made his resolution about the small things and intended to keep it. For his family he would try to do better in manners and speech and dress. He would even try to get up earlier. Perhaps he could hold himself to these if he wrote them in his diary as a sort of commitment, but it all ended up in a scrawl because he had to run to escape his birthday licks. Johnny did overtake him and in their wrestling Robert suddenly discovered something wonderful —that finally, after years of trying, he had a good chance of throwing his brother. He felt so good about this, even after their grandmother stopped them, that he went to the office to make a proper capital entry for the new year. On this birthday he had $15.25 in his pocket. That was more than some homeseekers had when they came, many without even the $14 filing fee—grown men with families.

But that $15.25 wasn't all. He was a creditor too. His father and Grandmother Julia and Johnny all owed him money—making almost $21 with the cash from his pocket. Later he found it came to $21 even; he had made a mistake in addition. Apparently he needed to work on his arithmetic too, as well as his spelling, because that would be another small fault that could set people's backs up.

Still, he was happy about the $21—that meant he could afford to go in with John Robert on that $1.75 croquet set in Dr. Ogden's drugstore window. Together they prepared the croquet ground and started to play. First Robert beat his cousin and then Johnny and Lewy Owens too. Their horses were all faster than his Darby, but he swung a truer mallet, at least for now.

The next morning the Cozad boys rode out to the bridge early to look at the flood that had stopped the work, and perhaps to help their father and Mr. Swepston. They found the two men dragging up brush, shouting that the high water had cut a dangerous hole through the first fill-in, between the bank and the first line of pilings, and that the ground was caving away, the whole fill going if it wasn't stopped.

Johnny grabbed some boards and a hammer and ran for the hole. While Robert gathered up more lumber, his brother kicked out of his clothes and dragged one board after another into the swift, churning water and dove down near the hole with it, carrying the hammer and nails in his teeth. He got several boards and planks worked out across the bottom, fastened in place as solidly as he could manage—enough to shut out half of the water at least. But the increased surge and pressure against the boards broke the lower ones. It happened while Johnny was under the water and the sudden suck of the current caught him, dragged him halfway into the hole, thrust him hard against a plank that still held, his legs swept out underneath it, his head and shoulders forced over the top. He was caught there, bent double against the stout plank, the flood pouring over him, holding him far under.

Horrified, John Cozad and Swepston saw it happen, but they were helpless while Johnny struggled for his life out of sight below them, caught so that not even his most desperate struggles cleared the top of his head from the gray torrent washing over him.

When it seemed he must die right there in less than ten seconds more, be held over the plank until he was torn in two by the flood, Johnny made one last mighty effort to throw himself back and down. He managed to shift the thrust of the water against him just a little, enough to increase the power of it against his thighs, his legs, forcing them ahead. Suddenly he was jerked down and under the plank, the power of the flood knocking his head against one piling after another, turning him end over end and finally sweeping him through the hole and out, to whirl along like some pale log until he was drifted into shallower water and turned slowly into an eddy full of floating brush and trash and one naked body.

By now Robert and the men running along the bank could get to him, drag him out. They emptied the water from his lungs and slowly he became conscious. They got him home, worn out, battered, with his head throbbing, but the doctor was away, so they put him to bed. By night the headache was much worse, he retched and then shook as with the ague, and retched again. Theresa sent Robert to the doctor's office for a pint of whisky and made a stiff Southern toddy. Then she piled the comforters over him and after a while he slept.

Robert sat beside his brother, up at every change of breathing, any stirring out of the troubled dreams. But after a while he dozed off to be awakened by his parents.

"Go to bed, Son," Theresa said. "It was a hard day for you too."

Within a week Johnny was up and able to go to the doctor to talk over his injuries and the chills that made the father uneasy, with so much consumption in the family. It would pass, the doctor thought, but now Theresa, very distraught, finally dared say what was in her heart.

"Take us away," she begged of her husband. "Isn't it enough now? With all the enemies you have here, you may well be killed any day. And a hundred dangers besides. I know we will never get our money back if we leave, but we almost lost our son!"

Now for the first time John J. Cozad rose against his wife in the anger that he had turned upon so many men since he was twelve. Theresa stood still, the tilt of her head the same as for any polite reply or discussion, and before this poise, this quietness, the black eyes of the man softened and turned away.

But his determination was firm. "We stay; the rains have just begun," he said.

XVIII

THE FOURTH OF JULY was upon them and not at a good time, with so much barefaced animosity in the town. Whenever anything came up there was a revival of the gossip about King O'Dell and his Kitty, and then the rumors of the faro games in the livery stable, with, some liked to say, some who weren't there, that a deputy sheriff had been bluffed out when counterfeit money was found on Cozad's son.

"Where there's smoke there's fire——"

Then there was the bull whip taken to Handley of the other livery stable, and Riggs thrown out of the hotel, but the real local animosity seemed to come from men like Alf Pearson and most of the other Cozad settlers who were going into cattle. True, the trouble with Pearson started before that, back when he tried to tell John Cozad where to put his bridge. Many, now that they had their land, their start, were suddenly against any more settlement, particularly against anyone locating homeseekers on government land. Many forgot that only a few years ago they were peppering range cattle with rock salt or worse, often from a borrowed old double-barrel ten-bore, owing Cozad for the very land under their feet.

With so much feeling in the community, it seemed better not to try a large general celebration. Instead, the day was turned over to the Sunday school in the hope that this would keep troublemakers and trouble away. And send the spenders to Plum Creek or the roadhouse at the Plum bridge, so for finances Sam Schooley collected fifty cents apiece from the boys who had the money, and doled out small tasks to the girls, methodically checking off one name after the other.

By the first of July the crops were fine and everybody tried to shut out the memory of the gray shimmering clouds that had blighted so much of the other years. John Cozad brought back large hay contracts and this year he hoped to fill them all, keep range cattle out, become a real hay magnate.

With Dave Claypool, he drove homeseekers over his holdings, even those who frankly said they had no money for fancy meadows. He wasn't anxious to sell his hay flats just now anyway, but he wanted to show the newcomers what the country produced, pointing his buggy whip to the fine leaf of the grass, the rich seed topping the annuals. But it was the perennials that made the hay, standing to the shoulder of a horse most places in a couple of weeks, and taller by cutting time, with very little rough, inedible stalk—waste to clutter up the mangers.

Once more he saw signs of cattle running on his hay everywhere, grazed spots, fresh cow chips. Several places they had to drive out several hundred head—wild Longhorns probably brought straight from Texas by the big outfits moving in on them all the time. The stock was wild all right, practically leaving the country when Claypool got out and started toward them afoot, swinging the dust robe.

"But they'll be back soon's we're gone," he said. "Best feed in the nation. The Platte valley used to keep millions of buffaloes, the fattest and finest——"

That evening at the post office John Cozad spoke publicly about the cattle on his hay land. He would make the rounds, giving the owners fair warning to keep the stock off or it would be taken up. Theresa heard of this with real alarm. "Oh, John, you can't go to do this yourself, not with your temper—your proud temper," she amended. "Don't go among your enemies unless you take Traber and Dave along."

"Dave has his paper to get out and Traber is away."

"Then wait——"

"No, there's not a day to be lost—if they bluff me on this with the smaller herds they'll overrun all my land. The warning must go out tomorrow."

"Then send Robert," the mother urged, justifying her selection with the excuse that this son was well liked almost everywhere.

So Robert was sent, going uneasily, doubting whether he could make the cattle owners take much notice of any warning he carried. But it was a fine day and Darby needed the exercise. He removed the gun holster from the horn and slipped it into the slicker behind the cantle, tied the coiled bull whip with the lasso string and started northeastward, heading out along the meadows, to swing back by the bridge.

Near the edge of town he made an excuse to stop, put off the disagreeable task by a little looking at Mr. Swepston's crops. His corn and potatoes were considered the best in the region and Traber Gatewood, back this morning from a dental trip, said there were none better anywhere, not even in Ohio. Robert, with his growing knack of talking to his elders, visited a while with Lon Swepston, reporting the compliment from Traber, making conversation about the rain, the danger of grasshoppers, and Johnny's accident in the river.

"That showed real pluck—and the sense to hold his breath," the settler said matter-of-factly. "I thought sure he was a goner."

But finally there was nothing left to do but ride on, let Mr. Swepston get back to his work. At the Graham place the father and son were plowing corn, the unfenced field noticeably untouched by their cattle that they were running on other people's land.

" 'Corn knee high by the Fourth of July, farmer fly high,' " Robert sang as he rode up. His voice was plainly uncertain these days but perhaps that might help make his message less awkward. At least the Grahams stopped their horses but remained between the cultivator handles.

"Father says you must keep your cattle off our land as we want to cut the grass for hay."

"The hell he does!— And sends a boy on a man's errand to tell me!"

Robert Cozad drew himself up in the saddle. "This notice is really unnecessary, sir. As you know, stock found trespassing anywhere can be taken up by the owner of the land and held for damages and court costs. Nebraska Herd Law, you know."

He said this with the Cozad curl on his wind burned lips and worked to get the confident hardness up into his eyes.

But Graham just spit a brown trickle of tobacco juice between the corn rows and clucked to his team. He did lift his long-lashed whip from the ground and glance up at the boy. but with a twist of the arm, he flicked the lash over his horses. When he looked back, Robert was headed for the Cozad hay land to whoop the Graham cattle out and send them flying for the higher prairie with a few pops of his bull whip. Then he rode past the Grahams, the whip stock still in his hand, the long length of the rawhide popper caught up.

"Next time you will find those cows in our hay yard until the damages are paid," he said, and as the man started toward him, Robert touched Darby with the spurs and was gone.

He stopped at three more places. Two turned out about the same as at Graham's. At Pearson's cow camp there was nobody home and no cattle around although fresh cow chips were plain all through the Cozad hay plot near there. At the bridge Robert picketed Darby and then doctored his new attack of poison ivy with the niter solution. The heat made the poison very itchy and the inside of his knees were saddle-galled and stinging in the sweat. Afterward he oiled the cross-cut saw with a thin layer of axle grease and then tried to rest a little in the shade of the big cottonwood out on the bottoms. With his hands behind his head he watched the orioles feed their young in the pretty swinging nests, hoping to doze off. But he was still too nervous from facing the men who were deliberately destroying his father's hay crop. They had bull-dozed the son today, and he had let them.

Finally Robert got up and went back to the bridge. He looked down into the clear water until the bridge began to fly upstream and tried to think about his Runty Papers, the long continued story he was writing. He wanted another ad-venture or two for his minstrels, something to write up after supper tonight, with maybe a picture or two—gay colors, red and orange, to set off the blackface. But he couldn't concen-trate and his hands still shook if he didn't keep them in his pockets.

Two nights before the celebration those who were to sing gathered at Julia Gatewood's for a little practice. Robert was surprised to see two of the men he had been sent to warn about cattle on the Cozad lands pushing up around Traber Gatewood's folding organ with the rest, and singing as lustily. The group worked mostly as a chorus but Gene Young set aside a quartet and gave them a little practice on "Yankee Doodle" and "Home, Sweet Home."

When it was time to leave there was such a thunder and wind that none could start home. So they sang on, from "Carry Me Back to Old Virginnie" through livelier and more foolish airs, as Theresa called them, particularly after "Dixie," which was followed from the Union men by "Marching through Georgia." From his place beside Traber to turn the music when necessary, Robert saw the changes in many faces, the eyes darkened by the lamplight, people seeming to move apart although no step had been taken.

Old Matthews started up some of his old Irish songs, including "Jimmie, Go Ile the Cairs" and then "Father, Dear Father, Come Home with Me Now," forgetting about poor O'Neil's drunken death in the hotel fire not much over a hundred feet away, the newcomers roaring it out hilariously. From that is was only to be expected that some of the men from around Handley's livery stable would start up "The Bride of the Gamblin' Man," Traber chording it as he did many of the others, his face as unmoved, his heavy shoulders bent forward over the small instrument as his feet worked the treadles.

So they sang until after midnight and still the street was a gray rushing stream in the downpour. Those who lived nearby made a run for it under bumbershoots, slickers, or even tin washtubs and dishpans. Four or five stayed with the Cozads, the boys doubling up.

The next morning water stood over the prairie. Old buffalo wallows that had been barely noticeable because they were long overgrown suddenly became ponds dotting the Platte valley much as they did when the buffaloes deepened them by rolling in the mud against the gnats that burrowed through the wool to the tender skin.

The Independence Day celebration wasn't too exciting for Robert and the other young people. A sort of brush arbor fifty, sixty feet long and about as wide as a room had been set up on the school grounds. In this shade benches were made of some of the planks bought for the bridge laid on nail kegs and blocks of wood. The wagons and horsebackers came early, even some walkers heading in from as far as fifteen, twenty miles—those from the south hauled over the river in a duck boat borrowed at Willow Island. At noon boards were laid over salt and flour barrels and covered with varying napery, the fine damask of Theresa Gatewood's girlhood next to a tablecloth of flour sacks bleached and hemstitched together by a settler's wife.

The elders ate first, then the young people and the children. Afterward there was a patriotic address by Ed Young, Gene's brother, and more speeches, one by a professor from Indiana out looking the country over, and another by a nurseryman ready to take orders for shrubs and trees, both flowering and fruit. There were the candidates running for office too, this presidential year, men speaking for themselves or for others of their party.

Mrs. Gatewood sent Lewy Owens over from the store with a bucket of lemonade to sell at five cents a glass. Robert and his cousin helped, the boys free to drink all they wanted. They did so well that the grandmother sent over figs and cigars to sell when the lemons were gone.

The picnic went off smoothly enough and broke up around four. Those living far away had to hurry home to the cows to be milked, the hogs to slop, the hens to lock up against the varmints. Skunks, weasels, and coyotes were getting very bold now that some of them had tasted the sweet meat of dominicker pullets. It was as well that the picnickers scattered early because with dark there was another thunderstorm.

The morning of the fifth John Cozad went to the bridge and found the uprights of the pile driver broken off close. It looked like the work of the storm, although it wasn't as violent as half a dozen that the big hammer had withstood without losing so much as a match-sized sliver of wood. Many suspected that this was some villainy against John Cozad and his town, perhaps by men from the picnic or from among those Robert had warned to keep their cattle off the Cozad hay lands. Perhaps some of the Plum Creekers hired some rascals who unfortunately were common enough around the Cozad neighborhood to destroy the pile driver while everybody was celebrating. From now on the work at the river must never be left alone, not even on a day of patriotic duty.

While Johnny and his grandfather moved to the bridge, Robert stayed to help his mother get ready for a change in their way of living. Mrs. Gatewood's business was flourishing so, now that there were crops, that she had no time or space for her boarders. Next week the Cozads would set up housekeeping in the hotel, with Theresa cooking the meals, the boys to help with the serving and the dishes.

But there was still a little time for Robert's writing. Theresa Cozad saw to that. The blank book he ordered for the extention of his comic Runty Papers came, and he started to rewrite them, with pictures across the tops of the pages, showing Bones, Banjo, Tambo and Fiddle, Bones and Tambo cutting monkeyshines, the others funny too. When it came Robert's turn to stay with his grandfather at the bridge the Platte was little more than a shallow fanning of tepid water meandering over rain-dappled sandbars. The old man cooked the meals, mostly very simple, just meat and bread, with perhaps a can of tomatoes or peaches, but his coffee was better than Robert's mother made and, besides, the youth liked the stories his grandfather told. Why, Robert Gatewood had gone along the Overland Trail there south of the river twenty-five years ago—captain of a wagon train that had to stop for days to let the buffalo herds pass.

"Was Pa along?" Robert asked, but the old man didn't reply and the boy was not brought up to insist.

By mid-July John Cozad had settled some good sturdy German homeseekers, and Robert wondered if they had families, perhaps a young daughter with thick blond braids and the dark blue eyes. There was a promise of a shoemaker for the town too, and a discussion about a saloon, although some said there was enough whisky around now, and saloons would only attract more gun-packing cowboys. Let the roadhouse, the hogranch at Plum Creek bridge, deal with them.

"I don't think Mr. Cozad's for saloons here; he don't do any of his gambling around his family, don't even talk about it, I hear. I never saw him touch a card, even socially," Sam Schooley said.

What the community needed, however, was more sociability, more parties and get-togethers at something besides the horseshoe games out in front of Mrs. Gatewood's store or the unending seven-up and pitch games going on at the livery barns. Some said there was blackjack and a little crap-shooting on a horse blanket down there too.

Yes, there should be more parties, both private and those on-the-wind, meaning by wind-borne invitation, with everybody who heard about them welcome to come. That might draw in some of the young ladies from the outlying settlements, and encourage more of them to make their homes right here in Cozad—more girls like Lulu Chase and Minnie Graves. Those two newcomers were beginning to make the town hum a little. First thing they did was get up a Phantom Party at the Cozad quarters in the hotel. "Planning to catch a husband——" John Handley told the men who played cards down at his place.

On the big night music from Traber's organ, a guitar, and a violin spilled out of the open windows into the July night. It drew more and more ghosts with much laughing and guessing of identity. Robert got into it too with a faded old calico wrapper, a big bustle and a flour sack over his head with holes for the eyes. He liked to think that everybody took him for a lady. The men did draw him into the quadrilles and promenades. Not even Johnny seemed to see through his disguise and asked for a waltz. He got it, but not a word of conversation. That Robert didn't dare risk.

Many thought the best thing was not the costumes but Mr.

and Mrs. Wolf waltzing and dancing the schottische together. It was like at Spiles in Cincinnati. Several times Robert felt a little homesickness for the old place in Ohio and the Friday night affairs at the dancing school that the brothers attended. The finest couple there were his parents, of that he was sure, now as he looked back upon it.

There was another event to draw customers to Cozad and to Julia Gatewood's lemonade bucket—a walking race that grew out of a bet between Traber Gatewood and Curtis, the newcomer who played the guitar. It seemed there were several local sports around willing to put considerable money on one man or the other. A track was laid out with two tents, one for Traber, the other for the opponent. The men came in costume, Traber in red, Curtis in blue—velvet caps, gold-fringed shirts, knee britches with gold trimming, and baseball shoes.

The contestants started out side by side for the first lap, then turned and headed in opposite directions, alternating this way throughout the race. From the start the Red, Traber, took the lead and by noon he was two and a half miles ahead, to Robert's whooping satisfaction. But in the afternoon the moderation of Curtis began to pay off. He overtook Traber and held the lead a long, long time, although Robert ran around beside the track, urging his uncle on. To keep his own spirits up, the boy ate a great deal of ice cream, his reward for selling it at the track. The betting rose as the afternoon dragged on, with several side races, short ones, outside the track, sprints, real foot races. All the time the crowd was getting noisier and larger, as though the wind really carried the news.

But in the end Curtis won, and Traber Gatewood had nothing but sore feet for his trouble. Robert looked in on the two men lying stretched out on the cool wood floor in the Gatewood dining room. He went away, determined not to watch a relative or friend in any grueling contest again. He couldn't stand to have those he liked hurt, even by a silly defeat in a walking race.

Then suddenly everything was changed. A horsebacker came spurring in from the north, yelling, the dust strung out behind him shining in the evening sun.

"Your dad——" he called to Robert, "Where's your dad? There's a scheme to kill him tonight——"

Slowly the boy took a step backward, then whirled and started for Traber, but he stopped himself, remembering his uncle stretched out on the floor, and some questions the man should be asked. "Who are you?" and "Who told you this?"

But the horsebacker was already reining down a side street and heading back north.

XIX

ROBERT LOOKED after the dust of the stranger who had come shouting that his father was to be killed tonight. He sneaked a glance toward the hotel, and saw no sign of anyone behind the curtains looking out. Not his mother or anyone, and suddenly he realized that those who might have seen the man probably thought he was just another drunken cowboy or perhaps someone sent to throw a scare into the community. Several children played hide-and-seek up near the brick kilns, one running hard for the schoolhouse corner. Several men were plodding up from one of the livery stables toward the Riggs hotel for supper. Minnie Graves' Persian cat walked idly toward a robin pulling at a worm.

It seemed that Robert must have dreamed the man and his alarm, except that there was still the thin, spreading haze of dust. Slowly the boy went homeward and waited for his mother to come in, probably over comforting his Uncle Traber. When she returned she took the father's place at the head of the table and while Robert served the plates she took out her napkin and exclaimed at the foolishness of men, sometimes.

"A walking race!" she said. "In the middle of the hot and busy summer."

Afterward Robert excused himself and prepared to watch through the night. But he fell asleep and the next thing he knew it was morning and no one had been disturbed. But he did not forget the warning and although he decided not to mention it even to his father when he returned with the excursion from Cincinnati, the son knew there were people, maybe many people, who wanted to kill the man who was settling up the government lands, lands the ranchers hoped to use for nothing forever.

Or perhaps the man yesterday really was just trying to scare them, to make the Cozad family uneasy with the father gone, as several of the more timid and remote settlers had been scared out. But usually that was by dumping a noose on the doorstep in the night, particularly just after Mitchell and Ketchum were killed, like the bullets in the tobacco sack at Grandpa Robert's door. Lately it was often a bullet in a Bull Durham sack tossed through a lighted window, or the bullet sent more directly, perhaps whistling over the head of a plowman ripping his breaker bottom through the virgin prairie like a pocketknife going up the belly of a Platte River catfish.

Perhaps the horsebacker was just amusing himself like a pack of boys dropping a .22 bullet into a flock of feeding prairie chickens, just to watch them scatter. But people could be a little like some prairie chickens. Sometimes the whole flock just looked up at the sound of the shot, even if one among them was hit and fluttering around, dying, some of the others perhaps coming up to pick at the wounded bird, as if to punish it for acting so silly. In the meantime more shots might come, more and more birds be hit, and the rest still only curious or reprimanding until finally one bird took fright and flew, the rest now following in panic, but too late for the dead and the dying.

Still, Robert decided to wait about telling anyone of his warning.

August came and although the rains had stopped, the grass-hoppers were barely plentiful enough to please the young fishermen of the valley. New signs were going up for old and new businesses: Wolf's shoeshop, the four livery stables that the town and the homeseekers were supporting, the new drug-store not far from Traber Gatewood's, the butchershop, and even a blacksmith shop open steadily now in addition to those rising out in the settlements. Mrs. Gatewood had new signs made too, a big one: DRY GOODS, for the west end of her barny frame building, GROCERY across the south, and POST OFFICE on the east, with a smaller one, CIGARS & TOBACCO beside the door. She looked at these with pride—all from the hundred dollars she had put into a few notions and goods six years ago.

The hay business was also booming. Out on the Cozad meadows the contract mowers were cutting around and around, the tall grass shivering and falling before the whirring sickle bars. The flowers went too, and late nestlings, young rabbits, and any snakes out of their holes, particularly in hay flats never touched by the roaring machine of man before. The hay was fine, leafy and curing fast so long as the rains held off. The little steam engine of the press, the baler, puffed steadily.

Work on the bridge had started again too, and Robert found his rides, his fishing, even his swims curtailed. There was talk about Johnny going to Denver to manage the sale and delivery end of the hay marketing but a kick by a horse laid him up and Robert took over his brother's work at the bridge earlier than had been planned.

"You sure have had bad luck this summer," he said when he came home and found Johnny in bed, his lean face tight with pain. "Almost drowned in the hole the flood made at the bridge and now that mean horse."

Theresa came in with a cold pack. "We need a doctor in the family," she said, but her light tone did not cover the deep agitation Robert saw in her eyes for his brother again, a concern he had never seen there for himself. Perhaps because he never seemed to get into accidents very often or those other difficulties of Johnny's, like the suspicion over the depot fires. Outside of the faro tramps—and that was very bad—his own troubles were mostly sleeping late and forgetting to speak to this or that personage. Not out of rudeness, he once defended, but because he hadn't noticed them.

"That is insult piled upon bad manners," his mother had replied.

By mid-August the bridge was being pushed in upon the stream from both sides in spite of the heat, the buffalo gnats, and the mosquitoes. There were usually seventeen, eighteen men and ten teams going now. The Freeman brothers had set up a cook tent and offered what Robert, the critical, reported were splendid meals.

"Hunger makes a good sauce," Theresa commented.

With the men working ten hours and the sons not able to spell each other now, Robert had to be up at five and keep going until sundown. He thought about his Runty Papers and the pictures of the minstrels he had planned, but there wasn't even time to join the Wolf boys in a little fishing or in their long, lazy swims. Perhaps it was as well, with poison ivy spreading even to the bridge workers now, from the sap of the cut roots where they scraped off the soil for the bridge, the doctor said. Robert mixed up buckets of the sweet spirits of niter solution for them but it didn't prevent contamination.

Although the hot south winds were curling the corn that had grown so lush and tall earlier, there was rain up the Platte, even cloudbursts, the river suddenly flooded so deep that Darby was in over his back taking Robert to the workers on the south side. At the height of the flood he had to cross over a second time to deal with some contractors wanting to put in the south dam of sod. The boy came back tired in the evenings but proud that he had discharged what was usually Johnny's job or Sam Schooley's, when Sam had time from his homestead. This was all in addition to Robert's own work at the hay press, keeping the books for the help, the output, and the hay cars being loaded on the siding, seeing that everything ran smoothly.

With the hay curing just right and more rain due any day, John Cozad put on a night shift for the press when he returned. Sam Schooley managed these but sometimes Robert stayed out too, catching a few hours of sleep in the hay. Perhaps to make the work seem easier to the boy, the father told Robert that he planned to take him to Denver for a short time to check on hay prices and prospects while he looked after a little of his other business, the money business, down around Larimer Street and up at Leadville.

But the time for the trip came and passed, with Johnny still weak from the horse kick. The father had written for boardinghouse accommodations at Denver for Johnny, at Leadville for Robert, saying he planned to bring his sons up to oversee the hay marketing. But Theresa reminded him that not even a responsible fifteen-year-old like Robert could be sent alone to the wild boom town of Leadville. Besides, John Cozad decided that the place was too high, at least 10,000 feet elevation, he thought, and mighty unhealthy for a boy whose father had fought consumption for years. But he needed a reliable helper to make the most of the mining-camp markets. Actually he needed a reliable man here too, one with the loyalty of his own sons and with Robert's judgment, his daring if trouble came. When the flood receded, Sam Schooley returned to the bridgework, leaving Dave Claypool alone at the *Hundredth Meridian* so he couldn't be away more than a day or two between publications. Besides, Johnny was still too weak to be much help in trouble, particularly the kind that the father's extra business in Denver might bring.

"Perhaps Traber can take the time to go up there with you for a few weeks," Theresa suggested, not for the first time.

Her husband gave no sign of hearing. There were things that he wished to keep from Theresa or at least from her overt knowledge, so he talked Dave Claypool into making arrangements to go along. The disappointed Robert helped Dave carry Johnny's little leather trunk to the depot in the sudden downpour that came out of nowhere, but the special tickets for the three had not come in from Omaha so John Cozad started west alone and then was back the next day. Out toward North Platte, where the river valley narrowed to a sort of canyon and pushed the tracks out upon the Platte banks, the flood yesterday had washed away a whole section. The colonizer was furious as a caged gray wolf, pacing, pacing at the delay.

The tickets arrived the next day and the three started again, Robert watching them go as he held the impatient Darby down. Then he hurried to the hayfield where Bill Claypool was to try starting the press after a breakdown two days ago. They were behind with the baling and Robert had been ordered to watch the machine start and to decide whether there was too much danger of tearing it to pieces, to stop it if it didn't seem to run smoothly. He listened to the clamor of the engine and the bang of the gears and ordered the machine stopped.

"No, go on, go on! John J. is in a hurry to have the hay ready for shipping," Traber Gatewood said.

Bill Claypool threw the baler into gear, and once more Robert commanded him to stop. "Father left *me* in charge here," he said firmly, his young face pale at his daring, but determined.

Bill dropped his hands from the starting lever. "Dammit, I can't work for two bosses and one of them a snot-nose kid!"

"You have only one boss. I was left in sole charge of the hay business," Robert said, trying to sound as much like his father as seemed possible.

"You're an overbearing whippersnapper!" his uncle shouted. "Get back to your bale counting."

"You get back to your tooth cobbling, sir," Robert retorted, and motioned the curious hay crew off to their work. When his Uncle Traber took a step toward the youth, Robert squared himself and pulled up the old knickerbockers he was wearing out at work, knowing that his uncle could send him rolling with one fist but standing his ground the best he could.

The man hesitated. "Your mother will hear of this!" he shouted.

"And father too. I shall wire him tonight," Robert replied coldly.

Knowing that it was over, the hay hands scattered back to their work, leaving the boy with his victory, but shaking so now that he had to ram his hands into his pockets to hide his shame from the grown men around him.

There was, however, still his mother to face, for surely his uncle would keep his threat. There might be trouble with his grandparents too, so the boy stayed out as long as he could, busying himself at the hay flats yet to be cut, driving out stock. Then he came upon a bunch of horses from a string of covered wagons camped on Cozad land, trampling down acres of the best hay, killing out a great circle dotted with fire spots. They looked like boomers, as his father called people like that—pretending to be seeking homes but preferring the road and living off the land, off any fields and gardens, chickens, pigs, and calves along the way, and not above picking up a milk cow or wagon horses. Robert spurred straight into camp and told the man who came over that they were trespassing, that the land was his father's, and they must move immediately, pointing out government land they were free to occupy now and forever if they cared to file on it.

The man looked at Robert's old knee pants and laughed, but the boy refused to go, letting his hand rest on the horn holster while more of the dark-bearded men stalked over, gathering around Darby in a threatening circle, shutting the boy in, one of the men with his hand on the sheath of his knife, the women standing off some distance, their arms wrapped in the security of their aprons. Many of the children, always quick to sense a conflict, had stopped their play and were watching, those nearby barefooted and half naked in their rags.

Before the hard-faced men Robert remembered Mr. Matthew's orders against drawing a gun on bluff and had a sudden idea. He unsnapped the cover of a saddlebag and, drawing out a pouch, poured a sliding palmful of rattles into his hand to show the watching circle.

"These represent part of over a hundred rattlesnakes killed around here this summer, over a dozen of them on the sandy spot off there toward the river," Robert said, pointing to where the small boys were digging and running.

After one disbelieving look, the anger-darkened eyes grayed in concern, in fear, the hands of the men showing their agitation, the women too far to see, to realize, but sensing the uneasiness. Some began to edge over as the men turned toward their children.

"Here, you, Cash, you Eddie!" one called to the boys.

The children everywhere stopped to look. As the identification of what Robert held in his palm spread to the women, the recognition of its meaning, its horror, moved into their sunburnt faces. Suddenly one after another gathered up her skirts and searched the ground around her feet, then the deep grass before her as she ran for the small children or stood at the edge of the trampled area calling in an anxious, high-pitched voice.

"Eddie! Eddie!– Dolly, come here!"

"Frederich, stand still, baby! Mama's coming!"

Robert nodded his head toward the road. "Go camp on some bare spot, or on short curly grass." Casually he poured the rattles back into the pouch, dropped it into the saddlebag, and slacked up on Darby's impatient reins. Half a mile away he looked back, to see the wagons already beginning to move out.

Robert felt good until halfway home. Then he recalled the spat with his Uncle Traber over the hay press, and doubted whether the rout of the campers would save him.

"Of course you had to protect the baler," Theresa said, when he came in at last. "But I cannot have you showing disrespect for your uncle or for any of your elders. You must know why it is so very important that my sons learn to control themselves, particularly you——"

Robert understood what she meant and all he could say was, "Yes, ma'am," but he was determined never to wear those old knickerbockers again.

The next issue of the *Hundredth Meridian* shocked Robert so he ran home with the paper spread between his outstretched hands. Mr. Claypool's name was gone from the masthead. Elijah Mosher's was in its place, and, much as Robert hated to admit it, the paper looked neater, the layout better, more pleasing. On the second page there was something else for Robert's eye, a piece about his father:

> The amount of labor that is now going on in this imme-
> diate vicinity is wonderful. John J. Cozad is now furnish-
> ing employment to scores of people, many of whom
> would be compelled to leave their claims to hunt em-
> ployment to get a means of support during the coming
> winter; besides the bridge work he is letting out hay
> contracts, so all that will work may, and at a fair price.
> A ride over the fields shows many willing. Mr. Good-
> year from Custer County has the largest contract, run-
> ning 4 mowers and expects to add 2 more in a few days;
> he is stacking from 30 to 35 tons of hay a day and will
> be at this about 3 weeks. He employs about 15 hands

> doing the work with a vim. Mr. Stonecipher is working on a 150 ton contract. Whipple & Chapin have a 200 ton contract. Several others also have contracted to put up hay. A hay press runs day and night for the western market, and occupies the attention of 16 to 18 men and bales 10 to 12 tons in ten hours. The press is run by steam. Will Claypool is captain of the Little Injun which runs steady as a top.

"Look!" Robert shouted, waving the paper in the doorway of his grandmother's store.

"Yes, we saw it," Theresa replied. "It is good to see some kind words for your father after so much malignment."

"But that's why Mr. Claypool could get away to go to Denver with Pa," Robert said in sudden realization.

"Yes, of course—but you knew the paper was up for sale or lease."

Oh, he had heard that for a long time, over a year at least, but he hadn't believed it—he hadn't believed that anything so close to their town as the *Hundredth Meridian* could be sold or even leased.

There was another editorial, one that Robert had missed in his excitement, a reply to a sarcastic piece about Mr. Mosher in the Dawson County *Pioneer* of Plum Creek. The *Pioneer*, John Cozad always said, was the mouthpiece of the rascals who opposed him ever since he came to the Platte, and was probably the outfit behind the breaking of the pile driver back in July, and a dozen other tricks. Of course a man like Mr. Mosher would irritate that stripe of Plum Creekers.

When John Cozad returned from the mountain towns he found two hundred tons of hay in stacks around town and over 3000 tons under contract to be cut, baled, and ready for the Denver, Leadville, and other markets. By then there was another outbreak of typhoid through the west, with several cases in Cozad and one death so far. This was Tom Stevenson, who died above the printing office. The jolly Irish immigrant was the father of John Stevenson, who had dragged Cozad into court some time ago in the hay-stealing case, claiming that Handley had been hired to haul away some of his hay to the Cozad yards. That was the trial Handley liked to tell about and brag that he knocked John J. Cozad down with a chair and broke his arm. But most people had liked old Tom, the father very well. He ran a threshing outfit and was as full of chaff inside, he used to say, as outside. Last year before the little grain grown was ready, he had helped Bill Claypool with the hay press.

John Cozad went to the funeral, conspicuous in his frock coat and silk hat. He even shook hands with the grieving son, and then walked back beside Robert, who was upset by all the tears and the loud Irish wailing of the Stevenson relatives.

"I don't like funerals," the boy protested. "I want to keep away from such sad feelings."

John Cozad looked down upon his earnest-faced son. "Sometimes you can't escape sad feelings—sometimes——"

But he was interrupted by Mrs. Riggs, of the opposition hotel across the street, and although he tipped his hat politely to her, there were no more words from him until they reached home, and Robert felt that somehow he had been cheated of a story from his father's early life.

Afterward Robert and the father made the rounds of the bridge and the haying together, the Cozad buggy team fat from disuse anyway, and shying at every weed or scurrying creature. But the man drove them with his customary close line and whip, the tassel just over the backs of the horses, always ready for a cut, swift and sharp. He said little until on the way home. Then he spoke of Denver, where Johnny was staying to care for the hay sales and collections. He had leased a big barny building to store the hay as a sort of supply depot for the mining towns. Denver itself was growing fast, livelier each time up, and building much better than the early cheap and shacky structures—too much like the old Elephant

248

Corral and the people that hung around there. Now fine buildings were going up, some by the English, like the new Windsor Hotel to be opened next year. But the building was not nearly swift enough, with hundreds of people, even families of some means, living in covered wagons and tents.

"I don't plan to station you at Leadville after all. No need for anyone there yet. But if there is a good school in Denver, I may send you there. I want a school that will develop your talents for writing and painting as you have developed into a manager of work and of men."

The boy flushed. "Then it's settled?" he asked, having to remember all the changed plans of his father.

"Well, Son, I hope to work it out, but we'll have to see. You have done very well here with the hay and the managing——"

The next day the press was repaired and started on a day-and-night run again. The first seven hours the men put out 240 bales—twelve tons. Although it was still the first week in September, the night seemed cold as winter. Robert stayed out until morning and almost froze. In a few days the weather warmed and the press was moved from meadow to meadow, the hay in fine green and fragrant windrows and cocks. Freight cars were shunted to the siding, loaded, and hauled out. Robert was very busy with the books, in charge of all the buying of provisions and repairs, and keeping track of the men, putting them on and laying them off as seemed best.

"My family depending for their bread on a kid in knee pants," one of the men complained, and others nodded. But they were glad, some of them, for even that much.

"You're looking thinnish, Bobbie," his grandmother complained one day when the boy slumped down on a bench in her store and dozed off right there before her eyes. "You're working too hard, and staying out there with the press all night, after a full day's work."

"Oh, I get a little snooze now and then in the hay. Besides, I take hardships as fun. I even hate to see Sunday come along," he admitted, and dragged himself off to bed, barely hearing Julia Gatewood's laugh. "He's a one, isn't he?" she asked of those waiting for the mail distribution.

Even some who were open enemies of the Cozads grinned a little, good-naturedly.

"You can laugh, but Cozad couldn't do without the boy here."

"Yeh, but he gets mighty big for his britches sometimes, and you can't knock him down like you could a man, like some has his dad," one of the hands from the livery stable pointed out.

"But you know that if Robert's keeping the accounts they're correct. He's always got his mind on his business," Bill Claypool said. "You know what he told me the other day? Same thing as here: 'My work, I make it fun,' he said. I think he's busting a tug to please his father—get him to take him to Denver."

In a few days things didn't seem to be running so smoothly. John Cozad fired Campbell and the Beardsleys and looked for another cook in place of Mrs. Beardsley, if not this fall at least for next year. Perhaps his temper was shortened by the rain, suddenly falling day after day, wetting the hay through, spoiling the color and the value. The rain soaked the men too and held up the work for a solid week. And when the sun came out and the press was thumping again, there was the perennial trouble of all the settlers along the Platte—the trail herds eating their way northward across the nation, taking grass wherever they found it. Settlers with corn patches or a jag of hay or even a garden patch had to stand out with their guns to turn the herds aside. Some put the children to

250

work at it but uneasily, knowing how reckless some of the cowboys were.

Then, in the midst of all the trouble and the delays, Robert heard a really disquieting rumor. It seemed that a secret petition was being circulated among the cowboys passing through, every name welcomed by the ranchers and their hands and by the Beardsleys, Campbells, Riggs, Handleys, Stevensons, Pearsons, and others. Robert decided it was something he should know about because everybody fell silent if he appeared while the long papers were being handed around for the name, or the X of the illiterate, somebody always hurrying to roll the sheets up, turning the talk to the weather or the delays in the railroad and in moving the national capital west.

After several attempts to find out about the petition, he tried to forget it and catch up on his reading that had been pushed aside for slacker times: Dickens, Jules Verne, Mark Twain, even Mary J. Holmes. But now and then he had to try one book after another to keep his mind from wandering and finally the painting failed too, so strong was his curiosity about the petition. Sometimes he recalled something else—the man who had come riding with the warning that John Cozad was to be killed. That must have been just a scare. Maybe the petition rumor was only more of that, the rolls of paper that he saw people signing just something about the county seat, the bridge or schools, or some other appeal to the county commissioners. But then why wasn't there something in the paper about it and why wasn't it passed openly, when Traber or Mr. Schooley or the Claypools were in the crowd?

XX

THE DAPPER YOUTH named John A. Cozad, with a business card identifying him as the Denver representative of the hay producer, John J. Cozad, wrote home almost every day, often to Robert. He suggested that his brother saddle up and cut across the country to Denver with Darby and Nimrod, the gentler of Johnny's two horses. Nimmy would be better for town than Forked Lightning, always faunching to run or buck. Robert could ride the horses in turn and be up in a few days. In Denver they could go for some fast canters in the park and along the fashionable bridle paths, called trails here. They would make a fine showing, a proper one for two young gentlemen in the mining capital.

But as Robert had foreseen, he couldn't get away. There were, however, some amusements even around Cozad. Not that he got to do much about these either. He didn't go plumming although almost everybody else did, taking day-long trips to the breaks off north or making a real outing of it, with tents or borrowed prairie schooners or at least bedrolls in the back of the wagon. Usually the boys and even a few of the girls, such as Mollie Claypool and her friends, went horseback with perhaps some of the homesteaders' daughters on the plumming trails too, probably riding bareback as they had most of the summer days watching their milk cows from straying, trying to haze the range cattle off the crops and the grass, perhaps even the melon patch this year, the best so far. True, the new invention, barbed wire, was coming in for the few who had the money to spend on loads of spiny wire spools for the four stout strands needed against the Longhorns. The posts could usually be cut somewhere on the free land up in the breaks, on the sly now, since the government started action against those harvesting telegraph-pole timber on the public domain. But many of the wild Texas cattle charged right through the fences, tearing them down, stringing the wire over the prairie. Apparently some of the cowboys didn't know what the wire was for either, although there was a fence war well started down in Texas. Cow hands ripped down any settler fences they struck, either with cattle or just riding across the prairie. They tore them down and left them down.

"No protection for settler property anywhere here," the sharp-tongued Handley, who had dared to take up range stock for damages, snorted when his fence was cut in a dozen places. "But there's ways of getting even." Nobody doubted that the Irishman would get even, good and even.

But plumming time came only once a year and seldom as fruitfully as this season, the thickets a lovely pinkish-red haze netted clear through the green from far off. Many usually tied down to hard survival managed to get away for this community event, somehow much more compelling even than the Fourth of July, perhaps because plumming was a sort of ceremonial to a fruitful year long before one furrow was cut from the sod of the earth anywhere. But most of the people who went out thought only of getting a little fruit for preserves and jelly if there was sugar, for scalding and spreading out to dry if there was none—any way to preserve it. Besides

253

they got at least one day's escape from the empty, treeless prairie and the monotony of far neighbors or none at all.

John Robert Gatewood and Lewy Owens and half a dozen other striplings from Cozad went, and Robert got the promise of perhaps a day or so, sometime later, when the big contractors like Goodyear and Stonecipher were done, the hay they cut all safely baled and loaded.

The wagons came back with tubs and blankets full of plums and chokecherries, some wild grapes just turning, and the strangeness of a day adventuring upon the pickers. John Robert and Lewy had to ride home slowly, their slickers full and round as yellow melons behind the saddles; so prodigal rich was the crop of plums this year that nobody could resist the picking. For several days the town and far soddies and shacks were fragrant with the rich smell of wild plum preserves, jellies, and butter, or collecting flies and wasps to their drying on canvas or papers or old sheets, under mosquito bar, or with perhaps a small girl shooing the swarming insects off with a leafed willow switch or a waving dish towel.

"There will be very little scurvy around our town next winter," Johnny replied to Robert's enthusiastic report of the plum preserves their mother was sending to Denver for a taste of home.

There were other plans for amusement and entertainment in Cozad during the coming winter. The Dramatic Club was reorganized and although Robert had to find out about it in the paper, and was hurt by that, he was told he had a place on the active list and Johnny too, if he returned. This year Robert was to be an actor, not just a scene painter.

During the weeks of rain Robert did find some time to catch up a little on his diary, with fewer pictures because by then John Cozad was gone again, off east, perhaps Omaha, leaving the urgent correspondence to Robert. He returned with a fine roll of greenbacks and a palmful of gold—not like the last time, when the curious Cozad luck failed him, some-how.

He had also called on the U.P. officials to thank them for the new hay spur built at Cozad and got the promise of another one. If his plans worked out there was to be a large warehouse to hold the loose hay, the hay press, and the ricked bales. Here the hay could be brought in as soon as dry and then baled when convenient, rain or shine or depth of winter storm. Such a place would have preserved the quality of the hay and a lot of the quantity too, when the rains stretched into October this year.

Robert thought about this while the cars were being loaded and the hay camp shacks moved to town for the winter, and finally the hay press too, with the smoking Little Injun drag-ging it along. There was one aspect to all the plans and activ-ities that depressed Robert. Evidently his father was concen-trating the whole hay business here, instead of expanding into Denver.

It was true that with his plans lagging at Washington, John Cozad had decided to spread out here in the valley, extending his options to more railroad lands. Then he hurried off to Denver to clear up some business there and later to concen-trate on excursions for the new places he could offer. Robert was uneasy about the Denver trip. He heard that someone, man or woman, who came to the supply station there was looking not for hay but for trouble.

Robert pushed this into the dark areas of his mind that he must not expose to light, back beside the mysterious petition he knew was still going the rounds, and the warning of the man that his father was to be killed, perhaps meaning any time, and always his uneasiness about such men as the faro tramps, come for blackmail at the least, more surely for a lynching.

Then there was the woman who got off the eastbound train last week, while the father was at Omaha. All the family ex-cept Robert and Julia Gatewood were away picking frost-sweetened buffalo berries and wild grapes. The woman was rather pretty, Robert thought, in a soft silk dress, blue with white speckles, and moving in a cloud of perfume that was as sweet as a spring rose patch with the wind on it. When Mrs. Gatewood saw her, she asked the woman to set her valise down, motioned Robert out, and brewed her a cup of tea. Afterward she put her to bed until the night train going east. Then the grandmother called Robert from his room to take the woman down, and behind her back held a finger across her lips in the gesture of silence.

It seemed the woman was looking for a man named John Cozad and that she didn't know who Robert was. "Your family came out with Mr. Cozad's colony?" she asked, and to this all Robert dared say was, "Yes."

"Do you know whether Mr. Cozad might be on the way out with another colony?" she wanted to know, and to this Robert replied, "No," volunteering nothing more. But he listened at the window of the depot and heard her ask for a ticket to Cincinnati, saw the glint of the gold in her purse as she paid for it.

When Robert returned to the lighted living room of his grandmother, his eyes were even darker than usual, even more than night-dark. The old woman stopped her furious knitting, her yarn finger arrested straight up with a twist of purple wool around it.

"You didn't say who you are?"

"No, just 'yes' when she asked if my folks came out with a colony of Mr. Cozad's, and 'no' meaning I did not know of a colony on the way now." This wasn't quite all the truth but the woman nodded an absent approval. "Go to bed—and forget that anybody was here."

Robert drew slowly away toward the door, his face troubled. But he hadn't grown up past fifteen as the son of John J. Cozad without learning not to ask questions. He wondered now if the story he overheard from a saddle salesman

256

out of Denver about a man looking for Cozad with a pistol, and the hurried note from Johnny about a troublemaker coming to the supply barn could have been connected with the woman in the speckled dress. Perhaps their father's awareness of her coming was behind that sudden run he made for the train to Omaha the night before the woman arrived. She had come out of the west, very likely from Denver or San Francisco, and somewhere far back in Robert's mind there seemed to be a memory of a similar occurrence in Cincinnati. He was small then, but suddenly now he connected his mother's illness in bed for a week or even longer with the appearance of that earlier woman. And since—there could have been a dozen other times, times he missed, or did not understand.

Robert watched Theresa Cozad when the fruiting party came home, with washtubs of buffalo berries and two flour barrels full to the top with wild grapes, layered between leaves to keep them from crushing, leaves good for the pickle barrels. He also watched the next day or so while she hurried around with the starched ties of her white apron flying out behind her. But if she heard about the woman she betrayed no sign of it and Robert had the sudden suspicion that she knew, that this had been a recurring circumstance of her life with their father. The possibility of this shocked the son's whole web of affection, his whole neat pattern of values that he had thought so final and finished. It shook the young complacency that had settled on him. Suddenly instead of being content with the work he did and with what he knew, considering it pretty much all that was important, this summer at least, he felt suddenly shallow and mean and ignorant of even the plainest events right before his eyes. Yet even now this self-doubt was just for moments between his rush of work as the only Cozad man around.

Almost everybody Robert knew seemed to be talking about the coming Dawson County Agricultural Society Fair, to be held at Cozad. There had been a lot of hope about that ever since last spring, with plans for a regular fairgrounds, a stripped race track for horses and one for men, with a $25 prize for the best walker and prizes for runners and long distance too, eventually, but not this year. And certainly there would be display buildings with eating accommodations and pens and sheds for the stock exhibits.

But somehow it all melted away like Cincinnati's ice palace did under the summer sun. The rag-chewing went on, with no agreement on anything, not even the date the fair was to open. Spinner, the coal, lumber, and hay-yard man, was president of the society and Traber Gatewood the secretary. They never agreed on anything and weren't ready to start now. Finally some of the townspeople and settlers around got together to prepare a place for at least a little something after a whole summer's wrangling. Instead of a fairgrounds they canvassed a lot of people to donate a day's work, mostly nailing together a few stands for the exhibitions alongside the schoolhouse. Some worked all through the night, sawing and hammering, and the next day the fair opened.

The people came early, the schoolhouse and the stands packed before noon, the empty lots somehow full of wagons, buggies, and saddle horses, but the quarreling officials didn't show up. David Claypool, so often the mainstay of Cozad the town and the man, took over and started some of the events going, now that the visitors were waiting. In the afternoon Spinner and Traber Gatewood finally came, a little sheepish. Few paid them any attention and Robert Cozad made a big point of ignoring them both, happy that he was no longer in knee pants. He decided to put his protest against their conduct into his diary, certain that the *Meridian* would not mention their unfitness for their position. He was disappointed that nobody, not even his mother, very pretty under her ruffled parasol, seemed to notice his conspicuous disapproval. Perhaps nobody was willing to give him that much satisfaction. This made him uneasy and reminded him of his father somehow, always feeling people were against him. The thought seemed disloyal but he forgot it as he strolled up to one group of men out among the wagons, hunting shade and talking, not about the fair officials but some about the exhibits, with an old complaint from John Handley.

"Did you see that bull whip of Robert Cozad's there? Getting more like his father every day," he said to the rest as the youth walked by with too much unconcern.

"He's steadier than the old man, and better handling people but just like a kid, he's took to feeling his importance so much you want to heat them damned new britches for him."

"Yes, I'd like to be around when he starts disapproving of old John J. Cozad himself."

Even the women, between the picnic baskets and talk of them, of children, chickens, and the gardens that had dried too fast toward fall, spoke some of the late crops and perhaps of the cattlemen eating them out. Nothing anywhere about the petition going the rounds that Robert could hear, nothing about the threat to kill John Cozad or the woman who came through last week.

After the prizes were awarded and most of the entries taken home, the Odd Fellows Hall above the schoolroom was thrown open for a big community dance. Goodyear, Erwin, the cattleman who hung around the town some, and Winchell, the big-talking, easygoing new storekeeper, came early but somehow everybody else seemed late, even the young couples. Robert had supper with his grandfather. Afterward they went to the hall, taking John Robert along, representatives of the town's builder, for certainly Theresa would not appear. There were still only two, three couples there, standing, waiting. The boys watched the door for some of the few girls and women in the region to come through it, but only stomping, laughing young fellows trooped in, and a few more men. Finally the couples left the hall to the noisy young bucks and the few older men like Grandpa Gatewood on the benches.

After a while somebody suggested a stag dance. Fiddler Ertile tuned up but at the very first pull of the bow the boys started a great yelling, swearing, and stomping.

Old Robert Gatewood, with whitening hair and leathered face, the oldest member of the local, ordered them to quiet down, dance right or get off the floor. Nobody paid any attention, particularly those who had been to the jugs hidden out at the wagons around the fair or down at the livery stables. They whooped and yelled through a quadrille that was more like a lot of milling, bawling Longhorns turned loose in a chicken yard. All the time Robert Gatewood kept getting madder, until he had to jump out on the floor and give them a good tongue-lashing.

All he got in return was a lot of saucy talk and Robert trying to coax him back to his bench. "It's not our business," he argued. "The officers of the fair and the lodge ought to be here. We don't own the hall——"

But the old man stood stubborn as a butcher's bulldog. "I'm a charter member of the Odd Fellows and I represent the rest. We want order in our hall."

Almost before he was done speaking, the door flew open to a kick and the two Finch boys and Oscar Ertile, the brother of the fiddler, burst in with a thundering racket, stomping their cowboy boots and cursing everything. The Finches divided, one stalking up each side of the hall, with Oscar pushing up the middle. As he passed Robert Gatewood he yelled out all the insults he could think of. The old man tried to shout him down, calling him a rowdy, a rascal.

"Oh, shut up, you old goat! You got no authority!"

"You're a liar!"

"You're another," Oscar roared out, "and you're going to get your damned old hide full of lead for this!"

260

Now there was a rush for the old man from all sides, all the tough boys and men there. It seemed he would be tromped down sure. Robert shouted for somebody to get Traber, and pushed in, raising his voice to outshout them all, including his grandfather. "You are all a pack of fools and cowards, to stir up such a fuss and talk about shooting a man as old as Grandpa. And Grandpa is pretty foolish to try to talk sense into your pudding heads!"

"We'll kill the old bastard!" Oscar Ertile shouted. "He's had it coming a long time; and all the rest of your damn outfit's going to get it too!"

Robert and his cousin hurried their grandfather out as fast as they could, glad to escape themselves. The next day it dawned on Robert that the Ertiles had planned the attack on the old man, to pay him for a grudge over something that happened at the bridge long ago, something that Robert never heard explained, something probably as foolish as the row up in the hall last night.

But Robert Cozad knew he had to be careful now, with the whole outfit from the dance probably waiting to jump him, pound him into the ground as men waylaid his father. Maybe he ought to carry his bull whip all the time, but it was still there among the exhibits, where it had won a prize. No, his pistol would be better, the one from his saddle holster, but his mother would never let him carry it in a cartridge belt, like a cowboy or a badman, and he had no frock coat yet to hide any gun on his hip, or even the smallest Lady Venger under his arm.

Robert hadn't been alarmed when his mother didn't come down to breakfast. But she didn't get up all day, or the next. The two Johns were expected in from Denver on every train but they didn't come, and when Robert went up to see how his mother felt, she turned her face to the wall, her dark hair a hiding cloud, loose and tangled.

"I don't want to see any of you," she cried out in anger.

"Not you or your father or my father either—not any of you!"

The boy stepped back, shocked at this loss of self-control. His mother must be very, very sick, surely delirious, to speak so. He ran down the stairs and out to the Gatewood store.

"Come quick, Grandma! Mother is very sick—out of her head."

"And no wonder," the old woman snapped, "with such a parcel of fools as the menfolks in this family." But she slipped the smelling salts into her apron pocket and went, her calico skirts flying out behind in her hurry.

There was rain that night, and the next two days, with the honking of geese and cranes high up somewhere, going south, while on the street there was the noise of political rallies and the flecker of a few torches in the rain as the parades fizzled out and everybody ran for the Odd Fellows Hall, to the meeting.

At last the two Cozads came up from the railroad carrying their gripsacks in the rain. The talk of many things went on late into the night, John Cozad getting more and more furious as he heard of the fair and the fiasco at the dance. There were more angry words, low but heated after the parents went to bed, their voices finally softening to a drone but going on into the morning. Several times Robert thought he caught the choking sound of a sob. He hadn't seen his mother cry, not every really, except the time the last baby died.

Robert listened to his brother too, but there was no movement there beyond an occasional turning, no soft step of a sleepwalker, no careful closing of a door.

XXI

ROBERT CARRIED HIS UNEASINESS INTO THE WINTER. He saw the woman looking for John Cozad in every youngish feminine figure that stepped off the train. Every bit of paper he saw passing among the men at the post office, the depot, or at a sale was a part of the secret petition until it turned out to be a letter, a sale bill, or perhaps a land patent handed around, proud proof of what seemed to be a man's deepest hope of attainment—sole ownership of a piece of ground.

But what disturbed Robert Cozad most now was any report of a man shot to death somewhere, openly or left face down on the prairie, always aware that the bullet might have been for his father, that bullet or the next one.

News traveled very slowly this bad winter of 1880–81. The warm fall rains had fooled the grass into starting up fresh as spring, and the cattle went into the winter full of new and easy fat, their jaws soft as from the tender grasses of May. Old-timers were uneasy too, about the great herd of elk that came clear down to the Loup in early December. Usually they straggled southward from the Black Hills country and the breaks of Pine Ridge down across the Niobrara to winter in the protected long-grass region of the sandhills. This year they came in one vast herd that broke from the horizon in a dark line miles wide, thundering southward, many stringing clear down to the bluffs and canyons north of Cozad.

"We're in for a killing winter," an old French breed from the fur-trade days told John Cozad at the land office.

Almost at once the rain started again, and when every creature was soaked to the hide, the downpour turned to sleet and then to snow as the temperature slid far below zero. Blizzards swept Nebraska and Dakota regions until late March. Even the couple of days now and then when the sun cleared to shimmer on the Platte valley, the whiteness of it might not be broken by the puff and soot of even one train. The drifts deepened to twenty, thirty feet in rougher regions, and lay eighteen inches to two, three feet deep on the level, crusted hard from the thaws.

Every day Robert Cozad checked the thermometer outside the post-office door, running out early with frosting breath. Once for ten days the mercury didn't rise to zero, night or day. With that much moisture crops would boom, and John Cozad worked up new excursion literature and started to Ohio. On the train and at Omaha he talked to cattlemen who had been out to their ranches and told stories of sore-legged stock plowing the crusted snow for grass as long as they could, grabbing a mouthful on any wind-whipped ridge, finally to be caught in the drifts, their noses reaching up until the running snow covered them too. After a while even the stronger started to go down anywhere, no more than piles of bones in gaunted and hair-worn hides that seemed hard as rusty sheet iron even before they were frozen.

In every storm some of the stronger cattle, shaggy, snow-caked, reached the Cozad region, their great horns crusted in ice until they struck a building, perhaps a settler's shack or a telegraph pole along the railroad. They crowded in around any cut bank or wall out of the wind, pushing in windows, doors, even walls, crashing through the roofs of dugouts. One steer fell in on a woman sleeping with her newborn baby beside her, crippling her foot and frightening her so that all the husband could do was hitch up the first possible day and haul her out in a bobsled full of hay and bedding, never to return.

In Cozad the drifting cattle packed in close around the buildings, humped upon themselves, not moving for yells, whips, and even buckshot. They gnawed at the siding and the few young trees and shrubs in yards and gardens. They ate up the shed Robert Cozad had made for his Darby from rain-spoiled bales of hay; they chewed at the wagon beds, harness, saddles and ropes, the hitching posts, and the wooden door-steps of Mrs. Gatewood's store. They jammed the streets, Longhorns once wild enough to stampede at a man's lusty yell or the flutter of a woman's skirt in softer air now cowered morosely together out of the wind or chased anyone for a newspaper held in the mitten or the clothing on his back.

Some of the townspeople joked about having spare ribs for supper delivered to the door. "And mighty spare, them ribs."

Every morning there were dozens of carcasses to be dragged away with frost-wreathed teams, the doubletrees lashed to the frozen necks or hooked to a hind leg, the hard snow complaining under the awkward load. The strip of brush left along the Platte was full of the dead and the dying, and many went through the frozen river seeking out the water that had retreated deep under the ice. When the wind whipped up the snow again, they started to drift southward out upon the river and more went through air holes or the open current, pushed down by the storm-blinded ones behind.

More and more cattle came to the Platte region, mostly the older, stronger of the southern stock, until Traber Gatewood and the Schooleys estimated around ten thousand dead through the town and along the river nearby, most of them mature range or beef stock.

Every time the sun came out a little, settlers rode in to make a few dollars skinning the frozen carcasses, usually for the brand owner at twenty-five cents a head. Some cattlemen placed little warnings in the papers forbidding anyone to take a hide burned with their mark, to avoid theft of their stock—as though anybody could be caught butchering cattle that were perhaps fifty even a hundred miles from their accustomed range. And mighty thin stew they would make for those who were driven to eating slow elk—stolen beef. Usually the hides of those with forbidden brands were stripped off anyway and shipped, for how were the hide buyers a thousand miles away to know or bother to pick the forbidden from the hundreds of thousands.

"Sure to be a great stink around here, come the first thaw," some of the skinners remarked at the Cozad stores, particularly the men far from town and perhaps envious.

There would be a stink everywhere come spring, with many cattlemen broke, particularly the new ones with no stock tied by familiarity to their range—only southern stuff up the trail the past summer and moving most willingly in the direction of their old home before the fury of such storms as they had never known. Some of the so-called American stock finally drifted too. The once deep-meated Durham cows and the heavy blooded bulls from Iowa or Indiana or Ohio, perhaps stall-bred, with shorter, heavier bones naturally well rounded, were just as gaunt and stumbling by mid-January and February as the poorest Longhorn that ever walked north from the Rio Grande.

By April some ranchers were estimating their losses at seventy and eighty per cent, perhaps cattle on which they were paying two and three per cent interest a month, much of it in advance. Often it was stock practically gold-plated that they were losing.

Such ranchers knew they were out of business when the storms really struck, but others didn't realize their situation until the snow thawed and the roundups showed nothing left to gather.

266

The winter was even harder on sheep, and some who bought their start from the herd that Haskell, the special friend of Robert Cozad, had brought up from the south were cleaned out. By mid-January those with a little money ordered hay shipped in at great expense and started their sheep to the railroad to eat it. That meant scooping trails not only through the larger drifts of twenty feet or so but on the level through snow two, three feet deep.

"Sheep's built too damn close to the ground," an out-of-job cowboy complained, one of those so hard up for grub that he finally took work with a sheep outfit for his board, for his found.

But there were no bare spots on the way to the railroad, nothing at all that a sheep could reach, and even the stronger finally began to stumble, scarcely blatting any more, many almost naked where others had eaten the wool from them in their hunger. Behind them the trail was marked by an increasing line of what looked like rolls of dirty snow—sheep that had dropped and died on the way, the night bedding grounds scattered thick in the mornings.

In some ways the winter was as bleak for the settler with no hoof or horn to his name. December had seen a major victory for violence, for the spearhead of the ranchers against the settlers. The man-burning Print Olive and his foreman were out of the pen—given a new trial on a technicality of sorts. By legislative oversight, the new county of Custer had not been attached to any judicial district when it was created years ago. So their trial, which ended in the verdict of guilty, had been held in the adjoining district but outside of Custer County, the scene of the crime. On this technicality the state supreme court ordered a new trial. Because, under their decision, no district judge had jurisdiction, the new trial of Print Olive was before the county judge of Custer. He was a cattleman too, and called court into session in a room packed with armed ranchers and their gunmen, a room not big enough to hold much more than the Olive outfit. There had been months of rumors about great rolls of bribe money carried around the region, with a choice of gold or lead. Anyway, not one witness came forward against the man-burners, not even the two who had turned state's evidence against them in the first trial, and although the mob that burned Mitchell and Ketchum had been a big enough one. Besides nobody ever heard Print Olive reject the credit for the lynching. But he and his foreman were released, turned loose upon the country.

The papers of the state and the nation joined in a loud chorus of denunciation, but there seemed nothing to be done.

John Cozad got off the train on one of the few clear days of winter. He gave Robert his handsatchel at the depot without much greeting. He looked up along the frozen street leading northward across the town and knew from the carcasses not yet dragged away that he could have doubled his profit by holding all the hay he shipped west for this urgent time here. But he had something else on his mind. He had come back in a dark anger because the power of the lawless element around Plum Creek had not only been restored but strengthened by the release of the man the newspapers from New York to California called the worst criminal in the nation. Print Olive was back walking the streets of the county seat that governed the town of Cozad, back in what had been called Olive Town ever since the Texan hit there four years ago—only four years, with almost half of them spent in prison, and yet he had built up such power in the state and its supreme court.

But surely many Plum Creekers were as disgusted and shamed by Olive and the renewed arrogance of his cowboys as anyone. Once more the gang was shooting up store fronts and saloon mirrors, dropping bullets through the night windows of settlers, and particularly effective this discouraging winter. John Cozad had heard about all this on the train west and realized that the situation was worse than before Olive was convicted of murder because now there was fear on the faces of those who had once stood against him.

Yet there had been men daring enough to arrest Print Olive in his own town two years ago, men led by the brothers of the dead Ketchum. Perhaps they were planning to lead a mob against him now that they had failed to hold him by law, the mob that the deputized Lawrence Ketchum had refused to lead two years ago, when he even handed Print Olive a gun and told him to use it if anybody tried to lynch him.

As John Cozad anticipated, he was accosted by talk of this nature the evening he returned. Some usually quiet, orderly men were now willing to face the guns of the Olive outfit.

"Better than waiting for old Print to have us picked off one, two at a time," some of Cozad's friends argued. "You might be the first, locating settlers——"

But the colonizer rose in anger against them. "I won't hear of lynching!"

"Now, Mr. Cozad, you know they been bulldozing you too," Sam Schooley said, "half a dozen of the Olive cowboys at a time. They ate out a lot of your hay land with the herds when they first moved in. Even bedded stock from over toward Ogallala down on your best hay bottom couple years ago. Print's making his brags that he's taking over everything to the river. I'm against lynching too but when the law fails——"

"I won't have lynch talk from anybody in Cozad. I forbid it under any circumstances!"

"You can't forbid nobody anything," Ed Winchell told him. "You don't run this town any more."

But John Cozad's opposition was still enough to cool the urge to such unaccustomed violence. The more reasonable of the group did point out that this was a time for alertness. Perhaps releasing Olive might help them to take the county seat away from Plum Creek, help rid the county of the evil influence from outside, from the Custer County ranchers. Properly presented at election time, this might be made the winning issue.

"There's no denying that Cozad is a much more orderly town, more law-abiding," Gene Young said, to nods all around him.

"Yes," one of Winchell's friends agreed, "the town would be just about perfectly law-tbiding if it wasn't for one John Cozad. If we wipe the blot of his name off the town we may get the county seat."

After one stunned moment John Cozad drew himself up in the dignity of his frock coat, his diamonds. "Maybe you want to lynch me, like that poor half-wit Fly Speck Billy got when he went up to the Black Hills?" he demanded, his eyes very dark in the sudden whiteness of his face. "Or that outfit that came to plant counterfeit on my son!"

The men stood silent before him and his lifted cane, grasped midway, the heavy golden knob a sturdy weapon, most of them aware of the loaded pistol waiting under the tail of his coat although perhaps only Robert, helpless behind his father, knew of the other gun.

As usual Traber Gatewood stepped forward as soother. "Now John J., don't take everything so personal."

"Silence!" the man roared upon his brother-in-law.

Traber shrugged his stout shoulders. "You can try to shout us all down but that just means you have fewer on your side."

Robert heard more talk of this around town the next few days. He tried to occupy his spare time with his own work but his writing did not go well when his mind was uneasy. He designed a few greeting cards and painted them. He had been ordering chromos through advertisements in his mother's magazines for several years and used to think he did pretty well selling them for a share of the money and some premiums, mainly because his grandmother let him display them in a wire rack on the wall that his relative, Alex McIntyre, had made. That was before that family went back East, convinced that grasshoppers were a regular cycle of the country, as Alex insisted to his wife's relatives, the Gatewoods.

Robert had made some decorated signs for the rack of chromos, changing them from Thanksgiving to Christmas. By then he had received many suggestions that he make the cards himself, so he ordered a lot of good board stock of different colors and put in long evenings drawing little decorative designs that he could do rapidly, with the illuminated lettering he liked. Before long these were selling much better than the chromos and the money was all his.

"You know, you are quite an artist," Mrs. Young told him. By now her husband was county school superintendent and the compliment made the youth's face burn and sting as from an overclose shave. He tried to think she said this because they were old friends, from back when she first came as the gay young bride to the hotel, eating at the table with them all, or to run antelope, sitting her sidesaddle like a bird, back before her children came, except that one time when her horse stepped into a badger hole or something.

Robert knew that his embarrassment, and most of his joy too, over her compliment was the memory of the photographer who had come through with the black wagon and his talk of becoming an artist.

By now both of the Cozad boys were through everything that could be taught them in the town school. Johnny was studying Latin with some plan in his head, something too unsettled to discuss, it seemed, and saying little about it to anyone except Sally Ann back in Cincinnati, the sister of his best friend there. Robert suspected that his brother hadn't found Denver too pleasant, perhaps because of their father's trouble over the woman, something never explained to Robert and something he tried to think might vanish if he never let it settle in his mind.

Johnny spoke very little about Denver except that he liked the mountains and had taken some long trips up there with hay customers, even a pack-horse ride up above Leadville to the Divide, where the summer nights seemed to be as cold and stormy as mid-January in Cozad. Johnny had been mighty glad there once that he had learned a little about curing exposure and frostbite from the old freighters and hunters around the Platte, and from the talk after Elisha Clark froze at Powell Canyon. When the whole pack-horse party was lost in a sudden August blizzard up at the Divide, he recalled the first rule: keep dry, and the second: don't wear yourself out. Better hole up and wait the storm through. He also knew that after exposure the patient must be warmed as soon as possible and the circulation worked back into any damaged appendages. He had heard this often around Cozad and even seen it done. True, gangrenous spots might break and remain festering a long time, as old Matthews said he discovered after he froze his feet, but if the deeper circulation could be saved the dead tissue might slough off and the holes refill, the flesh not so firm, perhaps, but there. Matthews once told about the ends of all his toes rotting off to the bone tips from frostbite, the nails horny as hoofs but he kept whittling at them with his hide ripper.

"Gosh, Johnny, I don't remember him saying all that," Robert exclaimed.

"You were right there when Mr. Matthews pulled his boots off to show us. You were probably staring in his face, like you do."

The mother laughed over her Battenberg. "You do go in for the morbid, Johnny," she said mildly, disapproving but unable to be stern. The boys had enough laid upon them, and more to come, she knew.

The spring brought one of the biggest settler booms of all time, and John Cozad was out almost every day with his two-seater rig, showing the land that was soaked to such rich blackness as the snow went off, the grass shooting up in sharp green spears, early and thick as never before. Not one settler, not even half a dozen women among them, seemed to mind the stink of the dead cattle.

With so much snow going out at once for hundreds of miles up the river, the Platte spread over the bottoms and endangered the bridge, particularly when river ice and bloating cattle choked the end gaps. The Cozad sons worked with prods and pry poles to break the jams, Johnny's face so strained, working so desperately to save the bridge, that suddenly Robert suspected that his brother knew some unhappy things, perhaps about the petition against their father.

The river kept on rising as the thaw spread farther into the western foothills and then the mountains. The ice was gone but the long softening process was making the bridge fills crumble. The boys worked to protect them, throwing bundles of brush on the upstream side and rolling rocks and sod upon them to weight them down. It would have been hard, back-breaking work even for grown laborers and very difficult for the young Cozads with their long, delicate hands. Then suddenly one steamy afternoon Johnny flung his picthfork down. "What's the use——" he said, speaking out of long and angry resentment.

Robert nodded. There didn't seem to be much. Afterward it looked almost like a premonition of some sort, for when they got back to town, Ed Winchell had tacked up a notice announcing that he was to be the new postmaster here and that the name of the post office had been changed by petition from Cozad to Gould.

"Gould?—why Gould?" an Eastern landseeker asked.

"I'm hoping that Jay Gould will be pleased enough to help the town get ahead more than all the Cozads put together been able. Might even use railroad influence to get the county seat moved to the town named for him."

People came to look at the notice and walked silently away, even signers of the petition requesting the change. Everybody watched for John Cozad's return from locating settlers, for his return to the town that had cost him so much in money, in thought and effort, in plain hard work and sorrow.

Theresa and her family were all out to meet him, the sons pretending to be busy with their own affairs, even wrangling a bit, as they never did under normal circumstances because their mother would not tolerate any of it.

Toward evening John Cozad pulled his shying, sweating team to a stop in front of the hotel, setting them back upon the doubletrees with his powerful jerk on the lines. Even before he got out, Robert was at the heads of the horses, trying to quiet them, but barely able to see the bridles for the watering in his eyes, or his father climbing heavily from the seat.

"So! All out waiting like buzzards on the fence to see the old bull die!" John Cozad roared out, looking all around the family, his eyes smoky dark even upon his wife. "Well, the old bull has heard the news."

None of the family dared look to each other and when not even Theresa could speak, Traber finally managed it. "Now, John J., be reasonable."

"Reasonable? Get out of my sight before I— I——"

But the man could not say it, and after a stiffening as from a vital shot that must not be admitted, he held himself firm. "You knew this was going on all fall and winter, and you did nothing. You didn't even think enough of me to warn me. Now git!"

Theresa Cozad started to speak, but had to remember the watchers behind every curtain, at hitch rack and farther off, on and on. She held herself quiet and with herself the sons too and even her mother.

Finally Traber moved a little, reluctantly turned to go to his drugstore. "You have no right to order me or anybody around," he said softly. "But you won't be troubled with me much longer. I am going. Maybe you know I bought into the drugstore over at Plum Creek. I'll be moving there soon."

"To Plum Creek——" John Cozad said the words as though tasting a strangeness, his gaunt cheeks sucked in almost speculatively, without identifying the meaning or recognizing even the sounds. Then at last he seemed to grasp the sense. He stepped back, steadying himself against a wheel.

"To Plum Creek——" he repeated, and now not even Theresa could have dared go to him, not after the desertion had begun again as it did as Cozaddale and before, but this time by one so very close.

They still stood there, even the horses quiet, but in weariness, when the evening train whistled the approach. Without stepping through any door of the town named for him until today, and without a sign to any of them at all, John J. Cozad stalked gauntly, stiffly down the middle of the dusty street to the depot and was gone.

Now even Robert was seldom seen on the street, perhaps no more than for a swift striding to the stable for his horse and back late in the day. Then the morning came when he tried to put off stepping outside the door entirely but finally he had to go, knowing the longer he waited, the more people would be there to see it. Everything was as he had expected: a new sign over the post-office door, a new piece of pine board with black stove-polish lettering: GOULD P.O.

A solid row of men were leaning against the weathered wall, a few of them in town clothing but mostly in worn and patched blue denim overalls, with the burnt, stubbled faces of men working in the raw outdoors. There were some boys too, mostly from out of town, in blue jeans and ragged shirts, with shaggy drake tails at their necks. Today Robert's barbered hair, his clean-shaven cheek, made him more than foreign in his own community, on his own block.

"Welcome to the city of Gould!" one of the men called to him, and all the rest standing around laughed.

The youth tried to hold himself to his usual gait, quick but not running, although his neck burned and grew even hotter when one of the Ertile boys called out, "Where's your bull whip now, Mister Cozad?"

Robert wanted to turn on them, call them the cowards he considered them all. Then he remembered that his mother would have to pass these men and a fury that was like his father's shook him. But he was helpless, helpless now. Yet his time would come—he was determined the time would come when he could show all these people that none of the Cozads was to be laughed at.

For the present he was grateful that his father had taken the train away immediately; was seen in Washington, a friend wrote Theresa, a friend perhaps not aware that there had been no word of him to anyone here. Of course John J. Cozad understood very well that there was little hope of changing the name of his town back to the original before the next presidential election, still more than three years away. Post offices were political plums and fell to those who managed to get a hand on the tree to shake it. Most of the Union veterans here were his enemies now, men like Handley, who had broken the colonizer's arm in court; Al Pearson,* whose cattle ate up the closer Cozad meadows, and had been working against him almost from the start, from the first disagreement over where and how the bridge should be built, and Pearson's good friends too, the Buckleys and the rest.

Among the few old Union men still on Cozad's side was the sandy-haired energetic Sam Atkinson, who had built the very first house in the new settlement, back during the winter

---

*Alfred Pearson, called both Al and Alf in letters, newspapers, and documents, and by those who remembered him. Used here as in the sources.

of 1873–4, and was still a hustler for his community. He, with Sam Schooley, were the solid and true friends that Robert used as models for his new series of stories planned to ease him through this difficult time, to help him forget the still face that their mother turned upon them all.

In reality Mr. Schooley was studying law and giving his legal advice free to those of the town. He had worked for his board and room the first two years on the *Hundredth Meridian* when he could have made more elsewhere, but the paper needed a man, Dave Claypool had no money, and Sam was very grateful for the first good health he had ever known. He would have made a good postmaster, Robert thought, but then he was a Democrat——

It seemed to young Robert that almost everyone was deserting his father the same moment: Traber going into the partnership at Plum Creek, where he knew his sister's husband had been promised a bullet in the gut if he stepped within the city limits, a bullet for both his brother-in-law and his nephew. And the Claypools were dropping away too, Dave deserting his Uncle John J. although the two families went back four, five generations side by side, back to the early days in New Jersey. Now he was tying up with that fence-crawling, johnny-come-lately, Ed Winchell, the new postmaster of Gould, at the post office started by Traber Gatewood and named for the community builder.

Truly the town seemed to be going like a bridge fill-in when the floods once got a hole started. But would this matter to his father now? Robert wondered. Would John Jackson Cozad go on spending his money to build a town or a bridge for a community named Gould, even if he came back, ever returned here? Ever returned to any of them?

When Robert managed to get past the post office with the new sign, he had no real destination, not even his Darby horse. All he could do was keep walking. Prince, Grandpa Gatewood's big shepherd dog, came trotting along from an alley, not looking toward Robert, perhaps sensing that the youth did not wish to be seen today, perhaps joining the deserters. Farther on, young Norsworthy, a friend of the croquet games last summer, which seemed a hundred years ago now, was taking General Grant, the big steel-gray stallion, to the shipping pens where he stood for the farmers bringing in their mares. Last year Robert would have hurried over for a pat at the fine powerful neck and a joshing word with the stallion's keeper, and perhaps some plans for a swim or a game. Even a month ago, perhaps. Now Robert pretended not to see the youth or the big handsome horse bowing his neck, prancing heavily, graceful as a gray and exuberant boxcar, shaking the red satin riboon braided into his mane, sniffing the wind, snaking his neck out in the direction of the waiting mare, then bowing it up thick and magnificent as he dragged his keeper along.

To Robert Cozad it seemed that he was not here at all but walking through some strange town bordered all around by some darkness, like a town laid thin against a painter's canvas, the sky and horizon almost black, the street deserted except for a figure that he could not recognize at first. Then he saw it was a girl, one with thick braids yellow as summer wheat, her eyes indigo dark.

XXII

I N A FEW DAYS only the outsider, the newcomer, seemed to notice the sign over the post-office door, to see that it was different from the large COZAD at the depot, as very few had noticed when the old hundredth-meridian sign finally went down in the blizzards of last winter. Those who kept an expectant eye on Theresa and her sons, wondering when they would pack up and quit the region too, found a new interest when two women moved into the little house up near the old brickyard, the man with them drumming up night trade.

"Huzzies parading on our streets already!" Julia Gatewood said with tight lips, and everybody knew that she laid the blame for this looseness in their town not to her son-in-law but to his enemies.

The two women brought cowboys riding in the night, many the declared and overt enemies of the town and the settlers. The young fellows around were slipping up that way too, the curious Robert Cozad and his cousin among the rest. But the sixteen-year-old son of the community builder was too concerned about his father for hanging around the women much, concerned, too, about the way his mother had gone back to her restrained but easy way in the town, in and out the Winchell store, even stepping through the despised post-office door much as always, her skirts lifted to clear the splintery floor and the increasing carelessness with the spittoon.

Robert found himself growing critical, and reasonably so, he thought, of all the treatment given their John J. Cozad—defrauded, cheated of his town and the honor of it, and no telling where he was now, or who was comforting his unhappiness and defeat.

Then suddenly the town builder was back, calmly walking up from the depot and past the post office, carrying a new handsatchel. He spoke to Mrs. Handley and lifted his hat to Mrs. Riggs too, then kissed his mother-in-law and went into the hotel to his wife and their sons.

He did all this almost as though nothing had happened, as Robert tried to say when he came riding out to the grandfather at the bridge with the news of his father's return.

"He's full of excitement and plans. Hay orders, plans to finish the bridge," Robert said, almost in complaint.

"I remember back when we had the hotel at Malden——" the grandfather told the youth. "To the gamblers losing was almost like oats to a hot-blooded horse. That's the real gambler every time."

"But this isn't gambling—this is the community he built!"

Old Robert measured out the coffee, with an extra grinding for the pot. "Same thing," he said judiciously, and when Robert protested, he repeated the words, "Same thing! I never seen John J. more excited than the night he left Cozaddale after a big blowup you could hear clear to Cincinnati. He was stepping so high you'd think he'd bucked the tiger out of his everlasting striped old hide."

Within two days the prostitutes who had moved in up near the brick kiln were gone and the summer and fall settled down to a sort of calm, but with a tentativeness about it, a waiting. Looking ahead, it seemed that 1882 must be a year of extra violence, starting as it did with the hanging of Guiteau, assassin of President Garfield, and closer to home, a spreading strike at Omaha broken by the militia, as was now the custom. The Great Plains boomed in a gold rush, a beef bonanza, although the cattle were mostly the same Texas stock that could scarcely be given away ten years ago. That fall the unsalable herds, after the long walk north and the longer, hungrier wait for buyers around the shipping pens at the Kansas railroad, finally had to face blizzards anywhere from Abilene to the Platte, the cattle thin as washboards and dying by the thousands.

But that was past now, and forgotten, with some of the Eastern and foreign investors suddenly making as high as forty and fifty per cent on free-grass beef, beef born and raised on the public domain that was the property of the country, not an individual, except as taken up by bona fide settlers in 160-acre chunks—not enough to buy up supreme courts, or even town constables. But with the boom in beef homesteaders cutting into the public domain must be kept out, those already settled driven off by every discouragement, every scare, the more terrifying the better.

"Even a flock of hungry old horned owls'll quit the county if you hang out a dead one or two, to stink," the settlers warned each other.

Because there had been some uneasiness in the beef market last fall, a little sagging at the top price, many held their steers over. These, added to the overexpansion the big profits encouraged, made range very scarce, the hungry stock harder to fight off the least shirttail patch of crop. By spring ranch cattle pushed in around Cozad, and only constant herding kept them off crops or hay or gardens, with the Herd Law useless so long as the cowmen owned the courthouse.

By now Robert realized that it might be up to him to save the Cozad meadows and perhaps help the nearby settlers some too, if he could. He went to Sam Schooley to get a little clarification of the Herd Law situation, and had his impressions verified. No good—not with the cattlemen flying high as eagles around Plum Creek these days. Any rancher whose stock was taken up could carry the case to the county seat, to a courtroom so filled with armed cowboys that a settler would scarcely dare show his face.

"It's not only your father who's been promised a bullet in the gut if he steps inside the town limits," Sam Schooley reminded the boy. "Others been included, you know, like a certain young Cozad with a bull whip——"

Robert nodded. He hadn't forgotten the threat. Besides there was another danger in taking up cattle for damages with the courthouse in rancher hands. If an owner found stock with his brand in a homesteader's corral, perhaps taken up for damages under the Herd Law, he charged the man with rustling, with theft, and had a good chance of making it stick, if he troubled to withhold his bullets and go to court instead. Sam Schooley knew of cattle planted in a settler's field at night, to trick him into taking them up, and so be caught at dawn with the stock in his corral by the owner and witnesses. Or, as some claimed, the Olive outfit did with Ketchum, dragged calves into the settler's corral to be discovered in the morning with the cows bawling outside.

"Such tricks work mighty easy if the officials are against you," Robert admitted. "Why don't you run for office?"

Sam lifted his old hat to scratch. "You think I could get elected to anything?—not from Cozad, or even Gould."

That was probably true. Although it was ten years since John J. Cozad walked west to the hundredth meridian, nine years since the town was started—the second-largest community in the county—there was still not one man except the school superintendent from the Cozad region at the courthouse.

The possible agitation by the town named Gould to move the county seat was met by the more solid citizens of Plum Creek with determination. They were encouraged by the vote against saloons. Somehow they would shake the Olives and their kind, Sam Schooley heard. They even planned to change the name of their town.

Robert thought about that a while. The railroad was stubborn. It kept the COZAD sign up at the depot and on the time-tables in spite of pressure and a bucket of black paint used to blot out the name.

The land-hungry of the world flocked to America like the passenger pigeons Robert remembered seeing over Cincinnati once, long ago. They came seeking homes, individually and in companies, but they came. A large colony of Germans arrived in tourist cars set out on the siding at Cozad. Their stuff was unloaded, teams hitched to the wagons, and with eight, ten people in each they struck out northeastward, over near the Danish settlement, not far from Alf Pearson and his family homesteads. In spite of his protest they filed on a whole block of land, threw up sod houses, broke out garden and corn plots, and were welcomed to the Danish church that lifted its little belfry toward the windy sky, paying their share of the $100 a year that brought the preacher out once a month.

Robert talked his brother into riding over that way for church one Sunday, hoping to find more girls with the timid, dark blue eyes. But these were a darker, a brown-haired people, and without a daughter among them who might hold out her hands to a strange boy for a wild little witches' dance.

Work on the bridge moved along slowly, usually with enough new settlers to keep Sam Schooley busy. It was a good thing that he was a pleasant man, because his workers, all tossed out of their old life one way or another, included the troublesome and the difficult. Even some with hungry children made slurring remarks about the bridgebuilder, whom they had perhaps never seen at all, telling one story over and over, of a man who came to the bridge for work. John Cozad had none but he knew the man's family was hungry and so he hired him to move a pile of planks and then the next day ordered him to carry them back.

"I quit!" the settler had shouted. "I won't work my hind-side off for a fool!"

The bridge hands seemed to think this was a fine joke on John Cozad and if anyone remembered the man's children were hungry, it wasn't mentioned.

One day Robert, who had just ridden in from the hay cutting, overheard one of the men telling the story, making it a ridiculing of the bridgebuilder, who was right there. It was a little like old Robert Gatewood exploding up at the Odd Fellows Hall, except that here the remarks were made on John Cozad's property, on his time. Yet when he roared out, "Shut your mouth until you know what you are talking about!" the other workers backed up the storyteller as the wild youths had backed up Oscar Ertile at the dance. In a moment all the long brooding animosities and hatreds were out in the open here too, and if it hadn't been evening anyway, practically every man except the foreman would have been fired on the spot. Or quit.

Robert didn't sleep much that night, uneasy about the bridge and the stupid storyteller, but his father didn't seem much disturbed after he cooled down. Trouble like that faded out like a preacher's luck, he said.

But when John Cozad drove out to the bridge next day, he found the plows idle on their sides, their polished shares catching the sun. The scrapers were idle too, belly up, the sod wagons besides each other, tongues down, and not a team or a man around except Sam Schooley.

The foreman was sharpening shovels, holding one between his knees, the big file poised over the back of the blade when the prancing team drew up beside him.

"Where's the crew?"

"I don't know, Mr. Cozad. Nobody showed up."

So it had come to that. Slowly the builder unlimbered his

long legs, got out and tied his team. Then, pushing his hat back and smoothing his beard with his handkerchief, he settled in the shade to take stock with the man who was also from Vinton County, Ohio, but long after John Cozad threw down his tedding fork and got a job on an Ohio river boat with a man he had to see hanged later.

By the time Sam was born, John Cozad had a reputation as a dangerous man at faro and had a neat little fortune sprouting. He had long been threatened by the consumption that killed so many young Cozads. Now he must act, perhaps move west, the doctor said. So he tried California but the dampness of San Francisco only aggravated the disease. Finally Nebraska, considered very good for lungers and stomach cases, was recommended and he had found it truly so, whatever the cost in money and in grief.

"You sure don't get much credit for what you done, Mr. Cozad," Sam said, thoughtfully chewing at a bitter cottonwood leaf. "But I think things will straighten out. People have to get used to you, to understand you."

"Some of them have known me all my life. The Ertiles who threatened to kill Mrs. Cozad's father are from my home township, near Cozaddale. Most of them I've known for years, brought them out here when times were hard, some at my own expense, helped them get land, financed them for years——"

"Yes, I know. Still owe you money, I hear. And some of the men missing from work today will be needing it mighty bad before winter. I guess they'll be back, maybe tomorrow."

Maybe, but the story was getting old, the same thing over and over, John Cozad let himself say angrily to this young foreman listening so politely and hearing more than even Theresa ever was told in the twenty-three years she had been his wife.

Toward noon Robert rode in from the haying and settled down to the sandwiches from his saddlebags with the two men. Still the father spoke, almost as freely as before, although Sam Schooley gave him a look once, motioning slightly toward the son with his stubbled chin. But John Cozad disposed of this in his usual highhanded way.

"I think I can depend upon Robert. He doesn't have to like what I do, just give me loyalty."

The young foreman nodded uneasily, perhaps a little ashamed that he seemed to be pushing his own loyalty here today, the only one to show up for work.

Sam was right about some of the men sneaking back to the bridge the next few days. "Sorry I couldn't come to work yesterday. Wife was sick," one explained. Or the horses had the colic, the well caved in, maybe a trail herd came through and had to be run off the land and watched all day.

To most of them Sam nodded as though he listened and put them back on the payroll, but a few he refused and they, with others, muttered around town about "that bastard Cozad! He ought to be run out!" Some spoke of a tar-and-feathering as though they hadn't gone begging to the bridgebuilder after Sam Schooley refused to take them back, and were told that Sam was running the work out there. He knew what he needed.

One man even watched for young Robert, stepping out from the wall where he had been waiting when the youth led his Darby out to mount. The man was incredibly patched and wash-faded, his face weathered as an old piece of bullhide, his knotted hands fumbling at the bib of his overalls.

"I hear you got a lot of pull around here," he said. "I got to have some work, bridge or hayfield, I ain't particular. I got a girl, fourteen——"

"We don't have any work for children," Robert told him, the reins ready in his hand at the saddle horn.

"Not for work——" the father said. "I know how they done down where the Gatewoods come from. She ain't black, my girl ain't, but she ought to be just about as good for wench-in'——"

Robert looked over the saddle at the man, at the watering faded blue of the eyes, the twitching, weather-burnt lips, and swung into the saddle. Because he did not answer immediately, the man pushed himself forward, ready to offer more induce-ments, probably, or descriptions. But Robert set his spurs, Darby leaped ahead in surprise and anger, ears back, making a couple of bucking jumps of protest.

When he was halfway to the bridge, Robert Cozad's mind cleared enough so he could think about the man and his offer, and felt the hot flush of shame and pity come up his neck. The man must be mighty, mighty hard up——

But it would have given Robert something more than the shack at the brickyard to talk about when the others bragged about going down to the place near the Plum Creek bridge, or tried to prod Johnny into telling about the girls along Larimer Street in Denver, and the one that he was writing to up there, her picture in the back of his gold watch, a win-some face, with a neat curl over one bare shoulder, one naked shoulder, as the boys called it. And here he was, Robert Henry Cozad, sometimes the only man in the Cozad family around for weeks at a time and without any far adventuring to his name.

Early in October there was a triple murder in the papers. The outlaw Dick Belmont and three of his gang after stealing horses in north Kansas, were located at the hotel in Minden, eating supper. Sheriff Woods, who had chased them from a neighboring county, went to arrest them. Belmont, fast with a gun, put two bullets into the sheriff while the others fired around the smoke-filling room, killing one man at a table and another as they ran out and then wounded one while holding off the astonished townsmen until they could get to their saddles and off southward. They got clear to Kansas, keeping

287

ahead of the posse by stealing fresh horses every few miles through the thickening settlements.

The Kearney *Gazette* complained loudly about the general lawlessness. First there was Doc Middleton's gang, then the killing of Mitchell and Ketchum by the Olive outfit, and now this, and none of the culprits seemed to be brought to any real justice.

By now it was known around the country that John Cozad had received several warnings to get out of the region just like any common settler or small locater. Bull Durham sacks with bullets in them were thrown into his buggy while tied to the hitch rack in town or out around the settlements. Notes were slipped under his office door in the hotel and finally a noose hung to the knob although no one admitted seeing this done, right in the hotel lobby.

The noose showed up right after a fight with Al Pearson over his cattle running on Cozad land, and after catching him mowing hay on one of the meadows, raking it up half green and hauling it away. John Cozad drove him off with violent words, the man claiming it was a mistake, that he didn't know he was on the colonizer's property, although the government corners were plain to see. Afterward it was rumored that Pearson said he had made sure that even Robert was away, but that old wandering John had come home and caught him.

Although these weren't his first time for such infringements, Al Pearson promised they would be his last.

"They better be. If we catch your stock on my land again we'll take them up and hit you for the damages."

"You do and it will be the last time you bulldoze anybody!"

John Cozad polished the gold head of his cane with his gloved hand. "Law's on my side, Pearson," he said. He said it with the usual Cozad assurance but he knew that at Plum Creek he didn't stand the chance of a hoptoad in a Longhorn stampede.

John Cozad was packing to go to Denver about the hay and with an eye to branching out in Colorado. He had had more trouble than usual to save his meadows this year, with range so scarce, even with the barbed-wire fencing. It had demanded keeping Robert in the saddle most of the summer, so much that the boy was getting as bowlegged as any old cowpuncher. He should be in school, making something of his talents, his determination, and his spunk. To give his sons everything he had missed, give them every opportunity to make whatever they wished of themselves, had been the hope of John Cozad and his wife. Now the father planned to look around for a good school, in Cincinnati perhaps or farther on, although he despised the East. He hoped it might be Denver, with a place for a new colony in Colorado somewhere, although there would never be another place as promising as Cozad.

Perhaps there might be room for a colony up along the new railroad heading through northern Nebraska for the Black Hills or up in the North Platte valley. But the advantages of railroad lands were no longer offered, and the cattlemen were entrenched almost everywhere, he heard, with pistoled men riding range protection, as they called it, keeping homeseekers out of the government land that their cattle grazed illegally.

Naturally he had not given up Cozad entirely. Perhaps a new excursion could still be started up, and with the bridge finished in one more good season to bring trade from the south the place would boom, no matter what the name was over the post-office door. Inevitably there must be a political change, nationally and locally.

Robert had heard his father speak of these things and tried to be hopeful, but he couldn't forget all the cattle troubles of the summer, with Pearson and others, in addition to the big outfits. Still, they had mailed out a great bundle of a special homestead edition of the *Hundredth Meridian* and several hundred broadsides neatly decorated by Robert's designs, calling Cozad the Heart of the Land of Opportunity.

The father was upstairs above Mrs. Gatewood's store dressing for the westbound train that would be along after a while. Robert brought up a new run of the special edition to pack into the luggage and then went back to the press.

Suddenly there was a commotion out in front of the store where Julia Gatewood was piling empty boxes for her customers. It was Alf Pearson, roaring in a violent rage, as though he had been to one of the jugs down at the livery stables.

"I want to see Cozad!" he shouted. "Right away!" and went into a long and threatening tirade.

Julia Gatewood was alone at the store and frightened by Pearson's anger, even before he said he had come to kill her son-in-law. She ran upstairs to tell John J. what was happening. He turned from the mirror and said to inform the man he would be down presently.

"Is it safe?" the old woman asked, her agitated hands rolling themselves into her apron. "He sounds almost insane."

"I'll be down presently," John J. repeated quietly.

When she was gone he retied his cravat, brushed his silk hat, selected his gloves, checked the chambers of his two pistols, and slipped them back into place. Then he drew on his beaver-collared overcoat and with his gloves in his hand he came striding down. Ignoring the threats that had been made, he spoke casually. "Let us step outside to dispatch any business you may have with me. I have no wish to disturb Mrs. Gatewood further," he said, and held the door for Pearson.

At first the man spoke quite reasonably. He said he must have more feed for his cattle, more winter range, and wanted the meadow down along the river, where his stock was always wandering any way.

"You can have it, but only by rental."

"You skinned the hay off for the year——"

"It is still my land, and winter range, as you say. It is only to be used rented."

Finally they agreed on a price and the terms of the lease.

Then Al Pearson began to shout that Cozad owed him money for work he had done long ago.

"You know you were paid long ago, and on top of that your stock has eaten a thousand times the amount in my hay flats. If you deny this you are a liar."

"Don't call me a liar!" Pearson shouted, his red face suddenly swelling.

"If you claim that I owe you money you are a damned liar!"

As though waiting for this opportunity, Pearson drew his fist back and struck out. Cozad, clumsy in his heavy overcoat, ducked back and stumbled into the empty packing boxes Mrs. Gatewood had just put out. Pearson pounced upon him, pounding him in the face, kicking him as he struggled to get up. Finally the colonizer managed to stick a foot out. Pearson half tripped, and when he came up there was the flash of a naked knife in his hands. John Cozad saw it, grabbed under his greatcoat, and as the knife was raised against him he fired without aim. The bullet struck the man's head as with a blow, jerking it back. The knife clattered among the boxes as he staggered and went down, a hand to his cheek, blood streaming between the fingers.

Inside, Mrs. Gatewood had seen this happen, crying out as her son-in-law was knocked down. She ran out to help him pull himself out of the pile of boxes and with blue and stinking powder smoke around them, they stooped over the unconscious man.

"Run for a doctor!" John Cozad ordered the people hurrying up, coming from everywhere, friend and enemy alike, murmuring, everybody standing off.

But Traber Gatewood, who had seen all this from some distance, was already gone. The doctor was known to be away but Traber brought a man from the lumberyard, one who had been a hospital orderly in the war. Together they pushed through the crowd and lifted Alfred Pearson from the pool of blood gathering in the dust and dripping in regular spatters from his face and mouth as they carried him away, the man beginning to moan and speak, the crowd murmuring louder now, dark-faced in the October wind.

For one moment John J. Cozad looked after the wounded man and then around the crowd pushing in upon him, against him. With the warm pistol still in his hand he backed into the store and ran upstairs and then came right back down carrying a small handsatchel as his wife ran in through the door, the white-faced Robert just behind.

"Oh, John! Oh, my dear, what have you done?"

For one instant the man stood on the bottom step, very tall, his face white and sharp-boned, his eyes far back and burning. Then he lifted his arms and gathered his wife to him. But almost at once he pushed her away. "I must hurry. They'll mob me, lynch me," he said, and ran to the back door, glancing all around the windows that looked out upon the alley. "I'll try to reach you through Sam or Dave. Traber will be watched——" he added, and started away.

But there was running behind him, and with his hand on the gun under his coattail John Cozad turned, to face his son.

"Wait," Robert whispered, taking the man's handsatchel, his arm, "you can't go out this way now," motioning off along the alley with his chin, to where men were already peering around corners. "They have ropes, I suspect. I don't think they would try to take this place with women here."

Slowly the man looked around, saw the watching faces, and hesitated. Then he let himself be turned, led back into the house and upstairs. Weary, suddenly spent, he let himself be pushed into his big chair in the bedroom.

"Now," Robert said, matter-of-factly, "first we have to send a telegram."

Oh, yes, the father agreed, nodding his head vaguely. Yes, perhaps a telegram to the county judge—no, that was Plum

Creek. Better to the district attorney or somebody at Lincoln, maybe. Or— or——

Robert looked at his father in sorrow, seeing the hesitation, knowing there must be action now. He would send a telegram to the sheriff, yes, to Plum Creek. A brief telegram but stating his father's case, from Pearson's loud threats to Mrs. Gatewood that he had come to kill her son-in-law, through the range deal and the attack while encumbered, knocked back into a pile of packing boxes, the blows, kicks, and the knife while down and finally the shot in self-defense and the wounded man's consciousness. Also that he, John J. Cozad, would deliver himself into proper and effective custody in time for the trial but that he did not propose to be taken by a mob and given the customary Plum Creek rope. The telegram had to be sent immediately, in case Mr. Pearson, as Robert still called him, worsened. It must be written out neatly, better, he would print it with his broad-stroke pen so the station agent could show it around, with John J. Cozad's signature at the bottom.

After the firm promise that his father would not try to get away until Robert returned, the youth started for the depot with the telegraph blank open in his hand, once more walking through an antagonistic crowd, but darker-faced this time, and making no joking, no noise at all beyond the sullen rising murmur of angry people not yet quite ready to move, to act.

He hurried back, past his uncle and Dave Claypool at the door, nodding to him, indicating that they were armed. Upstairs the father was hunched over on the edge of the bed, his hands in his black hair, the mother in the rocker at the window, silent, speaking only to ask whether the train from the west was late, hoping that somehow Johnny might come in from North Platte, where he had gone with some settlers. But he was headed to Denver from there, to look after the hay business and prepare for his father, due tomorrow.

293

Now there was the planning for their future. Plainly John Cozad must be gone when the sheriff arrived, or he would end like Mitchell and Ketchum or worse, if that was possible, go without more trouble with anyone, and stay away until they knew what must be done next. Robert approached this as he did his stories, planning it out as he would a plot, doing nothing without purpose and meaning, and always with a romantic eye.

He had thought this over on the way up from the depot. To avoid extradition, his father must use another name. Robert's grandfather, Henry Cozad, had selected the name of Jackson from the Stonewall relatives living near his birthplace in Upshur County, Virginia, for the middle name of John Jackson Cozad, so why not use an honored name of the Gatewood region in Kanawah County now—say, Richard H. Lee. He was a relative of General Lee but prominent in his own right back when John Cozad married Theresa Gatewood there. Robert had often heard what a fine man he was, tall, spare, and a very gallant figure at the wedding.

"But my appearance? I will not bare my chin——"

"Oh, if we must——" Theresa interrupted.

No, not his chin, but he must get away, John Cozad insisted, anxiously going to stand at the window to peer out from behind the draperies.

Robert considered his father carefully, striding halfway around him, squinting at him from this direction and that, rubbing his own short chin. "Maybe you better keep the goatee, just let it grow longer, stragglier, maybe spread out some, spaded off a little, and your mustache bushed out. Maybe you ought to trim your eyebrows pretty close to make your eyes look lighter, but keep the bearding. They'll go hunting for you clean-shaven sure. You can change back after you have a fair trial."

A fair trial! They didn't give a trial of any kind to the

two settlers taken to Plum Creek four years ago and strung up and burned. Not long before that Hallowell was dragged out and left hanging from the Dawson County's own courtroom steps. "There's much more hate out for me than any of them. Just being known as a gambler makes it bad. There's old Tom Gaynor, to be hung at Pueblo next month because he shot a cowboy who was cracking him over the head with a poker. It's the law that's hanging him, and there's a lot more feeling around against me, ready to be stirred up."

"Maybe Mr. Pearson won't die," Theresa tried to comfort.

Her husband did not answer and Robert realized that it would not matter one way or the other if his father had been given a Dawson County dance, a Plum Creek swing, in the meantime.

So Robert Cozad tried to hurry, going over everything once more as he would rewrite a story, but swiftly now. When everything seemed done he went out to hitch up the buggy team while his parents said good-by, perhaps for months or even forever, if something went wrong. He couldn't let himself think of his brother away, not here to see his father for what might be the last time, and no telling what might be happening to Johnny at North Platte, with the cowboys who attacked John Cozad a couple of times around up there. They would be a lot bolder now if they got the news of the shooting before Johnny got away to Denver, be on him like wolves on the biggest buck if his foot slipped.

Robert drove around to the front and stopped the team, doing it with the usual Cozad flourish, although the crowd was pushing up, wanting to know what was going on, Traber and Dave Claypool still standing on the steps against them.

"Sheriff's coming down on the next train, I hear," one of the Pearson sons shouted.

"I've got the ticket for Plum Creek ready," Robert replied, holding it up.

Then, while the son held the horses, John Cozad appeared in the doorway. He kissed his mother-in-law and then came out with Theresa beside him, clutching a shawl about her shoulders to hide the shaking of her hands. Dropping his little gripsatchel in ahead of him, the man climbed into the seat beside Robert. They turned, went down the dusty fall street at a smart trot but kept on, past the depot, and toward the bridge, stopping at Robert Gatewood's shack. There, with the old cottonwood over them almost bare of yellow leaves, they got out and stood facing each other a moment, Robert and his father who was a potential murderer, even if in self-defense. Although he was a large landowner, the builder of a strong and most orderly community, he had to flee from practically certain lynching by his enemies, if not by those he brought here himself then most surely by the hirelings of the cattlemen whose herds he had resisted all this time—the whole illegal grazing on government land that his settlers had practically shut out of a region more than twenty miles in every direction, and many, many more by example.

To Robert the father was a man giving up a dream, yet now, at this last moment, John Cozad did not seem defeated at all. Instead he was almost exultant, his red lips smiling slyly, his eyes burning as with reflected sunlight, no, not the sun but a sort of inner flame blazing through. One would think he had succeeded entirely, made the metropolis he dreamed of Cozad-dale, of all the other far places, and now of Cozad in Nebraska.

Suddenly the seventeen-year-old son felt a great pity well up within him, like a flood filling in all the bridge. It was not over his father's necessity to go, to leave, or even his necessity to kill in order to live. That was self-defense and by some of the rumors Robert had heard, it was not the first time for John Jackson Cozad. No, this was something deeper, something that made the son feel protective, fatherly, wanting to shield this man who was never so precious, so beloved as at this moment.

With a strong handclasp, one moment of naked eye upon eye, and the man was gone into the fading October brush, leaving only the sound of dry leaves under hurrying feet.

And now Robert Henry Cozad could have wept if he had been a crying man.

XXIII

Now the father was gone, carefully leaving without a word of his plans for the next month or two, so none need perjure himself or risk betrayal. For a long time the son stood beside the buggy, staring into the brush where the few yellow leaves still fluttered as from a man's passing.

But the same wind, chill and moist as with a coming storm, was making the matched bays stomp with impatience. Finally Robert climbed in and drove to the last brush patch south of town. There he drew off the road in the gathering dusk and waited until he felt the far vibration of the train coming in from the west. At the brightening gleam of the headlight and the far whistle, he started back into the road and reached the depot just as the train stopped. He drew up south of the tracks, opposite the depot, so, for the moment, some of the gathered watchers might think John J. Cozad was sneaking into a car from the far side and heading for Plum Creek on the ticket that Robert had held up earlier in the day for all the watchers to see.

But the train switched to the siding as a Hunters Excursion Express roared in out of the east. "Making a special stop," the agent said as he ran out to check the signals.

The express stopped only a couple of minutes, long enough

to drop off the sheriff from Plum Creek, a doctor, and a reporter from the Dawson County *Pioneer*. Then it puffed on toward the moose, elk, grizzly, and the few remaining buffaloes waiting for the hunters out in Wyoming. The train on the siding started too, and slid away before the sheriff got to search the cars. But that could be done just as well by his deputies at Coyote or at Plum Creek, particularly with the wounded Al Pearson still alive.

The sheriff got the story of everybody he could find, even Lewy Owens, the youthful friend of the Cozad sons back when they had time for such games as croquet and horse racings over the prairie. Lewy had seen the fight as many others did, from far off. The story of all was substantially the same: that John Cozad had come out of the store in his heavy overcoat and talked to Alf Pearson until they both got to shouting. Then Pearson knocked Cozad back into a big packing box, on a pile of boxes, and was pounding and kicking him, some said choking him too. Others said they caught a glint of metal, a knife just before the pistol shot, with Pearson falling, and blue smoke spreading around Cozad's hand and where Pearson had stood. It was in their interpretation of the motives during the last eight years that they differed. Cozad was an overbearing bastard. Pearson let his cattle run on Cozad land every little while, even mowed off some of the hay.

But the main story seemed to be the bad blood between the two men from the earliest days, increased as the Pearsons went into cattle and joined their sympathies to those of the ranchers, against any settlers coming in after they had their claims safely filed. There were foolish stories too of a boyhood feud over Theresa, but that was unlikely.

While the sheriff went to scout the region, Robert slipped out to listen at the livery stables. Not a horse left anywhere. Many must have sneaked out during the investigation. Perhaps the deputies had wired that John Cozad wasn't on the train.

Next forenoon silent men straggled into town, two, three at a time, their horses worn, without a prisoner, Robert saw, but could tell nothing more from their faces. For days the region was flooded by a cloudburst of rumors. First North Platte and then Omaha heard that Pearson had been killed instantly and that Cozad was overtaken by a mob and strung up to the old hundredth-meridian sign that had drawn him there in the first place. When the railroad conductor pointed out that the blizzards knocked the sign down long ago, the story was changed to a lynching to a telegraph pole, then to a windmill, perhaps in Cozad's own back yard.

But finally the news that Pearson was still alive spread. Shot in the face, the cheek, with the bullet lodged at the base of the skull, he was alive but dying fast. No, recovering. Or seeming to recover.

There were more reports about John Cozad too. He had been seen north and south, in Deadwood, Denver, and in Cincinnati where he was hiding out with Dr. Donough, the dentist who had come to the new Nebraska colony for a while, back in the earliest days, and to whom John Cozad had been taken when Todd broke his jaw. Then it got out that Dr. Ormsby Donough was in trouble himself, charged with assault and battery by Page, a rural schoolteacher who had rejected the doctor's two children as outsiders. The Donough farm, not far from Cozaddale, belonged to a farther school and even after the doctor got permission from two of the directors to send his children to the one close by, some of the other directors and Page, the teacher, ordered the children home a second time. Then, it seemed, the husky dentist went to the teacher's boarding place, grabbed the slim young man by the throat, and pounded him. Some said he threatened to kill Page, others there denied this, but finally Donough had to pay $20 damages and the court costs.

"They seem to grow 'em overbearing back there," Costin from Willow Island said. "Doc used to big-bug it around with Cozad those first years, but the grasshoppers killed the tooth-cobbling business. Anyway, Traber was a dentist too, and the brother of Cozad's wife."

Some said that the fleeing colonizer had been seen in Denver with his old acquaintance Dick Hargraves, the Cincinnati gambler gone west for his health too. John Cozad was seen walking along Larimer Street holding up the dying Hargraves to get him a little sunshine.

Others reported seeing Cozad back in Ohio, at the grave of old Mrs. Ertile, a long-time friend even if the younger Ertiles whom he helped to find homes out in Nebraska turned against him. Then someone saw him at another cemetery, at the grave of his cousin George Cozad, night editor of the *Register* at Wheeling, and comforting the dead man's two daughters.

But more thought that John Cozad was really hiding out somewhere near his town waiting to see if Pearson died before doing anything as drastic as deserting his dream. This rumor ran over the region like a fall prairie fire in a high wind. Robert didn't realize its seriousness until the night he was late coming in from showing the railroad lands to some of his father's homeseekers. It was dusk when he started back, riding fast in the cold wind around by his grandfather's shack to pick up the bridge books. He was so chilled that he built up a swift little fire to thaw out before he finished the ride home.

The lantern was out of coal oil and he sat in the glow of the little cookstove, the dry willow snapping and roaring in the pipe. Several times he thought he heard some movement outside but decided it was his impatient horse that should not be left standing in the wind after hard travel. But the warmth and the small play of light from the stove's hearth nestled by the darkness of the room was the first comfort Robert had found since the shooting, and he put off leaving it, poking more dry diamond willow into the firebox.

Suddenly the door was kicked open and a man's voice roared out, "Stick 'em up, Cozad!"

Robert jumped back from the stove. In the darkness he could see the firelight playing over the barrel of a Colt and touching the cautious eyes and hat brims of several men peering in around the doorjamb, keeping most of themselves out of gunshot.

"Who are you—bursting into a man's home like this?" Robert demanded.

, One of the men struck a match and held it up into the empty little room, showing only the figure of the youth, but holding it until the stick curled to the man's fingers and he dropped it in a red streak to the ground. In the flare of it Robert had seen three men he knew vaguely from around Plum Creek, deputy sheriffs probably, looking for his father and the reward one of them said was being offered for his apprehension.

"By the Pearsons, or all the cattlemen around Plum Creek?" Robert asked.

"Planning to take a pop at anybody that does with that bull whip you been carrying, or that gun I seen on your saddle?" one of the men said, swaggering into the room now that there was only a boy there.

Robert refused to acknowledge the *schneid* as they called it over in the German settlement. Afraid, not certain that they might not lynch the son in the father's place, he made himself turn his back up to the fire again, trying to warm the chill from between his shoulder blades.

The men talked low among themselves a while and finally went out. Saddles creaked in the dark and trotting hoofs faded up the road, but Robert knew the place would be watched. He let the fire burn out and then rode home, stroking the shivering neck of his horse, ashamed that he had let him get so chilled. Plainly none of the family would be free from spying eyes for a long, long time, if ever now. Angrily he determined that so long as he lived no deputy sheriffs should be given any excuse whatever to come kicking in doors over anything he did, and then was immediately shamed by his disloyalty.

As he rode across the tracks, passing the dim light of the station window, he remembered something his grandmother once said to a woman who offered her sympathy over the gambling, violent-tempered son-in-law that John Cozad was.

"Can you be sure what your own son-in-law will do before you are dead? Certainly it won't be community building, finding homes for the many, many poor and unhappy families as our John J. does."

When the first shock of the shooting was over, Theresa Cozad started making plans, automatically when Alfred Pearson seemed worse, hopefully if he had improved a little or even seemed the same. She wanted to go to call on the family, fortunately somewhat grown, but as Robert pointed out, she could not expose herself to their anger and insults, and who could blame them for these? So they waited for Johnny to come in from Denver where he had been sent, knowing little beyond what he read in the papers and the terse note from his father. "Put the caretaker of the hay barn in charge and come home as soon as you can get some settlement on the larger contracts. There is urgent and delicate business for you at Plum Creek."

Under no circumstances was Robert to go there. He had his warning, as his father had, even though it was their county seat too.

"Oh, won't it be very dangerous for Johnny also?" Theresa had demanded.

Yes, it would, and Johnny must conduct himself with utmost reserve and caution. But he had never been in any of the troubles at Plum Creek or had much contact with the cattlemen, never been sent to order their stock out of Cozad lands, and was not involved in any of the fights, such as the one with Handley or the trap Robert had walked into at the livery stable. Johnny was practically unknown at Plum and with his Uncle Traber in business there he should be safe enough. Someone must go to the courthouse for John Cozad, no matter what the risk.

Robert met his brother at the train, feeling the strangeness that mutual tragedy seen by only one puts between even the best of friends and brothers, with the little edge of resentment of this exclusion. They said nothing for the watchers at the depot to overhear, just gripped hands a moment and then, each carrying one of the valises, turned up the street. Almost no one was in sight but here and there a curtain moved a little or an edge of temple and a peering eye showed at a corner or a wall, and then was gone. None of the usual dogs were on the street, tied, perhaps or looking from far off, as upon suspected strangers.

"Even Uncle Traber's dog acts like we're poison," Johnny said bitterly, and in that moment Robert felt that the name *Johnny* did not fit his brother now, that he really had become John Cozad, John A.

There was a tearful meeting between the elder son and his mother. Robert made an errand to his Uncle Traber's store. There had been less warmth between these two since the day Robert ordered the hay press stopped because it wasn't working right, over his uncle's command that the work continue. In the exchange of abuse Robert won, and Traber had not forgotten that public challenge by a fifteen-year-old. Now, with more of his interest and his time transferred to Plum Creek business there had been less and less contact.

But most of this split had been healed by the Cozad bullet, and to Robert's unspoken question now, Traber shook his head, meaning either no news or no news that he was free to tell.

"Do you think it would do any good if you went with John A., Johnny, to Plum Creek? There are some papers to record at the courthouse, taxes due and——"

"The attorney to see——" Traber filled in.

"Yes, the right attorney to see about chances for a verdict of the self-defense that it was, as a dozen people could swear."

They talked a little longer, Robert giving his mother and her elder son time together. To avoid annoying his brother and embarrassing everybody, he had learned to do this very early in his childhood.

John A. got on the morning freight for Plum Creek. Robert went down to see him off with Theresa beside him—her first appearance on the street since the Pearson shooting. She wore a heavy black chiffon veil and black gloves to make the trembling of her hands less noticeable than in white, although Robert was certain she could not have explained why she should even consider white gloves for such a short walk down a dusty street that was no more than a road.

Evidently John A. didn't get his business completed that day for the westbound train that evening dropped off only a couple of landseekers. Nor was he on the caboose of the freight the next noon. Robert met the late afternoon passenger too, but only a drummer with a heavy sample case of work clothes got off.

The man brought news and told it at the cigar counter at the Gatewood store. There had been a big fire at Plum Creek last night—the Johnson hotel burned to the ground, he said. A young fellow named Cozad too, like the station here, was hauled off to jail, accused of setting the fire. Put up to it by his father, they claimed—old man who was a hairy-eyed hellcat.

Julia Gatewood looked up from her thread case where she was matching spools to a tiny swatch of raspberry-colored cloth. She pushed her heavy gray hair back from an ear to listen. There were so few customers now that she hesitated about losing even the thread sale but still she had to excuse herself and run to call Robert. He was away but Theresa came to stand outside the storeroom door, not showing herself, but trying to listen.

"The man says a Cozad boy is in jail at Plum Creek. It might be some of the others up north or from Iowa," Julia Gatewood had whispered, "but a fire——"

Theresa leaned against the wall and thrust her palm hard to her mouth to choke back a cry of horror when she heard the man tell of the fire, the young man named Cozad, one of the first out of the hotel, almost before the flames showed up. She turned and, forgetting all caution, picked up her skirts and ran out the back and down to the stable where Robert was scattering new bedding in the stalls for the night. She ran like a wild woman, frantic, crying out for him at every step.

"Oh Robert! Robert! They have Johnny in jail at Plum Creek. Claim he burned down the hotel, the Johnson House!"

At the look of her pale, distrait face, Robert let the fork slip from his hands and slide, tines up, into the bedding straw, his young face suddenly greenish under the sunburn. Then he hurried his mother home and ran out to Traber Gatewood's place. But he was gone, away until night on dental work.

Robert found his mother walking wildly up and down the sitting room, crying, "Oh, my boy, my baby! He'll be dragged out and hanged!"

The other son stood perfectly still a long moment. "Do you want me to go?" he made himself ask.

"Yes, oh yes! Saddle up and ride!"

Still the son hesitated. "Wouldn't it just make more trouble for John A.—Johnny? They're mighty down on me too, at Plum——"

The mother stopped her agitated walking for a moment, staring at Robert in the afternoon light, a desperate nakedness in her eyes. Before it he knew he must be judicious, as his

306

father had commanded before he left. "I'll go find Uncle," he said, and ran for the stable. On Johnny's Forked Lightning he struck off across the country for Traber Gatewood. They were back as the overcast dusk came in. They found Theresa still walking the floor while her mother was packing a valise for her.

"She insists on going, but I don't see what good that can do—except expose her to indignities and insults."

Traber gathered his sister in his arms and laid her on the sofa, holding her there, gently but firmly. "I'll go immediately," he said. From his dental bag he mixed up a powder to put her to sleep. She would drink it only if he promised to get Johnny out and away. "No matter what it costs," she said. At her command Robert brought a check. She signed it and stuffed it into her brother's breast pocket. "Any amount —just get him out," she said.

On the way to the stables Traber told Robert that he was afraid his friend, the sheriff, was away. If so all he could do was watch, stand such guard as was possible. Then with his antelope rifle in the scabbard, the saddlebags full of loose cartridges, he spurred out east but soon drew the horse down to a gait he could hold to Plum Creek.

The next two hours were very, very long for Robert, sitting motionless on the bench of the depot to catch any telegram coming in, any news. The westbound passenger dropped a couple of relatives for the Danish settlement, two young women standing quietly beside their bundles until one of the sunburnt homesteaders from up there came in his wagon and took them away. There was no one from Plum Creek, no news, and no movement on the street outside except old Robert Gatewood plodding in every ten, fifteen minutes, always with the same words, "Your mother sent me——"

"I'll come up the minute there's news——" Robert told him each time.

"I guess she's afraid you'd try to keep it——"

But any news from Plum Creek before Traber got there could scarcely be good, and so once more the stiff old man, stiff in the dampness of the cloudy night, plodded back up the street.

Then suddenly, when it seemed something must have happened to Traber, perhaps been turned back at the town limits by some of the lawless outfits up there as the district attorney had been before Hallowell was lynched, there was a sudden busy, self-concerned clicking at the telegraph. The agent dropped his paper and scribbled out the message that Robert read from the sound as it came.

Arrived stop horse acts mean but still tied stop friend out of town Traber

Robert took the pale yellow sheet to his mother. Plainly all it meant was that Traber had reached Plum Creek, that although there was danger, Johnny was still alive but the sheriff, whose duty it was to protect his prisoner, hold off a mob, was away.

So once more all they could do was wait. Robert settled in a chair beside his mother, trying to quiet her a little, now that the sedative was wearing off. He thought of Traber out there near the jail, probably in the patch of weeds that always grew up, dead now from the frost. He would have his rifle handy, waiting in the chill darkness that was strong with the stink of dead fire and ashes where the hotel and some other buildings had stood. "Horse acts mean" had been their signal for anger in the town and talk of violence. Perhaps at this very moment Traber was trying to stand off a mob. If he could get Johnny through to tomorrw, he could work, as a businessman of the town, a partner in the drugstore, for Johnny's release— try to delay the trial for arson, get it away from the anger and excitement of the Pearson shooting and the ashes of the hotel still drifting along the windy streets.

And if Pearson died tonight, or tomorrow, or any time before Johnny got out——

It seemed to Robert that he must ride to his brother's rescue as Johhny and their cousin had saved him from drowning under the ice that time they went to Willow Island. The time the girl with the eyes of such dark blue had drawn him into the whirling moment of a witches' dance and then dropped his hands and ran.

Yet what could he do for Johnny at Plum Creek except make things worse for him, perhaps precipitate violence, even a lynching? It wasn't only that he had been promised a bullet in the gut if he tried to cross the city limits, but now it would bring on a crisis, a sense that they had to act against those overbearing Cozad bastards, which up to now, meant John J. and the son Robert.

Toward morning the youth went out to look into the sky, wondering how his brother was, and about his father. Where was he—still fleeing as he had run through the brush that evening, or had he been overtaken somewhere, shot and left for the wolves and to rot, or, more likely if overtaken, left hanging from some remote cottonwood?

Suddenly the son could not stand the waiting with his hands idle and empty. He tiptoed down to his den and laid out a pad of thick paper and began to work with his paint box and colored pencils, taking up this one and that, throwing the pencils down one after another and then wetting up the color pans to bring depth and highlights to the pictures here and there. When he was done he had half a dozen sketches—his mother, Traber, Johnny, his father, all with the sudden appalling realization of what had happened to them all, the horror of it in the dark depths of their eyes.

Slowly Robert stretched the cramp from his arms and his back and then stopped to look down at the sketches spread out over the desk and against the wall. Suddenly an excitement rose in his arms, ran through his veins like a cloudburst roaring down the Platte. He could scarcely believe that he had made these sketches, they seemed so much the work of an artist, the artist the man selling the studio photographs a couple of summers ago suggested that he might become.

Three days later there was a telegram from Traber, and Theresa Cozad sat down to write a letter whose time and place of delivery she could not guess, or even if the letter would be delivered at all. She did no direct blaming. She had said many things to her husband's face, particularly in the early years of their marriage. But after the failures in his earlier undertakings and the deaths of their three young children, she learned to bury her griefs too, and to look to the tomorrow, comforting herself with her sons who must live and grow up with their father's idealism, his dreams of building, but not the other traits.

Now she must know how it was with John Jackson Cozad, or make the effort to know and to tell him what had been done here. Even now she was deliberate in the unfolding of the correspondence folio, drawing out a sheet of eggshell paper, wiping the fine golden point of her pen and dipping it carefully. Then she began:

> My Dear, wherever you are:—
> My heart bleeds for you, having to flee like a common felon after your brave defense against the vicious and cowardly attack upon your person. The man is living but the reports are not the best. Johnny thinks the doctors have been neglectful, have let infection start and spread.
> Regretfully I send you bad tidings. Our ill luck with fires remains with us, and I have had to draw out $6000 to try to save our Johnny from mob violence, which he could not, perhaps never could have, escaped otherwise. Johnny traveled to Plum Creek as you planned. While there at the Johnson House, the place burned down and our poor son was immediately jailed as an arsonist. I

have been frantic. Naturally there was immediate talk that you, in final revenge, had sent him to burn out the town that had stood against your will so long. We heard that there were immediate calls for a rope, for a hanging. Even some from here, several of our neighbors and formerly called friends, rode rapidly to Plum Creek not to miss it.

Fortunately Traber was able to go up soon after we heard, yet even as a partner in business there, and a friend, so he says, of the sheriff, he could not get Johnny released. The danger from lynchers is very great and Traber says he must watch the jail every night from some weeds, with his rifle and his pistol at his side. I have given him a blank check to be filled in for whatever is needed. He has succeeded in getting a mention of possible bail at $5,500, with an additional $500 to be applied in such useful places as may recommend themselves.

I should not have put this additional burden upon your laden shoulders if I had not deemed it necessary to inform you of the withdrawal. We trust that you are as well as can be expected, and have found a safe pillow for your troubled head, Robert sends affectionate greetings. He is like a soldier in this time of sorrow, very staunch, and calm, perhaps too calm.

Your affectionate spouse,
Theresa

The epidemic of violence in the middle Platte valley ran on into winter. The outlaws who killed Sheriff Wood and the other men in the Minden hotel were finally cornered in a dugout deep in Kansas by the men who lost horses to them. Belmont was shot dead and Zimmerman came out with his hands up and was sentenced to be hanged at Minden in April if the higher courts didn't turn him loose too. In the meantime there was another attack by the Olive cowboys. Schreyer, a German homesteader with a big family, in the South Loup region since 1875, had tried to stand off the cattlemen. They had stampeded a herd over his dugout with the family inside and accused him of shooting at any cattle or ranch hands he caught on his land ever since, although nobody had been hit.

Because Plum Creek was the cattleman town, Schreyer usually came to Cozad station to trade and to buy the barbed wire for his fences that the cowboys cut to pieces. Now two of the Olive hands, feeling a little high as they all did since Print was turned loose, drove their horse herd through a settler's cornfield and then went to Schreyer's place nearby, looking for a man who, they said, had made remarks about one of them. There were hard words and with guns drawn the cowboys backed out of the settler's house as Schreyer himself came around a corner. He grabbed for one of the cowboy guns and was shot through the breast.

This time the Plum Creekers were aroused, tired of the violence of the Olive gang. The solid citizens, many of good Pennsylvania stock, got up a purse of $50 for the capture of the cowboys who jumped Number 3 going west and didn't show their faces around Plum for some time.

By then Traber Gatewood had John A. Cozad out on $5,500 bail but the news of Alfred Pearson was not good.

"I think they are letting him die," young John A. complained. "He's not dying of the wound after all this time, but from the infection, from careless treatment and poor diet."

"So you think you would know better than the doctors?" Traber said, very impatient with the youth over the trouble he had got himself into.

"Maybe I would know better, and maybe I'll prove it, someday," John A. replied sharply. He was sharp-tongued most of the time now, and thinning down alarmingly, with a cough. He ought to get away from the worry and anger of the town, away from the worsening reports of Alf Pearson's condition, and from his trial for arson coming up in April.

Robert helped him pack a saddlebag with a few things he cherished, including the madstone hair ball and the skull of the picket-pin gopher that once stook up straight as a stake on the prairie to look. Johnny nested the skull in his palm a moment—neat, self-contained as a nut and no bigger than a butternut.

Then one thick snowy night Sam Schooley came to the back yard with a couple of storm-whitened horses, saddled. He brought leather chaps and yellow slickers for the ride to the south railroad. Even if John A. were recognized as a Cozad before he got out of the region, his tickets were in four blank envelopes, probably different railroads, with changes in unlikely places.

"He is to go to his father?" Theresa asked fearfully, and with some anger, some resentment.

"I don't know anything, nor do you. The tickets came with a railway postmark and a penciled note 'For Johnny' in one corner."

"Where to?"

"I didn't open the envelopes. Not you, I or the boys know anything."

John A. bundled himself up well and said good-by in the dark kitchen. Then the two slipped out into the softly falling snow and were gone without even a creak of saddle leather. That was the first night that Robert slept without a nightmare, free of the haunting, pleading, the hunted eyes of his father. Now he knew that John J. Cozad was alive, and with the loyal and resourceful Sam Schooley, his brother would surely reach the railroad and his destination.

It was several days after Sam returned before anybody seemed to miss young John. To questions about his brother, Robert said he had gone on some business errands. It was well that he went when he did. Just as winter settled down to stay, Sam Schooley came to the back door one cold dawn, breathing frost as they let him in.

Alfred Pearson had died.

So now it was called murder. Once more the newspapers carried items that Robert had to see. One that the *State*

Journal picked up for the December 30 issue seemed to reach everybody:

> A Colorado gambler named Cozad is worth about $300,000, half of which is in Denver real estate. He won it all playing faro, and has become so noted a breaker of faro banks that he is barred from all games where he is known. He is now a fugitive from justice and accused of murder.

The next news was that all the town lots owned by John J. Cozad were attached for damages by the estate of Alfred Pearson. William, one of the sons, had filed a petition that letters of administration of the estate be granted to him. Before this Theresa Gatewood Cozad had quietly sold the town property to Hendee of Illinois, sold it with papers that carried John J. Cozad's signature, sworn to by A. T. (Traber) Gatewood—sold the property in haste and so at a great sacrifice. She demanded and got immediate payment in cash—gold and currency. That night would have been a fine one for holdup men, for thieves. Robert laid out the big Colt his father had left with them when he fled and the pistol from his saddle holster, both handy. Then, with Julia Gatewood and Robert to help, Theresa worked for hours lining her widest underskirts with currency and sewing gold pieces into a pouch to fit between her breasts. The rest of the money went between the linings of Robert's jacket and underjacket. It was a scene for a story, one the youth was never to forget, one he knew he could never surpass in anything he might write.

They left before dawn in Sam's double-bed wagon layered deep in hay between the family trunks, held apart by planks. Blankets were spread on the hay for Theresa and Robert to lie in. The oats for the horses was stuffed into half flour sacks and well heated in the oven, to warm the feet on the long trip to some distant railroad. The entire wagon was covered with Sam Schooley's old hunting tent. If anyone passed him sitting up in the seat, he would say he was headed down into the

Republican River country to get a few buffalo hides and meat, and maybe some mink and beaver and gray wolves too, if he could, for the hide and the bounty, with money still scarce these days.

At the far depot Robert and his mother took no public notice of each other or on the train and the changes to Chicago. There they went to a hotel, indvidually, and in Theresa's room they snipped the threads holding the money, gathered it into a handsatchel, and went to buy new outfits for both.

There was no saying they didn't need them, with Robert's wrists and ankles hanging out of the suit he wore.

He bought a man's outfit and looked old and competent enough to vote, to file on land, if he were returning to the west. Theresa was fitted out in a new costume with a sealskin muff and toque. The lovely French rose in claret velvet at her brow added a little color to her ivory cheeks, and was very different from the blue summer bonnet with yellow daisies framing her face that she had worn the one time she was in Chicago, sixteen years ago.

After lunch they went to the bank together. As the wife of a western mine broker, Richard H. Lee, with their foster son Robert, they got drafts for the contents of the handsatchel.

They came away lighter in actuality and much lighter in spirit than they had been for months. Together they faced eastward and a new life.

XXIV

RICHARD H. LEE sat uneasily in an armchair in the high-ceil-
inged studio that was pungent with the smell of cigars,
pipe tobacco, paint, and turpentine. He stroked his beard,
graying now and much longer and stragglier than his neat
goatee the day, twenty-one years ago, when John J. Cozad
slipped off into the brush of the Platte River, leaving his son
Robert to look after him, the youth not certain that he would
ever see his father again.

Seventy-two now, the old community builder found himself uncomfortable in the new century with its curious notions. He felt an alien in a world where a place like Canfield's
over on East 44th Street could be raided as it was a few days
ago. Run by the prince of gamblers, Canfield's was a handsome, elaborate establishment, filled with works of art—statues,
paintings, and fragile porcelains. Here men of wealth and
position from all the world felt comfortable in a game of
chance, no matter how casual or how steep, for it was said
that Canfield treasured friendship and perhaps for that reason,
too, kept half a million dollars in ready cash in a secret wall
safe to cover any serious winnings immediately. More important was the confidence, the assurance, that here gentlemen
encountered gentlemen and were safe from the importunes,

even the casual presence, of cardsharps and vulgar cheats as well as from the poor-skate loser. Here they had felt secure from the recent custom of the police to come battering doors down, with the exposure to public gaze in the daily press if not the actual indignities of the hurrah wagon and the glare of night court. It seemed that when the recent raid did come, Canfield's first, he managed it so he was the only person in the place, protesting when the police smashed a window in, pointing out that a genteel tap on the door would have opened it to them at once.

Next thing they would be shutting down Saratoga, which Richard Lee would also regret, even though he never expected to make another entrance there, well-known as he was, and welcomed, even during the years of anger and lawing down in Jersey.

It was not only his own world that Richard H. Lee no longer understood. He barely knew this son who was preparing to paint his portrait. He did not understand his leaning toward a writer like Bakunin and the philosophical anarchism that Robert and his students and the other artists gathered around him read and chewed over for long hours. At the suggestion of Robert and the others, he had read *God and the State* and then realized even more that his son was a stranger, an alien.

But he cherished Robert's gifts in painting. He had sent him to the Pennsylvania Academy of Fine Arts to study soon after the flight from Cozad, Nebraska, to work under Thomas Anshutz, and then to Julian's in Paris, under Bouguereau and Fleury, and finally the Beaux-Arts. Robert still admired Rembrandt, ever since he saw the small painting that Duveneck showed him when he was a boy back in Cincinnati. Now Robert had added Hals, Goya, Velàsquez, and the newcomer Rouault. But he was the true son of his father and of pioneer America. He had chafed under the academic rigidity and dryness, feeling as tightly restricted as the hay that came

317

through the press out on the Platte, the bales safe and salable for money that way, but with no life possible inside. So Robert struck out for himself, through Britanny, Italy, and Spain, looking into the faces of the people along the streets, on the waterfronts, along the peasant roads. And finally he returned, for the boy with all the broad sweep of the Platte valley in his breast could not endure the narrow confines of Europe.

Back in Philadelphia he attracted a group of young illustrators to his studio on Walnut Street, became an instructor in the Women's School of Design, where the girls adored him. But he found not one with the dark blue eyes of the Richter daughter out on the Platte, the shy girl who could not lift her eyes to him but held out her crooked fingers for the whirling little dance.

Richard Lee liked his son's paintings. He admired their darknesses, the rich reds and purple-reds against the blacks and near-blacks—the colors so familiar and so compatible from a lifetime around gambling houses, particularly the better ones, known for their dark wealth of velvet hangings and drapes, of carpets and upholsterings. He disliked the paintings that were called impressionistic or impressionism that Robert and his students and friends derided so, pictures made by millions of dots that were like buffalo gnats buzzing around on a quiet, hot day out in Nebraska, those with larger dots unhappy reminders of the pale grasshoppers that clung to everything in their shimmering fall, making it hard for him to breathe. He did not say these things, because Nebraska and any connection with the region were never mentioned, but the experience could not be shut from the mind.

But now Richard H. Lee had to settle himself in his chair with some appearance of comfort while the artist in Robert considered him not as his father but as a subject for his brush. He scraped a palette and sorted out a flat pan of paint tubes, not hurrying, letting the light from 57th Street settle upon his father's face, upon the almost knife-thin nose and the gaunt, sunken cheeks, to bring the tight shine to the pale forehead, touch the upward twist of the brows and burn in the aging but still intense eyes.

Although Robert had been away from the brilliant sun of the Platte valley on snow or summer prairie for a long time, he still waited for more light then ever came, always finding Philadelphia, Paris, even Italy veiled as with a mist, and particularly New York.

But there was light enough to show the changes in Robert, the son of the community builder from the west. He was almost forty now, tall, very tall for the shortish face that seemed still shorter, cut as it was by the dark hair laid across the forehead, the heavy black line of the brows, and the dark mustache. There was a hint of Mongolian tightness of skin at his temples and across the cheekbones too, and yet with this and the old Cozad aloofness in him, there was humor about the face, even now as he considered, studied, his father with a curious shyness, perhaps because there was so much between these two men, so very much that was never told, never could be put into the crude vessel of words. Robert had said to his students back in Philadelphia long ago that to paint a portrait is to know the sitter, and that was perhaps why he hesitated now, not in doubt but in reticence, reluctant to invade the sacred premises that this man had kept inviolate so long.

Yet as Robert sketched in the first rapid outlines of the gaunt face he found it still very much like the one in the Brady photograph made almost thirty years ago, so much like it that the resemblance to anyone knowing John Cozad could not have escaped detection. Yet the story had not really ever come out, not even after Traber got the indictment for murder quieted and John Cozad made a short return to his town under his own name, hoping to win back something of the wide properties that had to be discarded so swiftly after

Pearson's death. The $10,000 it seemed he sacrificed to the Pearson family willingly enough, even though the shot he fired was in self-defense, but that was only one crumbling bit of earth in all the land that the flood of that day swept off. Nor had those who knew the background of the Richard Lee who fought the long legal battle with Atlantic City and the state of New Jersey ever revealed it widely.

"You never changed your appearance as much as we planned——" the son said, almost without thought as he selected one of the large brushes he liked to use.

There was a slight softening in the gaunt lines of the father's cheek, almost a smile on the hidden lips, perhaps. "You didn't expect me to, not with the hat, the cane and the little black handsatchel I took along——" But the lightness was there only a moment, and then the bitterness of the dream destroyed came back into the deep-set eyes.

"I hope they didn't make you too much trouble," the son said as he squeezed dark blobs of paint out around the palette.

Well, some, the father admitted, his eyes focused far off. He had waited in the brush until dark to wade the Platte and then struck south over the prairie like a fleeing animal, with only his cane out before him as a guide, like a blind man in the moonless night. It was so slow, and dangerous too, that he rested some, making a little fire down wind from a settler's shack whose smoke would cover the smell. At dawn he brushed himself off and started south, hitting a plain trail but ready to hide any moment. A few miles farther on a wagon turned in behind him. The fleeing community builder made the quick decision of a gambler. He stuck his silk hat into a badger hole, knotted a handkercheif around the gold head of his cane and hid in a plum patch until he was certain the man was a stranger. Then he stepped out to the road as a land-seeker whose horse got away from him in the night. Now he was heading back to Pennsylvania but returning in the spring with his family.

The man motioned John Cozad into the seat, even tried to talk him into becoming a neighbor. At the station the new Mr. Lee bought a sack of apples to send back to the man's family, got a slouch hat to cover his head, and took a train east. After that it was easier except the waiting, meaning about Pearson, Robert knew, although the name never passed the bearded lips of his father. There was the constant fear of recognition and extradition to Plum Creek, although he had stopped at a little Iowa town and bought an ordinary storm coat of small, neat black-and-white check to replace the beaver-collared broadcloth he had slipped, with the cane and the handsatchel, into a big drummer's telescope he picked up secondhand. He got a checkered jacket too, instead of the frock coat, and clipped his mustache and neat goatee into ragged edges with the tiny folding card shears he carried in his cuff links. Then with the cold snipe of a black cigar stuck into the corner of his mouth and his fingernails broken and dirty, he presented a pretty casual and negligent contrast to the John J. Cozad the law was seeking. He laughed a little at the memory, but harshly, and still Robert regretted that he never saw this.

But something in his father's face as the man talked seemed to disturb Robert about his sketching. He squinted critically at the canvas, not looking at the sitter. "We heard you were overtaken by a mob," he said, trying to make it easy and very long ago. "I wouldn't believe it but I knew there must have been a gang out for you that night. I sneaked down to the livery barns late and found them empty. Not a saddle horse around."

Slowly the man who had been a community builder flexed his long bony fingers. "Yes, I hoped to spare you that knowledge. The horses located me, nickered in the dark, and the outfit rode me down. Had a rope around my neck and up against a telegraph pole. I had been listening to their voices, an old trick from my earlier—ah, business. I knew most of them by voice and ticked off the names of those with claims not proved up, saying we had written out protests on all of them for non-residence, and on fifty more, all to be dumped in at the land office tomorrow if I didn't wire the code word in the morning. Be mighty expensive fighting the cases, even if they could win—with my pull at the land office, particularly after I was found strung up. No use torturing the code word out of me and hiding my carcass. Somebody in the mob standing around me in the dark would be sure to squeal. Men like that never trust each other. Later, with ranch cowboys it would have been different——"

"But they let you go! A bluff, a good gambler's bluff," the son said in admiration, but uneasily too, frowning at his canvas. The outlines, the bit of paint that was to be the eyes and the smudge of black hair and mustache did not please him, did not suggest anything of what he had just seen. Impatiently, as was his habit, he slopped turpentine over a rag and wiped it rapidly across the canvas, the outlines of the man's face melting sideways, streaking into a sort of angry blur of black mustache and brows. When the canvas was scrubbed clean, the painter started again with a stub of charcoal and more calculation.

After a while the father moved fretfully and Robert lifted an eyebrow. "You started over several times yourself, when one plan or another failed," he said, with the finality of tone that made some insist that the son was a domineering teacher and man, brooking no doubt from any quarter, accepting none but his own.

"My case was different," the father said bitterly. "I had outside opposition."

"It's the same. You started, weren't accomplishing what you wanted so you went away—to a clean canvas."

322

Robert longed to go on, drive the point farther. He knew that he would arouse something more of what he wanted in his father's face, make it burn through the death that sat so quickly, so heavily upon the man, but he could not. He wanted to capture something of the day John Cozad rose up in court and called Handley a liar and was knocked down with a chair, his arm broken for it. And later, when, with Robert behind him, he stepped out to bull-whip the man and both were chased with the pitchfork. Or the exultation of the evening he had to flee from Cozad, an exultation in defeat unequaled by anything of success the son had ever seen there. But this was something that the man could never admit and that must never be laid out naked upon canvas. There would be greatness in such a portrayal if he could capture it, but the price of such betrayal would be too high even for greatness.

Robert knew this because today he realized he must not push the old man very far, not even show the anger that he, the son, felt again himself, otherwise the father would be compelled to rise and stalk out, go down and out the marble portals of the Sherwood Studios and never return. And this last pride, surely his last remaining pride, no one could deny him now.

So Robert set out a large pad of paper and with his swift pencil caught what he could of the head, the sharp line of the cheek, the sunken temple, the mustache, the eyes, always the eyes. He drew a dozen of them, some glancing cautiously, boldly, or veiled with the smoke of anger, some sunken deep to look inward. He drew the eyes in pairs too, lifted to the son in curiosity, in annoyance, turned this way and that, eyes with a point of light set here, set there. But the expression he wanted would not come and as the evening softened and there was a trooping of feet in the corridor, he pushed the easel back.

"Tomorrow," he said. "There's so much I want you to tell me."

Gradually the sittings became a little better and the father began to talk in his old, rapid way, but without the hope, the unquenchable optimism of the early days. There was, instead, an urgency, as for one last thrust upon an enemy, one last communication, and Robert heard many things he had known only vaguely, or not at all. There was still anger at the leeching by a couple of the women of the long past, and attempts at blackmail more clever than King O'Dell's, more dangerous even than the counterfeit trick by the faro tramps, with probably lynching plans. There was particularly much of this while he was still in the good graces of the Union Pacific, with what seemed a fair chance of becoming the railroad senator. Or a millionaire anyway, if the capital had been moved west. What a long time ago that was——

Robert had never known much about his father's early attempts to locate a community in South America, about the time that many defeated Confederates went there. But the primitiveness of everything, the health hazards, including his own, with the obvious political obstacles, the internal jealousies—these killed the venture dead as frost on the watermelons. Even at Cozaddale the builder had been prevented from getting the factories for which the town was planned, which it must have. Then there was the Platte-valley Cozad and later his final undertaking, Lee's Pier at Atlantic City, a purely mercenary venture, an attempt to make a passable living for himself and his family by providing entertainment of various kinds on the Boardwalk. That brought the long years of trouble and lawing, ended, finally, by new legislation that froze him out.

Robert nodded. He had been away at school in Europe through much of this, but he knew that his father, with his talent for understanding population trends, had invested well the money that Theresa and Robert carried out of the Platte country sewed into their clothing. He bought a place on the Atlantic ocean front in the direct path of resort expansion.

A January storm in 1884 wrecked much of the beach front and Boardwalk, including the new electric arc lights. That summer a new Boardwalk was put in twenty feet wide, without railing and about two miles long. Unfortunately a portion of it collapsed under a crowd gathered to a streopticon show, dropping many of them down into the sand, with some injuries and much bad publicity. But none of this touched Lee's Pier, of course. Perhaps that helped bring a complaint against the scattered buildings outside the Boardwalk, including Lee's, claiming they shut off the sea view and the breezes. When in 1890 the Walk was extended, two of these outsiders refused to pull down their buildings, one of them the bearded Richard H. Lee. He had been operating quietly enough in the midst of the raucous and noisy resort front, and profitably. The city went to court against him. When the Walk builders reached the Lee property they found a barricade up, manned by Richard Lee himself with pistols, some said with a shotgun, his foster sons, as John A. and Robert were known, backing him up. Lee had made a run over to Saratoga, it was said, and came back with enough money to buy up the adjoining land, the whole now called Lee's Fort in the papers, and in the courts.

The new Boardwalk opened with a big celebration, a grand parade, and fireworks reflected in the glassy night waters, but everything had to go around the barricades. In the end the city got the power to condemn a right-of-way through the property of the holdouts from the legislature. Lee's Fort fell, and the owner left the community and moved to New York, seventy years old, without a dream—with nothing except the two sons making fine reputations, but never to be acknowledged as more than foster sons, never as his flesh and bone.

Johnny, as Dr. Frank Southern of Philadelphia, had even established a voting residence at Atlantic City, and Robert come hurrying back from Paris, but it had proved hopeless, and so now, after sixty years, John Cozad had no profession, no occupation, seemed without plan.

No one except Theresa could have been pleased. To her it was an end to public quarrelling, of lawing and anger and violence. If she recalled the shivaree back at Malden and the raucous version of "Bride of the Gamblin' Man" that night she may have been happy that the gambling too, seemed done. Except for brief business visits to Cozad, her departure from the Platte valley was her first separation from her parents and a complete separation it was, not only by distance but by name and necessity. Now that they were both dead there was no spot for even a brief release from the perpetual necessity to guard her tongue, her feelings. Cut off from those of any refinement by her husband's business on the Boardwalk, she had withdrawn more and more, taking satisfaction in those she must call foster sons, particularly in the good connections of Johnny, her Dr. Frank, who had married into the thread-company Clarks and gave her a lovely young granddaughter— the pride of Theresa's heart. But the Clarks liked to travel and were often abroad. Still, now that her husband had finally retired to New York, she was near Robert and his warm-hearted Linda, and Robert's artistic circles, his artistic causes and boilings.

Sitting for his portrait in the light of the long studio windows before the son who had so much of the Cozad fire, not for community building, but for the integrity and freedom of the painter, Richard H. Lee found himself reviewing the possibilities of one last venture for himself. He wished that it might be in a region not too rigorous for Theresa, although she had aged little, it seemed to him. The elegance of her handsome nose was unchanged, and the fine sweep of her neck to the soft pile of gray hair upon her head, the black velvet flow of her gowns. A fine figure of a woman.

But Richard H. Lee found himself reverting to 1872, when

he strode westward with silk hat and gold-headed cane to the sign at the hundredth meridian. Since the raid on Canfield's he had written to a man working to settle northwest Nebraska and the sandhills to which he himself had once gone with Dave Claypool about a railroad spur from Cozad to the Black Hills. Now there was a railroad survey through the heart of those sandhills, 250 miles up one long valley, surely with several good places for new communities. Not to be called Cozad—Traber had managed to get Gould P.O. changed back to Cozad in Cleveland's administration. Perhaps Theresa? Ironically, he might call his new community Plum Creek, since that town had changed its name to Lexington to escape the stigma, the shame of old Plum.

Since Robert started the portrait, Richard Lee had written more urgently to the sandhill locator who offered, for a $25 fee, to help settlers find homes on free land, the lines run and the corners located, the only other charge the government's regular $14. Robert had seen the man's letters in newspapers that went to laborers, farmers, and foreign groups, here and in Europe. He was sympathetic. He had painted such people all through Southern Europe and from back in his childhood understood their dream of a corner of land that was their own. He enjoyed reading his father's letters from this Sandoz, this sandhill locator, with a story so familiar to them both:

> The cattlemen still have most of the land covered but we are working with President Theodore Roosevelt who is determined that the hogging of the government range must stop. The illegal fences are to come down, the land thrown open to settlers without the danger of a bullet through the head from some blowout. If the planned 640 acre homestead bill is passed there will be a land boom here such as the country has never seen.

Richard H. Lee took the letter from Robert's outstretched hand and put it away in his wallet. He had a scheme to work up excursions, get Sandoz to charge a $100 locating fee to be split with him, in addition to a Cozad-built town on the new railroad survey. If he felt better in the spring he was determined to go out to see.

Of course it would be difficult to convince Theresa, content in their apartment across from Morningside Park, her husband knew. He realized it even more now as she came in with her furs flecked with the new snow, her cheeks still smooth and glowing with the cold, to take him home.

She brought two large scrapbooks she had made for Robert from his notices and clippings that she had collected all these years. "To go with your diaries," she said. "I gathered some about your teaching in Philadelphia and your Paris exhibitions, particularly the time the French government bought *Snow* for the Luxembourg, and about your medal from the Pan American and so on. Traveling around the way you do such things get lost——"

Linda came in, her tall pompadour lifting her warm features, making even her long thighs seem longer in her softly flowing gown, the curls from the coil at the crown falling to her nape, giving her neck a sweeping line too. She kissed Robert's parents and settled beside Theresa to glance through the scrapbooks, stopping at items she had never seen, particularly the silly ones of reporters and newspaper comment denouncing Robert as a radical painter because they didn't like Eakins and particularly not Anshutz and his darkness that came out in the work of his prize student.

Amused, she lifted her thick-lashed eyes in a teasing look to Robert. "Some of these crows sing pretty as nightingales now," she said.

"Yes," Theresa agreed, "but only since that Paris show."

Robert laughed as he would have out on the Platte when some criticism of his father was half disproved. He wiped the paint from his hands, slipped out of his dark smock, adjusted his bow tie, and smoothed his mustache. The scrapbooks were put aside for tea, but not the talk of art. Robert

328

was full of plans for a show next year at the National Arts Club, to be made up of some of the group from Philadelphia, perhaps seven or eight. John Sloan came in, and then some of Robert's students from the School of Art across the street wandered in too, and the talk went to the student days in Philadelphia and the gang that hung around Robert's studio .on Walnut Street.

The next day Richard H. Lee was almost loquacious, recalling Eakins and the shock he caused some Philadelphians by posing male and female models together to contrast their anatomy, and later Thomas Anshutz, Eakins' student.

"Tom was the only man that ever gave me a moment of jealousy over you——" the father finally said.

"But he was my teacher, and a great teacher, carrying on Eakins' search for the truth in the heart of American life—Eakins' and Walt Whitman's."

The old man looked away a long time, with a shadowing of regret in his black eyes. At last he stiffened and straightened himself for the sitting. "I guess I got a better look at it all yesterday, hearing you and the students talking. And John Sloan. John told me you make every painter feel like a genius. He thinks you are the leader, the great teacher who strikes fire in his followers."

Robert, always with a little western embarrassment over praise, wiped a brush carefully on a rag. "Oh, he was just talking, like you used to talk about the Platte valley."

"But I was telling the truth! Although John wasn't your student it's plain he considers you his father in art."

But Robert wasn't listening any further. He was working fast to catch the hint of regret he had seen in his father's face, grabbing at the big paint-tipped brushes, one after the other, held ready between his fingers, so many that his fist bristled with them.

"I sometimes think of you, a kid in knee pants, going out

to stand off those pistol-armed cowboys and their herds eating up my hay meadows, even standing off your Uncle Traber at the hay press, to keep it from being wrecked. Last night you sounded a lot like that boy, like you might drag out the old bull whip against some of the stodgies deciding who'll be——" he started to say "hung," but even now he shied from the word that called up the lynchings of Plum Creek—"deciding which artists will be included in the shows."

"I still have the old whip. Used it once in those plays we put on back in Philadelphia."

The man who was John Cozad, gambler, nodded uneasily. He remembered the parodies that Robert wrote in those days and staged with Sloan, Shinn, Glackens and some others, Luks usually around, full of sports talk. There was *Twillbe*, a parody on the fantastically popular *Trilby*, with John Sloan as the girl, in a fancy wig and a huge pair of vaudeville comedian's shoes. Robert, as Svengali, made his father uneasy, even angry because in his getup the son seemed so thoroughly a caricature of his father as a gambler. Perhaps he also resented Robert's poking fun at established taste and slapping success, which was really slapping Lady Luck, sacrilege to the gambler. Besides, Robert had also offended what remained of the colonizer in the father because he seemed to be drawing people by tearing down instead of building up.

Now, sitting in the tall-ceilinged studio, John Cozad admitted that Robert was all the magnet his father had ever been, drawing the young illustrators of a Philadelphia newspaper into painting, and firing their deepest resources into flame. His humor, his fondness for intellectual horseplay, seemed important in this, perhaps most important in glossing over his domineering, his drive and force that compelled the young artists to see what he saw, outside and within themselves, even though he insisted that each one must paint in his own way, each one must see what was great in his native American tradition and take from that. Painting was a man's vocation, not for the tender-minded, the halfhearted, the fashionably superficial, the dilettante.

As Robert scraped at the portrait of his father, repainting here and here, starting over again, and again, the man who was John Cozad finally burst out in impatience. "What do expect, Robert? What is it you want?"

The son did not lift his head for a long time. He had the reply ready, one he had thought over for himself a hundred, a thousand times the last few years. What did he want? He wanted most of all to live his life as himself, not only as the final of the Three B's his mother taught her sons years ago: "Be yourself," but he wanted to live the truth, live it as Robert Henry Cozad, the son of John J. and Theresa Cozad. Be what he was; yes, live his life as himself.

But this could not be, not in the face of that curious mixture of pride and fear that seemed at the bottom of the father's long persistence in his assumed name. That curious romanticism, perhaps inseparable from the gambler. As Robert thought of this now he laid his brushes down and reached into the cigar box, always open, waiting. When fragrant smoke crept in blue layerings along the room he spoke. "I want the truth, as near to it as possible. I want to grasp that esssence of everything which is its final truth."

The father thought of what this man before him had seen in his boyhood, the gun-carrying cowboys of outfits like the Olives, even Man-burner Print Olive himself, and the constant menace of such men. Then he had to see his own father and, yes, his brother too, fugitives from possible lynch mobs.

John Cozad knew how some of the Easterners, particularly art critics, were inclined to look upon this presumably pampered foster son of a wealthy family. He knew that some considered Robert's art the cry of youth untouched by sorrow.

"Untouched——" John Cozad thought. "Sorrow——" What did such words mean to those men.

The portrait was nearing the end. The father had not seen

it yet, perhaps because he had not been invited to look. But several of Robert's artist friends had walked around to stand before it a little, silent. Then one day a buyer who had heard about the artist and had seen his *Snow* in the Luxembourg stopped off to look over what Robert might have on hand. It was after the day's posing was done and Robert had remained alone in the studio, sitting hunched over, chin in his palm, considering his father's portrait. He got up to let the man in, showed him what seemed advisable on the walls and from the rick of canvases set face to back along a corner. The man made a few notes in a memo book, arranged an appointment for his colleague, and then noticed the canvas on the easel. He went over to it, sized it up this way and that.

"This is a fine piece of work," he admitted guardedly, "has great personal feeling. Is it commissioned or for sale?"

"Not for sale," Robert said curtly, suddenly shocked that there might be a price, a money price on this painting. And from this he knew that it was about done.

The next afternoon he brought his father's talk around to the long fight at Atlantic City, but there were few sparks. He tried Todd, Handley, the faro tramps, and finally even Pearson but there was less injured will, less hurt pride or smoldering anger and outrage than he had already seen here at the easel, seen, and had captured or missed. But it seemed that he got something else, a hint, a sort of sharp alertness coming into the eyes, almost as though the man were guarding himself against the son, against the artist's probing, and Robert recalled what he usually said to his students too. "Paint a portrait to know the sitter." Perhaps the sitter here realized this, and had put up barricades, as this man could, barricades with pistols of his own kind here.

A smile lifted the black mustache of the artist as he stood back and considered the painting, turning his head to this side and that, the heavy sweep of dark hair across his forehead unstirred.

"Come," he said to his father.

But the gambler who risked everything a thousand times in his life hesitated now. At last he came, bowed somewhat, and moving slowly, his eyes down as though considering every step. He stopped a little aloof from the son as though to keep himself free from any domination, free to see this in his own way.

A long time he looked at the dark intensity of the eyes, the whiteness of the face, the fine, thin nose, the heightened temples, the streaks in the hair and beard, the white linen sharp against the darkness of background and broadcloth. He began to tremble a little and his eyes to water as though suddenly very old. He shook his head hard, as when he had to shake back a mass of black hair falling forward in the heat of a big play. But it served now too, and in a moment he was steady once more, the impersonal gambler, as he held out his hand to the son, saying no more than he did the evening he slipped into the brush after shooting Pearson—leaving so much to the judgment and responsibility of a boy, a seventeen-year-old boy.

But when Robert took the hand in both of his, the man dared let his face soften.

"My son, my beloved son," he murmured.

Now finally, smiling into his father's eyes, the artist picked up a brush, dipped it into the black, and in the left-hand corner signed the portrait. He did it firmly, as always: Robert Henri, dotting the *i* very carefully.

The End